A Roman Rhapsody

Books by Sara Alexander

Under a Sardinian Sky

Four Hundred and Forty Steps to the Sea

A Roman Rhapsody

Published by Kensington Publishing Corporation

KENSINGTON BOOKS
www.kensingtonbooks.com

KENSINGTON BOOKS are published by

Kensington Publishing Corp.
119 West 40th Street
New York, NY 10018

All Kensington titles, imprints, and distributed lines are available at special quantity discounts for bulk purchases for sales promotion, premiums, fund-raising, educational, or institutional use.

Special book excerpts or customized printings can also be created to fit specific needs. For details, write or phone the office of the Kensington Sales Manager: Kensington Publishing Corp., 119 West 40th Street, New York, NY 10018. Attn. Sales Department. Phone: 1-800-221-2647.

ISBN-13: 978-1-4967-1551-7 (ebook)
ISBN-10: 1-4967-1551-9 (ebook)
Kensington Electronic Edition: September 2019

ISBN-13: 978-1-4967-1550-0
ISBN-10: 1-4967-1550-0
First Kensington Trade Paperback Edition: September 2019

10 9 8 7 6 5 4 3 2 1

Printed in the United States of America

For Mum & Dad, thank you for the piano

Music was my refuge. I could crawl
into the space between the notes
and curl my back to loneliness.

—Maya Angelou

I Movimento

1

Overture
a piece of music that is an introduction
to a longer piece

When her brother opened his eyes, Alba was convinced she was present at his wake. Her mother, Giovanna, knelt on one side of his bed, forehead resting on her thumbs whilst they crawled over the worn beads of her rosary. In the corner three wailers sobbed their own prayers, in warbled unison, invoking Mary, Jesus, and any saint who wished to assist. On the other side of the bed, their neighbor Grazietta held a bowl with oil and water. She told the women that the way in which the liquids mixed confirmed that Giovanna's firstborn, Marcellino, was, in fact, yet another victim of the evil eye. There could be no other explanation as to why he had been kidnapped alongside his father, Bruno, who was still held captive, whilst his son was released by the bandits the night before, after three days of white panic for all their family and friends. Grazietta grasped her wand of rosemary twigs and dipped it into the liquid, dousing the sheets like a demented priest. The wailers let out a further cry, which trebled across the sheets. A droplet fell on his forehead, from another swing, this time a close miss of Alba's eye. With his wince, everyone at last noticed that Marcellino was in fact conscious.

Giovanna jumped to her feet and held her child into her bosom. Alba could smell the reassuring scent of *sofritto* in the folds of her housedress, even from where she stood at the foot of the bed, those tiny cubes of carrots, onion, and celery fried in olive oil before making Sunday's batch of pasta sauce for the week, cut through with the sweat of her panic beneath.

"*Biseddu meu,*" she murmured in Sardinian, rocking Marcellino with such passion that Alba knew would induce a vague seasickness. This was a woman obsessed with omens. If the sauce boiled too fast, three starlings rather than two screeched their morning tweet, or a feather fell unexpected from nowhere, her particular strain of logic would portend horrific visions. She sang prayers to Saint Anthony at the crossroads in their Sardinian town when they needed something specific, accepting that it would lead, by necessity, to her forfeiting something in return. Alba had faded memories of her mother praying to miss her cycle one month because there was extra work to be done, only to be doubled up in excruciating pain the following. Saints gave to those who prayed, but at a cost; the original protection racket. It sat at an uncomfortable angle in Alba's mind, this idea of bargaining with a saint, the very thing she'd been taught was the devil's speciality. Alba's prodding at this point met only with the stone-setting stares of her aunts at best, physical harm at worst. She chose her battles with care, and made a silent pact with herself never to be indebted.

The Fresus asked neighbors' cousins' friends to say secret prayers—known only to those who dabbled in this branch of acceptable religious magic—at midday on the second Tuesday of a month if they lost something. These initiates then relayed a dutiful list of everything they heard on the street in order to find said lost item. One day, when twenty lire had gone missing from her mother's kitchen drawer, one such prayer had returned with the word Francesco repeated three times. Alba remembered her mother pinning the unsuspecting laborers working on the house next door with her Sardinian glare, black eyes like darts, thick eyebrows scouring a frown, when she found out they were from out of town and all shared that very same name. After that incident Giovanna stitched her cash into her skirts like her grandmother used to do.

None of these accepted manias were woven into the morning of May 27, 1968. No red sky in the morning to warn the shepherds, no burned garlic, curdled milk, dough that wouldn't prove, solitary nightingale calls. It was a joyous late spring day, the kind that teases you with the golden kiss of the Mediterranean summer to come. Giovanna had shrieked at Alba to return in time to accompany her father to the vineyard, her brothers Marcellino and Salvatore needed a rest and besides, it was her turn, but the familiar trill of her mother's voice fell on deaf ears. Alba had lost track of time, or rather decided never to pay much attention to it to begin with, and when she sauntered home at last, was met with the kind of pummeling from her mother that should have been reserved for the making of bread or churning of butter alone. Marcellino had been sent in her place and because of it, he now sat wrapped up in bed with her family facing a daily terror of a missing father.

Giovanna drew back and clasped Marcellino's face in hers. "Eat, yes? Oh my *tesoro,* did they hurt you?" More questions tumbled out, but the noise spun around the room like a gale. Grazietta muttered another snippet of a prayer before crossing herself and leaving, oily water in tow. As news spread to the crowd downstairs that the firstborn had, at last, awoken, more women came upstairs and filled the room. Alba was shot a look that she recognized as her cue to bring the tray her mother had prepared. She pressed past the well-wishers and returned with the feast in hand, setting it down on his bed; fresh *spianata,* Ozieri's renowned flatbread, enough cheese for a small football team, a handful of black figs, two long slipper-shaped *papassini* biscuits, and a glass of warm milk with a splash of coffee in it. If he wasn't dead yet, it seemed the army of mothers were to kill him off with overfeeding.

"*O Dio mio,*" one of the wailers cried, "his eyes, Giovanna, the look in this poor child's eyes!"

They took another breath in preparation for a further fervent chorus when a shout tore through the pause. The door flung open. Grazietta reappeared, face flushed, her circular wire glasses askew on her nose. "Benito's on the television, Giova', *beni*—come quickly!"

Giovanna followed Grazietta out, with the tumble of others close behind. Alba followed down the stone steps to their small living room. She'd never been in a room with so many quiet Sardinians. Even in church or at funerals words couldn't fail but escape, a titbit of gossip here, a grievance about the lack of flowers or the ostentatious abundance of them, the age of the priest or lack thereof. Now the dozen or more neighbors crammed into their room made Alba feel like the charred aubergines her mother would squeeze into jars throughout the summer.

On the small square of screen in the corner, above a chest of drawers topped with a lace doily, was her father's brother Benito. The angle of the camera pointed up toward him; beyond, the familiar outline of the Ozieri valley in silver tones. He seemed relaxed, even though Alba was sure the words he spoke were some of the hardest he'd ever have to say. "I speak on behalf of all my family," he began, "the bandits have picked on the wrong man. Our family is not rich. We don't have the money they are asking. We will not pay the ransom to release my brother Bruno."

The lump in Alba's throat became a stone. A murmur rippled across the room. Then the scene snapped to men signing a form at the police station. The neighbors took it in turns to shout at the screen as they recognized their husbands, brothers, sons. The clipped voice of the Rai Uno journalist began to describe a town in revolt. The scenes flipped between the main square with men huddled in groups back to the police station where the men were being described as signing on to a counter army to uncover the whereabouts of Bruno Fresu. Their firearms were being registered. Shepherds from the surrounding hills had come to town to aid the search efforts, citing the fact that they knew their Sardinian hills better than any bandit. All this was happening for her father. The rescue efforts were coupled with a revolutionary protest about to take place, the journalist said.

The noise inside the stone room began to rise, the voices ricocheted over their heads to an unbearable volume. Someone called out from the street and the room began to herd out of the small door onto the cobbles. People lined the road outside her house. A cry pelted down from farther up the *vicolo* just before Alba saw the first of the banners. A sea of schoolchildren from the upper years snaked around the corner, wooden signs above their heads. They were chanting and so were their teachers. There were decrees against the bandits. Someone shouted they had gone too far this time. Another screamed Fresus were one of the people, not rich folk. Even Alba's teacher, the most prim woman she knew, waved a sign high above her head yelling like she'd never heard her do before. The sea of students and teachers paraded past their house; there were shouts to not give up, to not give in, that Ozieri would stand against the criminal disease eating their island, that the bandits must not be bullied into taking one of their own by mainlanders. Alba should have been with her father when the men jumped out of a vehicle in the twilight. She should have been huddled with him in that damp cave, not Marcellino. A swell of guilt. Her father was the man who made her town revolt. No one marched when the rich landowners were kidnapped a few months back. There was little more than hand-wringing when the fancy American heir was kidnapped on the northeast coast the year before. There were even some hushed whispers that the rich had it coming to them, that their bandits maintained a warped equilibrium in society; the wealthy had no right to run their island as they pleased.

This time, however, they had gone too far. Her father was a hard worker; his father, Nonno Fresu, had accumulated huge debts to gain the first Fiat dealership in town. For this they were captured, for a ransom that none of them had. Bruno and his three brothers worked around the clock at the dealership. There was not wealth to speak of yet; it was swallowed by the bank. That's why Giovanna cleaned villas in the periphery, took on extra washing, fed the babies whose mother's milk had dried up, all to keep her own family fed.

Alba's father was now a celebrity. He had started a revolution. Was it wrong to feel proud? Alba shook off the sharp twist of guilt, because thinking of her father in this way was the only way to stop herself picturing him shot through the head with his blood seeping out onto the fennel-scented dirt beneath him.

Alba woke to find her school *grembiulino* hanging on the door of the wardrobe she shared with her brother. This apron she wore over her own clothes looked like a relic from a distant past: one in which Alba played in the street, fought with her brothers, and recited poems by memory under the glare of her teacher. Life after Marcellino's release and her father's continued captivity was disorienting. Each time it seemed to tease reality Giovanna would yell at her daughter for picking a fight with poor Marcellino as if his recovery rested on Alba's behavior alone. He was served his favorite breakfasts every morning. Neighbors would stop their whisperings as he entered the room. It was like living with a recluse celebrity, and Alba suspected that her brother's ability to mine the situation for all that it was worth, with more than a little performance thrown in, was apparent to no one but his younger sister. *Thank God it wasn't the girl,* women would lament over the never-ending pots of coffee bubbled to calm the nerves of the tormented wife, but their voices were a constant reminder that she was not guiltless in all of this. If she'd been home in time, they might have gotten to the *vigna* earlier, missed the bandits perhaps. The life Alba once knew was nowhere to be found.

That morning the familiar dread of school awaited. Her black apron with the scalloped white collar a promise of normality. Giovanna took extra time saying goodbye to Marcellino. He walked beside her and Salvatore, only running ahead as usual when his friends caught up with him and enveloped him with their bombardment of questions. By the time they'd reached school Alba was sure that he had embellished his story from how it had begun in half sentences back at the house on that first day, when he'd arrived a scruff, mute, in silent shock. Alba stepped through the tall gates of the elementary school, lit by the promise of life easing back to recognizable order. She took her place at the third desk from the front.

That's when all her classmates stared. Unhurried Sardinian glares. Dozens of dark eyes pierced her. Her own darted across the once familiar faces, but they seemed waxen, the disembodied type that haunted her dreams, people she thought she once knew who might spin off their axis on their own accord, or shape-shift into monsters.

Somewhere in the distance there was an echo of a familiar voice. Her gaze swiped to the front of the class. Her teacher peered at her over the glasses perched on the tip of her nose.

"Well, Alba? What do you say to that?"

"To what, Signora Maestra?" she replied, trying to ignore the wave of dizziness.

"Our class wishes your brother well. It's polite to say *grazie*."

Alba sipped a breath. Her whispered thank-you felt like it was warbling out from under water.

When the bell rang for morning break at long last, Alba shot out of the room to her usual spot in the concrete playground. The sun beat down. The noise was deafening; she'd never noticed how much her school friends shrieked. A hand tapped her shoulder. She twisted round. Mario Dettori stood before her, not a soul she despised more, his familiar sideways smile plastered over his face. "There she is, boys! The bandit girl!"

Alba pinned him with her hardest stare. He laughed.

"What? Your brother spends a few nights in the woods and you've forgotten to speak too?"

He turned to the pack of snotty boys gaggled around him, cackling.

"What do you say, boys? I think she looks wilder too now. Surprised you managed to remember how to get dressed. My uncle said they hung Marcellino naked in there!"

A snip-spark of something flamed in Alba's chest. She didn't remember throwing him to the ground, or swinging at his face, or breaking the skin, or the wild cries of the other children as they crowded around her.

Giovanna sat beside Alba. Her feet tapped nervously. Her bottom spread over the edges of the wooden child-sized seat. Alba stared down at her bruised knuckles. One of the cuts seeped a little blood as she bent it into a fist. Giovanna slapped them flat. Alba winced.

"Thank you for coming, Signora Fresu," her teacher began, slicing through the room and perching on her desk. "Today has been difficult. For everyone. You and your family are under a lot of pressure, I know, but that is no excuse for the violence she instigated."

Alba could feel her mother stiffen beside her.

"Let me be blunt, Signora. Alba is not a bright child at the best of times. She's now missed two weeks of a critical time in school. She will never catch up to where she ought to be. And, to be frank, I think the experience you're all going through is making her a danger to others. Let us recall the tussles back in the spring, the recurring altercations during the winter. Her ability to deal with typical childhood challenges is poor. At the slightest provocation she fights. This is not the kind of behavior I am trying to instill in the girls in my class."

Alba's mind streamed incessant images of all the times her brothers fought her. The way her mother would admonish her for partaking but never them for instigating. She recalled the fights ignored by the teachers between two boys. The way Mario would always get palmed off with a disapproving stare whilst she would stay inside writing line upon line about why she should never fight. Her face felt hot.

"So we are agreed, yes, Signora Fresu?"

"*Si.* I know you know best, Signora."

"I do. I will make allowances, but only if we expel Alba for this last month and have her retake the missed classes throughout the summer to catch up. If I allow Alba to stay in the class now, what kind of message am I giving to the others?"

Neither Giovanna nor Alba had an answer for that.

Their silence pleased the teacher.

The vise that strangled Alba's household continued to tighten. Sometimes her mother looked like she was close to breaking, even though a stream of women flowed through the house delivering never-ending trays of *gnochetti*, sauce, *pasta al forno*. Grazietta swept the swept floors, dusted where there was none to remove, and incanted prayers where necessary. Sometimes Alba would find her clapping into the corners of the room, shifting the menacing energy. Her brothers left for school each morning. Her uncles would come by for lunch, when they would update Giovanna on the search efforts. Alba wafted around the house like a ghost, finding comfort in invisibility. Grazietta would give her stitching to occupy her, but needlework was her nemesis, and after a while even Grazietta grew impatient with her.

Everyone's prayers were answered a week later.

Her father's release was the miracle the entire island had been praying for. Her town threw a *festa* in his honor the following day. It was the first time in their history that a captive was released unharmed and without a paid ransom. Bruno Fresu had left an indelible mark on Sardinian history. This, along with him remaining intact, unlike other victims whose ears or digits were cut off and sent to relatives as warnings, gave rise to nothing short of a national holiday. Tables lined the length of the *vicolo*. Every family cooked something for the feast. Her uncle Benito built a firepit at the end of their street and spent the entire day overseeing a suckling pig, dripping its fat into the moist flesh, caressed with rosemary wands dipped in olive oil, its salty scent curling down the street. The feast was bigger than any wedding any of them had ever been to.

Her father sat at the head of the snaking tables. He was thin. His skin pale. His eyes no longer the sparkling onyx Alba remembered. He shaved away his thick beard that had grown the past month, on Giovanna's insistence. Without it, his face looked smaller still. Everyone raised their glasses. There were tears. Alba even noticed several of the older men wipe their faces, then place their flat caps on their heads to shade their emotions.

The party trickled through the night till the wine-infused singing began. The men warbled in their thick Sardinian voices. The sound rang up the stone fronts, echoed down the *viccoli* to the piazza. Alba imagined the valley beyond, plains humming with the distant rumble of their celebratory voices. And beyond farther still, the empty caves where he had slept, the damp crevices where her father had been stowed. Her heart hardened trying to clamp her tears from escaping. Everyone was celebrating now, it was no longer her time to grieve for her missing father. The tears crystallized into a heavy weight in her chest. She wanted to feel the happiness surrounding her, but it felt like she was celebrating a family she knew, not her own. She hated herself for begrudging everyone's fawning on her brother, or rather, the flicker of infuriating pride she saw in his eyes as they caught her own. Marcellino was crowned the prince after all, and Alba, as always, the disappointing renegade. All the faces along the long table joined in her parents' disapproval of the girl who should have gone through this mortal test but failed even to show up. Her father seemed happiest that his son had survived more so even than being reunited with his family and having been released himself. Where Alba grasped for any feelings close to pride, relief, love, only anger surfaced, a bitter taste in her mouth, burned artichoke, singed pigskin.

Her father was closeted in quiet. After his return, the house became a hushed mausoleum. Alba had never seen her mother so stilted; tiptoeing around her kitchen so as not to make any sudden noise. She waved over at Alba, who was on dusting duty.

"Come on, get a move on, I'll be late!" Giovanna whispered, emphasizing every vowel with a theatrical movement of her lips.

"For what, Mamma?"

"You're to come to work with me today. I can't leave you here. Babbo needs to rest!"

Before Alba could ask anything further, she was bundled out of the door and the two began marching uphill. The sounds of the market awakening clanked up from the main square. Giovanna stomped at full speed. Alba was glad the morning heat had not fully cooked. By the time they reached Signora Elias's villa Alba could feel the droplets of sweat snake down the back of her neck. Giovanna gave her daughter's shirt a tug or two and it curled back into its original shape. She smoothed her work apron. The door opened.

Signora Elias appeared behind it, the doorframe encasing her like a painting of an aging Madonna, black hair scraped off her face into a low bun, streaked with waves of gray. Her face wrinkled into a grin. The tiny woman, with the sharp intelligent eyes of a bird, snapped her gaze from mother to daughter.

"*Buon giorno*, Signora. Sorry I am a little late today," Giovanna said, breathless.

"Nonsense. Your husband had quite the celebration last night. I fell asleep to the sound of it!"

She stepped back a little to let the two inside.

"This must be your girl, yes?"

"*Si*. She won't make any trouble, Signora."

Giovanna's face creased with streaks of worry. Did her mother fear Alba might pick a fistfight with this old lady too?

"*Piacere*, Signorina," Signora Elias said, reaching out a hand for Alba to shake. No adult had ever done such a thing. Alba felt Giovanna flick her shoulder to reciprocate.

Signora Elias's hand was small but strong. Her fingers were assured, muscular, belying her size and age. She looked straight into Alba, without the pity or mistrust she was more accustomed to receiving from older Sardinian women. They shuffled through the darkened hallway, along the cool of the tiles, which opened out into the biggest room Alba had ever seen. At the far end three sets of double glass doors framed the Ozieri plains. Parched yellows streaked with ochre beneath the graduating blues of the summer sky, and they stood as if floating in the space above it.

"Stop gawking!" her mother spat under her breath.

Alba scurried behind her mother as they worked their way through to the utility cupboard beside the kitchen and removed all the cleaning supplies for the morning's work. Her eyes slit sideways, registering the paintings on the walls, the huge Persian rug that covered the center of the room. As Giovanna flew out through the kitchen Alba had just enough time to see the enormous range, the double oven below, the bold, colorful designs on the tiles surrounding it. Giovanna headed to the upper floors only to discover she'd left the broom downstairs. She ordered Alba to fetch it.

That's when she heard it for the first time.

A golden sound; uplifting like the first light, reassuring as the afternoon sun's streaking glow through the fig trees. In silence Alba's feet stroked the carpet lining the stairs, not wanting to interrupt the cascade of notes running toward her, the mesmerizing trickle of a creek as it winds its way around mossy boulders and uncovered tree roots, cooling, comforting, ancient.

At the foot of the stairs she reached stillness. In the far corner of the room Signora Elias sat on an upholstered stool, facing toward the enormous glass-paned doors and the expanse of their burnished valley. Her fingers caressed the keys of a deep mahogany instrument. Its lid was lifted at an angle like a sail, the mirror sheen of the wood reflecting the paintings on the opposite side of the room. Bright yellow notes of birdsong followed by sonorous, melancholic blues. Alba couldn't move. Elias danced on further carousels of notes till, at last, her fingers eased down onto the white and black, peaceful, heavy. The song reached its final rest. Alba couldn't quite count all the different tones and sensations that wove out of the piano, but she knew the ending made her think of a sunset dipped in orange and ruby, or the memory she had created of her father before the kidnapping, edged with the silver-gray tinge of a farewell.

2

Pianoforte
1. formal term for piano
2. mid-18th century, "soft and loud," expressing the graduation in tone

Alba couldn't force the following week to pass quickly enough. The days dripped by unhurried, excruciating, as if she were listening to a leaking tap's droplets echo into a metal watering can till it reached the rim. Her restlessness did not go unnoticed by Giovanna, who admonished her for hurriedly rolling out the *gnochetti* from a large lump of dough, sweeping the floor without noticing what furniture she banged against in the process, and eating her food without chewing it first.

For Alba, the sounds around her became a claustrophobic symphony of erratic percussion, orderless, out of time, passionless. Her brothers rushed in from school each lunchtime, with stories of whom they had defeated in the playground, peacocking their self-appointed celebrity status amongst their peers for being sons of a hero. Her father would give them a swift glare, but his eyes smiled. He still spent his days in his room, but somehow the cacophony of her brothers brought him pleasure where the smallest noise of Alba's broom would make Giovanna wince at best, swing her hand at her daughter at worst.

Alba tried to bury the worm of envy inching around her belly. When the feeling deepened, she thought about Signora Elias. The sounds of hungry boys and crisscrossing conversations then hushed into the near distance as the memory of her song rippled closer.

"Alba! Do as your father said!" Giovanna's voice pierced the reimagined musical haze.

"What, Mamma?"

"Clear up. They've finished, can't you see? Bring the cheese from out back."

Alba stood and reached the cool stone cupboard toward the back of the room where several *perette* cheeses hung to form a hardened skin. She reached one and brought it to her father.

"What's got into you today, Alba?" he asked, grabbing a knife and wiping it clean on the tablecloth.

"Nothing."

"You're a wet cloth. This is how you thank your mother? She's supposed to be taking it easy. Lord knows we've put her through enough."

We. The way he slipped that tiny word into his sentence made Alba feel like she was folding down into a tiny parcel of tight paper. *We.* Giovanna had wanted her to go. The events had all been, in part, her fault. Bruno gripped the round-ended cheese in his palm and carved a slice. The boys eyed him as if they hadn't just licked their bowls of *gnochetti* clean. Bruno passed each of them a peeled piece, which they prized off the tip of his knife, then started to peel the rind off his own.

"Well, don't just sit there, Alba. Go and help your mother."

Alba left the room for the narrow kitchen beside it. Giovanna was filling a plastic container inside the deep sink with suds and water.

"Is this how you're helping him get better?" Her words were swallowed by the sloshing water. Alba could hear the force of it smack against the side, thwacks of cascading frustration.

Replying was pointless.

At last, Wednesday rolled around. Giovanna's calls for Alba not to run on so far ahead fell on deaf ears, or rather ears that were attuned to the treble of birdsong, the metallic click clang of the house at the end of the street whose upper terrace was being rebuilt, or the bee that buzzed close, which Alba watched land on the passiflora creeping up a neighbor's front door. As they wove farther uphill toward Signora Elias's home, the sun bore down and the cicadas hummed. Alba noticed their perfect synchronization, how their notes shifted but nevertheless sang in unison.

Alba rang the bell before Giovanna could stop her. And Signora Elias's smile silenced Giovanna before she could yell.

"Good morning, Signora. Alba is with us again today, I see?"

"Sorry, Signora, it won't always be like that."

"It's been too long since I've had children in my house. I've been looking forward to it all week."

She welcomed them inside. This time the smell of the silent house was powdered with a sugary vanilla scent. Alba's mouth watered.

"I've made *sospiri* this morning. I hope you'll have some, Alba. If Mamma says it's alright?"

Giovanna shook her head. "We'll get on with our work, Signora."

"Very well, Giovanna, but I want you to send Alba down when you begin with the bleach in the bathroom. Those smells are toxic for young noses. She will sit down here in silence, of course, until you come down again, yes?"

This time Alba knew her mother could not refuse. A victory. She would have grinned if she knew it wouldn't lead to mild physical harm.

Giovanna raised her eyebrows in unspoken agreement. When Signora Elias turned away to walk to her piano, Giovanna gave Alba a glare. In the utility cupboard Alba found all the cleaning equipment from the week before. This time she took a moment to commit the kitchen to memory. The white-tiled counters stretched one length of the facing wall with a window at the far end, which opened out onto the valley. Beyond lay the purple hills of Tula surrounding Lake Coghinas. A small wooden table beside the wall opposite the range was covered in baking parchment and topped with perfect medallions of almond paste *sospiri,* dipped in white icing. They were uniform in size and the morning light cast a tempting gleam across the tops of their perfect leveled surfaces.

"Run on up to your mother before she calls now, won't you, Alba." Signora Elias's voice made her jump round. Her guilt dissipated off the old woman's grin. "You'll have some when you come down, I promise."

Giovanna gave Alba several more chores to do before she at last allowed her downstairs with a squinty-eyed Sardinian glower. Alba left, trying not to look too happy about the fact.

"There you are at last!" Signora Elias called out, coming in from the kitchen with a porcelain plate of *sospiri*. She placed it down on a lace doily, which sat at the center of a spindle-legged side table, a pink velvet hall chair beside it.

"Do sit down, Alba, we were never meant to digest standing up you know."

Alba took a tentative seat.

"Those are for you. And yes, I will be offended if you don't finish them all. You've lived on our island long enough to know that, surely?"

Alba wanted to join her laughter, but the corners of her mouth clamped down the impulse, in case her mother heard.

"This is my practice time, Alba. If you don't mind, I will carry on as I always do. I don't do very well if I don't stick to my routines. I don't go to church often like the other women my age in town. But if I miss my morning practice my day does go off track somewhat. Perhaps I'm getting old after all."

Her smile lit up her little face, her eyes a dance of sagacity and infectious childlike joy. Alba took her first bite. It was perfection; sweet, nutty, smooth.

"Glad you like them," Elias said. Alba looked up. The *signora* must have other magic powers beyond the songs her fingers made.

Signora Elias sat on the piano stool. She turned away from Alba now and let her hands rest on her lap. Alba watched her breathe in and out three times. For a moment she wondered if maybe the old lady wasn't falling asleep. No sooner had she thought that, the woman's hands sprung to life. Her wrists lifted and her fingers touched the keys, soundless, elegant as a ballerina's silent feet.

They gave a twirl upon the keys, followed by a fierce, effortless run of notes. In her left hand, the notes spaced at even intervals undulating up and down toward the center notes. In her right, her fingers trilled into ripples of watery movements as if the two hands fought to be heard over each other; a heated conversation. The music rolled on, in waves, urgent, chasing, till Signora Elias reached up for the higher notes, spreading her palm wide and playing stacked notes at the same time. The tune from the earlier passage repeated, fuller for the addition of the lower notes, emphatic. The scarlet sounds burst with passion, insistence. And then, as quickly as the storm blew over the instrument, it fell back, like a tide fast retreating. The reds were replaced by golden yellow tones, making Alba think of how the sun shines all the warmer after a summer downpour. Yet beneath the hope, Alba heard nostalgia, as if the song harkened to a lost peace. The tune was a bitter balm. An involuntary tear left a wet streak on her cheek. Then the waves crashed in again, Signora Elias's fingers racing, till, at last, her rocking hands wove an ending, the repetition of the midsection playing over echoes of the tumultuous start, reaching a truce, both points of view sounding in their own right.

And then it was over.

Signora Elias looked at Alba's face.

"The first time I heard Chopin's *Fantaisie-Impromptu* I cried like a baby. You show remarkable self-control to shed only a solitary tear."

Alba laughed at that, in spite of herself.

"That's the piece which made me want to become a pianist."

Signora Elias held the silence, unhurried, as unflustered by it as the great splash of sound she'd just made. Then she stood up from her stool. Alba took it as her signal to leave, and she jumped up from her seat and pounced toward the stairs. Elias called out to her.

Alba turned back.

"My piano. Would you like to play it?"

Alba wanted nothing more than to know how that magic poured out of her fingers, but she stood, frozen between terror and embarrassment.

"Mamma will be busy for a while yet. I can show you some things. Only if you like, of course."

Alba glanced toward the stairs, imagining the look on her mother's face if she came down to see her daughter fingering this magnificent instrument.

"Here, take a seat and I'll adjust the stool to your height."

Alba felt the thickness of the plush rug beneath her feet. She walked to the stool as if drawn to it by an invisible cord of golden thread. She listened to the metallic squeak of the stool as it rose.

"Now, just place your hands on the keys, see what they want to naturally do."

Alba did. They reflected back to her in the polished wood; twenty expectant fingers.

"Have you ever sat at a piano, Alba?"

She shook her head.

"Goodness. You hold your hands as if you have, my dear." Elias reached over and lifted her hands and moved them a little to the right until they seemed to be at the center of the keyboard.

"Why don't you go ahead and play a few notes then?"

Alba turned to face Signora Elias, feeling like a trespasser.

"Any note at all, any order, doesn't matter, just feel the weight of them."

Alba looked down at her hands. She pressed her second finger down. A bright sound rose up from beneath the lid, a fizz of yellow.

"And another," Signora Elias encouraged.

Alba pressed her little finger down. This one was higher, prouder, more certain of a sound.

"What happens if you play one at a time starting with your thumb all the way up to your little finger, do you think?"

Alba felt the smoothness under the pads of her fingers, the thickness of the key, and let her fingers press down on each note in turn. A ladder, stepping-stones, sounds stacked on top of one another like building blocks.

"Now come back down," Signora Elias said. Alba did. Her fingers were hot. They ached to touch every key, to hear the color of each note, to race up and down like Elias.

"Very good, Alba. Your fingers look quite at home there, wouldn't you say?"

Alba looked up at Signora Elias. She hadn't felt this safe since before her father's ordeal, or perhaps ever. Her eyes grew moist. This time she swallowed her tears before they escaped.

"Alba Fresu, what do you think you are doing?" Giovanna cried, waddling down the stairs with buckets and brooms in tow. "Signora, I'm so, so sorry—this won't happen again."

"I think it would be criminal if it didn't."

Giovanna looked at her, unsure if she was about to be fired.

"Giovanna, I would very much like to teach this young lady, if you and she were agreeable to the idea."

Alba looked down at her fingers on her lap.

"That's very kind, Signora"—Giovanna flustered a laugh—"right now we must get on and finish your downstairs and get home to make lunch. I'm so sorry if she made a nuisance of herself." Giovanna's gaze flitted to the *sospiri* crumbs on the doily. Alba's cheeks burned.

"Very well, Giovanna, but once you're finished you'll take some of these *sospiri* home to your family, won't you? No pleasure without sharing."

Giovanna nodded. Alba jumped up from her stool.

They mopped the kitchen and downstairs bathrooms in silence.

Outside the heat swelled. The cicadas were in operatic form and the tufts of yellow fennel blossoms on the side of the road gave off their sweet sun-toasted anise scent. It was of some comfort ahead of Giovanna's tirade.

"What exactly did you make that poor old woman do? Did you ask her to play on that expensive piano?"

"Of course not, Mamma, she asked me."

Giovanna skidded to a stop. She pinned Alba with a glower. "Alba Fresu, we don't have much, but I work every hour under the sun to teach my children one thing: honesty. You stand here lying to my face and think you won't be punished? You wait till your father hears this."

"She asked me to listen!"

"Maybe she did. But that's no excuse to push your way in like a peasant. You know better."

Tears of injustice prickled Alba's eyes.

"I've been waiting for the moment where you show some kind of thanks, for your father being alive, for having escaped this ordeal. But nothing! You float around like you're invisible. Like a princess. It's disgusting. You don't talk. You help, but I have to redo the things after you've finished. Is this how I've taught you to be?"

Alba would have liked to cry then and there, to spit out that her night terrors were more than she could bear, that the feeling of a cave's dampness skirted her dreams and waking hours, that she didn't know how to describe the way her heart thudded in her chest for no reason during the day. That every bush held a secret promise of bandits lurking beneath. That their job was unfinished. That they would return for more. She longed to be held by her mother, told that everything would be fine, that one day she wouldn't have the sinking feeling of dread trail her like a menacing shadow, that the dusk wouldn't seep white panic through her veins. Instead, a sun-blanched silence clamped down.

"There, you see? More sulky silence. Well, this has got to stop, Signorina. You hear me?"

Alba swallowed. Her throat was hot and dry. The pine trees farther up the hill swished their needled branches. Their woody scent wafted down on the breeze. Alba longed for them to be the comfort they once were.

3

Fantasie

1. a free composition structured according to the composer's fancy
2. a medley of familiar themes with variations and interludes

The following week, just as Alba was starting to speed up her run toward Signora Elias, her mother handed her a crumpled piece of paper. On it was a detailed list of vegetables she wanted Alba to buy at the market. Alba looked up at her mother.

"Don't just stand there. Get on down before it gets too hot. You can clean the artichokes and cut the potatoes. Get a can of olives from the shop and see at the end of the list I've added a few strips of pancetta. I'll make *pasta al coccodrillo* for a treat, I know how much your brothers love that. They'll be hungry after the morning at the *officina*."

Giovanna's words tumbled out in one blast of breath. Alba's stomach growled. She wanted to think it was because she'd only eaten half a roll with her milk and coffee. Signora Elias was the highlight of her week. Her mother had just robbed her of it.

When they both returned home, Giovanna took her frustration out on the unsuspecting white-skinned onion she massacred into tiny pieces. Next, she launched an attack on the slices of pancetta, thwacked open the lids of *passata* from their glass jars, and ripped into the can of drained black olives that turned into little disks in a brusque breath or two. Alba was instructed to chop the slab of semisoft fontina cheese into tiny cubes whilst her mother whooshed a pan with warmed olive oil and the softening onions. Pancetta was thrown in soon after, and the smell in their galley kitchen would have filled it with the promise of a comforting lunch if it wasn't for Giovanna banging every pan on the range. Alba knew better than to ask what the matter was. Instead she eased her knife down through the cheese, taking her time so that she wouldn't have to lay the table yet. Each blade splice, Alba half expected her mother to tell her how Signora Elias was that day, what she'd played, if it had been a swirling piece like the others. No descriptions of her morning were offered, but the way Giovanna threw a fist of salt into the boiling water of a deep stockpot for pasta made Alba worry she'd been fired for her daughter's impoliteness after all.

Alba's brothers returned soon after to bellows from their mother to scrub their hands. Alba carried the huge pot of pasta onto the table. The fontina cheese had melted over all the *pennette* mixed in with the pancetta red sauce and olives. As she scooped the spoon down toward the base and up onto one of her brother's bowls, strands of fontina oozed off it.

"*Cocodrillo*, Ma?" her elder brother, Marcellino, yelled from the other end of the table. He reached out a hungry arm for his bowl. He had entered his teenage years in earnest and Giovanna moaned about having to cook almost two kilos of pasta for their family these days. His thick black hair was like his father's, and his crooked smile, and the way his eyes twinkled with unspoken mischief. His voice was deep and broad and he held the weight of an heir upon his wide shoulders with pride. Beside him sat their younger brother, Salvatore, who had their mother's moon-shaped face and never fought to step out of his elder brother's shadow. Salvatore had his grandfather's patter and a speed of speech and reaction to match Marcellino. Neither measured the volume of their voices.

"It's a treat for you all today!" her mother cried from the kitchen.

When all the bowls were full and Giovanna and Bruno took their places, silence replaced the gaggle of voices. The boys were sent out to play after lunch whilst Alba helped clear the table. Her father took his time to peel an early peach and chop it into tiny cubes, which dropped into his tumbler. When it was almost full, he reached for a slice of melon and did the same. Then he poured wine over the fruit-filled glass and began to swirl the mixture, pressing the soft fruit down with a gentle spoon until it was submerged. He scooped up his first spoon of wine-infused fruit. The smell made Alba's mouth water. She found herself, as always, hanging to her place waiting for him to cast her a story, share a secret. Since his return home, none came. He was in his faraway place that Alba was instructed to never interrupt.

"Let your father eat his *macedonia* in peace, Alba, and finish up inside."

Alba followed her mother's instructions. Her parents' voices became muffled all of a sudden. It made her tune in through the doorway; when adults whispered there was always information that would be better known than not.

"And Signora Elias wants Alba to go every day to do this?" she heard her father say.

"Yes. I don't know why. She has a car. She likes to walk into town every day. But she says it would be a big help. And the extra money wouldn't be so bad, would it? Get Alba out of the house doing something too."

Her father harrumphed.

"So shall I tell her yes, Bruno?"

"Is this some kind of charity bone for us poor down in town, Giovanna? You be sure that Alba works for every one of those lire, you hear me? We're workers not takers, you hear me?"

Alba heard her father's feet climb up the stairs for his siesta.

Giovanna didn't mention anything more of that conversation for several days. At last, over breakfast one morning, Giovanna looked up from her little coffee cup, which she had been stirring without stopping for several minutes. Alba couldn't remember if she'd even put sugar in it yet.

"Signora Elias would like you to do a job for her over the summer, Alba."

Alba looked up. The bit of bread she'd dipped into her hot milk and coffee split from the roll and fell into her deep tin cup with a plop.

"You will collect her morning rolls from the *panificio* and newspaper from the *tabacchi* each day. She wants you at her house by seven and not a minute later."

Alba blinked. The woman who forbade her to go with her was now sending her to that house on daily visits. It was better than any Christmas.

"Well, say something, child. 'Thank you for the job. Yes, Mamma I'll do that.' Anything!"

Alba nodded.

"I'll take that as agreement to do the best job you can. Now, you and I both know that the poor lady is taking pity on me. Everyone knows what I've been through. Now my only daughter, the girl who is going to look after me in old age, who will make me a grandmother, doesn't speak? That's not how daughters are to behave. From the boys I'd understand. They need their father. But you? A shadow."

The tumble of words were hot, like the boiling water that wheezed through the packed coffee grounds of their morning pot. Alba held on to the hope that her own silence would be like lifting that screeching pot off the gas ring.

Her mother stood up. "You start tomorrow."

Alba jumped out of her bed the next day, prepared the coffeepot for her mother, set out the cups for all the family, and ran out of the door for the *panificio*, across the cobbled street that ran in front of their narrow four-room house, clustered in the damp shade between a dozen others behind the town's square. Down the *viccoli*, washing draped in waves of boiled white flags of surrender across the house fronts. After a few hairpin turns along stony streets, meant for donkeys and small humans, not noisy cars, she reached the main road, which funneled around their town, snaking out toward the hills that encircled the valley. The baker gave her a milk roll on the house and filled a small thick brown paper bag with a slice of oil bread and two fresh rolls. At the *tabacchi*, the owner,

Liseddu, handed her a copy of *La Nuova Sardegna* over the counter, and then told her, with a wink, that she could have a stick of licorice for herself. With her load underarm, she swung up to Signora Elias's, feeling like the plains opening up below were a promise. The cathedral steeple shone in the morning light, its golden tip gleaming at the center of town. The huddles of houses, narrow town homes, clustered together straining for height, top floors encased with columned terraces, now gave way to firs and pines as she climbed toward the *pineta,* the pine forests of the periphery, the cool sought by young or illicit lovers, shadows protecting their secrets, their desires permissible for a snatched breath or two. Behind them the *piazzette* of the town, the greengrocers hidden within the stone ground floor of houses, the shoe and clothes shops for which the town was famous sheltered in the crooks of shady alleyways. Up here, in the fresher air beneath the trees that lined the hills surrounding her town, the men traipsed the ground for truffles or edible mushrooms. And in the unbearable heat of August, families would climb to seek respite from a punishing sun.

Alba loved the smell of this part of town. She turned her face out toward the trees, feeling their spindled shadows streak across her face, her mouth open now to the pine air, its earthy scent whispered over her tongue. On she strode, her feet crunching along the gravel that led to Signora Elias's front door. She pulled down on the iron handle. The bell rattled inside the hallway. Signora Elias appeared. Her face lit up.

"As I suspected. Your timing is, indeed, impeccable."

"*Grazie,* Signora," Alba replied, and handed her the packages.

"Lovely. They smell divine as always."

Alba had never heard the daily bread described with such delight.

"Do bring them into the kitchen, Alba, yes?"

She knew better than to do anything other than what she was asked. The kitchen was laid for two. At the center were two porcelain dishes, one with a white square of butter and a smaller one with jam. A large pot of coffee sat on the range. The windows were open. The room filled with birdsong.

"*Grazie,* Alba. Now, do sit down and have some with me. I'm sure you're thirsty after your climb, no? Judging by the shine on your forehead I'd even say you ran."

"I did."

That Alba knew something about this woman's house made it easier for her to breathe, to speak, though it was impossible to decide whether it was the crisp, clear air, the light that flooded in from the surrounding gardens, or the peaceful silence of the home itself.

"Here, do sit down after you've given your hands a wash, yes?"

Alba hesitated.

"You won't be late home."

Alba watched Signora Elias light the pot and cut her roll, butter it, and smear it with jam. She handed half to Alba.

Maybe it was the homemade fig jam, the sound of the medlar tree leaves twirling in the light breeze just beyond the window, or the sensation of being in this lady's kitchen, but Signora Elias was right: It was divine.

Once the pot simmered to ready, Elias poured herself a cup and signaled for Alba to follow her into the next room.

"I think we ought to learn your first scale today."

Alba looked at her, trying to mask the thrill soaring up her middle.

"Only if you'd like, of course?"

"I would love that, Signora."

She took her seat. They repeated the stool dance from the other day. Alba looked down at the shiny keys. She'd remembered where Signora Elias had placed her thumb last time and laid it back there.

"Very good, Alba. You have a keen memory. That is wonderful."

Alba turned her head to look at Signora Elias. She looked a little younger today.

"Now, like the other day. Just five to start. Then we'll reach up a little more."

Alba was soothed by Signora Elias's voice, firm yet gentle, like being under the protection of a queen. It felt far safer than the constant dodge of evil eye, that quiet but incessant terror that trailed Alba now that at any moment things might change, or be lost.

Signora Elias's voice turned mahogany, rich tones that guided her up the familiar notes and then directed her thumb to scoot beneath her third for her to trace further notes still. Her fingers spidered across the new and familiar sounds, the sunlight streaming in from the double doors and lighting up the backs of her hands as if they too had been dipped into a little of the golden magic that overtook those of Signora Elias.

Throughout the summer Elias spun tales about numbers, their families, the way the notes were grouped together and why. Elias painted pictures with her voice and hands that described a cosmic symmetry. The mathematical patterns bewitched Alba, and the more Elias explained the more Alba yearned to know. At night, her terrors ebbed away as her fingers tip-tapped upon her sheets; up to five down to one, up to eight, down to one, one, skip to three, skip to five, down to three. She made up her own patterns too, which she showed Elias with great enthusiasm the next day. When the white notes sung out with confidence under her fingers, Elias introduced a few black ones too. This time the scale shifted mood. Here was a moonlit forest, a bad dream, something hidden in the dark. The scales peeled open like the pages of books, unfolding pictures of far-off places, imagined worlds, miniature stories of heroines in the wilderness. Elias showed Alba how to recognize the key notes within the scale, how they were all linked by intrinsic tone, vibration, and mathematics. How it repeated up the keyboard, each eight notes resonating at double the speed as the same note eight notes below. Alba hung on to every word, every nuance, sepulchring the musical secrets, as if she and Elias were standing before an enormous map of the universe feeling her reassuring hand at her back that told Alba it was safe to sail.

1975

4

Battaglia
battle. A composition that features drumrolls, fanfares, and the general commotion of battle.

For the seven years that followed, Alba's fingers were in perpetual motion. Giovanna gave up yelling at her to cease their incessant tapping. Over time the compulsive movement paled into mild irritation because Alba performed her duties at home. The silent melodies became just another tick to join her other obsessive behaviors, like wiping a clean counter, scouring a gleaming range, or checking the taps were twisted tight. The more her fingers percussed, the less Alba spoke. The silence cloaked her in a guarded invisibility, a cocoon from which she could witness the world at a safe distance. After dinner, she would sit beside the record player and piano albums Signora Elias had lent her and play without stopping. When Giovanna started moaning about the constant music, Signora Elias also let her borrow some headphones. The pieces she studied wove into her mind like a dance, and after listening for an evening several sections would escape from her fingers onto the keyboard with ease. It was like repeating a conversation, almost word for word, and where discrepancies remained Signora Elias took time to make the necessary corrections, of which there were often very few.

Each morning Alba rose with the dawn she was named after, striding down to the bakery and back up through the hills of obsidian and crimson-streaked winter sunrises and the peony-orange haze of the summers. Signora Elias greeted her like a cherished granddaughter each of those days, never once forcing conversation, nor prying. The space they created every morning was a secret Signora Elias and Alba held close, clasped in complicit trust like the two photographic faces of a snapped-shut locket.

When her teachers crowbarred their way into Alba's personal and mental space, yelling from their desk, haranguing her out of her self-imposed silence, Alba replayed minute details of Signora Elias's mornings on a loop. The images squared into view, ordered, yet singular, like the family slides her neighbors would project onto their white walls, the mechanical clicks between each image a metronome chasing time; scales, morning light, gleaming floors, fresh coffee, arpeggios, the taut strings of the piano, their vibration, their frequency, their power.

May of 1975 was in full bloom. The grasslands surrounding Ozieri were splattered yellow with blossom. In the crags between the granite along the roadside leading up to Signora Elias, rock-roses grappled with gravity, their fuchsia-purple blossoms widening to the sun. Giant wild fennel swayed on the gentle breeze, scenting the air with anise. Minuscule orchids appeared in the cracks between the boulders; Alba gazed at their petal faces, minuscule mournful masks. By Signora Elias's gate, tufts of wild poppies greeted Alba, and each day she visited, another unfurled its blood-splat petals.

Shafts of morning light cut through Signora Elias's large room and across the open piano lid, striking a golden gleam across its polished top. Alba could feel its heat trace her outline and light up her fingers. She looked down at the keys. Her fingers sprang into action.

Signora Elias interrupted at once. "You took a breath, yes, but it was high in your chest, snatched. You cannot expect to be able to keep up with this Bach fugue in this way. Bach is stamina, precision, absolute clarity. He is the source."

Alba tilted her head back, blowing a puff of air out from her lower lip, which lifted a few strands of hair that had fallen onto her forehead.

"And there's no use in succumbing to frustration either. We can't create or practice from that place. Sorrow? Yes. Feel the pain of those notes escaping from under you. Then simply work out what you must do to fix it."

Alba wanted to say sorry, but the words stuck in her throat, a knot of silence.

"Don't apologize," Signora Elias continued, as always, intuiting what Alba longed to say but couldn't, "this is the work, Alba. This is the constant reminder that you are merely human. What Bach is laying out for us is the entire cosmos, layers of mathematics, interweaving with glorious symmetry. Then he twists it in on itself, reveling in the asymmetry of those rules. It's a kaleidoscope of patterns. We know this. So we honor this."

Alba was accustomed to Signora Elias's tempo increasing as she charged through her corrections, sometimes striding beside the piano, then drawing to a curt pause when the pinnacle of her thought was reached, a mountaineer charging toward the peak. She stood still now, in the spotlight of the sun's glow. "Will you return to the beginning?"

"Slower."

"And?"

Alba swallowed. "Then I'll play these first few measures, repeating at speed, playing with alternate rhythms."

Signora Elias raised her eyebrows, waiting for the end of the thought.

"Until my fingers play me," Alba whispered.

"Until there is no space between those patterns and you," Signora Elias added. "I don't want to see Alba Fresu play with her fingers. I want to see the music ripple out of you. That's when we know that you truly know the piece. When we have stripped it to its core, asked what it is, why it is, what it needs to tell us, and then step inside."

Alba looked at Signora Elias and allowed herself to smile in spite of a sinking in her stomach. When would these exercises become instinctive?

"It's about learning to control every minute movement of your body to produce the precise tone the piece requires," Signora

Elias began, "and then, in performance, being able to shift that focus on control alone, and simply allow your technique to be in place, so your musicality can soar. We want to hear the music, not the practice. Music is about control and the loss of it at the same time, a beautiful contradiction. At this moment, from your flushed cheeks I see you are still grappling with the sensations of losing control in the first instance."

The past seven years Signora Elias had sat beside her each and every morning leading her down these waterways of her music. Now, at eighteen, as Alba approached her final year at school, their lesson together was a cool balm before class. After it, Signora Elias would permit her to practice unguided.

"I want to apologize," Alba replied, her voice dry.

"I know. Hold on to this thought—my corrections are leading you toward your music, Alba, they are never criticism alone, however it might feel."

Signora Elias invited the silence for a moment as if it were an unexpected yet welcome guest. Alba lost herself in it. Her breath dropped down into her abdomen, warm, deep. She felt her lower back unlock, each vertebra separating a little, rising up out of the top of her head. Her fingers lifted back onto the keys. As she exhaled, they became heavy, assured, curious. The first few measures tumbled out effortless, precise. Alba stopped, then began again, each time her breath deepening a little more, each time her feet finding the reassurance of the wooden parquet rise up to meet them. As the cascade of notes became equal, controlled, her hands began to relax, speeding up without tension. Her fingers sank into the ivories, weighted but free. The glorious symmetry of the sounds and patterns washed over her, shining light. She was no longer in Ozieri. She was far beyond the plains, above her turquoise coast. She was deep in the forests of Gennargentu, beneath a gushing waterfall, icy cold electrifying her body. She was everywhere but here. And the feeling lit her up from her feet and lifted up out of her head. She was inside her body and far beyond it at the same time.

The final run descended and landed, in perfect alignment, both hands announcing the last chord. The vibrations lifted out of the piano thinning to a faint blue glow somewhere in the air above the strings.

And then it was over.

She returned back to a stark awareness of the room, once more a piano student surrounded by the landscape paintings on the wall around her, the promise of the spring morning outside sketching hope. She looked over at Signora Elias. Her eyes appeared wet, or perhaps it was the morning light, which caught a spiral dance of dust motes in the space between them.

"You and I both know our lessons will reach their end after the summer. Your father has made it quite clear that you will be working at the *officina*. That will leave little or no time for you to be coming here."

Alba nodded. The thought of the minutes ticking away toward a time when the piano wouldn't be part of her daily life made Alba feel like she was suffocating.

"It's time at this crucial point in your training that you are allowed to perform. At the very least once. Every performance I gave taught me something I needed to learn, and stayed with me forever. I want to give you that."

Alba felt her chest crease into a tight knot.

"Don't look so terrified, Alba. Perhaps in preparation you might play for my friend first? She is staying with me at the moment and her favorite thing is to listen to piano music. Would that be alright? After next lesson would be the perfect time."

Alba nodded, though the idea sent a sliver of terror scorching through her.

Signora Elias looked into her. "When you practice in the way you have today Alba, anything is truly possible. When you can acknowledge that fire and channel it with humility and passion, this instrument, and you, will sing."

The next morning Signora Elias instructed Alba to use their lesson time to warm up and run through her repertoire. "Take all the time this morning to repeat whatever you need. What have I told you?"

"A piece soars only when it's shared."

"Why?"

"Because it's then that we find out what we really feel about it, how much careful time we've given it. Whether our practice has been well directed."

"Which, of course, it has. You have the most wonderful teacher, I hear."

They laughed at that.

"We'll be down in a little while so you aren't observed during practice. I have a gentleman coming to work on my car shortly, but he shouldn't make too much noise, I'll look out for him so her doesn't ring the bell."

"*Grazie,* Signora Maestra."

Signora Elias closed the door behind her as she left. The doorbell clanged soon after. "I spoke too soon! I'll see to it, you carry on."

She thought about the anticipation brewing in her house for Marcellino's upcoming wedding. The way her mother insisted they practice her makeup. The way every breath of life seemed to be directed toward their firstborn, the boy who could do no wrong, now set to marry the most beautiful young woman in town. The town was electric with the imminent nuptials. Alba was tired of the incessant talk of it after the first day back in the freezing fog of January, when all of a sudden, both families had agreed the marriage should go ahead sooner rather than later. Her mother clawed at her attention now, the picture of her demanding she return at a good hour today to help set up the luncheon with the closer family members as they sampled all the food the caterer was planning on providing. Giovanna, Grazietta, and several other women would already be at their *vigna* now, setting up a long table in the one-room cottage, the wood heaving.

With a breath, Alba wiped her thoughts clear. In her mind's eye, she pictured the surrounding vines, the gnarled rows that grew to eclipse the terror of what first happened there. The grapes had exorcised those memories and now the *vigna* would be the center of more celebration for the boy who was kidnapped in place of his sister. She pictured the cottage behind her as she walked through the vines, down the hills toward the plains, across them, past the Nuragic towers, onto Lake Coghinas, its glassy surface urging her to step in. She imagined turning around in the water with the jagged mountains surrounding her, breathing in the juniper and toasted thyme air.

Her breath fell deep, down into the watery bed of her thoughts. Her hands lifted. Her fingers stretched along the piano keys. Her left hand began a wave rolling deep currents of passion and longing whilst her right soared above. She was a bird swooping toward the lake from above, ripples shooting out from the flick of her tail upon the crystal liquid. The music tugged her deeper into thoughtlessness. She was diving into her sea, unfathomable, powerful, free. Her skin flushed, her arms hot and fast as they stretched up and down the keys. Now she was the lover yearning to be understood, to be forgiven, to be heard, to be loved with every fiber, to be touched, tasted, savored, honored.

The door creaked. Her fingers lifted.

A shattering silence: Mario's face was in the slit of the opening.

Splintering currents of electricity fractured the space between them. She felt naked. Stinging vulnerability crawled up her calves. He didn't blink. Neither breathed.

He was the last person in town she would have liked to be spied on by. Now he had the ultimate arsenal for his incessant attacks. Alba snapped into panic. The person she trusted least was privy to the biggest betrayal of her parents. She sat, motionless in cloying dizziness, as if her feet were sticky in almond brittle before the tacky molten sugar sets.

Signora Elias and her friend swept in, and she watched Mario tumble a clumsy apology for being inside the house rather than outside with his father. The women closed the door behind them. Mario's face disappeared.

Signora Elias's friend was a reed. Long, thin, with an elegant bearing about her. A woman Alba desired not to cross. Yet as she spoke, her voice wove out like a clarinet, woody and warm. Her face lit up listening to Signora Elias, crinkling the wrinkles on her thin white skin deeper still. The many colors of her dress undercut her poise. Here were washes of blues and reds, a scarf swooped across her with a tropical print. Geometric earrings clasped her earlobes in colorful anarchy. She reached a hand out for Alba's. The nails were painted fuchsia. Her hand was firm, unapologetic.

"I'm Celeste. So very lovely to meet you, *tesoro*. Elena has told me so very much about you. I'm terribly excited to hear you play."

Alba flushed, embarrassed by her embarrassment. She was about to play for a lady who appeared to value confidence and Alba wished she could find some. It was impossible, having just heard that Signora Elias had already spoken about her to a distinguished friend. It made their lessons at once less private. A secret had been divulged elsewhere too.

"I would absolutely adore it if you would play?" Celeste asked. Signora Elias turned toward her too. There was a different buoyancy to her this morning. Perhaps she was lonelier than Alba had thought?

"*Si*," Alba replied, "do you have a preference on which one I play first?"

"Not at all," replied Signora Elias. "You must play what you feel is right for you this morning."

Alba nodded. She scooted the stool a little way from the keys and rolled the knobs at the side up to where was comfortable. She'd never played for anyone else. Signora Elias was right. Doing so was the hardest thing. At once she was exposed, filled with doubt without knowing why. She turned back to Signora Elias, annoyed for seeking reassurance. Signora Elias responded with the calm and clarity Alba needed; an effortless smile, as if Alba playing for a stranger was the most natural thing to do this morning.

Alba took a breath. Mario's face crisped into focus. She blew away the picture, though it remained at the fringes, like a spider's sticky silk. "Clair de Lune" was one of her favorite pieces. She allowed mind to be soothed by the fact. She began, fingers light, silver tones sparkling in a starry Sardinian night, silent, fragrant with sun-cooked rosemary and myrtle. She wove toward the midsection letting her body move into the melody supporting her fingers. Mauves and violets replaced the metallic shimmer from the opening and then returned home, like waking from a dream. Alba lifted her fingers off, unhurried.

She turned toward the women.

Celeste was nodding her head. Signora Elias was a sunbeam.

"My second piece is a Chopin."

"I should hope so too," replied Celeste with a twinkle.

The further two pieces wound out of Alba's body like a story she'd lived and retold a thousand times. Then the final staccato of her last Bartok piece leaped off the soundboard with the perk of a vibrant orange. The energy of the frenetic rhythms hung in the air when she turned back to the women.

"That's all I have ready to share just now," said Alba, thrumming with a mixture of elation and relief.

"No 'just' about it, Signorina," Celeste replied with a grin that stretched her thin crimson-painted lips. She stood up, wafting her silk caftan behind her as she did so and planted two kisses on Alba's cheeks.

"And what, may I ask, do you intend to do with this talent? And the years of service my wonderful friend has invested in you?"

The question was so absurd Alba almost chuckled. Off the woman's serious expression she stopped herself.

"I don't really know. I'm not sure how I could ever repay my debt."

"No debt to me, Alba," Signora Elias said. "Celeste is asking you whether you think you would pursue a life in music. Should you have the chance."

Alba's mouth opened then shut again.

"You have undeniable talent, Alba," Celeste began. "You have a light inside you and it streams out when you play. It is unfettered. Unaffected. I listen to a great deal of young people play and very few have this, an affinity with the instrument. A respect. A lack of desire to be watched, but rather an ability to communicate with brutal honesty. Believe me when I tell you how rare that is."

Alba longed for words, expression, something other than the numbing silence fogging her body.

"When Signora Elias and I met at the Accademia of Santa Cecilia in Rome we were told the same thing."

Signora Elias chuckled now.

"It is a great responsibility—talent," Celeste said. "You were born with something to honor, nurture, share. And this fabulous woman Elias saw it right away. I can see that. She's not as much of a fool as she looks, no?"

The women laughed in unison now. Celeste's laughter tumbling out like a scale, Signora Elias's voice warm, like *papassini* fresh from the oven.

"It is so wonderful to meet you, Alba dear." Celeste stretched out her hands and held Alba's. "Tell me one thing. How do you feel when you play?"

Alba took a breath. Signora Elias nodded.

"I've never been asked really."

"I'm asking you now. And I want to see if you can be as honest with your answer as you are when you play."

Alba let the words reach her like a lapping wave.

"I'm not sure I can. I'm not a person who likes to describe things too well. I think that's why I love the piano." Alba longed to be able to form her sensations into sentences, but the words slipped away like rivulets of water at her fingertips. She longed to explain that when she sat at Signora Elias's instrument she had a voice to express feelings and thoughts it was impossible to in real life, when she was Bruno Fresu's daughter, the sulky girl who couldn't control her temper, or get through school without coming from a family that grew in influence each year. That when she played she felt protected by the music and ripped open at the same time. That the music told her things, secret stories, coded messages of what it meant to exist, in all its brutal unfathomable glory. That it lifted her into blissful invisibility. That feeling was what she loved most. Powerful because of what the music fed her. But instead of sharing her tumbling thoughts Alba felt her expression crinkle into an awkward frown. "I love the piano." Her voice slipped out plain, without ornamentation, like a starched linen tablecloth before the plates and crystal glasses have been laid.

"Music is mathematics and heart," Celeste replied, "it can't just make sense nor can it be just emotional. It's a tender, intoxicating balance. That's why so many people give their lives to it."

Alba let her words reach her like a longed-for promise.

"I suspect you ought to, too."

"Sorry?"

"It's been a great honor to meet you, Alba."

"You too, Signora."

Up till this very moment Alba had no inkling of what she was capable of. Each time Signora Elias encouraged her, she never shook the feeling that it was an act of kindness, that her playing was good in context, for a girl who knew nothing of music, and learned in secret against the wishes of her parents, listening to the recordings on a loop till her body knew the tunes better than anything that had happened to her in real life. Did Signora Elias know that she ate all her meals, attended all her school classes, finished her chores at home with the carousel of pieces and exercises spinning in her mind; weaving incessant patterns, articulations, melodies, countermelodies?

"You'd better head off to school now, Alba. I would hate for you to be late," Signora Elias said.

Alba felt she had overstayed her welcome. Her cheeks flushed in spite of herself.

"I'll see myself out, Signora. Thank you so much."

She left feeling that the heat and light scoring her chest as the door closed behind her had little to do with the sun batting down from above.

Alba swung her class door open so fast that the wood banged against the concrete in the same spot as the week prior when she was sent out of class for arguing with Mario.

That morning, her teacher, Signora Campo, was not in a mood to let her inappropriate entrance slide. She slashed through the clatter of students setting out their thick textbooks onto their desks, staccato thuds echoing in the stone-walled room. "Why are you late, Fresu?"

Alba twisted back to her teacher's squawk, answerless.

"Well?"

"She's doing shows at the old witch's house, Signora! Thinks herself quite the little maestro!" Mario called out from his desk next to hers. The boys around him fell into confused whispers. Alba shot him a look. It made everyone but him avert their eyes.

"I will speak to your mother if this continues to affect your school day in this way, mark my words."

Bull's-eye. Alba sank.

"Does she make you play for all her cronies?" Mario whispered out of the corner of his mouth as Alba swung onto her hard chair. His friend on the next desk sniggered. She gave an extra lift of her backpack and it missed Mario's face by a hair.

"Go to hell," Mario spat.

Alba let her biology textbook thud onto her desk, hoping she wouldn't be the first one called on.

"Fresu, you may come up for *interrogazione,* seeing as you wish everyone to notice you this morning." Alba felt her shoulders heave an involuntary defeat. She stood up, ignoring Mario's smirk. The teacher took a breath, pulled down her light brown sweater over the mounds of her breasts and abdomen, peered over the rim of her glasses, and launched her assault. As Alba returned to her desk, relieved she had memorized the chapter on osmosis better than she had expected—much to the frustration of her teacher, who was looking forward to having an excuse to send her out—she couldn't ignore the smart of shrapnel left by her threat.

When the bell rang at one o'clock, the concrete building thrummed with the swagger of sweaty adolescence, corridors thick with hormonal bodies pushing for escape. Alba adjusted the strap on her backpack, feeling the weight of her textbooks pull down on her shoulders. The throng was an unbearable cacophony, walls of intersecting discordance pushing in like a vise. A familiar panic bubbled in her abdomen. Her fingers raced up and down her thigh, clinging to Bach like a mast, the quicker they scurried the louder the music in her head rose above the din like a white light.

The music came to a violent stop as a boy was pushed toward her, falling onto her back. Her knees buckled. The concrete met them with a painful blow. She reared underneath the weight with such force that the teenagers around her pressed back against the corridor walls. Her jet-black hair flung out in all directions, a horse flaying against the stable door. She twisted underneath the boy. He fell beside her, banging his head on the ground.

That's when she recognized her only friend.

"*O Dio,* Raffaele—I'm so sorry." They stood up, sniggering teenagers pushing around them.

"Look at the lovebirds," someone shouted.

"Don't talk shit!" Mario yelled from the opposite end of the corridor by the door to the yard. "He wouldn't know where to stick it even if you told him!"

Thunderous laughter now. Alba's cheeks deepened.

"Don't listen to those cretins, Alba," Raffaele whispered, scratching his head. Alba watched a few flakes of dandruff tumble down from his scalp over his forehead.

"Did I break anything?" Alba asked, feeling the sea of hormones wash behind her, blotting out the crackling voices, loose coins jangling in a pocket. Raffaele looked down at her, his huge black eyes sullen in his white face, small eruptions of acne threatening his cheeks. He launched into typical high-gear chatter. It reminded Alba of the passage she'd practiced that morning. As always, he deflected the situation with a long explanation of algebraic logic from his morning's math class. His familiar patter was reassuring. His rhythm rambled, sprouting shoots of tangential thoughts like weeds, filling the air Alba left bare.

"So if I decided that if I switched my approach, I could actually unpick the correct calculation. I think it just proves that math is inherently a creative art. Like people always like to split us into artists or scientists, don't you think? But it's all bullshit because when I'm asking myself 'what if,' it's just the same as someone dreaming up something. Because that's what I'm doing. Seeing an imagined list of outcomes and calculating which one is going to get me the result I need. You following?"

Alba watched Raffaele pull a skim of skin from around his nail with his front teeth.

"Want to walk?" she asked.

They crossed the forecourt, cutting through the cackles of the young girls and the clattering jeers of the boys. The noise grated, treble, discordant.

"Hang on a second," Raffaele said, swinging his backpack round and reaching inside for a *panino*. Despite near constant eating, the boy was a spindle. He ripped the bread in two, a flap of prosciutto hung out the side beneath a thin slice of fontina cheese. He reached it out to her. "You want?"

Alba took it and sunk her teeth in.

"Mamma won't stop checking my food. I swear she knows when I throw it away. Which of course I don't, because that's a waste, but what do I do when I'm not hungry? Seriously, feeding you is the only way I can stop Mamma launching into her lecture about the dangers of calorific and vitamin deficiencies in adolescence."

Alba laughed. He was the only person who could make her do that.

"Algorithmically speaking it's complete nonsense. But she's a Sardinian mother and she doesn't care about the fact that I love numbers more than her. Correction, she is in fact threatened by that. She doesn't even try to understand that. But she wouldn't because she's a doctor and she fixes things. And so do I. Only with my pencil and my brain. I got top marks for calculus today. There are people who do that all day. Did you know there are people who do that all day, Alba?"

They fell into hungry silence for a moment, chomping down on their halves of crusty roll, flicking off the flakes crumbling onto their sweaters as they strode downhill from the high school. Its large yellow concrete façade rose up behind them, overlooking a small park space with a rusting slide and metal seesaw. They reached Piazza Cantareddu, where the buses pulled in to take students back to the neighboring smaller towns. Raffaele ran a hand through his floppy hair and sighed. "I don't want to go home yet. Absolutely don't want to be home."

Alba drew to a stop and wiped her mouth of a final crumb. "Come to mine?"

"What will your ma say?"

"Eat."

"I could—is that okay? I mean is that a bit weird or maybe rude just showing up again? Are your brothers going to give me that look like I'm-the-boyfriend look because I don't know how to deal with that look like they're going to eat me or kiss me or both or worse, I don't like that look. Mamma's visiting a hospital down in Nuoro. Dad's in Sassari at the office."

Alba pictured her mother's face if Raffaele turned up on her doorstep. She made it no secret that she loved the boy. The fact that his mother was a doctor and his father a lawyer only served to cement her affections. Alba ignored the sensation that her mother had crafted secret plans for him to become her son-in-law at the soonest opportunity.

Alba grinned. "My brothers share a brain. My mum loves you."

"I thought you loved me for my physique." He pulled a face then and curled his bicep, which peeped up under his shirt in a feeble half-moon.

"I love you because you were the only boy in kindergarten that didn't try and mutilate my toys."

They began the climb behind the main square, passing several schoolmates. One girl looked them both up and down, scanning for gossip; she leaned into her friend and whispered something. They giggled. Then both of them, catching the eye of someone beyond Alba, separated, lengthened, and pushed their chests farther out displaying their breasts as a prize. It made Alba feel nauseous. The facile rules of adolescence were exhausting and surreal. She scanned the kids hanging out in groups waiting for their rides, picking up the whispers in the air; who kissed whom, which eyeliner was best, which Levi's showed off their hips. Another girl threw a look her way as she passed them with Raffaele, checking for makeup and chosen style, both a drawn blank. Alba wore whatever lay on her chair in the morning from the day before, ran an impatient hand through her hair, and left the house. The other girls' expressions told Alba that such an intimate friendship with an awkward boy like Raffaele was beyond their understanding.

A voice yelled out from behind her toward the peacocking girls. "You asked her out yet?"

Alba swung round to see Mario jeering at Raffaele with a group of friends. She heard the girls simper pathetic laughter, high notes on a piano played with too frothy a touch.

Alba shot him a look.

"Lover girl sticking up for her man. How sweet!" Mario caressed his cheek with a girlish giggle. The pack of boys around him chuckled, thwacks of broken voices bracing boyhood.

Raffaele straightened. "Don't talk to her like that."

"What you going to do? Write a calculation to shut me up?" Mario snapped back, delighted his bait had been bitten.

The girls' laughter spiked.

Alba watched Raffaele's cheeks turn.

"Don't look at me like that, nerd," Mario jeered.

Raffaele's frown creased in confusion.

"I said, don't look at me like that!"

Mario pounced from his throne at the metal table outside the bar where the teenagers congregated for soda, waiting for their buses home. He pushed off with such force that it tipped, sending the glasses smashing to the floor. In a breath, he was on top of Raffaele, pounding his back. Two of Mario's friends jumped up and began kicking into his side. Alba watched her only friend being pummeled. Her chest burned. The sounds tunneled into a pounding silence undercut with a familiar echo of scuffing feet, men's voices. Her hand reached out to a large glass bottle on the table beside Mario's. Her fingers tightened. She swung. The glass smashed against the back of Mario's skull. A splat reached her face. Water? Blood? She didn't care. Her arm cut through the air again and again. A hand on hers clamped her to stillness. The silence became a bass note, slow vibrations waving through the heat. The wetness on her hands turned red. A drip on her trousers blotted crimson. Someone held her.

The smash of the half bottle as it slipped from her hand onto the cobbles brought her attention down to Mario at her feet. There were men around him now. Some hollers. There was a cry, a beige blur of confusion.

Alba didn't remember getting into the car until she noticed the heat of her grandfather's passenger seat. The leather squeaked as Raffaele scooted into the back. They wound the *viccoli* to her house in silence but for the metallic simmer of the engine. As they stepped inside, Giovanna's expression blanched into panic.

"Found them in the square, Giovanna, killing each other like dogs." Her grandfather's voice was a scrape of sandpaper.

Giovanna disappeared into the kitchen and came out with a

bowl of warm water and some cloths. She sat Raffaele down and lifted his chin. He winced. He tried to swallow a tear before it tipped over his lashes but failed.

"Which cretin did this to you?" Giovanna puffed in between blotting. "You tell me who and we'll sort him out."

"We will discuss this when Bruno is home," her grandfather answered, "you just get on and clean him up. Don't want his father to think we'd sent him home without that. The very least we can do after what your child did."

Alba didn't meet his eye.

The door swung open. Alba's brothers bounded in ahead of their father from the *officina*. Marcellino undid the two top buttons of his shirt; at nineteen he'd become the newest executive of the *officina*. His hair was black and thick like Alba's, but his eyes lacked the probing intensity of hers. To him, life was a game and one that was sure to deal him a good hand. Her younger brother, Salvatore, flung his tie and shirt off to sit in just his vest, throwing the discarded uniform to the sofa in a thoughtless crumple. He ran his hand through his floppy light brown hair.

As he caught her eye his expression changed. "Christ! What the hell happened?"

"*O Dio*—who did this?" Marcellino bellowed, seeing Raffaele's face. "Tell me his name and I'll crumple his face for you."

"Back off," Alba hissed, her lips opening into a thin line.

"That's enough from you, Alba," her grandfather overruled.

"What's happening?" Bruno asked, his voice urgent as he stepped in by the table.

"I caught your wild daughter attacking our mechanic's son, Mario, in the middle of the piazza just now. Any more swings with that broken bottle and she'd near enough killed the boy."

"He's a cretin!" Alba blurted.

"Quiet!" Bruno spat. "Every week you have to make a fool of yourself. Of us!"

"She's hurt, Bruno," Giovanna eased.

"You've spoiled this girl and you see how she turned out? I've told you and I've told you again, but no, you let her do as she pleases. And now look! Running around town like a demented urchin, picking fights. She'll be at Marcellino's wedding next week looking like this!"

"Take it easy, Bruno," Alba's grandfather murmured.

Giovanna's hand began to shake. She pressed the cloth a little too hard onto Raffaele's face. He took a sharp intake of breath.

"*Scusa,* Raffaele," Giovanna whispered, "are you alright?"

He nodded, biting his lip.

"And the boy?" Bruno bellowed a breath away from Alba's face. "Don't tell me you hit him too, for God's sake?"

Alba's head didn't move. Tears rolled down her cheeks.

"Say something, for Christ's sake!"

Bruno's shouts ricocheted against the surrounding stone walls, creeping closer with every hot second that pounded.

"What you asking her for, Babbo?" Marcellino jeered. "You think she's going to answer for once?"

"I'm not talking to you, Marcellino," Bruno replied, "or you, Salvatore."

Alba noticed her younger brother swallow an interjection.

"What in God's name is this family coming to? You know what I do all day for you at the *officina?* What we all do? And you just float in and out of this house as if you weren't here. You run out of the house before dawn for that old lady on the hill, doing her every whim like a servant girl and in here you're like this! What am I supposed to do with someone like this at work?"

A knock at the door. Everyone turned toward it. Salvatore opened it. Their neighbor Grazietta poked her head around the wood. She took a breath to begin her usual prattle but the angry eyes pinning her at the doorframe stopped her train of thought in an instant.

"Raffaele! *Dio!* Who did this? This boy needs a hospital! Giova', I'll come with you to the hospital," she flapped, "my nephew is on shift today, he'll help us."

"Stay where you are," Bruno interrupted, "my lawyer's son is being looked after just fine." Grazietta turned pale. "Sick and tired of you women telling me how to look after this stupid child! Alba did this. All this. You women have no idea how to bring her up. You bring shame on all of us!"

He reached for the jug of water and filled a glass, emptying it in two gulps. He set it back down too quickly and it almost cracked. His eyes drifted over to the wide dish of fresh ravioli, fast cooling as the argument steamed on, the pecorino hardening to a congealed mess.

"Bruno," Grandfather stepped in, "eat your lunch, then decide what needs to be done. And something drastic. You can't get away with this any longer, Alba, you hear me? Time you learned how to behave as part of this family. People respect us. We've all worked our guts out to give you children a good life. You don't throw it in our faces like this, you hear? Your father got taken by the bandits and we fought against them. I won't stand here and watch my granddaughter become a spoiled brat. I won't let you ruin my name, do you hear?"

Bruno yanked a chair out from the head of the table; it screeched along the tiles. "Eat with us, Papà." He flicked a look at Giovanna. She pulled the cloth away from Raffaele's face.

"I'll stop by later then?" Grazietta squeaked into the charged silence.

"And before you go," Bruno snarled, "and think about going around the rest of the street telling them what you just saw, just remember this is me when I'm calm. No one wants to see me angry. Hear me?"

Grazietta scurried back out onto the street.

The boys sat down in the shadow of their father's suffocated ire.

"You going to help Mamma or what?" Marcellino hollered at Alba.

She stood up. Her fingers gripped the ladle.

"Talk to that old woman Elias, Giovanna," Bruno called out to her as she returned to the kitchen for a basket of bread, "tell her Alba has to stop working for her immediately. No knowing what she'll do."

His words tore right through Alba. A thin line of high-pitched whir in her head grew in volume. Alba scooped up three plump parcels of ricotta and spinach. Marcellino lifted his plate. She pulled the spoon over past the rim and let the ravioli fall onto his lap. Marcellino jumped up, yelping. Giovanna rushed out of the kitchen. The room skewed, piano strings twisted out of tune. Alba didn't remember flinging the door open, the cries of her mother, the sound of her feet pounding the toasted cobbles as she dragged her friend behind her and ran toward the road for the *pineta*. She remembered only the salt of her angry tears wetting her lips and the sound of her brothers like hungry hounds, echoes swallowed up by the distance.

It was Alba's favorite time to be in the *pineta*. The shade didn't hum with the fringes of summer, there was a pleasant cool. They found a stump on the needled floor and sat in silence fighting to catch their breath.

"I don't know who's going to kill me first. My father or yours," Raffaele murmured.

Their breaths eased toward normal.

"What are we going to do, Alba? I mean we can't just sit here. And when Mario sees me tomorrow, he's going to kill me completely, I mean not just like this, I mean absolutely no breathing, as in dead, do you hear me? And dead is not what I want to be right now, can you understand that? Do you have any idea how terrified I am right now?"

Alba picked up a dried needle and started twiddling it between her fingers.

"Tell me what to do!"

Raffaele's tears fought for their freedom and won. Alba reached for his hand and squeezed it. The bruises on his face were starting to form, blushed bougainvillea pinks, crushed grape purples.

"I don't know," she murmured.

"You have to."

"I don't remember any of it."

"You saved me."

His eyes warmed into an expression she didn't recognize. Her brow creased.

"Are you going to kiss me, Raffaele?"

He swallowed. Neither moved.

"You're my brother."

"I know," he replied. His stillness unnerved Alba.

"Don't you just want to get all of this out of the way? I mean, it's like I don't care about any of it and just want it done. Cleared up. Is that weird? It's a bit weird maybe. I just want to stop feeling like I should be having feelings about it? And I do want to kiss you. Well not really, but you're sort of the only person I could if I had to. Not that we have to. I want to get some sex out of the way before I fall in love with someone. Sorry. I mean, not sorry, but sort of." His fingers reached up for a pimple on his cheeks and started twiddling. "Help me anytime you want, Alba. I'm drowning here."

"Sort of how I feel, I think."

Raffaele looked up.

"That makes us both weird, I guess," Alba added, smoothing the hair off her face. He was the only person she could be honest with. It was an orange glow in her belly.

"We could try?" she began, feeling the absurdity of the moment heat her cheeks.

"Really? I thought you were about to hit me."

"Make sure you get out before you—you know."

Raffaele swallowed. "Yeah, course."

"Will you know when?"

"Think so?"

They looked at each other. Alba moved her face toward his. Raffaele sneezed, splattering his T-shirt. A speck of saliva flecked Alba's wrist.

"Sorry," he murmured, wiping his arm across his face.

He took a breath and Alba knew he was about to launch into a punctuation-free sentence. She stopped him with her lips. He didn't move. After a moment, their heads switched incline. The kiss was stilted and angular. It dissolved the hissing red in her ears. She twisted out of her jeans and he out of his. She felt his penis harden on her thigh. It felt like two friends marking their hypothesis ahead of a scientific experiment. He eased himself inside Alba. They stopped for a moment.

"Is it awful? Does it feel weird?" he stammered. "Does it hurt? I'll stop if it's hurting."

"Stop talking."

An expression streaked his long face. Alba reached up with her hands. "I'm not saying it's not nice. Try moving."

He did, slowly at first, tentative whispers in his hips, reluctant, stiff. His breath quickened. His eyes closed. He looked like he was listening to a far-off call, a pianissimo section. Alba thought about the ferocity of a demanding measure of Liszt, her hands defiant, full of longing. But as her friend became urgent on top of her, it was like watching him through glass. The sounds and feelings muted, an echo reaching her, diluted and distorted. He pulled out. His semen spilled in spurts across the needled floor.

It was over.

They lay upon their backs gazing up at the pines above them, crisscrossing lines of green against the pure blue.

"I don't know how I'm feeling, Alba."

Their silence creased. The cicadas raised their cry. Congratulatory or mocking, Alba couldn't tell.

"I don't know if I want to do that again," he said.

"Me neither."

Alba propped herself up on one elbow and looked down at her friend's face. "Your face looks awful."

"The idiot staring at me saved me. That's all I care about."

His narrow chest rose and fell as his breath deepened toward normal.

Alba smiled. Her headache had gone at last. "I love you."

He smiled with relief. "No one I would have liked to get all that out of the way with other than you. It's a minty freedom."

Her face spread into a grin. "One try at sex and you speak poems, not algorithms."

"No," he replied, his voice dipped in a sudden seriousness. "Love does that."

Alba laughed and fell onto her back. She reached her hand for his.

When they returned to their spot the next day, Raffaele broke down whilst revealing his love for his neighbor Claudio. Alba held her weeping friend as he described wanting to suffocate his desires by having sex with her. Her strong fingers wrapped around his shuddering arms as sobs spilled from him. Their foreheads touched. His tears streaked her cheeks. His secret was out and safe. Would she ever be able to say the same?

5

Accelerando, accel.
accelerating; gradually increasing the tempo

At last, the week from hell reached its welcome end. Both daughter and parents stood firm, retreating into stubborn silences. Alba was accompanied to school by Marcellino, and returned flanked by Salvatore, both instructed not to let her out of their sight. The notes she'd written to Signora Elias in her mind would never reach her. Raffaele tried to talk with her but each time one or other of her brothers would intervene, as instructed. Alba ignored her mother at her own peril, because if she'd paid more attention, she may have noticed Raffaele's father at the house more often. She might have thought that Raffaele's mother coming round was odd. But she didn't. She baked the *papassini* as her mother asked. She sliced melon thin upon a plate. She poured the coffee when asked and attended to all her usual duties, trying to mask her bitterness so as not to give them the satisfaction of them seeing how much they hurt her. She returned from school that Friday to find her mother leaning over her father with a needle in one hand and a red thread hanging from it. She mimed stitching her father's eye, as if joining both eyelids together. The thread lifted through her father's thick eyelashes several times. He had another sty. This was the tried and tested remedy.

"Good, you're back. Your father has come home to talk to you before your brothers get home. Sit down."

It was the first time Giovanna had looked excited about anything other than Marcellino's wedding, or directed anything to her for that matter.

Alba's suspicion peaked.

"Your father and I have been talking."

Bruno patted her mother's hand. They smiled at each other. Their loving moment should have filled Alba with relief. Had they decided to let her work for Signora Elias again? Had they mistaken her sullen quiet for obedience? Something stirred in her stomach.

"I've been asked to give permission for you to marry," Bruno said, taking over the exposition of wonderful news.

Alba sat motionless.

"Say something," Bruno murmured. "A smile would be a good start."

"By who?" Alba blurted, her cheeks' creasing, making the bruises from the fight still ache.

"Who?" Bruno asked, perplexed. "How many are you leading on at once?"

"It's perfectly normal to be nervous!" Giovanna piped up. "I was a wreck when your father asked me. It's what girls do. It's a big step. You're young, I know. This week has been difficult, yes. But having children young is better. And I will help of course with the children so you can keep up your job at the *officina*. All the modern girls do that now. You don't have to stay at home like I did. You can have it all, Alba. Freedom! And such a good family. I'm going to cry."

Alba watched as her mother lived her proposal on her behalf. All the tears she ought to be shedding, all the excitement for a life revolved around work at the *officina* and babies. A delightful seesaw of obligations to guarantee fulfilment.

"I said yes, of course," Bruno added, trying to steer the conversation back.

Alba looked at her father. Whose betrayal was worse? Hers for sneaking out of their sight under the guise of aiding an old lady or theirs for coordinating the rest of her life? She couldn't protest because she was too guilty. She couldn't accept because the thought was absurd. Why had her friend done this to her? He was saving them both from the fate of small-town living, but had he not stopped to think that their fate was inscribed in the stone streets of the very place they needed to careen away from? Was his love for Claudio so deep that he would do something as stupid as this? Love was not blind, thought Alba. It was sheer self-destruction.

Giovanna's arms wound around her now, squeezing what little hope there was left. Celeste rose into Alba's mind, her dancing eyes, her voice filled with spring and floral celebration. That room felt like a place she'd touched in a dream.

A knock at the door tore the trio's attention away from the absurd plan. Alba opened the door, more to escape the enforced celebration than anything else. Signora Elias stood on the street. She looked smaller somehow. Without words Alba tried to describe what had happened. She watched her teacher look at her face, still marked with the fight, registering the cuts and bruises.

"I couldn't come," Alba said, feeling tears sting her eyes, watching her teacher read in between her breaths.

"It's quite alright, Alba," she soothed. "You're not to worry. I had to come now though. I have a letter for you which you must read."

"Signora!" Giovanna called out, stepping in behind her daughter. "Please, come in, you need coffee? An *aperitivo* maybe?"

"*Grazie,* Signora, but I can't stay. I have a shopping order to pick up at the butcher. Actually, might Alba just help me to carry it to my car? I won't keep her more than five minutes. I know she'll be helping you with lunch."

"Bruno is here, he can help. I'll call him!"

As Giovanna turned to call for him, Signora Elias insisted. Alba suspected she was the only woman who might do that to her mother. "I won't have you trouble him. I know how hard he works, Alba will do just as well."

Alba tried not to look excited at the prospect and it appeared to serve as enough to convince her mother that running the errand would not upset her father. She gave a terse nod and Signora Elias didn't waste any time.

Alba hadn't realized how fast the old woman walked until they were striding downhill. Anyone who might have seen would have been as confused as her father as to why this nimble woman needed a young girl to run her morning goods up to her each morning. It made Alba love her even more than she already did. Nothing stood in the way of Signora Elias's will. Besides her playing, that was a dark art in and of itself.

Signora Elias led them to a bench in the small Piazza Cantareddu, where next week the fires would be lit for St. John's celebrations. Alba and Raffaele would always leap over the embers together with the other teenagers. This year would be different. If she didn't strangle him before then for not stopping this harebrained idea of marriage before it got out of hand.

They sat beneath the acers, sheltered in their mottled shade. Alba knew better than to ask about the butcher. There was no shopping to collect. Signora Elias had prized a little privacy for them, that was all.

"I have something important to tell you, Alba."

Alba's heart lurched.

"I have a letter here."

Signora Elias was about to elucidate when Alba's tears compelled her attention.

"*Dio,* whatever is the matter, child? What I have to say is the most amazing thing I've ever had to say to any of my pupils."

Alba looked up.

"Whatever's the matter?" Signora Elias asked.

"They want me to marry," Alba sobbed, hating herself for not being able to talk like a sensible person, to stretch her back, deepen her breath, hold some kind of center. She was behaving like the very girls she never longed to emulate.

Signora Elias wiped her tears. Her thumbs were smooth and firm.

"I didn't know you were courting?"

"I'm not. He's my best friend. It's not our idea. It's all so stupid I can't believe I'm even telling you. I'm so sorry, Signora."

"Nonsense. I would be hurt if you didn't. Here." She handed over a neat folded tissue from her pocket.

"*Grazie.*"

They sat in silence for a moment. Alba grew aware of the sauntering teenagers beginning to fill the *piazzetta,* still parading after the end of school before returning home. It would be better if none of them saw her like this, even if Signora Elias had picked a bench a little way from the main drag.

"Perhaps when they find out what I have to say everything might change?" Signora Elias soothed. "You may want to cry again, and that is absolutely fine with me, do you hear?"

Alba nodded, but her words were a dying echo. Signora unfolded a letter. It was cream paper, embossed at the top, which Alba could make out from the sunlight hitting it from behind Signora Elias. Her teacher began reading.

When she finished she looked up.

Alba could hear nothing but the galloping thuds in her chest.

"Do you understand what they're offering you, Alba?"

"I want to but I don't think I believe it."

"A full scholarship, Alba. This is only offered for exceptional students at the *accademia.* Celeste has also offered that you might take a few classes at the *conservatorio,* the adjoined school, which prepares pupils from the basic level up to a standard where they might try out for the *accademia.* These extra classes would only be for the first few months, just to bring you up to speed on the theory side of things. I've covered most of what you need but she thinks it would help you. Only a handful of piano students are chosen each year."

"What?"

"My dear friend is the head assessor at the Accademia of Santa Cecilia in Rome. What she says goes. It is highly unusual, which means your first year will be very important. As with all students, there is no guarantee that you will stay for the whole three years unless you maintain a high standard. If you do not keep up the work it will be in their rights to ask you to leave, you understand? Especially with such an atypical admission process."

"I'm trying to hear what you're saying but it's like it's so sunny my ears are blocked. Does that even make any sense?"

Signora reached forward and wrapped her arms around Alba. She wasn't sure which one of them was crying now. As Signora

Elias pulled away her face lit up. "I knew it from the very first moment. Something about the way you sat. Something about your curiosity, humility, power, passion even you don't fully understand just yet, I suspect. And I don't mean that in a patronizing way—it's not a reductive remark, I mean that you are just at the start of your potential and it fills me with grace and hope and pleasure that has been lacking in my life for too long."

Alba watched her wipe her eyes, feeling waves of gratitude and embarrassment and grief and excitement.

"I will be happy to let your parents know. You won't do this alone. This has a lot to do with me and I will take the responsibility, you must trust me on that, yes?"

"How?"

"All you need do is play. You must leave everything else to me, *sì?*"

Sunday arrived and the Fresu household became a tense allegro. Alba's fingers ached for the instrument in the house she'd been barred from. Her heart raced with the prospect of when and how Signora Elias would explain her offer to her parents, which they'd decided to delay till after the wedding. Giovanna ran up and down the stairs remembering and forgetting, her feet stomping the stone as she switched scarves, exchanged earrings, begged her sons to wear what they had agreed the night before. In one hand, she clutched a cloth bag of grains and in another a basket of rose petals. She and Grazietta had stayed in the previous evening, plucking them from their stems, listing the wrongs of the neighbors and the fanfare with which Marcellino's prospective mother-in-law had dealt her demands for his wedding to her daughter Lucia. Alba noticed her mother's streaming thoughts had more in common with the discarded thorny stems than the petals as they released their delicate scent between the women's tugging thumbs. At last it was the morning of the largest wedding in town to date, a triumph Alba's mother bore with pride and panic.

Alba heard her mother fly up the stairs one more time and took the chance to step into the kitchen for some water. Marcellino leaned against the tiled counter.

"You look like a ghost," she said.

He glanced up and gave a half smile. He sighed, ran his hand over his black hair, cemented with gel.

"Break the habit of a lifetime and say something nice," he replied.

Alba noticed his skin was salty with nervous sweat. She returned his half smile in reply. Marcellino ruffled her hair, nearly pulling out the flower Giovanna had insisted she wear. She felt like a hedge trying to dress as a rose. Her mother had painted over her bruises, but they still blushed through the makeup.

Bruno poked his head around the doorframe. He reached out a small shot glass to his firstborn, filled to the brim with *acquavite.* There were no words to accompany the gesture, only a complicit silence. Marcellino's eyes widened with the fire coursing down his throat. Bruno laughed and took his son's cheeks in his hands. Alba couldn't remember the last time she'd seen her father so happy. Would he do this to her once he heard her music? Would he understand the gift Signora Elias had given her? It was the first time Alba could remember seeing his smile take over his face with complete abandon. Her heart twisted into a knot. Bruno shot her a glance. A warning? She would have liked to find the words to reassure him that she wouldn't be starting a fight at the party, but a stubborn silence froze her face into well-rehearsed diffidence; the night before she'd heard her parents argue over where Mario's father, Gigi, and the family would be seated to make sure that Alba wouldn't cause unnecessary problems.

The men left and bundled into a large black sedan Fiat. Giovanna, Grazietta, and Alba scooted onto the leather back seat of a smaller vehicle. At once the line of cars waiting outside their house started sounding their horns. The caravan of trumpeting cars wove through Ozieri, announcing to the few people who were not invited that the son of one of the most successful families in town was about to marry the love of his life. The narrow *viccoli* were filled with the bombardment of metallic orchestration, the rumble of the engines, the treble of the obnoxious Klaxons. The cars filled every nook around the cathedral, a metallic cluster of ants upon the cobbles. Cars were eked into narrow spaces at angles, double-parked, a breath of space between them, whilst the Fresu clan headed up to Lucia's flower-strewn house for Marcellino to collect his bride. Lucia's mother greeted Giovanna with two kisses. Wine was passed around. Voices collided like currents bouncing off the marble floors and up the stone walls and concave ceiling. The eldest aunt threw flowers over Lucia's head, a face floating in a meringue of lace and tulle. Grains were thrown over Marcellino for fertility. A plate was smashed. The cheers were an assault on Alba's ears, but her mother's face streaked with tears and Bruno's infectious smile made everyone believe him to be the proudest of fathers.

Violent happiness thundered around her. The claustrophobic energy reminded Alba her music might swerve toward unavoidable disappearance. Her father made no secret that her destiny lay behind the counter at the *officina*, learning from Mario's father no less, overseeing the parts and books. Alba decided it was his prolonged punishment for what she'd done to his son. Every Saturday from now on was to be spent beside him learning every detail of the job. What pleasure would be found in the quiet order of nuts and bolts? The idea of listening to the customers and their mechanical needs made her heart ache. To Mario's father, customers' car stories elongated into detailed descriptions of domestic concerns, delivered with mechanical precision. He oiled their worries, wiped them clean off their conscience, and then replaced them with new thoughts. Alba couldn't picture herself doing the same. The knot in her chest twisted a little tighter.

In the cathedral, the priest intoned a mass they all knew by heart whilst the echoes of the crowd rippled whispers up the stone like a September sea caressing the white sands of the shore. The couple were blessed, then stepped out into the glare of the midmorning sun, where they were showered with more grains of rice and petals and hollers. The snaking parade of cars then curved through the valley, pumping out their triumphant cries with a further blast of horns vibrating the sunny stillness toward the plains. When they reached the new headquarters of the *officina*, waves of people flooded the hangar where the cars were usually stored, now moved and parked outside, filling the surrounding tarmac, to allow shelter of the seven hundred invitees. Tables stretched from one end to another with a central one heaving with food.

Vast trays offered every kind of salad, sliced meats, and cheeses, which the guests dove into as if everyone had refrained from eating for the entire week in preparation. Servers swarmed the tables after that with trays of fresh *gnochetti*, linguini with bottarga, and fresh ravioli. The king prawns that followed were almost punishment, but the guests soldiered on, plates heaped with discarded pink shells, fingers sticky and happy with parsley and garlic juice. Wine sloshed between glasses, onto tablecloths, onto some men's shirts. When the roasted suckling pigs were pushed in on a trolley, they were met with cheers.

Alba watched her town before her from her seat at the head table, ignoring the knowing stares at her bruised face beneath the layers of pink blusher. Her father swayed between tables, shaking hands, laughing full bellied, her mother's feathers sprayed with pride, her brothers among the guests greeting everyone like princes. Several tables beyond theirs Raffaele sat beside his parents looking his usual pale self, his own face a healing map of surface wounds. Alba shot him a look, counting the seconds until she could get him outside and lay into him for being in any way complicit with the obnoxious plan for them to marry. They had to stay visible at least for the meal before she could find a quiet corner for them to talk.

A chorus of glass tinkling rose from the tables, to yells for the couple to kiss. "*Bacio! Bacio!*" the guests belted, a canon of bass and tenor, soprano laughter. The tempo quickened, till it galloped toward consummation. Marcellino and Lucia leaned into each other, pressed their lips together, and the room exploded with applause.

Once the first feast reached its end, Alba took the opportunity to escape. Outside the air was hot against her skin. The sun was beginning its golden descent toward the mountains, their purple silhouettes rising into focus.

"I've been going crazy not being able to talk to you!" Raffaele called out, breathless.

Alba turned. He stood a few steps behind her, his vanilla skin turning amber, the sun streaking across the healing scrapes on his forehead.

"You've lost your mind!" she blurted. "I don't want to talk to you. I want to hurt you."

"Yes, I'm fine, thanks, my friend, how are you?"

Alba shook her head. "You're the insane one here, not me."

"Actually I've accepted our escape route."

"For someone so clever your common sense has some seriously arrested development."

Raffaele grabbed her shoulder. "You want to die here?"

"No dramatics, Ra'."

"We get married—we get to do what we like with our lives. *Real* lives. What town do you think we're living in, Alba? We both know what plans they've made for you. And they don't involve Elias."

Alba stiffened.

"You don't think I've put two and two together? The way you speak about music. The way your face lights up like a flame when you've played me some of the records she gave you at my house? Come on. You don't have to be a detective to know that spending every morning with a music teacher insinuates you are her pupil."

"Save your smart-ass for someone else, Ra'. They stopped me going after the fight. Why do you think I've had my brothers following me like shadows?"

"And it's killing you. Alba, this is me. Not some idiot. I'm not going to tell anyone. Obviously. Crazy that we're even having this conversation."

Alba pinned him with a stare.

"Don't be like that. I'm just . . ." His voice trailed off for a moment.

"I thought you were my friend," she whispered, fighting tears of frustration and almost winning.

"I wouldn't be here if I wasn't."

Alba turned her gaze away from him, playing chess maneuvers in her mind to escape her corner.

"My parents will be expecting a good match for me," he said, undeterred, releasing his hands from her. "I don't want to spend my life with another woman. It makes me feel like I'm dying. You don't want to spend your life behind the counter of an *officina*—so why don't we cut our losses, do the stupid thing, and then move away from it all?"

Alba turned to him, eyes stinging. "You're talking shit."

"At least I'm talking."

Her breaths rose in her chest.

"I got the acceptance letter from the University of Cagliari yesterday. I don't know how I'm going to cope without you, Alba. We know each other's secrets."

Not all of them, Alba thought.

"I don't think there's a soul out there I could trust like I do you. And it terrifies me."

Alba held her friend's cheek in her hand. His skin was soft even where he had shaved. She took a breath to tell him about her offer from the *accademia*. Mario's sneer interrupted before she could. "People normally go someplace private to do that shit."

The pair twisted round to him as he threw a cigarette into his mouth and lit it.

"People normally don't interrupt conversations they're not part of," Alba snapped.

"Planning on swinging for round two, Alba? Your papà would love that. At your brother's wedding of the year and all."

Alba pinned him with a stare. Mario flicked his ash down onto the dusty earth by her shoes. "Don't know what you see in her, Raffaele," he jeered.

"Your dad's pissed as a fart, Alba," Mario said, flicking her a diagonal grin.

She watched Mario take a deep drag on his cigarette, the orange-ruby light dipping his skin a richer olive, the thick mass of eyelashes potent shades for his jeering eyes.

"Anyway, get back to your necking. Your dads will be organizing your big day in no time neither." He scuffed the dirt. "What?" he asked, taking another drag. "Frustrating to have to hear it as it is and not be able to throw a bottle at me?"

He turned back to the hangar, which hummed with song now, a

call-and-response chant, each verse interrupted by the throng in unison.

"He likes you," Raffaele said.

Alba shot him a look.

"I know you'd like me to say he's straight out terrified of you. But when you're a stupid boy choked by the feelings you have for someone you behave like him. Pretty much how I deal with Claudio on a daily basis. Either that or I act like I'm totally indifferent."

Raffaele's smile was fringed with sadness.

"The next few months are going to be intense. I know it. Dad's got big plans for me. I'll do anything to take the heat off."

"I need to talk to you."

"That's what we're doing," he replied, just as Salvatore came bounding out of the hangar.

"Alba, Raffaele! Babbo says to come in, they're about to toast you!"

Alba couldn't get her response out before they were dragged inside to deafening applause.

"Please God, these two will be the next!" Bruno shouted. The crowd stood, gleaming eyes that Alba felt were seeming to wish imprisonment on them both. Her bones felt brittle, as if they'd never felt the response of a piano's song beneath them, calling out all that was hers to utter in secret, filling the air with melodic freedom, nor never would again.

She tried to swallow, but her mouth remained dry.

6

Fuoco
a directive to perform a certain passage with energy and passion. *Con fuoco* means with fire, instruction to play in a fiery manner.

A few days later, Signora Elias dropped by to speak with Giovanna and offer a cordial invitation to come to hers for coffee, an official thank-you for all the time she and Alba had worked for her she'd said, in a way that Giovanna was left with no power to refuse. The date was set. During the weekend, after school had reached its end, Alba and her parents would come to her house. Never had five days felt so close and far away.

Now, at the beginning of the week, all of Ozieri crowded around the huge bonfire in Piazza Cantareddu to celebrate St. John the Baptist. Beside the fire, people sat upon wooden benches drinking wine and carving slabs of cheese from other enormous pieces, wrapping them into blankets of bread and toasting the feast. Applause began from one end of the square and rippled up to where Alba sat with her mother and Grazietta.

"*Abaida!*" Grazietta called above the din. "Isn't that Gigi's boy? I didn't know he was singing with the men now!"

Alba shot a look across to where a group of men were tightening into a circle intoning a chord before their song. She scanned the familiar faces and there, beside his father, was Mario. His flat black hat flopped over one ear, his white shirt billowing out from beneath a black tunic. Their voices vibrated with a warm, burnished sound, glistening copper tones. Then they stopped, took a breath in unison, and began to sing. She listened as Mario's voice lifted up above the group, the purest column of sound she'd ever heard. His timbre woody yet crisp, golden and bright, full of yearning. It was impossible to match this voice with the imbecile she loathed. This couldn't be the arrogant boy flicking ash toward her feet. Where was his snarl, the sideways grimace, the unattractive swagger? He took a deeper breath and his voice rose higher still, enhanced by the earthy bass chord beneath, the crowd hushed at the sound. The others men's voices glowed blood red and ochre and above, the sky blue of his love song. Alba felt the tears in her eyes but stopped them from falling. Her mother mopped her own with a frenetic hand. Grazietta wound an arm around her.

"People are born with this gift, Giovanna," Grazietta whispered, thrilled, "you can't teach someone that. God bless him. What a voice. From God I say. What a sound."

His eyes lowered from his upward gaze and found hers. She watched, her stare impenetrable. It was her turn to gaze through a crack and he knew it.

The crowd burst into cheers. Gigi's friends patted him on the back. Some of the boys in their class knocked Mario's hat off his head and whacked him with it. Then the group merged toward the other end of the piazza where a smaller fire edged toward embers. The children lined up on one side. One of the parents belted out instructions most wouldn't hear above the noise. The first child burst into a sprint, then leaped over the flames. The crowd cheered.

Raffaele slipped in behind Alba. "We have to do it you know, it's our last year."

"I think we need more than a leap over flames to get us out of our mess."

"Now who is being dramatic?"

"*Prag*matic."

"We're officially not kids next year, Alba. Besides, you want Mario to think you don't have the guts?"

"Why would I care what he thought?"

"Saw you watch him singing."

Alba thwacked an elbow into his side. He grabbed her wrist and ran them on, pulling her behind him, laughing in spite of herself, till they fell into line. Mario and his mates were coercing one another with shoves and pelted insults. One of the parents screamed to stay away from the embers and the younger child ahead of them, impervious to the kerfuffle behind them.

The music from the other side of the square was louder now, belting through the speakers. Alba thought she caught sight of her parents waltzing. All of a sudden, she was at the front of the line. Raffaele's voice hummed in her ear. "Remember, you've got to think of stuff you want rid of! St. John will sort it. Take away the bad."

"You don't believe that shit and I know it," she screamed back.

"And you love it more than you'd admit, pagan-girl."

He knew her better than she'd like to admit. Besides, there were only a few days between now and her parents discovering her daughter had received the most prestigious invitation they could have ever dreamed up. A marriage to a local wealthy boy was nothing compared to that. And yet. She brushed off her unease, loosing herself for a breath in the fire, as it burned, insistent, free.

A snatched breath, then she charged toward it. The summer air kissed her cheeks as she cut through. Her legs felt powerful. Excitement rose up through their fiber, her chest light and free. She leaped. Time melted. Below, the dancing flames. The sounds of voices swallowed up by the dark. There was only the red lick of the light beneath her. She rose higher. The amber glow upon a face on the opposite side of the circle huddled around the leapers met hers. The moment hovered, hot, hidden. Mario's eyes were inscrutable. Then the cobbles rose to meet her with a thud as her gum soles landed. Ozieri crashed back into her ears, a fanatic crescendo, a sforzando chord full of authority, defiance and rebellion. Mario disappeared into the crowd.

Signora Elias's piano room smelled of vanilla and almond. Giovanna agreed to let Alba go ahead of her, whilst she waited for Bruno to accompany her a little later. Alba arrived to practice finding the kitchen counters topped with several baking trays. There was a neat parade of fig jam–filled *tiricche*, fine white pastry twists cut with a serrated wooden wheel leaving edges like lace. In a ceramic dish Signora Elias's famed *sospiri* were laid in a circle with a tiny space between each so that the heat wouldn't melt them and make them stick together. These were Bruno's favorite, but Alba knew no amount of sugar would sweeten the betrayal they were about to reveal.

"Don't hover in your nerves, Alba. You leave this all to me. All you must do is warm up and play. Everything else rests on my shoulders, do you understand?"

Alba wanted to but she knew her father better than that.

"At some point our secret had to come out, no? This is the nature of secrets. They have a lifespan of their own. Eventually they too must die, as they shift from the dark into the light."

Alba felt her eyebrows squeeze into a frown.

"Goodness, my metaphors will do nothing to ease your mind, I'm sure. Off you go, I have things to do here now."

Alba let herself be shooed back out toward the piano. She took her seat as she had done for all those mornings up till today. Her scales began a little slower than usual. Her mind began to percuss the fragment of space between the notes, the middle quiet where one note ends and another begins, the subtle shifts in frequency urging her toward the instrument and away from her rattling nerves. As her fingers spidered up and down the keyboard Alba felt the warmth of that wordless place, one she was always being criticized by her father for living in most of the time but the very strength this instrument required. She didn't hear the bell ring until it jangled for what must have been the fourth time. Her fingers lifted off the keys as if scalded. Signora Elias appeared at the kitchen doorway wiping hers.

"You stay exactly where you are, Signorina. I will let your parents in."

Every sound thrummed like a chord cutting across a silence: the creak of the door, its solemn close, her mother's footsteps along the shiny floors, tentative clips toward the piano room. Giovanna entered. She registered Alba seated upon the ottoman.

"Please, do get comfortable, Signora Giovanna," Signora Elias said, leading her into the room she cleaned once a week. "The coffee is just about ready. Alba, do help me with the sweets, *si?*"

Alba was relieved to be asked to do something other than sit beside her mother, who looked stiff. She scooped up two plates and returned to the table in front of the ottoman. Giovanna gave her a peculiar look, swerving embarrassment or perhaps pride, Alba couldn't decide which.

"And Signore Bruno?" Signora Elias asked without a trace of emotion, though his absence made Alba feel more uneasy than before. She placed the coffeepot on a holder and poured Giovanna a dainty china cup and handed it over.

"He's got caught with a terrible customer, Signora," Giovanna replied, breathy. "I stopped by at the *officina.* It's awfully busy. There was simply no way he could get away. He sends his apologies. It's just us women together. Probably best. You know how he is, Signora."

Signora Elias smiled, unruffled. Alba shifted along the velvet, which prickled her bare legs below the hem of her cutoff shorts.

"Do have a sweet, Signora Giovanna, I made them especially. It's wonderful to have someone to bake for. Try one of each."

Signora Elias and Giovanna performed the ritual dance of refusal and insistence, and, as always, age won out and Giovanna ate as ordered. Watching her mother do as she was told filled Alba with hope that what was about to happen might not be the disaster she anticipated.

"Very well, Signora Giovanna."

"Please, Signora, just call me Giovanna."

"You're not working today, Signora, today you are the respected mother of this wonderful young woman. What I would like you to enjoy now, is the fruit of my time with Alba. She has helped me a great deal, and I know there have been times over the years where you have considered taking her job away as punishment, an understandable measure considering, but I first of all want to thank you, from the deepest part of my heart, for not doing so. When I came to you after the Mario debacle you listened to my plea, and, as an old woman living alone, I can't tell you what that meant."

Giovanna shifted in her seat. Alba saw her eye the *sospiri*. Signora Elias lifted the dish right away and insisted she take another. Her mother never told Alba it was Signora Elias who had saved her lessons from her father's threat to terminate them. Alba clung on to the belief that he'd spat it in the heat of a temper, nothing more. Giovanna had let Alba believe that she'd permitted her to continue working for Signora Elias out of the goodness of her heart, and for a while, Alba had believed her mother understood her friendship with Signora Elias was the most important part of her life. Now she watched the subtle shadow of betrayal cast a gray over her mother's face. It made her own lighten for a breath.

"But enough prattling from me, I invited you and Signore Bruno to hear something quite marvelous this morning and I can only say that I hope you will enjoy it as much as I do. It is my wish, that when Alba has finished what she has prepared, you will understand what a wonder it has been working with your daughter."

Giovanna took a breath to speak. Signora Elias interrupted. "Do get comfortable. And enjoy."

Signora Elias nodded at Alba. The metallic ache in her stomach piqued. She stood up and took her seat at the stool. As she pushed it a little farther away with her feet she caught sight of her canvas pumps. They were the ones she'd worn that day she'd had sex with Raffaele in the *pineta*. Giovanna forced her to scrub them clean once a week, but Alba felt like a little of the pine dust always remained. No amount of water could take that away.

She caught Signora Elias's eye. It sent a wave of calm over her. She let her breath leave her chest and deepen into her lower back. The soles of her feet rooted onto the floor. The room shifted into her periphery. Her fingers sunk down onto Chopin's notes she had played countless times. A purple melancholy swept over her. Wave after wave of measures rolled on with ease, the notes a cocoon around her and the piano, dancing light. The mournful melody swirled out from her, weighted, familiar, describing the longing and silence she could not articulate with words alone. The ending trickled into view, an unstoppable tide urging toward the shore.

And then it was over.

Alba lifted her fingers with reluctance, holding on to the space before reality would have to be confronted. She placed them on her lap and looked at her mother.

Giovanna's eyes were wet. Her breath seemed to catch somewhere high in her chest. Signora Elias didn't fill her silence. Alba looked at her teacher. Her eyes glistened with pride. Whatever happened now, that expression was one Alba would cling to. In the golden gap between this moment and their next, Alba felt like her mother cradled her life in her lap, petals of possibility that might tumble and crush underfoot if she rose too quick, or be thrown into the air, fragrant confetti of celebration.

"Signora Giovanna," Signora Elias began at last, "in return for all the errands your daughter does for me I offered what I could, besides money, in return. You see, the moment she sat at my instrument I knew I would be failing my duty as a teacher if I didn't protect and nurture her talent."

Giovanna opened her mouth to speak but her thoughts remained choked.

"Your daughter has become an exceptional student and pianist."

"I've never heard anything like that," Giovanna murmured.

"Alba has been offered a full scholarship in Rome to pursue her studies further. She has what it takes to become a professional, Signora Giovanna."

Her mother's expression crinkled through confusion, pride, concern, a troubled spring day between showers.

"I don't know what to say," Giovanna replied after a beat.

"I can't tell you what to say, Signora, but in my professional capacity I would urge you to permit her to go. I have friends there who will be able to arrange her accommodation, it will be simple of course, but clean."

"In Rome you say?"

Signora Elias nodded.

"Alone? A girl *alone* in Rome? She's going to be married."

Alba's eyes slit to Signora Elias, the prickle of panic creeping up her middle.

"Take some time to think about it, Signora, but I can reassure you that I know people who can help her in the early days and that many young people make the same pilgrimage every year. For their art. For talent that they have a duty to share with the world."

Giovanna looked at her daughter. Alba persuaded herself that the flicker she caught in her eye was one of a mother almost convinced.

Giovanna said nothing on the walk home, nor as they prepared lunch. She cut the cured sausage into thin precise slices without a word. She handed Alba the six plates to set the table without even looking Alba in the eye. She washed the fresh tomatoes and placed them in a bowl without the slightest evidence of emotion of any kind, other than a robotic repetition of their regular rhythms. Only when she tipped the salt into a tiny ramekin for the table and it overflowed onto the counter did Alba spy any nerves. When Giovanna made no move to clear up the salt flakes Alba's sense of impending storm peaked. She gave the linguini a swirl in the simmering water.

Salvatore came in soon after, world-weary and hungry as he always was after Saturday mornings at the *officina*. He slumped onto his chair.

"Why all the plates?" he grumbled.

"Marcellino and Lucia are coming," Giovanna shouted from the kitchen.

"When's Babbo back?" he called back.

"Didn't he say at the *officina?*" Alba said, laying down a bowl of chicory on the table.

"He wasn't at work today."

Alba wanted to check her mother's face for a reply as she brought out a hunk of Parmesan and a grater, dropping them onto the table with a thud, then thought better of it.

The door opened. Marcellino and Lucia strode in, taking over the space as they always did. Lucia stepped toward Giovanna and greeted her like her second mother. Then she swished over to Alba and gave a dutiful kiss on each cheek, almost touching the skin.

"Nearly ready, Ma?" Marcellino harangued his mother.

Lucia gave him a playful tap on his belly.

"What?" he guffawed. "A boy's hungry!"

"Not a boy for long," Lucia purred, her blue eyes flashing with something Alba struggled to identify. She did look different today, but it was hard to pinpoint why. She sashayed across the tiles with her usual perky sway, her jet-black hair lustrous even in the dim light of the shady room.

Giovanna yelled for Alba and handed her the pasta pot. The family took their seats. Bruno stepped in just as the first bowl was filled.

"*Buon appetito!*" he called, his walk a playful swagger.

"Get changed, *amore, sì?*" Giovanna insisted. Bruno stopped and grinned at his daughter-in-law. "Don't get any ideas now, Lucia? You see how old married men are? Do what their little wives say at all times, *sì?* Watch out, Marcellino, it's the beginning of the end."

Alba thought her father sounded a little drunk. It wouldn't be unusual for him to have an *aperitivo* at the bar with his cronies after the morning at the *officina*, or to drum up more business over a Campari soda or two, but there was more sway than usual about him that afternoon. Only when he turned for upstairs did Alba spy a fleck of lipstick on his collar. The clang of the metal serving fork upon the bowls as her mother tipped another portion of the pasta brought her back into the room. She watched the steam ribbon off the strands, fragrant with anchovy, garlic, chili, and fresh tomatoes.

Just before the figs were brought out at the end of the meal, Lucia asked for everyone's attention and announced she was pregnant. Alba's father needed no excuse to crack open a bottle of *moscato* and the sweet wine frothed six glasses like it was Christmas. When Lucia was asked her due date, she shied around a direct answer. It wasn't until Alba brought out the coffee that she understood Lucia's pregnancy was almost five months along. Women on the cusp of marriage were granted different rules, it seemed.

When everyone left, the house dipped into a sleepy quiet. Bruno snored upstairs. Salvatore lay on the couch. Only the percussive sloppy grating of Giovanna washing at the tub outside cut through the stillness. Alba stepped outside into the narrow courtyard garden. Above a canopy of wisteria wept purple blooms. Giovanna plunged a shirt into the sudsy cement tub, then lifted it and began attacking it along the ridges of the washboard, which lifted out at an angle. Her mother's knuckles were red.

"When are you going to tell Babbo?" Alba asked, before realizing that it was her father's shirt Giovanna was waging war on.

Her mother looked up at her, eyes bloodshot from dried tears.

"Leave me now. I've had quite the morning, don't you think? Sending me up there to be shamed by my daughter who has become a charity case? Have you any idea how I felt? I told you loud and clear what I thought about imposing on that kind woman. After everything she did for me when we were struggling? All those years I've been cleaning her house. Meanwhile you've been pretending to work there when all you've been doing is plonking that instrument. And now you stand here, silent as a cave telling me to tell your father. You've got another thing coming."

She plunged the shirt into the tub again, though Alba sensed Giovanna was picturing submerging something, or *someone* else.

"That's it, stand there like a rock. I'm used to it now. I could have lost my son that night with your father. Do you know that? Or was it just a game to you? You think you're the only one who has nightmares of that time? I did everything I could to raise you right. Do you know what your little secret means for *me?*"

Now her mother wrung the shirt as if it were her daughter's neck. Alba stepped inside. She sat at the deserted table fingering her letter. When her father came back down an hour later, dressed in a new shirt and smelling of sandalwood, she asked him to sit down. He did. Alba put the letter in front of him.

When he finished, he folded it and handed it back to her.

"Giova'!" he yelled.

She stepped inside wiping her suds on her apron.

"What do you know about this?"

Giovanna looked at the letter and then at her daughter.

"I haven't read it."

"Tell him, Mamma," Alba interrupted.

"You be quiet, I'm talking to your mother."

"It's what Signora Elias wanted to talk to us about today," Giovanna replied. "I know you were busy. I told her that."

Bruno twisted away from Giovanna and ran a hand over his beard.

"Why did they write to you, Alba?" he asked, flames flickering the fringes of his tone.

Giovanna stepped in and took a seat.

"Tell your father, Alba."

She looked between her parents' faces. For a moment a spark of optimism; a fast-fading firework.

"I have had lessons. They want me to study in Rome."

"I can read, Alba, I'm asking you to tell me the truth."

Alba's swallow felt hollow. "Signora Elias taught me."

Her father's smile was crooked. "Took pity on the poor town mute, did she?"

Alba took a breath, but her stomach clasped tight.

"And you sit here, telling me you've spent all these years studying music, wasting your time at the old woman's when your father has been building a business that will take care of you and your unborn children? Is that what you're saying? Are you actually telling me you think it's a good idea to run to Rome and play an instrument? Now I've heard it all. You are even crazier than they tell me. What do you have to say about this, Giovanna? You sitting there wringing your hands? You going to sit there mute as well?"

The corners of Giovanna's lips stretched as if she were clamping whatever words were fighting their way out.

"This is all *your* fault, you know that, don't you? I said so when she nearly killed that boy! And did you listen? You both sit there with no words! You're the most stupid women I know! My own family, imbeciles! What happened to this family? Everything I do, and this is how you thank me. Selfish, stupid little women."

"I had no idea!" Giovanna blurted.

"Even worse!" His voice rose, a crescendo, sweeping treble notes that ascended into a painful octave. "The girl's mother not knowing what's going on under her eyes! How did that feel? Watching that old woman shame you like that?"

Giovanna took a breath to speak, but Bruno swung his hand across her face. She cried out. Alba stood up. Bruno grabbed her chin.

"See what you did? That's all you. You and your surly little game. Over my dead body you go. You're not going to make a mockery of me like that."

He pushed her down. The wood thwacked the crease between her calves and the back of her thigh.

"I won't hear another word of it." He scuffed his chair back, swung his sweater over his shoulder, and slammed the door shut.

The silence could not suffocate Giovanna's swallowed sobs.

7

Piu mosso
a directive to a performer that the music of the indicated passage should have more motion, it should move more quickly

Rena Majore was a small town tucked inland of a blustery, rocky coast and a winding drive north of Ozieri. Alba and her family had visited many of the smaller sheltered coves along the eastern coast before Bruno and his brothers had settled on this place for their shared second home. The sea was rough, unpredictable, and uninviting. The town was sleepy and woke up, groggy, during the summer months with a half-forgotten piazza that whispered the promise of a town center. It was a town that attracted those in search of shelter from holiday crowds. Alba hated the place, more so now, because it was where her parents had decided to celebrate Alba and Raffaele's engagement and graduation.

"Go on, Alba!" Giovanna called from the kitchen window that opened out onto the terrace, "go and have fun already! You've worked hard enough! This is your day too, you know!"

The words were ridiculous droplets of forced maternal altruism, an impeccable performance enjoyed by everyone it seemed, apart from the person to whom it was directed. Her mother's gushing happiness held the same violent edge as the woman's disappointment. Since her parents put a definitive end to her visits to Signora Elias, the offer of her place at the *accademia* had not been mentioned again, and Alba couldn't help feeling that the whole experience was a warped dream, or a memory she had been taught to remember. But her fingers ached. They hadn't played since the letter was torn up in her kitchen. The deeper she sank into the numbness the more alive her mother became; her own fading life force was feeding her. The music had spun out of Alba and into her mother; she sang of summer and love and weddings and feasts. Her pans and pots and ladles and spoons percussed joy and hope.

A towel landed on Alba's face. She looked across at Raffaele, who was grinning, performing on her behalf. A wan smile threatened her lips. Marcellino took the helm in Bruno's newly acquired British jeep, delivered from England by one of his cousin's foreign husbands. The teenagers crammed into the back, some on the metal benches that lined the sides, others on the space between them. Mario's sister sat on his lap, Alba sat cross-legged on the metal floor by Raffaele. Lucia, clutching her protruding belly, yelled at Marcellino as he bombed down the white roads oblivious to the bumps and his wife's discomfort. After passing the scant smattering of shops edging open for the season, onward through the *pineta,* they arrived at the beach at last. Tall white dunes rose into view as the party negotiated the steep incline and skidded down toward the coast. As always, the wind whipped, and the fine sand prickled Alba's calves as it flew across the beach. The other people on the beach had long since given up on their umbrellas and lay them down, closed, beside themselves as they worshipped the glaring sun above. Nothing about this section of the coast was an alluring invite. The others in the group yelled in the water now, dashing toward the edge and diving into the deep. Lucia planted herself onto the sand, propping herself up on her elbows.

"I'm surprised your mother let you out for once, Alba."

She looked down at Lucia beneath her huge sunglasses. Two miniature concave Albas reflected back to her on the glass.

"Enjoy your freedom while you can, no? Soon you'll be making babies like me and then all this jumping around will feel like a story your grandma would tell you at bedtime."

A blank space formed where the image of a kind grandmother ought to materialize. Alba nodded, to close the start of a conversation she could not relate to, if nothing else. The older women in Alba's family shared whispered gossip, dabbled in magic and superstition in equal measure. They did not weave soporific fairy tales.

"For heaven's sake, Alba, go and have a swim. You stand there like the world's ending already. I'd do anything to have just graduated from school again!"

And with that Lucia let out a breathy laugh and eased herself down onto the warm sand beneath her towel.

Alba peeled off her T-shirt and shorts and let them fall to the ground. She slipped out of her flip-flops and felt the grainy heat under her soles. The white slid away underfoot till she reached the water, waves rushing up to her, white foam curling into clear. She dove in, feeling the cool envelop her, head racing to the bottom desperate to drown the noise around her. Her body rushed to the surface for air and then her arms beat through the surface without pause. Three strokes, one breath, repeat. The turquoise rose into view for a snatched intake of air, then down into the sloshing blue, pounding a beat in her ears. Her arms wouldn't stop. All these weeks without her music had built up an avalanche of physical frustration, more than she could bear. Her hand cupped like the shape of a pianist's diving into the water, pulling it away from her. The repetition was the closest way to reach her scales, to sense the symmetry of those exercises in her muscles, to feel the pulse that had greeted her every morning and now lay buried in a not so distant past.

She may have heard voices, which she chose to ignore; the shouts of her brothers, their cousins, Raffaele, Mario, all unnecessary interruptions. The ache for the solitude and complicit dance of music burned. With each stroke, each tension and relaxation of her muscles, her body fought to drive the feeling out further like a tide. She reached the first curve of rocks and pulled herself up onto them, the sun pounding down, drying her salty skin. Raffaele swam over to join her.

"Need company?" he said, hauling his dripping body beside her. "Well, you don't have the choice right now, sorry. I've had just about as much as I can take of your cousin's ball throwing. Mario's swum out to catch squid so at least I don't have to listen to him for a bit."

Raffaele stopped mid-flow. "Alba?" he murmured, watching her fat tears roll down her face. "Have I bored you to tears already? I've got to stop doing that. I think it's becoming a habit."

Alba snorted a laugh.

"Okay, a glimmer of hope in the dark, no?"

He reached his arms around her wet shoulders.

"You can tell me. Right? Of all the people here today, you can talk to me. If I actually shut up, that is."

He smiled at her second laugh. Her sobs ebbed.

"They're killing me," she whispered.

Raffaele held the silence. It caught Alba off guard. She took a deeper breath.

"Mamma. Papà. This insane wedding talk."

Raffaele interlinked his fingers in hers. "Only until we get to do what we want with our lives. We don't have to stay here, do we? We get to be who we really are if we're together."

He lifted her chin with a gentle finger of his other hand.

"I love you, Alba. I don't want you to be that wife in the kitchen. We know that. Our marriage is a refuge. From all the things they'll force on us if we don't stick together."

"I don't want to be a wife. I want to be a pianist."

Alba withdrew her fingers from inside his hand.

Her words splat out in starts, competing with tears. "Signora Elias taught me more than I can describe. She passed on magic, in secret. Mamma and Babbo found out after the Accademia di Saint Cecilia's in Rome offered me a full scholarship. They burned the letter. I'm still not out of their sight for a minute. I've started full-time at the *officina*, but you knew that already. I haven't played for days."

Raffaele held her. Alba caught the slosh of turquoise water rise up toward their feet upon the ochre rock.

"I feel like I'm disappearing," she said, shuddering.

"Why didn't you tell me before?"

"It was my hidden life. I'm dead without it. Can you understand that?"

His smile was a silver streak of grief.

"The only person who can help me now is you, Raffaele."

"How?"

"Help me get to Rome."

Raffaele's face was struck with disbelief.

"I need to buy a ticket for the boat. Once I'm there I'll be okay."

"You want me to help you escape?"

"This is a once-in-a-lifetime chance, Raffaele. We can't stay here and wither away. Is that what you really want? For yourself? For me? I love you, Raffaele. I don't want to destroy your life with a fake marriage. I want you to be free. I want us to set me free too."

Raffaele dropped his head onto his hands. Alba's chest creased with spidering panic and the intoxicating liberation of unburdening her secret.

Mario's head appeared around the rocks. He pulled his snorkel mask up to the top of his head, his eyes reflecting the glint of the sun-kissed water. He pedaled water and reached his full net of squirming squid overhead.

"Full catch!" he yelled, triumphant.

Alba watched him register the tears drying on her face, Raffaele ashen.

"Don't look so sad! They didn't feel a thing, *sì?*"

Raffaele offered a half-hearted laugh, to make Mario go away if nothing else.

"Your ma's going to be happy, no?" Mario asked, flicking his mask back onto his face and racing back to the shore to show off his hunt.

Raffaele and Alba waited for him to be out of earshot.

"Your parents are one of the wealthiest families in Ozieri, Alba. You've been working for Signora Elias for years, you can't find the money?"

"Mamma took everything. There's no way she'll give me a single lira toward this. You're crazy to even suggest me asking them."

"How much do you need?"

"About two hundred thousand lire. That will be enough for the fare and my first week. Just till I find a job. Signora Elias and her friend told me my accommodation and tuition is all covered by the scholarship. If I don't go now, I will never play again. I can't live like that."

Alba watched Raffaele's expression spin through a spectrum of colors; uncertain blues, doubtful grays, flecks of amber hope.

"You're my last hope, Ra'. If we love each other, then let's do the right thing for each other."

He held her. She could feel his heart pulsing beneath the thin skin of his chest.

"So you're asking me to raise a load of money, in secret, without rousing suspicion, so that you can live your dream and I'll never see you again?"

Alba looked at him squarely. "I don't want to hurt you, Ra'."

"You are."

When the party returned to the beach house, salt crusted, sun toasted, the table was laid with ramekins of gherkins and tiny pickled onions, olives, trays of sausage and cheese, piles of *pane carasau*, thin crisp bread drizzled with olive oil and a sprinkling of coarse sea salt. Mammas shooed their overgrown offspring toward the outdoor showers, hurrying them up. Fathers put their worlds to rights around the fire, passing around bottomless glasses of wine, clinking toward the embers whilst Bruno eased the flesh off the skewers and onto large trays of cork, with stems of wild myrtle branches upon it, letting the tender meat and its juices soak onto the fragrant platter. Ceramic troughs of *culurgiones* were paraded toward the hungry guests once everyone sat, at long last. The little pasta parcels, pinched-together dough in the shape of wheat, filled with creamy ricotta and spinach drizzled with fresh tomato sauce, arrived to cheers and clinks and the promise of happiness and wealth and health. The guests congratulated her parents' generosity, their hospitality, oblivious to the fact that the person they appeared to be celebrating was their mute prisoner. The hypocrisy of this pounding celebration made Alba's throat scratch. A swell of salty water popped in her ear.

Dinner was an indeterminate age of gluttony. At last the watermelon arrived and the eaters stabbed the red flesh, poking out the seeds, some cutting perfect staircases of sweet crisp fruit, others vertical splices. Alba ate half of hers before the teenagers and younger adults were urged to leave the elders in peace and make trouble someplace else.

"Come on, Alba, you'll come out with us, right?" Raffaele asked. "Please, God, don't leave me with all these cool lot. It's like sending me to purgatory. Dear God, don't do that. They'll all be eyeing up the girls in the square and jeering me on. I'd rather not commit social suicide without you beside me, *sì?*"

Raffaele filled her hand with his and led her off the table. They shuffled toward the back of the pack, slow stroll widening the gap between them and the group.

"Have you thought about what we talked about?" Alba asked.

"You ask just to make me cry on the street in front of these lot?"

Raffaele's voice eased away from his nervous tempo. They walked a few silent steps, the scuff of the dusty white road underfoot, the streets dark save for sporadic streetlamps, surrounding bungalows alive with the clinks of other parties.

He drew them to a stop in the dark between two streetlights.

"I love no soul in the world more than you, Alba."

Alba swallowed.

"It terrifies me to help you leave."

The cicadas' warbled beat intensified. Alba smelled juniper and wild myrtle on the whisper of breeze. "It terrifies me to stay."

"What will I do?"

"Follow your own dreams."

"Since when do you talk like those stupid movie girls?"

Alba shrugged.

"Our marriage plan was our escape. Now you go off to your music and I'm here marooned."

An ending and beginning opened up in the breaths filling the space between them. She could hear his muffled tears in the dark. Her arms wound around her best friend.

"I love you, Ra'."

"I want to help you. I'd be a shit if I didn't. And the thought of you hating me for not doing it is worse than being abandoned by my best friend."

Alba held his hand.

"Who will I talk to about Claudio?" he asked.

"You'll write. Long letters. Gory details."

Raffaele's smile was wan; the streetlamp caught its fade.

"When do you need the money by?"

"Late August."

His looked toward the darkened end of the street where it reached the piazza. "Do I look like a magician?"

They joined the others in the piazza, eating gelato, watching the visiting clowns warble through a half-rehearsed comedy routine, which delighted the younger children of out-of-towners and left Alba longing for solitude. She slipped away from the crowd. Her body needed to move. She didn't notice the houses fall away in her periphery, the darkened woods didn't fill her with fear. The dunes rose before her after a while and at last the moonlit water. She sat down, feeling the sand peel away beneath her, tipping downhill. The waves lapped in rhythm like a sleeper's breath.

"You should be careful running about alone like that in a strange place, Alba."

Mario's voice startled her. She twisted round to him. He was seated, far enough away to not have noticed him, cradling his knees, watching the water.

"You should be careful scaring young women who need to be alone for a change," she called out.

"Sarcasm is a killer. Probably the only fact in this world, I'd say," he replied.

Alba watched his chin raise into a smug grin. His humor was more disarming than his aggression.

She sat in defiant silence. So did he.

"What's all that stuff about music college they were on about?" he asked after a while.

Alba shook her head.

"Alba, we're alone now, no one has to know that we're actually able to talk without a fight. You don't have to let anyone see the fact that you can answer a real question with a real answer."

"I don't want to talk about it."

He retreated into her imposed silence.

"I never forgot about that time, you know."

His tone dipped burned ochre. She turned to face him.

"When I heard you play at Elias's."

They looked at each other for a breath.

"You going to pretend to forget?" he prodded.

She turned to face the water. They watched the curling laps disappear into the dark.

"Never heard anything like it in my life."

He stood up. Alba waited for a further snide gibe to follow his unexpected admission. The water rushed up to the sand fighting the pull, then acquiescing. Her breaths followed their rhythm, an incessant seesaw of advance and retreat. Whose battle was to be won?

She turned back.

He'd gone.

8

Nocturne
a composition inspired by, or evocative of, the night, and cultivated in the nineteenth century primarily as a character piece for piano, generally with three sections, often slightly melancholic in mood

After the party returned to Ozieri from the coastal town of Rena Majore, Alba waited a few days and used her parents' siesta to run to Signora Elias. She arrived, as planned, thanks to a note Raffaele had passed to her on Alba's behalf.

"You look like a ghost, Alba," Signora Elias cooed as she ushered her inside, closing the heavy door behind her against the heat.

"I haven't slept properly in a week."

"Understandable," Signora Elias replied, whilst leading her to the kitchen table where she poured Alba a glass of cold water.

"They won't change their mind."

"That's their prerogative. What does *your* mind say?"

"I have to go to Rome."

Signora Elias took a long sip of her water. "What if I said that's what you must do then?"

Alba's face creased with desperation. "Mamma has all the money you ever gave me. I don't have a lira."

"And what will you do about that?"

Alba's eyes lowered. She summoned a breath to say what had been eating at her the entire journey home. "I need help."

"I know. Raffaele told me so. Actually, he asked me to."

"For help?"

"For money, yes."

Alba shifted in her seat.

"If you want to make decisions on your own, Alba, and for yourself, you will have to work for them and then, the hardest part, stand by them. I could give you the fare and be done with it, yes. But what kind of betrayal would that be of your parents? We've already come this far. They've been very clear about how they feel. If you want this, I mean really can't live without this, you are going to have to put in the work. Choosing this life is a huge commitment. Not just hours of practice, but all the other real responsibilities around it. The work starts now."

Alba felt her eyes sting with tears she refused to let fall.

"I'd pay you back," Alba whispered.

"I know you would. I don't think I can buy your ticket, Alba, send your parents' girl away like that. This has to be your decision. All the way."

The next day Alba begged Mario's father, Gigi, to give her extra shifts on the pump. She nagged him to let her work through lunch even though there were no customers, asking to sort parts ahead of the next day, clean some of the ones brought in for repair, any little extra he would allow her to do.

"Why all the hours, Alba? I'm not expecting you to pay for your own wedding, you know that, right?" Bruno joked, loud enough for Gigi to hear and be forced to laugh.

"Your father's right, Alba. You look exhausted."

"I'm fine," she said, trying to suffocate the panic bubbling.

"You can today, but then I reduce the shifts. Doesn't look right, a girl on the pump."

Alba knew better than to start an argument then and there. Once her father left, she would convince Gigi by herself. She watched Bruno walk away and headed straight for the pump. Mario was already standing there.

"Go home," Alba called out, "your dad's put me on today."

"Says who?"

"Who does it look like?"

Gigi stepped out of the showroom with a fresh cloth for Alba. "I told you about the shift change, son."

"No, you didn't."

"I'm not going to argue. You're on the late shifts."

Gigi turned and walked back inside.

"What the hell has got into you, Alba? You hate the pumps, you hate me, now you're like some kind of gas junkie. Anyways, shouldn't you be looking after your piano fingers? Lots of accidents can happen around here if you're not careful."

Alba willed herself to ignore the snarl creasing his lips, but it was impossible. Another day she might have smacked the nozzle she was cleaning over him. She was desperate to save up enough for the fare to Rome. If she carried on at this rate, she still wouldn't make it. That's when her expression gave away more than she would have liked.

"Someone told me they'd heard you were going to that fancy music school anyways. What you hanging around here for?"

"Shut up!"

"I won't as it happens, because I know you're not going to lose it here."

A car pulled up much to Alba's relief. The driver rolled down the window and she set to work filling the tank, offering a clean of the windscreen too, which didn't interest the driver until Mario piped in with his patter and convinced him of a quick clean wash. He paid Alba, handed her a five thousand lire tip, and drove off.

"Fifty-fifty, right?" Mario asked.

"What?"

"You're desperate for money and I don't know why, but I'm enjoying the look of desperation on your face."

Alba felt anger surge through her bones.

They worked in brittle unison for the next two weeks, sometimes even through the lunch hours to catch the odd stray traveler or commuter returning to town for lunch and siesta. Tiredness crept around Alba, tightening like a vine, but she charged on because the alternative was incomprehensible. Dizzy from the heat and lack of sleep she slammed the pump back into its slot and caught the tip of her finger. Blood spurted out. Panic bolted through her as she examined the tip, then unexpected tears followed. Mario came over to her.

"What the hell's going on?"

"Nothing!" she spat.

"You bleeding?"

"No, it's fine."

He left and returned with a crushed clump of toilet tissue and threw it at her.

"Don't thank me," he said.

"I won't."

She blotted her hand and watched the droplets spread along the fibers. When she saw the cut looked superficial, her panicked tears became those of relief, and then smarting embarrassment. She tightened the knot of tissue.

"You look like crap. Go inside and clean up before your dad thinks I did it."

"I'm fine," she managed, just before more tears fought their way out. The tarmac heated underfoot; she longed for it to become molten so she'd be swallowed inside.

Bruno walked across the forecourt. He looked down at his daughter's hand.

"Get home, Alba."

"I'm fine."

"You're a mess. Get home. Now."

Alba refused to look at Mario's victorious expression. She walked over to her dad. "Please let me stay," she begged under her breath so Mario wouldn't hear. "I'll be more careful. The customers like me. I'm doing well."

Bruno leaned in. She could smell aqua vitae on his breath. "Be happy we're not at home so my hands can't say what they'd like. If I say go home, you go home. You want to work? You've got to listen to your boss. You barely know what you're doing inside in the office. I'm not having any child of mine make a fool of me outside too. Do you get that into your thick skull? Walk with me to the car. Now."

Alba felt his hand on her elbow, pressing harder than he needed. He slammed the door after her. Alba could picture Mario's face now. They stepped into the cool of the house, Alba's face oil-smeared, her overalls damp with gas stains, her hands still smelling of the metal pump.

"*O Dio,* look at the state of you, go and get clean, child!" Giovanna yelled.

"And don't come down until we've finished lunch!" Bruno added.

Alba shot a look to her father.

"You heard! You should have seen the way I had to drag her away, Giovanna. Talking to me like I'm some idiot. You think that's alright, do you?"

"I just want to work!" Alba blurted.

"Why? You have a house! You'll have a rich husband soon enough once he graduates with his finance degree. What is wrong with you?"

"Nothing is wrong, Bruno," Giovanna interrupted. He swung back to her so fast Alba almost didn't see him take his hand to her face. "Shut up! The girl is not right. Never has been!" He switched back to his daughter. "If I didn't know better, I'd say you're trying to save up to get the hell out of here!"

"That's crazy," Giovanna whimpered, her cheek red, "she's going to be a good girl now, aren't you, Alba? Everything is planned out." Her begging descended into sobs. Bruno grabbed her chin. "I told you quiet!"

Alba lunged at him. "Let go of her!"

He swiped back, pushing Alba against the wall.

"If I find out you are lying to me," he spat, pressing his thumbs either side of her clavicle so deep it made it hard to breathe, "if I get even a sniff of that being the reason you're so desperate for money, you will not be my daughter any longer. You hear me?" He gave her a shunt and she felt the wall hit the back of her head. Alba fought the ferocity of her tears, the red heat of anger cramping her chest. When he pointed toward the stairs, she did what he asked because her bones ached, because she craved solitude, because the thought of her dream being bullied away from her made life one she couldn't trust herself to bear.

The next day Raffaele came into the *officina* during her morning shift at the spare parts counter. On her break they scurried to the bar next door and ordered a couple of espressos.

"You look awful," he said, dipping into a concerned whisper. "What's happened?"

"My dad knows."

Raffaele blushed.

"What did he say?"

"More what he *did*. Or threatened to." Her eyes filled with angry tears. "I'm working like a slave up here, Ra', but I'm never going to have enough. He's forced Gigi to cut my shifts. Doesn't want me on the pump. I've only got a few days before I have to get to Rome. I'm falling apart, Ra'."

Raffaele hugged her. "Meet me at the cemetery this evening after you close up."

Alba's eyebrow raised.

"It's the only place I thought your ma would let you go without her. Signora Elias asked me to get you the message."

Alba's eyes stung with salty excitement.

Raffaele was right. Giovanna let Alba leave without a second glance. She even gave her some coins for fresh flowers. Bruno's mother was laid to rest in a tomb that since her death had been developed into a small but elaborate house, an ornate iron gate to match, angels swooping with grief on either side and within, a minute chapel with glass candleholders. Alba lay the yellow chrysanthemums inside. They sprouted in hapless angles out of the heavy glass vase.

"Glad you're keeping up the charade to its potential, Alba."

"Swallowing my guilt," she replied, the iron gate creaking closed.

"Follow me," he said, leading them down the central aisle of the walled cemetery toward a far gate that opened onto a patch of unattended grass. Signora Elias sat in her car parked in the shade of the wall. Raffaele opened the door. They both got in.

"Well done, Raffaele," Signora Elias began, "have you got the envelope?"

He nodded and pulled it out of his leather satchel. Before Alba could speak Signora Elias ploughed on, "Alba, here is a ticket for the crossing to Civitavecchia. Raffaele has helped you with the balance you need to afford it."

Alba felt her face blanch with disbelief and excitement.

"How?"

"No time for questions just now, Alba. We can't stay here long. Talk to him about it once I've left, yes? This ticket is for this Friday. There's enough there for the train to Rome's Termini station, and the rest will see you fed and watered for a few weeks, until you find a small job to support you beyond the tuition and lodging that the *conservatorio* has arranged. Celeste will meet you at Rome Termini at the end of platform two, which is where the trains from Civitavecchia pull in. She estimates that you will catch the eleven a.m. train from the port and arrive with her in time for lunch. I understand this will all come as a bit of a shock. Time is of the essence. You cannot wait another week or your offer will be withdrawn. You know this. I know the hell you have been through these past weeks. Simply getting a message to you was difficult enough, let alone buying a crossing ticket without news of the fact reaching your mother and father. You've worked hard for this, and your friend has been your angel. I know you want this more than you'll ever be able to describe."

Alba nodded, determined that her tears fall ignored.

"There is a paper with her number and mine. Everything you might need."

Alba smiled and felt her cheeks become wet.

"You have a very special friend here. I don't know what we would have done without him."

"I won't take all the credit," Raffaele whispered from the back seat, his face scarlet.

"I will meet you here on Friday at this hour. It will give us enough time to reach Porto Torres for your night crossing."

Alba forced a breath. "I don't know what to say. You're giving me my life, Signora."

"And you mine, Alba. Don't dwell on me now. This is about what you want."

"How do I thank you for all this?"

Her eyes twinkled with irrepressible joy. "You already have, *tesoro*."

Raffaele glanced at his watch. "We'd better go, if you're here too long they'll get suspicious." Alba kissed Signora Elias on both cheeks and cranked open her door. They watched her maneuver over the grass and turn back toward the town.

Alba couldn't decide if it was the light, the danger, or Signora Elias, but Raffaele stood taller just now, like he'd conquered a mountain and was surveying his land below.

On August 11th Alba Fresu boarded the Tirrenia line ship for Civitavecchia. Raffaele point-blank refused to say how he'd got the money, but assured her he hadn't stolen it, nor begged for it and that it hadn't been Signora Elias to foot the bill, of that he needed her to be clear. Alba sepulchred the memory of her father announcing she was no longer his daughter if she entertained any further the idea of leaving. She let her brothers' final insistence that she was making the biggest mistake of her life lift like dying leaves on the wind. She blocked out the pictured of Bruno slamming the door closed in front of her, blocking her inside, the way he lunged at his wife for not controlling his daughter, and how Alba used that as her chance to run out. She thought only of the way Signora Elias's face had crinkled into the easy joy of youth, explaining that sometimes life shunts people to a fork in the roads, forcing them to listen to the muffled little voice that always knows which way their compass points. She held on to the feeling of her best friend wrapped around her, trying to swallow his tears and failing, muttering promises of visiting, writing, protecting their getaway plan. She felt his clammy fingers in hers, the quiet insecurity within the tiny beads of sweat upon their palms. Alba took a last look at her island, the port of Porto Torres and its primary jagged freight-stained noise around her. The people saying their last farewells, others leaving their lives behind for another, or returning to reality from their island escape. She heard the memory of her mother's wooden rosary beads click-clack against one another. Her prayers would not be answered. All these pictures rose like a mid-measure swell, a crescendo exploding toward an unexpected space, a measure of expectant silence before the orchestra sings riotous life. Alba hung in that soundless place for as long as she could, as the ship pulled away from the turquoise bay, as her family became an ever-decreasing haze, disappearing into a past she decided was no longer hers.

II Movimento

9

Sostenuto
a very legato style in which the notes
are performed in a sustained manner
beyond their normal values

The huge wooden doors of Santa Cecilia on the narrow Via dei Greci were opened and a river of new students flowed through. Alba pressed into the center of the crowd, listening to the reverberating nervous voices, trying to quash the sensation that everyone knew one another and none felt the same fizz of disorienting terror and excitement as she did. The throng wove on through the courtyard just beyond the doors, the grass stretching the length of the open space, fruit trees in enormous pots at regular intervals providing sporadic branching shade.

"You a starter too?" a girl asked her.

She turned toward the voice, her face a sun, lit from the white light above and luminous with uncorked enthusiasm. Alba nodded, blinded by the young woman's unrestrained effervescence.

"I am a total mess," she flapped, before Alba could answer. "I've worked all my life to be here, now it's actually here I think I can hardly remember how to breathe, let alone play, right?"

Alba smiled, noticing the way the rays played upon the rainbow of tiny beads dancing down from this girl's ears. Her neck was adorned with worn leather strips aching with the weight of several crystals wrapped in fine wire, projecting purple and orange citrine light upon her chest.

"I'm Natalia. My parents named me after a Russian violinist. Sort of mapped out my life from day one, I guess. Do you believe in all that predestination stuff?"

Alba swallowed, trying to comprehend how to mirror this stranger's effortless dip into conversation, as if she was watching her step into a warm sea.

"Not sure," Alba mumbled.

Natalia stretched out her hand. "I didn't catch your name, sorry. Should have asked before. I trip into the middle of thoughts all the time. Rude, I know. It's a compulsion. I'm rubbish at the order of things. All the how-do-you-dos and don'ts feel so dull, don't you think? I like to jump into the middle of people. Your eyes are amazing. Where are you from?"

"Sardinia."

Natalia took in a sharp breath and let out a warm sigh of pleasure. Several students ahead of them turned to see who was expressing at great volume.

"Only my family's favorite place in the world! We camp there most summers. The most beautiful place I've ever been. Serious. Oh God, what's happening now?"

Natalia's attention was directed to the bottleneck ahead.

"I guess we're having the talk first, then they're dividing us up into some smaller groups. That's what my brother's friend told me. He studied here too. Gave me the lowdown. I hope I'm in your group. We have small study groups of mixed majors, you know, then we split into our personal timetables. I didn't catch your name?"

"Alba."

"Sunrise. That's so beautiful."

Alba felt Natalia's gaze penetrate a little too deep. Her abrupt intense stillness was unnerving, a sudden dam to halt her determined cascade of words and scissoring thoughts. Her attention diverted away just as quickly when another student waved across the throng to her.

"I'll catch you later, Sunrise!" she called out, swerving around instrument cases perched on the backs of the students ahead to reach her friend.

The students filed into the main hall, taking tentative seats upon the red velvet hinged chairs, expectant faces toward the stage at the far end where the silver pipes of the organ dominated the entire back of the stage rising toward the high ceiling. Alba gazed up at the heavy ornate squares of cornices and rosettes above, then traced the balcony that ran the length of the long narrow auditorium lined with fat white balustrades and giant swirls of stone supports below. It was like church, not only the palette of colors, the stony air, the marble and gilt presentation, but the same lofty feel, a space that had once sung with music. Instead of a dying man before her though, bleeding for mankind upon a cross, Alba saw an empty performance space, dominated by a full-size grand piano gleaming its open onyx lid like a languid invitation. Her body scored with white light.

A file of teachers walked onto the stage and took seats in the arc of chairs laid out in front of the piano. Alba spied Celeste at the center amongst the others who surveyed the crowd with dour eagle-eyed precision. She replayed their warm greeting earlier, a beam amongst the stone modernist anonymity of Termini station, so welcoming after the long, rough crossing, seated upon a brown velveteen chair, the memory of stale smoke in the air and waves of rosary intoned in her periphery by older, God-fearing grandmothers. She thought about the light bowl of spaghettini Celeste had prepared for her in her apartment before taking her to her new landlady. Her new home was a perfect cloister of white-walled solitude; a single bed, a long window with shutters that opened up onto a breathtaking view of the aqueduct that stretched out of the suburb of Lodi. Her landlady, Anna, greeted her with warmth but a cool businesslike handshake, reassuring Alba that she didn't have plans to become her second mother. Alba's bed was clean and comfortable, but sleep, that first night, had eluded her. She'd been awake to watch the dawn, the ancient stones of the aqueduct dipping red, orange, then tan, as the sun stretched its rays. The electric anticipation of her first day tingled through her.

A male teacher shifted on his seat beside Celeste, observing the students over the rim of his glasses. How much could he actually see beyond the cloud of white beard puffing out from his face? Several others appeared to find the whole process a painful display of mediocrity. Another tanned professor with a tailored sharp suit, white hair scraped back off his face, twiddled a gold ring on his little finger. After a while he stood up and walked to the center of the stage. He welcomed the new intake of students to the *accademia*. The remainder of his speech was a fuzz of names. Lists of classes, instructions on how to find out information, directions that wove around Alba like a thread of stave-less notes, her head too giddy to claw them from the air and put them into any succinct order. She felt a tap on her shoulder.

"We are together, Sunrise! I knew it."

Alba smiled, wishing she could have memorized everything as quickly as her new shadow.

"Signora Celeste Agnelli's group, right?"

"I think so."

"You alright? You look dizzy."

Alba nodded her head with a smile.

The crowd dispersed to find their tutors out in the courtyard. Natalia wasted no time in leading the way. Soon a group of twelve students huddled around the blaze of silken colors floating around Celeste's frame. Her arms raised in welcome, inviting the students to follow her. They wove into the main building, leaving the arched cloister walkways of the central courtyard. The wide stone staircase rose several flights before their footsteps echoed along a corridor tiled with granite, splotches of deep reds, creams, and blacks grouted with a bronze-colored caulk, the arched ceilings stretching the length with large glass lanterns hung at regular intervals from the apex. Celeste's office door opened and they each took a seat on the twelve chairs arranged in an oval, flanked by deep shelves of scores, biographies spanning musical history, and several huge black-and-white framed photographs of Celeste mid-performance. Her face in those shots had the same feline outline as now, hair swept up and off it, body angled toward a piano like a dance partner.

She lifted herself onto the edge of her desk, swinging her legs. "So! Here we are. I am delighted with the musicians in my group. We have a lot of work to do. We have a lot of fun to do too. There are some professors amongst us who like to terrify students into good work. That's not how I work. But I will not put up with laziness of any sort, of that you must be clear. Now, let's get the painful part out of the way. We'll take it in turns to say our names and what our majors are."

Alba's fingers curled inward toward her damp palms. She heard her name.

"You may start, Alba," Celeste encouraged.

Alba ran her dry tongue over her lips and croaked her name, then mumbled something about the piano. Going first was a blessing she soon realized, because it meant she was free to focus on the others. Beside her, Natalia poured out a carefree introduction with a pepper of self-deprecation that made the others laugh. There were two other violinists, a bassoonist, a trumpet player, all of whose names flitted in one ear and out the other. Opposite Alba sat a young man with a mop of black curls. He surveyed his competitors, chin lifted as if he knew who had already won. His turn came. He ran a hand through his locks that sprang back over his forehead.

"Vittorio," he announced, his voice warm but his delivery a flat line, piercing the space without target. "Cello."

A couple of international students followed the cellist and at last the room returned to be led by Celeste.

"So is that clear?"

Alba realized she hadn't heard the first part of what had been spoken.

"Alba dear, you're looking terrified. I reassure you this is a necessary evil. I like to get the initial performance for one another out of the way before we've had time to work and share our development. I want everyone to hear one another in their raw form before the work begins. It's the start of a steep learning curve for us all. We will continue to learn by watching others throughout our time here together. Before we talk, we listen. So too, when we play. Onward, my troupe! We will meet at the rehearsal room downstairs in half an hour. That's enough time for a swift break and to warm up."

The group filed out of the room. Alba was thankful Natalia appeared to have switched her attention away from her new audience and toward preparing her violin piece inside a small practice room. Alba retraced her steps back down toward the courtyard, then followed the signs toward the rehearsal room. She looked through the glass toward the empty space. In the corner was the piano beside the three double windows that lined the wall. Only a hint of the city wafted up into the room, not the incessant whiz of scooters and trams. She opened the door, reached the beautiful instrument, and adjusted the seat. Her finger traced the lip, feeling the warm polished wood beneath it.

Signora Elias's voice was in her head now. Her breath widened. Her fingers eased down onto the notes. A buttery tone lifted from the vibrating strings as the hammers hit. She'd never heard that tone. Her scales flew out of her. Everything was foreign about the day, the disorientation of the trip, the terse farewells, her best friend's tears, his unswerving support, but now all the pictures fell into white space as the new instrument sang. It was like coming home.

The door swung open.

Her hands flew off the keys.

"All the other rooms are taken. I'm going to warm up in here," Vittorio announced, leaving Alba wondering if it was his way of asking her to stop or reassure her to continue. He didn't wait for a reply, hauling his large hard case into the opposite corner, laying it gently onto the polished parquet. He popped open the catches and cradled his cello out of its repose.

"Give me an A?"

Alba didn't move.

"You never helped someone tune up?"

Alba shook her head.

"Just press A. Surely you know that much, no?"

She poked an A.

"Lower."

She lifted her finger.

Vittorio drew his gaze away from the bridge back across to Alba.

"You always look like you're going to hurt someone or shall I take it personally?"

She plonked a different A.

He plucked a string again. Alba listened to it twang up through the narrow space between tones. She'd never heard so many subtle shades between notes before. Much to Alba's relief, Celeste appeared, followed by the other students. There was a flurry of chairs and instruments and nervous preparation. At last the group was ready.

"So here we are," Celeste began, standing in front of the piano. "The worst part of your time here will be over in a heartbeat. I am not judging you on today, nor will you be judging others. This is simply setting a bar—for *yourself.* I want you to notice what emotions surface as you start to play today. Witness where your mind goes. After you've finished, consider how your body dealt with the stress, where it stored its tension. Today we start our journey as witnesses, this will be your superpower as you train—your ability to really see yourselves, your playing, under the incisive light of day. I will always be brutally honest with you. I will ask you to do the same of yourselves."

Celeste turned toward Vittorio. "Strings first, I think, Vittorio. Would you open?"

He rose, not a quiver of nerves evident. He took a seat at the piano for a moment and played his A himself. He drew his long bow across several strings at once, twiddling the tiny black knobs toward the base of the instrument, altering the pitch in minute increments. The sound was assured. It filled the space. Alba felt the notes vibrate across the front of her body.

He took a seat, the wooden curves fitting into his body like a lover. His long fingers cradled the bow now, arm weighty and loose. His other hand wrapped around the neck. A breath. Then his bow lengthened into life, caressing the strings with confidence. Alba heard a palette of earthy colors fly out of the instrument, mournful reds of grief, ochre tones of hope. The song sent a light through her middle to the stony gap where her tears hid. The piece ended, and she was glad; her eyes grew once again dry.

The students applauded.

"Wonderful start, Vittorio, thank you. We'll take it in turns to talk about our sensations in a moment. I want only the music, first," Celeste explained.

That's when Alba felt all eyes turn on her. She didn't realize Celeste was looking straight at her. The echo of the strings still sang somewhere in her bones.

"*Scusa*," Alba said, shifting her attention back to the room.

"Take your time, Alba," Celeste reassured, reaching out an arm toward the stool.

Alba sat. The eyes upon her became wallpaper. The light from the Roman street danced shadows across her keys. The fringe of a breeze lifted the hem of the net curtain beside her. Silence rose from within. She remembered little of Liszt's music after that, save the reassuring disappearance of everything around her. The blues and sweeping metallic tones of love and loss filled her, rising out of the strings that crisscrossed ahead inside the wooden body of the piano, like a cleansing waterfall. She walked through the piece she'd played a thousand times before, assured steps, like a wanderer tracing a well-remembered forest path, witnessing the subtle changes in air, the temperature, the different heat and angles of the light streaming through the ferns. At last, the final steps toward the open plains of the ending. The notes resonated, a hum of possibilities and, when it felt like the song had said all it needed to, she released the foot pedal and the piece was swallowed back into the empty space where it began.

The silence smacked.

"*O Dio*," Natalia whispered, puncturing the stillness.

Everyone turned to look at her. Natalia wiped her wet face. "Signora Agnelli, please tell me I don't play after that."

The class laughed, dissolving the trepidation on how their new professor would react to the interruption she had told them not to offer.

"Let this be our first lesson then," Celeste replied, without missing a beat. "That which terrifies you the most is the very thing you are being drawn to overcome. Have I answered your question, Natalia?"

She sighed a laugh. "Thank God I'm a violinist is all I can say!"

The room rang with laughter. Alba stood in the glow; her colleagues' genuine congratulatory smiles filled her with song. Vittorio locked eyes with her for a snatch as she crossed back to her seat. She might have decoded his expression, but there was none, save a wisp of gray indifference.

10

Toccata, Quasi Improvisando
a rapid keyboard composition for organ or harpsichord, dating from the baroque period, usually in a rhythmically free style

Alba stepped into Celeste's office. A memory of fresh coffee hung in the air above the papery smell of scores lining the shelves, hundreds of dormant notes folded into silence between the sheets.

"So tell me about this first month, Alba." Celeste sank back into her armchair, looking expectant. The leather squeaked beneath her skirt. Alba would have liked to describe the wrenching ache during her one-to-one sessions with the piano department deputy, Dimitri Goldstein, a Greek Jewish man who reeked of filterless Gitane cigarettes and the faint waft of last night's whiskey. She wanted to tell Celeste that she felt the school had made a horrendous mistake in inviting her. That her first month had felt like everything she thought she knew was being defragmented before her eyes and she had no idea how it would ever cement back together.

"Am I right in thinking that the experience is a little overwhelming at times?"

Alba nodded.

"I only say that because all the students I've seen today tell me that they think they are underqualified to be here. Is that something you're feeling also?"

Alba nodded again.

"Very good."

Alba cocked her head.

"Your time here is a process, Alba. Development of a musician means pushing into the unknown, *their* unknowns. We have a plan for you, but sometimes growing as a musician and seeing how far music will take you is not going to feel comfortable. It has to push beyond your comfort, otherwise you will leave the same as you arrived."

Celeste's words felt like swirling questions.

"Anything in particular that you're struggling with?" Celeste asked.

Alba thought back to her lesson with Goldstein, the way he huffed into the hidden beats at the end of the grand piano, sighing with frustration. She shook her head.

"This week we will begin work on your first quartet, you know that, yes?"

Alba's smile papered over her nerves.

"You will be working with Vittorio and Natalia, joined by Leonardo on viola."

"Yes," Alba murmured.

"Professore Giroletti would like you to work on Brahms Piano Quartet, number three, opus sixty."

The words wove around her, twisting her back to the record player in her bedroom, where she'd spent long evenings letting the music spin worlds around her. This was one of the pieces she'd loved best amongst the collection that Signora Elias had lent her.

"You appear to be delighted with our choice," Celeste purred with pride. "This is a good start. Here is your part." She reached over and placed a wide score into Alba's hands. "You may practice before class in the practice rooms by making sure your name is on the sign-up sheet by the end of this week."

Alba straightened in her chair, expecting to be dismissed.

"What about your living arrangements? Have you found a job yet? Is your room comfortable?"

"*Si,* everything is comfortable. My landlady has given me the name of her brother who owns Bar Calisto in Trastevere. He's looking for some evening and weekend help."

"Good. Just be sure it doesn't interfere with your studies, that's all I would caution."

"*Si*, Professoressa."

Celeste nodded and stood up. Alba mirrored.

"Lastly, woman to woman, I'd like to remind you that you are not here to be intimidated by any of the other students or teachers, do you understand? Feeling daunted is perfectly normal, but it will require great discipline to not give in to despair. Most of the women studying here have had to make bigger sacrifices than the men. Music is still a world which appalls many. We receive the message that there are fewer opportunities for women in this world, and over the years I've watched that story breed a vicious strain of jealousy between the few of us who succeed, as if we all have to fight over what meager offerings there are. We can choose not to propagate that belief, which suits everyone but those very women carving out their journey in the music world, nor give in to the sensation of not feeling good enough, should it ever arise. Do you understand?"

Alba smiled, unnerved by the way Celeste had grasped what she was feeling, as simple as a wipe away of condensation from a cold windowpane to peer inside.

Goldstein must have had a rough night. He hadn't removed his sunglasses from the beginning of Alba's lesson. His movements were more jerky than usual. He seemed like a lion in chains, every now and then giving a flick of his beard mane, running a frustrated hand through his wiry mop of hair.

"Do you sit there hearing anything I have just said?" he barked with his cigarette husk. "Again. You stay on the surface of the notes"—he twisted his wrist in the air now, a marionette's wooden hand on a loose string—"plonk plonk, a skimming stone on water. No! This is a piece which can be confused as naïve, yes, but it is not. Stop playing it like a nursery rhyme."

Alba felt her neck become rigid. She sent it a breath, hoping somehow her body would comply to the request of relaxation. It did not.

He interrupted her almost immediately, swinging down onto the piano beside hers. “Stop, for the love of God, stop. Now *listen*.”

He lifted his hands and let them fall deep onto the keys. The sound was like a bell, ringing clear and free, startling in its simplicity and depth of tone at the same time.

“Now you.”

Alba echoed.

“Are you listening to yourself, Alba?”

“Yes.”

“No. You are imitating me. I want you to *understand*. There is a great difference.”

He stood up from the piano, flicked open his cigarette packet, and lit up. The filterless cigarette filled the space with thick smoke. Alba sneezed.

“What is my job, Alba?”

“Your job?”

“That was the question, yes. You are hearing some things, I see.”

“You are the deputy head of piano.”

“That is my title. What is my *job?*”

Alba took a breath, longing to play, longing for silence to experiment with the task at hand.

“My job as your maestro is very simple and complex. I am to discover who you are and show it to you.”

“Who I am?”

“That is my point exactly. Right now you are a naïve little Sardinian girl full of the countryside with a talent for music. I'm asking you to connect to this piece in a profound way. You are pressing the notes. Liszt wrote this because he couldn't put into words the great longing that drove him, the insatiable fire that ate at him to create, to say what we can't with letters alone. You have to express something eternal. You never felt anything in your life?”

Alba had no idea what reaction to offer. Her chest grew rigid.

“What do you know about fear? About loss? About rejection?”

His rhetoric held in the pungent air. Her eyes burned. He took a sharp breath.

"Ah. So we *do* know something about life. I see it now. There's the fire you Sardinians are famous for, no?"

Alba swallowed.

"So play from there. Right there. In your fury at me for prying. That's where you play. Now!"

Alba lifted her wrists. She played the cornered feeling. She played the claustrophobia. A salty droplet from her eye landed on her wrist. She didn't let it stop her. The metallic notes rang, simple, profound, cutting through the thick smoky quiet. She finished the phrase.

"*Complimenti*," he said, his voice a scratch of gravel, "now you've shown me you can listen. So now I hear."

Alba left the room with the feeling of failure trailing her like Goldstein's smoke. If her three years here were going to continue in this manner, she doubted she would survive unharmed. This was the failure her father had projected all along. This was the insistence she'd chosen to ignore. She couldn't do anything right at the *officina*, or at home, or at school, and she couldn't do much right here either. Effort wasn't enough. She wasn't enough. But failure wasn't an option. That was a satisfaction she'd never gift her father.

Instead of heading up toward Piazza del Popolo and past Flaminio to catch her bus back to the quiet of her landlady's apartment in Lodi, Alba turned left at the end of Via Dei Greci where the *conservatorio* entrance stood, and strolled down Via del Corso, passing the trawl of boutiques, cutting through the narrow side *viccoli* until she reached the toasted hazelnut air outside Giolitti's *gelateria*. Customers passed the early evening at small metal tables, served by waiters in white jackets with shiny gold buttons. Her funds were fast trickling away and it was crucial she secured a job within the week, even if she hadn't yet proved to herself that she was capable of holding one of them down. Her father had reminded her enough times of that. She followed the cobbles downhill until the road narrowed and La Tazza D'Oro coffee roasters faced her, customers spilling out onto the streets, clinking red bubbles of *aperitivi,* others arguing over tiny coffee cups, and beyond, golden in the evening light, the Pantheon. Goose bumps rippled up her arms. The temple columns of another world stood before her. She reached the marble fountain at the center of the square before it, tourists cooing over the age, snapping their memories into their metal boxes. Even after the month, she found it hard to believe that she was here at all. Her family rose into her mind, their picture swirling away as soon as they snapped into focus, overexposed photographs dripping blank in a puddle.

Her pace quickened a little now as she found her way to the Tiber and crossed over the Garibaldi Bridge to Trastevere. The evening was already hot with bodies and young students. The bars here lacked the pomp of those closer to her school. Here, the buildings fought for space, its Jewish ghetto past still clung to the fading painted plaster, the wooden shutters creaking with age, scarred with flaking paint. Bar Calisto took up the corner of a palazzo on the main square, facing the church of Santa Maria di Trastevere. The cobbled square was filling with young people, flicking their ash onto the cobbles, putting the world in order at great volume.

Alba stepped inside. It was heaving with drinkers, and the two waiters behind the bar performed a frenzied dance with precision, almost crashing into each other but somehow managing to retain the drinks inside their relevant glasses to reach their rightful owners. The noise was a belly laugh of politics and gossip. Alba wove her way through the Roman crowd and reached the high bar.

"What do you want?" the young man yelled, flicking coffee grounds into his espresso handle and screwing it tight onto the machine that whooshed into a temper.

"I'm here to see Antonio!" she yelled over the din.

"And you are?"

"Alba. A tenant of his sister. I've come about the job."

His eyebrows did a little dance, he swerved around his colleague, placed the two espresso cups onto the saucers, and held them out into the narrow space of air over the bar toward a couple. They swirled the creamy contents, downed it in one go, dropped a coin onto the marble, and left.

"You done this before?" the barman called to her, slicing an orange and flipping it into a glass with Campari and a large hunk of ice.

"No."

He slit his eyes with a smile. "Why you want to start now then?"

Alba prepared to answer, wishing he would call his boss and stop the carousel conversation. The waiter's attention was redirected to a customer yelling an order two rows of people back from the marble. A small man appeared at the beaded doorway behind the bar. The waiter signaled to him and then nodded his head toward Alba.

"You the Sardinian?" the man called out to her.

Alba nodded.

"You good at clearing up?"

"I think so," Alba replied, trying to make her voice ping over the trebled conversation over her head.

"Take this," he snapped, chucking an apron at her. "I'll give you a try because you stay with my sister. If you're no good, you don't stay."

He turned and disappeared before Alba could thank him. She stepped up onto the raised level behind the bar, feeling like she was about to sight-read a concerto. Some sections she played by ear, others she improvised, watching her colleagues and mirroring their tempo and, where possible, their precision. When the shift came to its end Antonio held out his hands for the apron. "Not bad for an out-of-towner. You're fast. You're quiet. You're hired."

"*Grazie!*"

"Don't burst a blood vessel."

Alba straightened, trying to subdue her excitement.

"Turn up on time or you go, you hear? Tuesday and Thursday evenings and weekends, *sì?*"

He turned before she could reply, disappearing up the stairs to the rooms above.

"Impressive, kid," the male waiter nodded. "I'm Dario, you ask me when you don't know something. Next shift I'll get you on the coffee machine, *sì?*"

"*Grazie.*"

"Don't thank me. We need the extra hands. I won't tell you what happened to the last girl."

He gave a wry grin. Alba decided it was time she got used to the Roman sense of humor sooner rather than later.

She stepped into the streetlamp-lit back streets of Trastevere. She wasn't ready to go home. The mild terror of jumping in to help at that busy bar had made her feel wide awake. Goldstein's lesson was a distant memory. If she could wrangle the Roman throng of Antonio's bar, perhaps conquering the piano might not be as hard as she thought? Natalia had invited her over to Leonardo's place tonight. She looked toward the Tiber and decided to join them. The first tinge of autumn hung in the humidity. Someone answered the door after she rang the bell several times. Natalia's face brightened on seeing her. "Yes! You came at last! Come on, we're needing some keys."

"What do you mean?" Alba asked, following her friend up the narrow stone staircase toward a door music was slipping out of, a ramble of improvisation.

She didn't answer but led her down the thin corridor toward a snug sitting room. Leonardo shouted a welcome. He was flanked by a couple of young men she didn't recognize, who took out their cigarettes to say hi. Someone put a glass of wine in her hand and before she could say anything more Leonardo started to wail a lament on his viola. The room's chatter reduced to simmer, before Natalia picked up her violin and one of the young men crooned his saxophone. Then a deeper melody resonated from the corner behind her. She twisted to see Vittorio, his head bowed as he bowed, swinging toward the sound of his strings. They swerved the key signature, every now and then someone skidded off at an unusual musical angle, offering a sketch off the theme, then returning to home. Natalia lifted her bow. "Alba, take a seat, we need you!" She gestured toward an old piano in the corner of the smoky room. "We're A minor," she added, before joining in with the others. Alba sat and lifted the lid. Several ivories were missing. She tuned in to the wash of glissandos around her, and gambled a start on A. She followed the others, intuiting their shifts, playing the neat threesome of main chords within the scale, and then, when Leonardo gave her a nod, she added her own melodic twist. The others paired away, till only the bold strings of the cello and her keys rang out. Her improvised melody tinkled up toward the upper registers, then back down to grounded chords, whilst Vittorio's cello hummed like a bass whisper beneath, steady as a drone, the warm hum beneath a lullaby. Then Natalia sang over the top and then the others molded back into the silence adding their own colors. They sensed the ending and came to a gradual stop. Their glasses raised as they clinked to one another. Her new musical family surrounded her in cheers, the dim light of the room catching the tips of the students' wine-rosy cheeks. Was this the tribe her father was so terrified of her joining? Was this warm feeling such a threat to him after all? Her happiness was the rebellion he'd sought to crush for so very long. She hushed the cruel resonance of his words into the echo of an almost forgotten memory.

Alba tuned back into the laid-back ease of the room. Was even Vittorio lured by it? It was impossible to tell, because as everyone sank back into conversation, she noticed that he'd already left.

11

Libero
a directive to perform a certain passage of a composition in a free, unrestrained style

Natalia met Alba outside their rehearsal room the following day. "So great having you there last night, Alba. You feeling as fragile as me today?"

"Maybe," Alba replied.

"I've listened to this piece I don't know how many times. My mother tried to get me to play it when I wasn't ready. We had the biggest fight of our lives over it. I mean bigger than the other two thousand fights."

Alba smiled.

"Did your mamma set your practice schedule or you?" Natalia asked.

"Sorry?"

"Who did your schedule? Like just after school or before too? I had to do one hour before school and one straight after. Then two half-hour practices spaced out between homework."

Off Alba's expression Natalia blushed. "I know, right. Crazy. Wouldn't be here today though. And actually I did love it. I just didn't like her reminding me all the time. She's a cellist. She teaches at home and at several schools. My father is with the philharmonic in Milan. I'm prattling again I know. I'm so nervous I think I'm literally going to throw up."

Alba let a laugh froth out.

"At least I'm finally making you laugh. The green flecks in your eyes though. Just like a gem. Oh, here's Mr. Happy."

Alba twisted round to see Vittorio saunter along the polished tiles. He looked straight at them without blinking.

"*Buon giorno,* Vittorio. I'm surprised you're not here before us," Natalia said with a sideways smile.

"Are you?"

"No. But I thought I'd show you how to start conversation. You know, before you tell me what you think of my playing like in music theory class the other day."

"Glad you think so much of my opinion. I'm flattered." He lifted his cello off his back and placed it onto the tiles with care.

"Don't be," Natalia added, making sure she had the last word.

Professore Giroletti greeted them from the opposing direction, his crisp linen shirt ironed to perfection, his white hair parted with precision. The students straightened to attention.

"*Buon giorno,* my quartet. Glorious day for a first rehearsal. Right now our quartet is a trio. Where is Leonardo?"

Natalia looked back toward the direction Vittorio had arrived from. "He said he was just grabbing a drink, Professore. He's on his way."

Giroletti nodded and opened the door. They filed in. Natalia and Vittorio tuned up around Alba, who by now had become well practiced in helping strings. Just as they finished, Leonardo flung open the door and flew across the space with his usual mix of apologies and the vague sense that he had just returned from somewhere more important. His T-shirt hung on in patches, worn away in some parts to where you could see his skin underneath. His jeans flared out over his pumps. Natalia flicked her fringe off her face, and it flopped back to where it started. Alba noticed her cheeks were more pink than a moment ago.

"What's your delectable story this time, Leonardo? Which political rally needed your undivided attention today? How about you channel some of your fury against the establishment into a spot of Brahms?"

"You read my mind, Professore!" Leonardo replied, breathy, whipping his viola from its case, reaching over Alba to press an A.

"Sorry I stink," he said, with a laugh. "Ran all the way here because the tram broke down. You don't know Romans till you've been cooped up in a hot tram with fifty of them!"

"Leonardo, let us leave the anthropology to another morning, shall we?" Giroletti interrupted.

Leonardo wiped his brow, tightened his bow, and sat down.

"Ladies and gentlemen, let us start with the first movement, *si?* Seems a ludicrously good place to start, no?"

Natalia looked down the neck of her violin. Leonardo locked eyes with her. Vittorio straightened. Alba played her first octave alone. She held the space, observing those precious inner beats Goldstein hammered on about. Then she played her second. The strings entered in unison, sighing pairs of notes as the one slurred onto the other.

Giroletti sprang to his feet. "I stop you there. And I ask you what these sighs mean?"

The four students looked between one another.

"Well one of you must know?"

Alba raised her hand. "Brahms was obsessed with Schumann's wife, Clara, sir."

Giroletti smiled, willing her on.

"Some people say that those notes are the sound of his yearning for her. They have the same beats as her name, if you like. Cla-Ra."

"Excellent, Alba! Yes. That is what I want to feel from you three. Again."

They repeated the first phrase several more times, Giroletti arcing his body to the sound, leading them toward the color he searched for. They skipped the second movement and moved on to the third section.

"Vittorio, what do we notice about this movement?"

Vittorio sized up the score before him upon his metal stand. He ran a finger along the first few measures. Alba noticed their length, the way the tiny muscles in his hand rippled beneath his alabaster skin, the veins scrawling deep blue tracks above the bone.

"It's the only movement that is not in C minor?"

"And?" Giroletti prodded.

"The opening theme here is pretty much a sequence of descending thirds? Brahms uses this a lot. The opening of Symphony number four, for example?"

"You always sound like a book, Vittorio?" Leonardo asked, winking at Natalia.

"Yes, very good, Leonardo, but don't let yourself be intimidated by your colleague's knowledge," Giroletti cut through, "you're not a conducting major, are you?"

"I'm conducting *A* major, does that count?" Leonardo teased with his heavy Roman slur.

"Not if I can help it, no," Giroletti replied.

"He's just jealous that the second theme is stolen by the violin and then Natalia and I basically take us home from there," Vittorio announced, his face creasing into a grin.

"Alright, that's enough now," Giroletti said, snapping to attention. "Let's hear it."

Vittorio stretched his arm and then rested the bow on his strings. The melody oozed into the space, then lifted up into the higher registers of his instrument with only Alba as an accompaniment. Giroletti listened for a moment, with his back to them. Then he flung out his arms cutting them short.

"Alright. Natalia and Leonardo, I'm going to use the rest of this rehearsal to work with these two cotton-tapped musicians, while you and Singsong here go next door and perfect your pizzicato in the final section, which I can tell from your work in the first movement leaves a lot to be desired."

Alba watched them pack away and leave. She turned to Giroletti, waiting for his direction.

"So. You two know each other?"

Alba and Vittorio alternated a "No" and "Yes" in unison.

"No confusion there then."

Alba and Vittorio looked at each other for a half beat and turned straight back to their maestro.

"Is this your first time accompanying strings, Alba?"

"Yes, Maestro."

Vittorio muttered something under his breath.

"Care to share?" Giroletti asked, his voice pointed.

"No, Maestro."

"Good. Now, Alba, you are the backbone here, your support will carry on throughout the next section when Natalia will echo Vittorio's theme, yes? So I need to hear your warmth, a grounding from which Vittorio can sing out, you understand?"

"Take my lead for when to come in," Vittorio added.

Alba looked at him.

"That means watch me, I'll tell you when to start."

"I think we need to think a bit broader than leader and follower, dear boy."

Vittorio twisted toward Giroletti's interruption.

Alba noticed the cellist's shoulders tense.

"Do you know the word for teacher and learner in German is almost the same?" Giroletti began, his eyes dancing. "The two terms are intertwined so that in the very language there is an understanding that the two roles are one and the same. When I teach I learn, when you learn you teach me."

Vittorio took a breath. Giroletti didn't give him space to speak. "And right now I am learning once again that the subtle art of cooperation happens only when two musicians can meet in the delicious quiet before the music, before melody, in the sensation that the melody must fight out into the space between them. Let us not talk about leaders and followers nor teachers and students. Let us meet one another in the glorious center. Where the magic happens."

Vittorio let the neck of his cello rest on his shoulder and ran his now free hand through his hair.

"A difficult pill to swallow sometimes, yes, Vittorio," Giroletti added. "This is your assignment before next rehearsal. Allow yourselves to converse a little, that way we stand a chance of chiming. Can you do that?"

"I know my part, Maestro," Vittorio replied, though Girloetti's prodding invited no answer other than agreement.

"No, Vittorio, I don't think you do. We are not four soloists. Each instrument's voice is part of the whole. *This* is the part to learn."

Giroletti nodded with a half smile, twisted on his heels, and walked out.

Alba sat in the stilted silence. Vittorio took a sharp breath. Natalia and Leonardo walked in.

"Giroletti throw the rule book at you?" Leonardo called out, strutting to his case and laying his viola inside.

"Go on, then, what he say?" Natalia egged on.

"He told us to talk," Vittorio replied through the narrow space between his lips.

"That's why you look like a storm, Signorino? Did you tell him you only speak through your strings?" Leonardo cackled now, mimicking Vittorio at his cello. Natalia threw her head back with laughter, her light brown hair catching the afternoon streaks streaming in through the small windows that faced the courtyard.

Vittorio packed his case in silence whilst the other two ping-ponged gentle insults. They watched him leave without a goodbye.

Natalia turned to Alba. "Take my word for it—not all strings are like that, okay?"

The threesome separated for their next classes. Alba reached her music theory room and took a seat at the back. It wasn't till the last few minutes that she spied Vittorio seated on the far end of her same row. His face looked deep in concentration on every syllable that Professoressa Simonelli was uttering, her treble tones staccato in the heavy closed-windowed air. Her glasses were perched at the end of her tiny nose, hair sprayed into statuesque stillness, her painted lips dancing over complicated patterns in harmonics. Alba let her professor's voice weave in as she described negative fifths, positive fourths, peculiar journeys from middle C, majors and their relative minors, the way twelve notes knitted together in concentric patterns, each connected to the web of others in astounding mathematical patterns. Her eyes, however, were focused on Vittorio's left hand as it twisted his pencil between each finger, deft and restless. Either side of her, students scribbled their version of Simonelli's words. Alba loved to listen and write her notes straight after the class, finding the act of writing drew her away from the details of what was being said; the physical task of absorbing the information becoming at once removed, cerebral, rather than understood somewhere in her bones. Vittorio's page was blank also, but his expression signaled complete engagement. It wasn't until Simonelli finished, somewhere at the end of the explanation of suspended notes within a chord, that he drew his gaze away from the large green chalkboard printed with staves and caught Alba's eye. His expression revealed he had seen her and then it wiped clean off his face, disintegrating like powdered chalk off Simonelli's felt eraser.

The students piled out of the class and filled the courtyard. Alba found a spot on a stone bench along the walkway and took a seat, the autumnal sunshine dipping the grass in a golden haze, mourning the inevitable disappearance of summer. She took a bite of her apple and reached into her satchel for her notebook to take down some of the key information from Simonelli's class. That's when she spied Vittorio on the opposite side of the courtyard doing the same. She watched him scratch across his page, his pencil leaving squirls of notation. His proud demeanor vanished for a hidden second, out of obvious view of the other students pounding past him. Her instinct to avoid broaching the subject of meeting up as requested by Giroletti urged her to stay seated, to wait for him to approach, but her pride told her there was no dignity in that. She hadn't escaped the unbending rule of her father only to be intimidated by a stuck-up Tuscan who thought himself far better than any of the others. She threw her notebook into her satchel and walked across the green.

"When shall we practice?" she asked, her voice weaving out with unexpected crispness.

Vittorio looked up. Alba noticed his expression stiffen. "My week is pretty full."

"Everyone's is."

He swallowed, irritated.

"Let's go and book a room now, I suppose? I've got my one-to-one in ten minutes, so be quick," he said, with barbed agreement.

Alba twisted away from him and walked toward reception, where a short line of students already formed, waiting their turns to reserve practice rooms. Vittorio stepped in behind her. The other students' chatter prattled around them. Neither of them said a word.

At last Alba reached the front of the queue. The receptionist was patient and calm, accustomed to working with the intensity of music students, but couldn't accommodate both their timetables with a suitable practice room.

"*Grazie,* Signora, not to worry, we can work something out," Vittorio replied, assured. He walked away from the reception and returned toward the courtyard, Alba catching up to his fast strides.

"I'm late for class now," he said, glancing back.

"No, we're not. We've got a few minutes."

"Listen," he said, twisting round to a sudden stop, "I can't give up my day practice times to work on this. I'm not here to carry people."

"Neither am I," Alba replied, determined not to be silenced. "Giroletti asked us to do this."

"You always do what people tell you to?"

Alba felt her cheeks deepen.

Vittorio let out a sigh. "Fine. I have a piano at my place. I'm not far from Calisto. We can work after your shift one night? That's the only time I can give you."

Alba hadn't asked him to give her anything.

"Fine," she replied, deciding to dodge the argument for another time.

"Give me your notebook," he said, glancing to the side toward the corridor that led to the classrooms as a violinist from another class wiped by him, her strands of black hair lifting on the wind like threads of silk.

Alba handed it to him. He wrote down his address, then looked up.

"Tomorrow works for me," he said, closing the book and handing it back.

"Me too, I think," she said, determined to reply even though he hadn't laid the offer out as a question so much as a decision. He left. The courtyard dipped into a sudden quiet. She reached her class panting, after sprinting the three flights.

Alba's shift was due to finish at ten, but in the short while she'd worked it was clear time was as fluid in this city as back home. It had never mattered until tonight, when she knew every extra glass she cleared and washed and wiped was a few minutes shaved off her practice time. That ached. At last, Antonio gave her the nod.

The streets off central Trastevere grew quiet, some hidden in near complete darkness so that Alba struggled to read the names of the *viccoli* on the tiled signs. The main square politics reverberated in the distance across the night air fringed with a threat of frost. At last, she came to Vittorio's door and rang the bottom bell. She waited for several minutes, trying not to notice that she was alone on the darkened narrow street. A smaller door within one side of the tall double doors, which reminded her of the cathedral in Ozieri, creaked open and Vittorio's head poked into the shadows. She couldn't tell if he'd just woken up.

"Is it too late?" she asked, feeling like he'd forgotten about their arrangement.

He shook his head. "No. I've been writing, takes me a second to be sociable—sorry."

Alba followed him down a wide flecked tile hallway, a door at the far end open, shafting a corridor of inviting light. He stepped inside. She did the same.

The first thing that hit her was the smell of caramelized onion and garlic that made her mouth water in an instant and reminded her she hadn't eaten anything since breakfast. Her eyes landed on the huge window that dominated the main wall, its arched sash fitted with curved white shutters. Beside them stood an upright piano with walnut veneer and a panel of carved screen across the face with two candelabras reaching out from it.

"It's no Fazioli but it's all I've got," he said, walking across the Persian rug swirled with intricate gold and black patterns, toward the opposite side of the studio room where half the wall was taken up by a kitchen. There was an impressive hanging of pots along the wall, a shelf packed with glass jars of spices and dried goods, a wide gas range and oven flanked on either side with two wide cupboards topped with a tiled counter. He opened a glass dresser at the farthest end and pulled out two wineglasses. It felt like he'd lived here for years. There was nothing of the transient musical anarchy of Leonardo's apartment. This was like stepping into a miniature creative cave.

"*Vino?*"

Alba was so taken aback by his seamless shift into host that it took her a moment to answer. He didn't wait and lifted his full one to hers. They clinked. Alba longed to unshackle her awkwardness, but it clung like briars.

"Here's the thing," he said, returning to the spiky patter she was accustomed to. "I don't play hungry. I was about to eat. Haven't had anything all day. You want?"

Alba shrugged.

"Well, either you watch me eat or you join in, but I don't work on empty."

Alba felt her lips unfurl into a smile. He'd already retreated into the kitchen. The skillet on the stove was where the sweet smell rose from. She watched him turn up the heat a little then tip in cubed *guanciale,* cured pig's cheek, from a small wooden chopping board. The studio filled with a salty sweetness. He fell into practiced silence, cracking three eggs and separating the whites with the deft hands Alba had seen slide up and down the neck of his cello. Into the bowl of yolks he tipped a heap of Parmesan and attacked it with a whisk.

"What do you want me to do?" Alba asked, never having watched a boy his age do anything in a kitchen other than complain.

"Warm up if you like, I don't care. I don't talk and cook at the same time."

Alba turned toward the piano. She took a sip of the wine and found a narrow space to put it down on amongst the manuscripts strewn across the wooden table by the window. His annotation was swift; scurries of marks and corrections danced along the staves.

The piano stool looked well loved. She lifted the lid. Inside there were sheets of old music, notated in pencil, some popular hits, a couple of books with gold lettering along the spine, Beethoven, gilt and written in sweeping elegance beside a collection of Bach's preludes and fugues. She closed it again without a sound, just in time to see Vittorio crack some pepper into the egg mix and tip in fresh *spaghettoni* into another larger pot of boiling water. His attention was the same that she had witnessed in class, but inside the four walls of his home he was a different version of that persona, his shoulders relaxed, his gait lacking the antagonistic poise of school.

Alba sat at the piano and lifted the lid. The ivories were colored with age. She let her hands trace several scales, with whimsical, curious fingers. She let them feel every note, but her eyes wandered over to the kitchen where the smells deepened and Vittorio's movements sped up, forking steaming strands of pasta into the egg mix bowl, twisting them this way and that, coating them with care. He tipped the contents of the onion and *guanciale* skillet into it and again scooped with a large fork, a helix of salty steam twirling up into his face. A few minutes later, she was presented with her bowl of carbonara.

"Thank you—sorry I interrupted your dinner."

"Just tipped in more pasta. No trouble. I always eat at this time."

Vittorio handed her a fork; she twirled her pasta around it.

"My brothers wouldn't even know where to find a glass of water in the kitchen let alone cook in it."

"Your brothers probably have a mamma who won't let them."

Alba stiffened. What did he know about her family? Who was he to comment? It didn't seem like he'd had anyone stopping him doing what he'd dreamed of.

"Relax. Just a stupid remark. You always get offended so easily?"

Alba wiped the picture of her family from view. She was starving but no longer wanted to eat his food.

She watched Vittorio take his first mouthful. "And before you say anything, my mamma didn't let me either. I learned all this from my aunts. If that serves as an apology, you can have it."

Alba felt embarrassed her expression had revealed so much. She switched her attention to the food and twirled a mouthful. It was creamy, salty perfection. An audible gasp of delight escaped before she could stop it.

"Really?" Vittorio asked without missing a beat. "I didn't put enough salt in the water, I think."

Alba shook her head, savoring the depth of flavor, the smoky intensity of the *guanciale* crisped and sweetened with the onion and garlic. "I've never tasted anything like it."

"Your first carbonara?" he asked, incredulous.

Alba nodded.

"You should be embarrassed," he replied, sensing her shift, "you've eaten your first cooked by a Tuscan! Don't tell any Roman friends, yes? They'll accuse me of desecrating their city's most famous dish."

They slipped into hungry silence for a moment, Alba waiting for the Vittorio she thought she knew to rise into view. Instead, he reached for the bottle of wine and filled their glasses. Alba became aware of her chewing and how loud it sounded. A few twirls later both their bowls were empty.

"Now I work," he said, lifting their empty bowls away and placing them into the ceramic sink.

"Your studio is amazing," Alba said, feeling the wine redden her cheeks.

"My aunt's. Mum's sister. Spent a lot of time here when I was a kid. We have an arrangement. She doesn't charge me what she could a stranger, let's just say that. You?"

"Me?"

"Where do you live?"

"Other side of town."

Vittorio nodded. Their familiar silence filled the gaps. Then he lifted his cello off its stand and brought it over to the piano.

"I'll tune it to this old thing," he said, nodding toward the piano.

Alba played the notes before he asked. She could feel the start of his sarcastic eyebrow raise. As soon as they sat at their instruments they returned to the students of the courtyard, but this time the wine relaxed Alba's muscles, more than she would have liked, the comforting carbonara sitting in her belly like a hug. She could have climbed up to the mezzanine bed and slept that instant. Vittorio stopped mid-flow during the andante section.

"It just sounds a little flabby, stuck, no?" he asked, dropping his bow.

"Should have thought of that before you force-fed me."

His face cracked into that of a stranger's when he smiled, unrecognizable from the taut version at school.

"Let's go back a few measures, from the reprise of the theme, yes?" he suggested.

They did. This time Alba took a few moments before she began to play, easing into the notes, the sounds weaving warmth into the space, like a carpet of copper thread, whilst Vittorio's cello line soared above. His vibrato increased, miniature folds of sound filled the studio, lifting up till the point at which the violin section would begin. They didn't stop there this time. Onward they flew through the rest of the movement, dipping into the shade of the midsection, rising toward the crescendo after that. It felt bare without the other two instruments, pared back to its skeletal core. Their movements were synchronized and assured. Gone was the tentative angular mismatch of their first rehearsal.

The final chord sang. Alba's hands lifted off the keys.

She turned to Vittorio. Neither raced to pierce the silence.

"I don't know what I'm most disappointed about," Vittorio said at last. Alba felt the hairs on the back of her neck lengthen in preparation for a provocative comment, one she'd already decided she wouldn't let pass without a fight.

"The fact that I was wrong to say what I did in our rehearsal," he began, "or the fact that Giroletti was right."

Alba felt her eyebrow raise. She caught sight of the clock above the range.

"*O Dio,* it's late"—she jumped up from her stool—"I've still got some work to finish for classes tomorrow."

"Me too," Vittorio said, setting his cello back on its wooden stand.

Alba pulled her sweater off the back of her chair and swung it over her shoulders.

"I'll walk with you," Vittorio said.

Alba knew she ought to be happy for the company but insisted he didn't need to.

"My friend lives toward our school," he continued, seeing her expression, "I promised him I'd swing by."

"At this time?"

"I get all my best work done after midnight. It's why I'm a bear in the day."

Alba reached the door and twisted the lock. They stepped onto the darkened street and began their walk back toward the Tiber, cobbles dappled with late-night condensation. The scuff of their feet echoed along the stone through the emptied streets toward the main square where sporadic groups still huddled, swaying with alcohol, pelting the world with their wine-infused versions of reality. Vittorio walked like a Roman, twisting down narrow streets and unexpected turns with confidence. They reached the Spanish steps and he climbed them two at a time. Alba paused halfway to catch her breath, the double towers of the church above her creamy in the half-light. Vittorio stood at the top waiting. She reached him and turned back toward the piazza at the bottom of the steps, breathing in the autumn night air.

"Come on," he said, "I know a better view."

He turned and started climbing up another twist of steps that led to a pathway. She fell into step beside him.

"Thanks for tonight," she said, matching his pace.

"No need to tell the others about my cooking, yes? Don't want them all begging me to feed them."

Alba sighed a laugh.

They walked in silence for a while. Then they reached a level ground and Vittorio stopped. Before them the entire panorama of Rome opened up, ancient metropolis scattered with streetlights, antiquity and modernity intertwined in chaotic beauty, a grand improvisation.

"Now, this is worth a Tuscan stopping and ordering a Sardinian to appreciate."

"You always order people around like that?"

"You'd know more about that coming from bandit country, no?"

Alba's stomach struck with steel.

"Whoa—don't be so sensitive, everyone knows what you lot are infamous for. Should I be scared?" he teased, running a carefree hand through his black curls.

"Don't talk about stuff you know nothing about."

"Nerve hit."

Alba wished she'd realized the relaxed Vittorio would expire no sooner had it appeared. "I know my way from here," she replied, turning away from him and starting to walk down toward the Villa Borghese gardens, huge Roman pines twisting up toward the moon, undulating silhouettes crossing the night sky.

She heard his footsteps catch her up.

"Christ, Alba, it was a joke."

Alba didn't reply.

"Come on, you're stomping right into the stereotype you're trying to escape, you know. Don't just run away. Defend yourself!"

"You know nothing about where I'm from!"

He upped his pace and stepped in front of her.

"So tell me."

Alba paused for a moment. His face danced in half shadow, moonlit tricks across his high cheekbones. She stepped around him and quickened her pace, angry that he had lured her into a false sense of relaxation back at his studio only to return to his typical snark.

"Alright—you want me to go first then?" he asked, unwilling to let her go without an argument after all. He walked backward to stay in front of her, stumbling on a stray root but regaining his balance straightaway.

"My mother died when I was ten. That's why I cook. That's why I play—she sent me to my first lessons even though I didn't think I'd like it. She taught me how to practice. She was a Roman. Carbonara is in my blood."

Alba refused to reply.

"She taught me to walk backward too."

Alba stopped then, out of breath, as he crowbarred laughter out of her.

Their eyes locked. Their breaths synchronized.

"My father was kidnapped when I was ten," she said, the words spilling out without a plan, a collapsed tower of cards. "The piano became my safety." Embarrassment clawed up her throat as she witnessed her admission escape.

He didn't race a reply. Their truths hung in the cool night air, stars twinkling in the broad gaps of the huge trees curling their branches to the moon.

"Perhaps," he murmured, "we're not quite as different as we'd like to believe?"

The cluster of trees stood stoic in the silence, barky majesty rising like emperors around them. The singular sound was his rhetoric, weaving through the dark air along a thread of electric blue between them. His voice reached her, measured, vulnerable, and woody, like the deep resonance of his A string.

12

Staccato
with each sound or note sharply detached or separated from the others; "a staccato rhythm"

Mid-November brought the first spray of autumnal rain, streaking the ancient ruins with dripping grief for the distant memory of summer. Natalia and Alba ducked into a bar to dodge the start of a further downpour. Natalia signaled for two espressos and gave her wet locks a shake. A droplet fell on Alba's cheek.

"So do you think Giroletti and his mob are going to mark us for heart or technique?" she asked.

Alba smiled and tucked her black hair behind one ear. "As long as we pass. That's all I care about."

"That's not *all* you care about."

Two espressos landed on the granite counter with a clang. Natalia tipped three spoonfuls of sugar from a metal pot into hers, the gyrations increasing in speed as she spoke.

"We worked hard, no? You and Vittorio sounded divine. Truly. What on earth did you do?"

"Practice."

Natalia rolled her eyes. "When are you going to let go of this sultry Sardinian performance, Signorina? Seriously, between the two of you I don't know how you would actually use enough direct communication to conduct a rehearsal. I think that's exactly what Giroletti was on about."

The young women sipped their coffee. Natalia lifted her hand for the waiter and ordered two small crème puffs.

"Don't be silly, Natalia, I'm fine with just the coffee."

"You're not, Alba. Their sweets are from heaven. You will eat."

The puff arrived, dusted with a snow of fine sugar. The *crème pâtissière* melted in Alba's mouth. Her friend was right.

"And you can put your purse away immediately. It's not a crime to partake in pleasure, you know. You're always so serious, Alba."

Natalia's soft laughter tumbled out one eyebrow raised in jest. "Let's run up to my apartment for a second. I left a manuscript there I should bring in today before we check our results."

Alba followed her out and down a twist of back streets till they reached her palazzo where Natalia rented a room in her sister's apartment. Wide stairs wove through the center of the hallway with a lift that rose up a metal caged shaft to the sixth floor, enclosed in an ornate wrought-iron cubicle with tiny double doors that the women had to skim sideways to fit through.

Natalia opened the three locks of their heavy wooden door and they stepped inside onto the black tiles. A comforting smell of minestrone greeted them. Alba had never been inside when there wasn't a pot simmering on the back burner. Today it was clouded with the pungent smoke of a patchouli incense stick weaving its scent from underneath Natalia's sister's door, a wail of music pumping out from beyond. The door flung open sending a further thick ribbon of smoky herb out into the hallway. A woman with a cropped head of jet-black hair appeared, smudged kohl around her eyelids and beneath her lower lashes, several earrings puncturing her ears like trophies.

"*Ciao*, Francesca," Natalia gushed, kissing the vision of defiance. "This is my friend Alba, from the *accademia*. Only the best pianist I have ever heard in my life. Truth. It's sickening, to be frank."

Francesca held out her hand and gave Alba's a tough squeeze, which she couldn't decipher as challenge or welcome.

"Francesca is my sister," Natalia said, filling in the gaps.

"It would be cool if we didn't have to say that *every* time you introduce me." Her voice was throaty with a faint rasp of someone who smoked and shouted. Natalia lit with an apologetic smile, then rolled her eyes at Alba once Francesca's back was turned to slope toward the soup smell.

Alba followed the corridor and stepped into their living room while Natalia commenced battle on the heap of belongings that was her small room. Two bookcases heaved with knowledge, Francesca's manifestos aching the shelves. The floorboards were covered with old sheets. All along them, banners lay face up, their wet paint drying. Rally cries for women's rights for autonomy over their bodies sat beside demands to make abortion legal. Alba could imagine Francesca shouting them as she traced the fat sticky font.

"Don't step in there, yeah?" Francesca's voice rose in a rumble from behind.

Alba turned toward her. "Of course."

"Natalia told you about the rally yet?" she asked, dipping her spoon into the hot thick orange liquid inside her bowl. Alba had never seen a soup that color before. Her mother's minestrone was always an earthy swirl of cabbage and root vegetable, the same soupy brown as a spectrum of paints drowning together.

"It's made from squash and lentils," Francesca said, finding Alba's obvious ignorance lift an oblique smile across her face. "You want?"

Francesca ate a couple of spoonfuls in silence.

"The demo is on December sixth. It's going to be big. If you care about the situation of women in our country right now, you'll be there."

"The situation?"

Alba felt the awkwardness of asking questions, but Francesca's spikes softened her own.

"In our country, Alba, women can get raped and are forced to keep the child. They're tied to their homes, housework essentially an accepted form of patriarchal slavery of which we are all victims, either by succumbing to it or turning a blind eye. Your mum work at home all day?"

Alba nodded.

"She get paid?"

"No, it's home."

"So you're blind to what's really happening. Most of us have been or choose to remain so. The fact is, women are locked out of the labor force but at the same time are forced to work twenty-four hours to keep that labor force going. It's slavery. We're fighting for the government to pay us as they do the men, for all the work we are expected to do without reimbursement. We're demanding that the laws are changed to make abortion legal. It's time to say that the crimes against women must stop and laws be put in place against the men who commit them."

Francesca's unexpected sermon finished with the same unannounced abruptness as it began. She took another slurp of her soup. Alba's crème puff was the first thing she'd eaten since a sandwich at lunch the day before and she wished she'd accepted the offer of a bowl herself.

"So you know, if you care about having a voice, if you're sick of the way men in your life treat you like a second-class citizen, you should join us."

The memory of her father crowbarred into view. The way he'd yelled about the Red Brigade in Rome, the anti-fascists causing havoc around the country with their assassinations, their demonstrations, their ridiculous attention-seeking bombs, throwing their country into chaos, an imminent toss to the dogs.

"I'd love to," Alba said.

Francesca nodded, as if she'd scanned right through Alba's mind and watched the replaying of all those pictures too; Alba's stone house echoing with the bitter rage of her father, the cynical snide of her brothers, her mother refusing to assert herself or contest their decisions, using herself as a physical buffer for her daughter and failing, leaving Alba stranded, unsupported, alone, with only the received message that she was and never would be right, or good or enough. That somehow her nature was formed with missing essential components and their anger at failing to train it into her could only ever be expressed through violence, spoken, and unspoken, in those vicious silences where love, acceptance, and encouragement might have breathed hope. Alba hadn't traveled all this way to let these phantom memories suffocate her still.

Natalia's face popped around the door. "Isn't it amazing? There's been all kinds of meetings here. I've learned so much. Mamma is coming down to join us too. I'll tell you about it on our way in, yes? Take my mind off our results."

Francesca sighed a condescending laugh with a shake of her head. "Go ahead and run back to your music. You still haven't answered my question from the other day, Natalia."

"Which one?"

"How many female composers are you studying?"

Natalia took a breath. "I don't have time to go into all this now, Francesca."

"Figures." Francesca slunk around them, swallowed back into the patchouli haze of her room.

Natalia bubbled through a stream of consciousness as they dodged the puddles along the walk toward the *accademia*. Alba twisted Francesca's question around in her mind, toying with it from different directions, a cat swiping its shadow.

"She has a point," Alba said, cutting through Natalia's patter.

"Who has? I'm talking about Giroletti."

"Francesca."

"What did she say this time? She's always upsetting my friends."

"She asked me how many women we study."

Natalia's expression crinkled curiosity.

"I've never thought about it at all. Take Clara Schumann, we talk about her as the woman Brahms was infatuated with, but we don't play her concertos as much as we do his, even though she was a phenomenal musician, better than her husband for sure. There's Fanny Mendelssohn. Her brother gets all the accolades, but her compositions have an intricacy that can't be matched by his work, and we barely hear of her."

Natalia stopped walking. "That's the most I've ever heard you say in one go."

Alba smiled, unguarded. "I suppose I wait until I have something important to say."

"If I didn't adore you so much, I would feel completely offended right now." Natalia hooked her arm into Alba's. They walked on in comfortable silence.

* * *

The corridor by the student board was rammed with anxious bodies. Several students ahead of Alba peeled away, tears in their eyes. Others stepped by her, inscrutable, not wishing to share their reactions with their competitors. At last the two women were before the typed list of names and grading. Natalia ran her fingers down the list until she reached their quartet. She traced the dotted line across toward the score.

"Not bad for beginners!" Leonardo's voice cut across the noisy milieu behind them.

Natalia twisted round. Alba heard their lips meet in a kiss, trying not to let her surprise register.

"What are you talking about?" Alba recognized Vittorio's voice swimming in between them. "The guys from the other section got two marks more."

"That's because their cellist was half decent," Leonardo teased.

Vittorio raised an eyebrow. "Like you could tell anyway."

"I love it when you get emotional, Vittorio," Leonardo laughed, kissing him on each cheek.

Vittorio almost blushed and a resigned smile lit his face for a breath.

The four of them moved away from the throng who lapped to the front, a shifting wave. Natalia and Leonardo disappeared behind the corner. Alba made her way toward the practice rooms.

"Your sound was perfection."

Vittorio's voice caught her off guard as much as the words themselves. She twisted around to him.

"It's a compliment, Alba. Most people don't look like thunder on the rare occasions I give them."

"That's most likely because you follow it with sarcasm like that."

"You're the one uncomfortable accepting praise. I'm giving it freely. Your playing was sublime."

He held her gaze. She matched it, wondering who might win this battle. Any second now he would glance away, like he always did. Alba was accustomed to him behaving as if he were always almost late for something, on his way to a better use of his time. The memory of him cooking flooded her senses, his confident, yet delicate movements inside his kitchen. It was soon followed by the memory of it feeling as if she had imposed on his private ritual, rather than him feeding an expected guest, however delectable the food.

"There you both are!" They twisted toward Goldstein's rasp. A draw. Their teacher's sunglasses were firm on the bridge of his nose, cigarette unlit in hand. "Serendipity—the Greek word for sublime, cosmic timing. They knew about it way ahead of those stuck-up Romans. That's why I'm here I suppose, to try and drill it into you imbeciles."

Vittorio glanced at Alba, then back at their teacher.

"I'm leading an open master class," Goldstein began, "and I'm recruiting some of our most exciting players. Before your heads explode with hubris, I add that two of them have had to pull out because they are representing our school at a competition in Turin so I'm asking if you'd like to step in instead?"

"What's the plan?" Vittorio asked, unwavering in Goldstein's shadow. Alba made a mental note to try and affect the same attitude at her next lesson.

"My plan is to pick Fauré's *Elégie* for piano and cello to pieces."

He'd be tearing her and Vittorio apart, rather than Fauré, Alba thought. Goldstein pecked at his protégés and this time he was threatening to do so before an audience.

"Alba and I have already worked together," Vittorio replied. "Do you want players who are new together?"

Alba bristled at Vittorio's precocious negotiation, as if Goldstein was the kind of professor to say anything other than thank you to rather than begin professional bartering.

"Cocky son of a whore, isn't he, Alba?" Goldstein asked, looking through her to see if Vittorio's peculiar brand of charm had disarmed. "It would be my absolute pleasure to dissect you two, I mean Fauré, for the benefit of our esteemed audience. We have people coming from Florence and Milan, and other students of course. But perhaps I should change the name to *The Vittorio Spectacular*?"

Vittorio's lips pressed together a little tighter.

"I'll call the printers and ask them to reprint the program."

He laughed at his own joke and pulled out a lighter from his pocket, lifting the flame toward his cigarette. "I'll leave a copy of the score in your pigeonholes at reception. You've got a few weeks to prepare."

He left, a waft of gray in his wake.

"Shall I take that look as a threat, Alba?"

"If you like."

Vittorio shifted weight to his other foot. "We'll stick with the same day as last time?"

Alba shrugged.

"I'm not cooking every time you step inside my place, you know that, right? To be frank I think it made me a little heavy. We'll stay easy on the wine too."

Alba watched him retract the spontaneous hospitality of their rehearsal. Their snatched confessions under the stillness of those Roman pines dismissed. Her Sardinian upbringing held fast; she couldn't imagine threatening a visitor into her home with a promise like that. Then again she couldn't imagine having her own home. Francesca's banners rose into her mind, her arch smile, her goading politics, followed by the echoes of Celeste's advice, clear and free and as insistent as a morning church bell.

"Your hospitality is overwhelming, Vittorio," Alba replied, walking away from him. "See you Tuesday!" she called out, without turning back.

13

Elégie
a poem or song composed especially
as a lament for a deceased person

By the last days of November Alba was at last feeling like she remembered where everything lived behind the counter at Bar Calisto. She'd learned to dodge Antonio's verbal bullets, anticipate when he was about to launch an attack, clear tables before he asked, and polish the glasses till they sparkled. He didn't go as far as to praise her but the odd extra thousand lire here and there, enough to help her buy a few extra groceries, made her know that he saw she was a good worker and one who could be trusted. It didn't matter that he called her his Sardinian shepherdess, a term of endearment compared to what he called some of the other staff.

The patrons of Bar Calisto came for his very peculiar brand of Roman swagger, his ability to say things as they were, and with such blunt passion that it was impossible to argue against it. Add that to the fact that his *aperitivo* snacks were the best and cheapest on the square, his Negronis mixed to perfection, and he had created a winning formula.

Alba cleared one of the heaving tables as the group of customers seated around it signaled for her to bring them another round of Camparis and a plate of Antonio's prosciutto-and-fresh-tomato-topped crostini, sliced toasted day-old rolls scraped with garlic, small cubed tomatoes and parsley tumbled over the top with coarse salt and a drizzle of his own olive oil he crushed at his farm outside the city.

Dario, the waiter she had first spoken to when she'd arrived a few months ago asking for the job, was behind the counter, pirouetting with various bottles in hand, the lion tamer of Antonio's espresso machine. "You going to go human pace now, Alba, or stay snail?" he called, lifting the bottle of wine up as he emptied it into a glass, throwing it into the bin behind him without looking.

"Two more Campari, table four," she answered, not taking the bait.

"Take that tray to Antonio," he called back.

She lifted the large metal tray that lay upon the counter. There were small bowls of peanuts and olives. A pile of crisps was surrounded by a rainbow of crostini, some topped with black olive tapenade, others with thin slices of boiled egg and a twirl of mayonnaise, a few with crumbled gorgonzola and surrounding them all, folds of thin-sliced salami and twists of deep red prosciutto. Her mouth watered.

The stairs behind the beaded curtain toward the back of the bar were wide enough for one person and rose crooked with age, steep as a ladder. They creaked as she squeezed up with the heavy tray. At the top of the stairs was Antonio's office, cigarette smoke filling the air just beyond and seeping out from the uneven gap at the foot of the door. There were voices of several men, their tone urgent, a group of people trying to argue without making noise.

"Signori, let's keep to the original plan," she heard Antonio say. "We go in, we surround, we plant what we need, and then let the chaos do its job."

"But Antonio," another voice interrupted, "you want it to be so obvious? It's like leading a trail of crumbs right to us."

"Isn't that the point, for Christ's sake?" another interrupted, more heated than the first. "We don't stand for hiding in the shadows! We're not the Mafia. If you can't get your head around that then you shouldn't be here in the first place."

Alba coughed, for want of a third hand to knock.

The men's silence was instant.

Antonio opened the door. Four faces looked up, their cheeks red with disagreement, an ashtray between them almost overflowing.

"Get back to the animals," Antonio said to her, grabbing the tray from her hands. The door eased shut to the sound of the men's laughter.

"Why the face?" Dario asked as he pushed the tray of Camparis over to her along the marble. "You didn't interrupt them up there, did you?"

Alba shook her head and lifted the drinks.

"One bit of advice," Dario began as Alba tried to recall a shift when he hadn't preached uninvited titbits of sagacity. "You go up when Anotnio's having one of his meetings? You act like you heard nothing. If people ask you what you know about what goes on up there you pull that Sardinian silence. Shouldn't be difficult for you. You get me?"

Alba nodded, but didn't. Or didn't want to.

"You going to use this practice with me to perform or do the work?" Goldstein's question hung unanswered in the suffocating Gitanes air, wafting through the wintry midmorning light shafting in through the windows. He looked over at her from his perch on the stool in front of his grand piano.

"It's a question, Alba. I'm wanting you to talk."

"I tried to find interesting ways to practice this section, like you said."

"Good. I can hear it."

Alba sat, expectant.

"Tell me why I've asked you to work on Schumann's overplayed 'Traumerei'?" he asked.

She shrugged. He waited.

Alba watched him run his square hand down through his thick beard.

"Be wary of the wrong type of perfection, Alba. Do not be dominated by that. Invulnerability is boring. It's not exciting. I don't want to watch a pianist perform their practice. I want to know that they are human. Our job is to allow our audience to feel. What you feel is not necessarily what they will feel."

Alba rolled her wrists. They ached a little.

"You must surprise the audience with the shift in harmonics. Keep us on our toes. Again, from this midsection."

Alba began the rolling wave of the left hand. The right hand cut in, high notes floating over the bass.

"So what is Schumann trying to say here?"

"Say?"

"We have studied together for this entire term, for crying out loud. We don't play black dots. We are pulling apart the composer's mind. Climbing into their skin. Finding out what they are trying to say, not just what they want us to hear. Christ, what on earth have I been preaching for the past hour?"

The familiar claustrophobia of his lessons closed in.

He looked at her, then twisted to his piano. He played the measures. His tone was wistful, ardent, and full of the yearning that ran through all the music of these Romantic pianists. His interpretation of Schumann sang a life of manic genius and periods of utter despair. Alba could hear the man who threw himself into the Rhine. She could feel a private moment of reflection in the deceptive simplicity of the melody, in the absence of an orchestral fanfare, virtuoso runs, and flashy trills. Instead, Schumann's pared-down contemplation drove the listener deep into a child's fading dream; innocent, yet fringed with the sadness of the inevitable, and imminent, loss of it.

He stopped.

"Schumann is intensity, introspection, lyricism," he said, his voice caramel.

Alba felt the weight and warmth of the words land without reply.

"Qualities you possess in spades if you were courageous enough to know yourself," he added.

He snapped his lighter to life. "The Greeks knew that the universe is music," he began, on a deep inhale, "and here we are, silent Signorina, before machines of vibrating strings. No more than that. Our Signor Pythagoras, from my homeland, developed a musical scale based on universal harmonies. Life is a song, Alba!" He breathed out a cloud of smoke, his wistful meanderings more disarming than his fire. "It is a symphony of major and minor keys, polarities, opposites that weave a harmony that unites us into a whole grand symphony of life."

He turned toward her. She took her cue to play.

He listened without interruption.

When she finished the first phrase, she lifted her hands. He smiled. She felt her shoulders soften down her back.

"Tell me you won't play like that at the master class next week."

An unexpected smart. They hurt the most.

"Vittorio won't waste the opportunity," he continued, "he already thinks he is a maestro. But you must match him. And not embarrass me—you understand that much, I hope?"

"*Si*, Maestro."

He crossed the room. The door snapped shut behind him.

The two silent pianos taunted her; faint sirens luring her sail toward watery annihilation.

The Piazza del Popolo filled with women as the December sun cut through the frigid air. Alba, Natalia, her sister Francesca, and friends couldn't feel the cold. There were too many other bodies around them, too much fierce camaraderie to feel anything other than the powerful rush of connectedness. Women with hair hanging at free angles, fists raised in provocation, their banners dancing as the early morning frost melted, breath escaping in steamy defiance. The voices swam together in the air, calls in unison. When the papers and television news reported it later that day, they confirmed numbers had reached upward of ten thousand. Alba didn't shout out with the others, but the energy around her wove deep inside. The immense vocal power, noise, of sheer space taken up by women made her feel the promise of invincibility, a sense of infinity that she'd only ever felt whilst playing. The idea that there might be an existence beyond her former understanding of life was an icy shower on a scorching day. Her chest felt luminous, light, hot, free. Natalia looked over at her, the chanting percussing the cloudless blue above their heads. "I've never been anywhere like this either!" she shouted.

An unexpected tear ran down Alba's cheek. The sheer power of the bodies around her, the safety in these great numbers, the sense that nothing was unachievable moved something deep inside her. She too had escaped. She had fled the very culture all these thousands of women were protesting. Without following a manifesto other than that of her music she had become one of them, part of this venerable tribe, trembling with thousands of years of oppression, humans who refused to be held down and now demanded to be heard. She knew firsthand what it was like to feel the smother of a bully, as they attack, fearing their loss of control over a woman. She knew firsthand the violent terror of an oppressor who cannot accept a woman choosing to chase her dream of entering the intangible world of music, its intense power impossible to be strangled, quantified, but able to move, to touch, to appeal to a feeling nature so strangled within themselves. For the first time, pounding the pavements next to these women, unafraid to shout, to use their sound, their hearts, their strength, Alba understood that this daughter was a threat to her father, and one he would always be compelled to obliterate, whatever the cost to either of them.

But Alba had a voice nonetheless. It was her music. Goldstein's bearlike coaching growled to mind, amongst the stamping feet, as the voices echoed up the palazzi lining the streets they marched, curious faces peering down from balconies, some waving in solidarity, others looking on, disapproving.

Alba had been gifted this powerful voice. It streamed out of her when she played. It was time to release the fear of its power. Her piano would set it free.

In the narrow wings that flanked the sides of the auditorium stage, the monitors, other student volunteers, clutched their clipboards. They shifted weight from foot to foot, glaring out toward the stage, their faces blanched in the white sidelights, then shifting back into the shadows where Alba and Vittorio stood.

"Please show your warm appreciation for Vittorio del Piero and Alba Fresu," Goldstein announced. A monitor signaled for them to enter. They stepped out into applause. Alba's noticed how loud her footsteps sounded as she walked across the wooden stage to the piano. Vittorio lifted his cello and took his seat. They tuned up.

The sporadic coughs and shuffles from the audience softened into silence.

Goldstein nodded.

Vittorio straightened. Alba felt her breath deepen. She lifted her wrists and began the opening chime of Fauré's *Elégie*, solemn church bell chords tolling a funereal melody, fading over a few measures like a painful memory. Vittorio took a breath and caressed his strings, the melody rising up toward the stone ceiling, a melancholic cry.

Goldstein clapped his hands. "So let us begin immediately, no?"

The audience laughed. Alba swallowed the sensation of being an accidental clown orbiting their ringmaster.

"The beginning, Vittorio—tell me where the emotion lies."

Vittorio shifted in his seat a little. Alba was relieved to discover it appeared he was as nervous as her.

"From the beginning."

"No!" Goldstein exclaimed. "It lies in the last six inches of the bow. That is where you will draw out this longing for the deceased. To play this you must know death, Vittorio."

Vittorio lifted his bow. Goldstein flicked his wrist for Alba to begin. This time Vittorio's bow made the string sing with a deeper mahogany sound, the texture of grief without balm.

"Yes!" Goldstein heaved, stamping over to the other side of the cello now. "And then we move on you see, the next section, tell me about this, Vittorio."

"It's pianissimo."

"He reads!" Goldstein declared, twisting to the crowd, lighting up with their laughter. "So we deduce what?"

Vittorio's head shook a little, as if he was rattling it for an answer.

"Vittorio, this is the quiet ebb of a cry, boy," Goldstein said, his voice dipping into warmth. "It is the out breath when you feel there are simply no more tears to shed. You ask yourself, do you have the courage to tap into those shades of emotions? Or do you choose to stay a young boy who simply wants to pantomime the feeling? We can hear when a musician tunes in or just shows off."

He raised his hands. "I want you to reach for a very French vibrato, Vittorio, very close, tight, elegant, this is not minimalist."

They began again. This time Goldstein moved them through another few measures, pinging vocal direction as they played, sometimes beside Alba *push through here, Alba, sing out now,* other times beside Vittorio painting pictures with words, swirling his arms through space, his black eyes glimmering with a passion that both ignited their playing and threatened obliteration.

"Enough!" he said.

They stopped.

Goldstein lifted a hand to a woman seated in the front row. She was wiping her eye.

"You see, Vittorio?" he said, as the woman laughed at herself, the crowd around her joining in soon after. "Our job as musicians is to allow the people listening to make our music take them to their *own* grief, their *own* memories. We don't want to see your perfection, or musicianship. We don't care about that. We need you to be a conduit for our *own* lives. We need you to know that Fauré wrote this for his dead wife. We need you to understand this middle section, which you danced through so elegantly, Alba, is him painting her alive, before we return to his interminable loss."

Goldstein lifted Vittorio's chin. "Look at you!"

That's when Alba saw Vittorio's eyes were wet too.

"This is the stuff of great artists, Vittorio, yes! If you can allow yourself to tap into the same emotion as the composer *and* feed it through the instrument, then you can allow their song to weave out—as it should."

He tripped them on through the swell of the midsection, a stormy interlacing of the piano and cello, then allowed them to hold a moment of silence before playing the piece once through in its entirety.

Alba heard those scuffs in the dark, the march through the Sardinian night with the hood over her head, felt Raffaele's hand by the port, the fading echoes of her father's tirade as she stepped out of her stone house for the last time. Signora Elias was with her now, urging her on, running a light finger across her tear-stained cheek. A halo of light spread across her back, down her legs, unlocking the knot in her chest like a powerful waterfall. She tumbled in its wake, surrendering to its power without a fight.

The final note was Fauré's wounded eternal sigh; a languid caress of the lower string of Vittorio's cello. Alba spidered her fingers up the keyboard, her piano's lament one final unhurried minor arpeggio. Vittorio's bow lifted.

Their shared grief hung above them, bleak, powerful, full of truth.

The audience stood. The auditorium ignited with applause.

Vittorio laid his cello down on its side and stepped forward. He turned back to Alba and reached out his hand. She slipped hers into his. His fingers wrapped around hers. Alba could feel the tension there, the tendons twitching with relief, with success. Their heads dipped as they bowed. As they rose his hand squeezed hers a little tighter. They turned to each other, a sketch of silence in the dizzying roar, an intense quiet at a storm's center. His eyes were dancing. The sidelights traced his runaway curls with a metallic outline.

They turned back to the crowd in unison. It wasn't the passionate appreciation from the crowd alone that sent refracting light splintering through them.

14

Tremolo
a wavering effect in a musical tone, produced either by rapid reiteration of a note, by rapid repeated slight variation in the pitch of a note, or by sounding two notes of slightly different pitches to produce prominent overtones

Natalia was waiting for Alba by the main entrance of the auditorium hall where the audience filed out into the night. She felt her friend wrap her arms around her, squealing into her ear.

"Alba! It was sublime! When my mother hears you, she's going to adopt you. You have to come and stay with us at Christmas now. No more *maybes*, and *I'll think about it*, yes? Now tell me, you work with Goldstein every week, right?"

"Got the bruises to prove it," Alba replied, still riding the giddy crest of the performance wave.

"Come," Natalia said, hooking her arm into Alba's, "Leonardo and I have reserved a big table down by Calisto at Zio Umberto's. It's cheap and amazing. A load of us are going."

Natalia registered Alba's expression. "Don't be doing that *I can't be with loads of people right now* thing. You need to adore your public as much as they did you tonight, *tesoro*. It's only polite."

Leonardo swung in beside them, wrapping his arms around both.

"Well look at this pair of talent!" He kissed each on their chilled cheeks. "Even managed to get Mr. Aloof to come along. Maybe with some wine in his bones he might break into song."

Natalia laughed, grabbed Leonardo's chin, and kissed him.

"You see the effect I have on intelligent, talented women, Alba?" Leonardo teased. "It really is a liability."

Vittorio stepped into line with Alba. She noticed his pace stall a little, not his usual determined swing, separating them ever so from the group of other students.

"Stringers can't hold their drink too well. Percussive players have much more stamina," he said.

Alba turned her face toward him. His smile was oblique without the usual harsh angle. They walked without talking for a moment, noiseless but for the scuff of their soles on the frigid cobbles beneath.

"I left my body," he murmured, puncturing the quiet.

His words were a light. She noticed the temperature of her cheeks change.

"I'd never felt like that before," she replied, the words escaping before self-consciousness could trap them inside.

Their footsteps kept time, whilst the sensations rattling around Alba's body zapped in opposing directions, a frenetic syncopated improvisation scuffing against the melody, both searching and dodging harmonic conclusion.

"Come on, divas!" Leonardo yelled, twisting back toward them. "The owner won't hold the table if we're late!"

They sped up and slipped back into the group.

Zio Umberto's was a rattling cave, stuffed with too many tables for the miniscule space and too many hungry bodies talking at the same time, clinking their glasses, hauling the oversized serving plates across one another as they each filled their own from the communal sharing dishes. When they'd arrived, the owner told them what to order. There were no menus, no prices, nothing other than the rough promise that they wouldn't be spending more than about ten thousand lire and that would include enough wine to make them forget everything and make everyone's jokes louder, faster, and funnier. Vittorio sat at the opposite end of the table, surrounded by Leonardo's classmates. Alba twisted the thick homemade spaghetti strands around her fork, the *cacio e pepe* oozing Parmesan and cracked black pepper sauce filling her with a depth of savory delight she'd never experienced. All the while, trying to convince herself she couldn't feel Vittorio's stare cut across the noisy table in her direction.

Natalia swapped stories with the other young men and women around Alba, but the sensation of having her every move committed to his memory persisted in her peripheral. It was the wine making her cheeks flush, that was all, the intense pleasure of the food, nothing more, the adoring company filling her with compliments and questions and queries on how she survived Goldstein. She even remembered, in the fog of the third glass of wine, discovering that she thought he was one of the best teachers she'd ever had, that he understood music on a profound level, cosmic even. That made the table erupt in laughter. On the outside he may have once appeared a brutal man, she persisted, to jeers, intent on making his students jump through hoops, but that was his quest for the truth and nothing short of that. The words rippled out of her in an unaccustomed string of effortless tales, twisting through the air to the obvious delight of her crowd.

More dishes appeared and disappeared at a hungry student rate. Someone passed her a shot of aquavit. She thought of her brothers' expressions should they have been there, then knocked it back. When all the tables were empty but theirs, and the owner Umberto had cracked a few more jokes, then told them to bugger off to where they'd come from, the singing group spilled out onto the small courtyard beyond the door. They began a roving zigzag toward the main square of Trastevere in the direction of Leonardo's.

Alba felt a hand slip into hers.

"This way," Vittorio whispered in her ear. A shiver skated up her arm. She followed his gentle tug.

He sped up now, his hand cradling hers.

"What's happening?" Alba asked, trying to cork her laughter and failing.

"Whiskey at mine."

Their feet tip-tapped the silent streets, a half skip through the giddy replay of their night. They reached his palazzo's door. It creaked open.

"Don't start any Sardinian singing, okay?" he teased, looking back at her. "I have neighbors to think of, *sì?*"

They stepped into the black. She felt him fumble for his apartment door key. It creaked open. A streetlight's shaft skewered across the darkened space through the half-opened shutters, traveling up and along the furniture; divergent pathways through the night.

He stopped. His hand slipped around hers.

The silver light danced across the visible half of his face. Their heartbeats filled the shadows between. His face edged closer. Alba didn't move. She felt his lips brush the narrow space where her jaw met her neck. She felt the strength of his elegant fingers cup her cheeks. His forehead pressed against hers. Their breaths plaited.

He lifted her face. She reached forward and felt the surprising softness of his lips play against hers, sending ribboning pleasure down her spine. Her mouth opened. His tongue wove around the tip of her top lip, then played inside, curious, ardent. His hands eased down her arms then around her back, tracing the base of her neck, playing through her thick hair. It sent a shimmering ripple around her skull.

She didn't remember every moment of the dance that followed. Only that it was legato, smooth, free, an improvised duet. She wouldn't forget the way he peeled away her clothing with care. The way he'd let his lips taste every inch of her bare body. The way he'd stopped her hand when she'd tried to do the same to him. She remembered the feel of the silver light tracing the outline of her bare breasts. The way his touch felt like he was savoring the texture, temperature, and contours of her body with the sensitive precision of a musician's hand.

The bare wall pressed against her. He moved his fingers down her stomach to the crisscross of her pubic hair. She let herself feel the tingling waves rise up through her, feeling the rhythm of his hand merge with that of her body. His breath was hot in her ear, yet patient. Here was the timeless space Celeste had spoken of in their lessons, the stretch of infinity essential to seek and revel in at the heart of a piece. Here was the roaring silence, the blinding light in the dark.

She let herself be played.

Her body was a spark that took flight.

Then the quiet curled in, a dying wave stroking wet sand. He held her naked body against him. She felt the wetness at the top of her thighs press against his trousers. She pulled away, a piercing vulnerability tensing her muscles, but he reached round to the small of her back and pressed her harder against him. His tongue traced her ear. His fingers eased down onto her sacrum, smoothing a figure of eight.

Their chests rose and fell, breaths hiding in the shadows. A further release bubbled up from her middle; waves of surprising tears that she let score out of her.

He tightened his hold. Wordless. Warm.

"The whiskey was the only thing I'd planned," he whispered into her ear, "honest."

She laughed into the crook of his neck, sobs jutting through in between breaths. She pulled away. He reached for her hand. She retracted from his and picked up the pile of her clothes crumpled at her feet, at once her nudity a stark nakedness she wanted to escape.

"I think I should go."

His eyes flinted a shade of disappointment, fast-moving clouds on a changeable day. "I would love you to stay. It's your choice, of course."

She bent down, fumbling with her clothes, wishing both that the light were on and hoping he wouldn't flick the switch.

He stepped forward. He lifted her chin with a gentle finger. She felt his mouth on hers. She dropped her clothes. Her hands wrapped around his face, filling with the width of his jaw. The heat in her chest burned past pleasure; a white heat, opening her up too much, too soon, too deep. It was as if he had stepped inside her. Revealed herself to herself, like shining a torch around the cavern of her body into the mercurial crags where her soul hid with an unforgiving light. It was a brutal awakening, one she hadn't practiced nor prepared for.

She pulled away again and jerked back into her clothes, though her body ached for more, muscles alight; the sensation of running whilst standing in utter stillness tripped through her bones.

She picked up her coat and scarf and, without putting them on stepped outside of his door meeting the frigid dark of the corridor. Her footsteps scuffed the dark. She heaved the main door open. It shut behind her. The sound of the closing lock traveled down the corridor beyond. Alba sent the memory of the last hour away from her along each tiny wave of the rippling echo.

Piazzale Centro Storico,
Cagliari
Sardegna
December 16, 1975

To my dear Alba,

Thank you so much for your last letter. What a special week. I need to meet this Vittorio. You've never described someone's music that way.

I'm looking forward to Christmas and dreading it at the same time. It's nice to get a break from the professor's interrogations (you don't miss them, do you?) but the idea of being around the table with Mamma and Papà while he drills me on every aspect of my university life is a dirge. He knows a couple of my professors, so even though I've had a taste of freedom it's like he's always watching me.

Do you want me to pass on any message to your folks? What shall I tell them if they ask? Papà says your father doesn't talk about the fiasco. Those first weeks of panic and anger are smoke. I think he's too proud to let on to anyone.

I'll be thinking of you when everyone's parading in the central square showing off their new furs. I'll remember the time you reminded me they were the skins of corpses.

I miss you more than I'd like to admit. Write again soon.

Your Raffaele.

PS I've met someone. I want to be able to try and describe him with the detail and elegance you did your friends but I'm not ready to do that yet. I might jinx it before anything starts.

PPS Stop smirking.

15

Amabile
a directive to a musician to perform the indicated passage of a composition in a charming, gracious, or amiable manner

Alba boarded an early train from Termini station toward Venice and from there followed Natalia's directions, catching two local buses up to the mountain town of Revine in the northern province of Treviso, where her parents had extended their invitation for her to join them at her grandparents' home. Natalia met her at the bottom of the driveway, her cheeks flush against the snowy meadows surrounding them.

"Dear God, is that the only coat you have, Alba? Hurry in, you'll freeze!" Natalia wrapped her arm around her friend, and they dodged the deeper parts of the snow along the path, bursting through the door with an announcement introducing the arrival of their new guest. An older woman appeared from the doorway that led off the entrance hall, wiping her hand on a tea towel. Her hair had the same effusive quality of Natalia's but was flecked with white. She moved across the space with the same easy grace of Natalia but void of the skittish diverging attention, and kissed Alba on both cheeks. Natalia took Alba's suitcase out of her hand.

"I'm Violetta," said the woman. "Natalia's mamma." Alba was struck by the gentle upward angle of her eyes, inflecting her face with curiosity and sagacity, their color lying somewhere between the sparkling blue of Natalia's and a warmer indecipherable auburn. Alba tried to stop staring.

"We've heard a great deal about you," Violetta continued, her voice assured, warm, void of the nervous energy that bristled her own mother's when new people arrived at their home, always the waver of insecurity at its fringes, desperate to pass the newcomer's presupposed judgment of her. "I'm so glad you decided to join us." There was an echo of an accent she couldn't place, something angular about the vowels, which didn't sound Italian.

Violetta signaled for her to follow. "Was your journey easy? I know things do get busy this time of year."

"It was beautiful. I've never been up here."

"I hadn't either," Violetta replied, "until I met Giacomo, Natalia's father." Her tone shifted then, a slide into languid adagio, then snapped back into the previous timbre just as Alba noticed it. "Now we come whenever we can."

"It's glorious in the summer, Alba. We get naked by the lake!" Natalia added, taking Alba's case out of her hand and into hers.

Violetta laughed with a shake of her head. "It's a choice, Alba," she said, registering Alba's expression, "not a requirement."

They stepped into the stone-floored kitchen. Francesca was standing at the table shelling chestnuts and chopping them into small pieces. Another young woman was beside her, hair scrunched up in an untidy bun, wisps falling onto her face. They wore thick knit jumpers the same shade as the nuts they were cracking. Francesca looked up and walked over to Alba.

"I've got nutty hands, sorry!" she said, kissing her on each cheek. Alba assumed she'd earned this newfound warmth by attending the rally. "This is my girlfriend, Anna." She reached out her arm toward the other woman, who looked up and smiled. Alba had never been introduced to another woman's girlfriend. She hoped her face didn't register the initial shock. Her mind flitted to Raffaele. What would he do to be able to stand amongst his own family and be open like this? Her island felt distant, locked in a different time.

A younger boy walked in from a door at the far end of the kitchen revealing stone steps beyond which was a cellar. He clutched a bag of potatoes. "These ones, Mamma?" he asked, slamming it on the table.

"Watch it, imbecile!" Francesca yelled.

"Easy, Francesca," Violetta called out, "your brother is helping." She nodded at her son.

He noticed Alba. "So you're the new friend, no? Natalia's been going on about you. Glad you're here. I was getting bored of listening to her."

Alba felt a laugh escape. "And you are?"

"Silvio. Try not to let my sisters run your life. They've practiced long enough on me." He ran a lackadaisical hand through his light brown hair, which flopped back from where it came.

An older man stepped in behind Alba. "*Ecco qua*, *benvenuta*, Signorina Alba!" he said. His voice was rich, resonant. The perfect treble-bass balance made the walls vibrate with a round sound. She turned and stretched out her hand.

"*Piacere,*" she said.

He took it and gave a firm shake. "I'm Natalia's papà, Giacomo. Now listen to me." Alba couldn't imagine many people wouldn't if he was speaking. "This *casa* is yours too for the next ten days, you understand? Don't be expecting us to wait on you and we won't expect the same from you."

"Christ, Papà, let the woman sit down before the lecture. I think she knows enough about us to understand we conduct our home with socialist ideals," Francesca interjected, fingers fast with chestnuts once again. Her girlfriend, Anna, laughed and kissed her on the cheek.

"If she's been around you, I think she's likely not had any choice," Silvio piped.

"Alright, that's enough," Violetta said, looking up from the large iron skillet in which she was melting finely diced onions. "Natalia will show you upstairs to your room and we'll have dinner in an hour or so, yes?"

Natalia left the kitchen and Alba followed, letting the warmth of the home and company heat her. Her Sardinian Christmases felt even further away than before. Along the journey she'd pictured their accustomed rhythms, the weeks of baking in her mother's tense kitchen, swiping all family members but Alba out of the small room. The women from along the street would be assembled around the kitchen table, rolling and cutting and coating pastries, icing with meticulous care, bemoaning the men in their lives, their aching backs, the scandals that befell the priests in the next town. Would they bemoan Giovanna's renegade daughter this year? Or would she remain an unspeakable? The daughter a disappointment so brutal that it would be best to have her remain a secret from a swallowed past, a ghost in the room or preferable even to that, erased? Watching the people around her lit up her own family's cruelty with stark truths, like the light snapped on in the back store at Calisto that sometimes made the cockroaches scamper to safety. Alba doubted she could bear these sensations much longer than her short stay.

Natalia led them up the narrow steps, beneath thick wooden beams. The inviting atmosphere from the kitchen wove through the whole house. The colors were muted and mellow, like the building itself was delighted to welcome visitors. There was an alpine aspect to the interior, ceilings aching with age, crisscrossed with thick pale trunks of oak. The windows were small, each framing a square of the white surrounds, undulating hills blanketed, dotted with barren trees, black branches reaching out into the gray frosted air.

"Natalia, this is beautiful!"

"I know," Natalia replied, not slowing her pace, "I absolutely love it here." She opened a door at the far end of the corridor. "This is you."

Alba stepped inside. A wrought-iron bed was plump with a thick pale blue eiderdown. In the corner there sat a ceramic washbasin complete with a jug and a small mirror, and beyond the foot of the bed stood a wood-burning stove, which had a small log smoldering inside. Alba's eyes lit up.

"I saved the best for you," Natalia cooed. "Leonardo will stay with me."

"Leonardo?"

"Yes. We weren't going to be together for the first holiday and everything. But then we realized it was an insane plan. He's coming up a few days after Christmas, for the Epiphany. It's a big deal up here. When I was a kid I lived for the *panevin* festival. They'll be burning a huge witch on the massive bonfire of old Christmas trees on the fifth."

"A witch?" Alba thought about the mustached women her mother went to when she'd lost something, had a stubborn wart she wanted to get rid of, or came down with influenza and felt desperate to be cleansed of the evil eye.

"An effigy, not the real deal," Natalia said, sarcastic.

"Right."

"Alba, you are funny. Everyone knows *real* witches can never be caught."

"*I'm* funny?"

Natalia kissed her friend's cheek. "It's an effigy of the *befana*, you know, the old crone who supposedly interrupted the three kings to see Jesus and all that? The one who gives fruit and nuts to the kids."

"Of course I know the *befana*."

"Yeah, so she's like a representation of the past year. We burn her. Out with the old and all that. Depending on the way the smoke goes tells us pagans, sorry, 'Catholics,' how our year is going to be. Apparently. I don't care so much about that. I just love looking at the wild flames redden the night. Neighbors' faces lit up orange. Hypnotized by the cleansing power of it all."

Alba raised an eyebrow.

"You know," she said with a tilt of her head, making her long beaded earring swish away from her neck, "that kind of thing."

Natalia lifted her arms above her head in the catlike stretch Alba was accustomed to her pawing into on impulse. "Come downstairs when you're settled in. Mamma will be opening wine most days as soon as it's *aperitivo* time. Then we can argue about politics and you can watch Francesca show off for gorgeous Anna. Standard evening at *casa* Cicchetti."

Natalia left the room and closed the door behind her. Alba walked over to the tiny window and gazed over the snowy hills. The wood spattered a spark in the stove. Burning away the past year didn't seem like too bad of an idea. Burning away the past few weeks was even better. Somewhere frozen beneath the white outside was the beauty of that master class, the shimmering memory of that night, clouded by the uncomfortable escape from Vittorio's, an ending neither had spoken of since, having avoided each other for the final few days of school that remained after the performance. All the fizz of intense pleasure now clouded by what she'd decided was an act of brutality disguised as a lover unfurling another with elegance and skill. Now, the thought of him fully clothed, igniting a charge so deep inside her, made her feel ripped of something special; he had uncovered something electric and hidden, the force of which scared her.

It hadn't felt like that with Raffaele. Theirs was a floundering between friends. But Vittorio was not her friend. She knew nothing about him in fact. She only knew his music, the magnificent way he communicated with his instrument so that it was almost impossible to tell where he ended and it began. She only knew the delicate, passionate intimacy he didn't appear afraid to share in front of an audience. She was dazzled by his talent, verve, his artful communication with wordless prowess, and felt ridiculous for having blurred that with attraction to the person behind it. How vulnerable he had appeared to her on that stage, how bare; it was as if she had seen through him right to the hot center of his soul. She had felt his light and heat. That wasn't enough to warrant opening up to him as she did in the shadows of his home though. That wasn't music. That was a one-sided game. She'd been played with a clumsy beat. And she hated herself for it, for confusing the person with their music. Goldstein's words now fought for attention, his insistence that her own spirit was the only thing that would play her piano to its capacity, after she had dissected the composer's intent, their desires, she, the pianist, must by necessity connect with a parallel to her own emotions. She had not thrown herself into the Rhine like Schumann, but she needed to understand and connect with the feeling that precedes that action, understand the person behind the music, seek a reflection of their intentions in her own life.

The log crackled again. If only it was as simple to smolder away the burned embers of her father's ire, watch her decision to abandon her family to follow her dream of being a pianist lift up into smoke, perhaps the ignored weight trailing her would disappear too.

Voices bubbled up from the kitchen below. Most likely Francesca had made another carved quip to the despair and delight of the family. What would Alba's siblings be doing now? Had her mother received her Christmas card? She didn't send any in return, of course, though Alba had made sure to leave her address clearly written on the back of the envelope to give her the option of replying. She hadn't written back to her after any of the other brief letters assuring her she was well and safe, so it was not surprising that the festive one had essayed the same effect. Perhaps her father had received it first and burned it? Perhaps it didn't matter? She wasn't asking her mother's approval, she'd written to reassure her, no more. Perhaps she'd even written to prove herself the stronger of the two? To show that she, unlike her mother, was free to live without her father's approval or suffocating smears.

Her eyes focused on a tree at the farthest point in the distance. It stood alone, a faint blue-black outline to its barren branches, delicate as one at the hand of a fine watercolorist, rising up from the white wash below and around. An unfamiliar warmth spread through her. She wondered how she would ever put all this into words so that Raffaele could understand that her first experience of feeling at home at Christmas was in the rambling old mountain house of the Cicchettis.

The days that followed were marked by a stream of food and sweet indulgences, settled by unhurried stretches of time where the family lost themselves in books and music practice. Alba sat at their piano each morning, which dominated the lower living room, flanked by a wide stone hearth, lit through most of the day. She played her scales and technical exercises for the first half and after a break, ran through her repertoire, repeating the same in the afternoon. Meanwhile, upstairs, Natalia made her violin sing. Her mother stayed upstairs in the study on the corridor of the bedrooms. Her cello resonated along the beams of the house, her woody rich sound filling the upper floor. It was the perfect antidote to the tumultuous first term at Santa Cecilia's, one she didn't even know she needed until now. Her mind was silent. Her doubts and embarrassment over Vittorio dissipated. She lost herself in her music as before, as it was supposed to be, as she had sacrificed her family for. Here was peace in its most wordless astounding simplicity; the promise of the true meaning of home, by traveling within herself, spiraling into the core of what she had set out to do, whilst allowing herself to be fed, in every way, by the people now surrounding her.

"I'm really glad my sister wasn't full of hot air about you, Alba," Francesca said, stepping into the living room for a book she'd left on the coffee table. "She gets so overexcited, you know? But everything she's said about you? On the nose. *Complimenti.*"

"*Grazie,*" Alba replied without taking her fingers off the piano.

"You gearing up for our annual concert, right?"

Alba lifted her hands.

"I didn't think Natalia would have mentioned it. Mamma loves showing off her kids' friends when they're musical. Silvio usually gets together with his mates and they do something and then Natalia. I might even sing. If they fill me with enough drink!" Her laughter rippled out then, stretching her face into a smile that lit up her face and eclipsed her usual pout. "After the *panevin* bonfire we all head back here and play until dawn. Pretty cool. You know, in a Cicchetti sort of way. Anna is a flautist. I fell in love with her the first time I heard her play."

Alba watched Francesca register her own admission, then stiffen back into her typical gait. "Forewarned is forearmed, no?"

Alba smiled, wishing she agreed.

By the afternoon Natalia was a twirl of skittish excitement. Her patter was double the speed of her accustomed tempo and Alba worried she'd be exhausted by the time her lover eventually arrived. Just after the deep afternoon lull the bell jangled and Natalia flew downstairs from her third practice of the day and flung open the door. Alba heard Leonardo's voice, followed by a silence in which she knew her friends would be wrapped around each other in their usual unselfconscious embrace. After a beat, Leonardo's head popped around the doorway.

"There she is! Hard at work—no one told you it was Christmas, Alba?"

He strode across the space, swinging his arms out in amazement at the literature-filled shelves, fire roaring in the hearth, comfortable chairs strewn with blankets and half-finished books.

He kissed her on both cheeks. "Everything alright?" he asked. "You look, how do I say, *happy?*"

Alba laughed. "Your lover has kept me fed and watered for the past week. Her mother has carved out silence for me to practice. I am literally in heaven, yes."

Another voice filled the hallway.

Alba heard Violetta's welcoming tone.

The door opened a little farther.

His eyes traced the length of the shelves, the beams, the deep red Persian woven rug. "This place is perfection, no?" he asked, catching Alba's eye on the ebb of his broad smile. She felt her jaw tighten.

Vittorio.

"Yes, Alba," Leonardo said, snapping their silence, "it's not a ghost."

Off Alba's glare, Leonardo twisted away from her and walked toward the door, swinging a playful slap onto Vittorio's back as he left. Alba heard Natalia lead him into the kitchen, and the rest of the siblings joining in with their welcomes like they had when she'd arrived.

Their eyes met. A static of silence crackled.

"Good to see you, Alba," Vittorio said at last.

His voice pierced the peaceful cocoon she'd wound around herself since she'd arrived. Natalia had betrayed her.

"I didn't know you were coming," she said.

"Neither did I. Leo's gift of the gab—plus the promise of Signora Violetta's hospitality."

He cast his face toward the fire. Alba could see the flames twist their light in his eyes.

"How long have you been here?" he asked, without looking at her.

"Week or so."

"Heaven."

Natalia swung her head around the door. "Come and meet the gang, Vittorio, Mamma is so excited to hear about your professors. She went to school with a few of them. I think she's been gagging for some juicy gossip since I told her you'd decided to join us!"

She left. Alba felt Vittorio turn toward the piano, but she didn't take her eyes away from her fingers, scoring through her scales as if it were just another morning in the mountains, in the hope they may prove a self-fulfilling prophecy.

16

Family
a grouping of instruments that
produce sound in the same manner
and are constructed in the same way
but in different sizes

Alba did a fine job of erasing Vittorio out of her periphery throughout most of the afternoon, until it was decided that she would team up with the token Tuscan to make *panforte*.

"I don't want to help make *panforte*, Natalia," Alba whispered as she led her out into the hallway from the kitchen.

"I've never seen you so passionate, Alba, apart from when you're playing."

"What's that supposed to mean?"

"Nothing. I didn't think him coming would upset you."

"It hasn't."

Natalia inclined her head.

"Don't look at me all puppy dog."

Natalia said nothing.

"You should have told me," Alba added. "It was underhanded."

"Last thing I saw was the two of you laughing down a side street in Trastevere. Now you're acting as if he's your nemesis again."

Alba straightened, desperate to share every detail of why she was behaving this way whilst hoping that refusal to express any of it at all would somehow make the feeling disappear.

Natalia softened. "It's a stupid cake, that's all. If it really bothers you cut some veg with us, it really doesn't matter."

Alba sighed with a shake of her head, stung with embarrassment at her childishness. "Sorry. It's fine. Your mum asked me to."

"She thinks you're amazing. You will play later, won't you?"

"The least I can do."

Natalia gave her a squeeze. Alba tried to imagine becoming the kind of woman who could unruffle another's feathers with such easy warmth, the images sifted together and fell away, like building a sandcastle without water.

Leonardo and Natalia arranged several side dishes. Violetta was in charge of the slow-roasted joint of beef. Giacomo dusted off wines from the cellar and Francesca and Anna argued over how to prepare the lentils. Silvio in the meantime alternated between playing records with his friends upstairs in his room and filling the kitchen with a late teenage mix of restless energy and feckless wit, pricking off cubes from the large hunk of cheese at the center of the table and being swatted by his sisters and mother in turn, till the young men took on their job of preparing the sliced meat antipasti with a quiet concentration that unnerved Alba. She tried to imagine her own brothers doing anything like the same. It brought a wry smile to her face.

"How are the silent duo getting on over there?" Leonardo asked, taking a swig of wine whilst stripping the hard base ends of a *cavolo nero*.

"Fine, noisy," Vittorio replied, not taking his eyes off the nuts and candied fruit he was chopping. "We're almost ready, Alba," he said, signaling for her to tip the honey, sugar, and a few tablespoons of marsala wine into the skillet warming on the stove. She gave the mixture a gentle stir. In her periphery she could see him at the table, sifting the flour, cinnamon, ginger, and cardamom over the chopped toasted nuts and candied fruit and peel, having tipped them into a bowl. His movements had the same fluidity, patience, and precision as when he played. As when he'd touched her. She felt a twinge of pleasure, followed by a cramp of claustrophobia. She focused her attention back to the pan. The space heated with a syrupy scent.

"Oh my God, that's divine!" Natalia announced.

"You use that word for everything," Francesca replied from the far end of the table, "and you haven't even heard Anna play yet."

"Me neither!" said Violetta, opening the range door to check on the roast, tipping the pan slightly to spoon up the juices and trickle them back over the caramelized crust.

"Signora, you're making me weep with pleasure right now, no, Vittorio?" Leonardo charmed.

"Once in your life, Leo," Vittorio pinged, "keep your cakehole shut so I can finish making something to do the job for me."

Vittorio gave the bowl another stir, a little too hard.

"He loves me really, Signora Violetta," Leonardo added. "I give him excuses to show off how clever he thinks he is."

Violetta stood back up and closed the oven door. "I'm just thrilled you're all here. It's made our Christmas even more special than it normally is. Listen, Vittorio, you can use the upper oven here, I've lined this baking dish for your *panforte* when it's ready to go in."

She cast an approving eye over her team of cooks and left.

"How's your honey looking, Alba?" Vittorio asked.

Anna looked up and caught Leonardo's eye. "Does your boyfriend always take everything Vittorio says as an innuendo, Natalia?" she asked, noting Leonardo's raised eyebrow.

"That's the kind of boy my sister is attracted to. I suppose she can't help it," Francesca replied. Leonardo flicked her a wounded expression.

"Actually, I think it's ready, Vittorio," Alba added, watching the sugar dissolve its final granules into the golden ooze. He stepped in beside her and tipped in the fruit mixture. She smelled the sweet coating lift the depth of cinnamon, cardamom's complex spice, and the heat of the ginger. He stood closer than he needed to, so that beneath the skillet's contents she could also pick up his scent; it made her think of pine needles, mint, wooden floors heated by the sun. His breath brushed her ear. They were back in the moonlight, lost and confused in the shadows of that wine-infused night in his studio, a disorienting pleasure.

"Here," he said, "I'll tip it in."

He reached for the handle and his fingers wrapped around hers for a moment. She slipped them out from underneath and stepped back, noticing the narrow gap between his jaw and his neck, where she'd buried her tears. Her chest was an ache of bittersweet; she longed to feel him close to her, but the sensation was the promise of something she might not be able to control, it was too unknown not to be dangerous.

When the feast was assembled, the table cleared, the room awaiting a languid feast, the family left to watch the bonfire in the main square. Natalia lent Alba more appropriate clothing. They all stepped out of the house, cocooned in scarves and hats and gloves and good cheer.

"I don't want to sound all playground, but are we still friends?" Natalia asked, hooking her arm into Alba's.

"I don't think I have a choice, Natalia, do you?"

"Don't know. You Sardinians take things so very serious. But I love you. And about what's his name, Maestro Vittorio, my mamma has been nagging me to bring him up ever since I told her about him. Plus, Leonardo told him you were here. Seemed to change his mind somewhat."

Alba nodded as if it mattered little to her, but her eyes fixed on his silhouette a little way in front of her against the blue white of the moonlit snowbanks.

All of Revine filled the main square, and, as promised, the upside-down Christmas trees hung on a pyre with a huge effigy of the *befana* made out of hay on top. Two local men lit several long torches and as the flames licked up toward the sky the town erupted in cheers. Soon the pyre was burning bright. Singing began, percussed with clapping, stomping, cheers, and laughter. Then the wind picked up and an expectant hush fell. The smoke twisted up, then from side to side till it blew out in a determined gust toward the west. The square shook with applause.

"See?" Natalia shouted toward Alba. "It's blowing west. So it's going to be a good year after all! Perhaps I'll believe it just this once, no?"

Alba smiled, feeling the heat of the fire on her cheeks.

"Time and place for superstition, don't you think, Alba?"

Vittorio's voice was a warm murmur behind her. She inclined her head back toward him.

"This light on your face," he said.

"What about it?"

He shrugged. She turned back away from him.

"It makes me ache to kiss it." His whisper wove through her, down to her feet.

She stiffened into their stilted silence.

"You know the only reason I've left my family in Florence for the Epiphany is so I can be near you."

Her heart thudded into a hidden gallop; the thrill and dread of the chase. She couldn't decide which sensation was the dominant, like the fifth note of a scale, the most important anchor of a piece, the one harmonic that leads the ear to the resolution. All of classical music theory rested on this dominant. Now her flailing to pinpoint her own made her feel like an unfinished piece, a composition scribbled in haste without grounding knowledge, without ease. She was an amateur in this game. That was the feeling after all, a stab of pride; the assumption that his desire was by necessity an eagerness to consume her, to make her appear brighter than before and disappear at the same time. He whispered the promise of her being desired. He would rob her of something more. He'd already taken more than she'd wanted, under the guise of giving her something. He'd peeled back her mask. The very shield Goldstein was at a constant bark at her to dispel.

She turned back. He'd moved away.

After a while, the Cicchettis and their guests wove a relaxed stroll back through the night. The feast was as delicious as it promised to be. After they couldn't eat any more Violetta summoned everyone into the living room, threw a few more logs onto the fire, and brought her cello down from upstairs. Giacomo sang a folk song, but his voice left no doubt he was classically trained. Violetta accompanied him and Natalia harmonized. It was a luscious lullaby, the words of which Alba couldn't fully understand because of the northern dialect, but Giacomo explained before starting that it was about a lost love, a mountain herdsman who left for the hills promising to return and wed his sweetheart.

Next, Violetta insisted Vittorio play. He made a peacock show of modesty, which Leonardo mocked him for, and then they tuned up together. Violetta invited them to improvise a little something and called Leonardo and Anna to join. They knew better than to refuse. Violetta signaled for Alba to take her seat.

"If the others are in you hardly have the right to refuse now," Francesca teased from her prone position on the sofa, twisting into the best position for a clear view of Anna.

Alba sat and let her fingers ease into the simple chord changes, following Leonardo's lead as he twirled through a phrase harmonizing with Natalia. Alba looked up from the keys. Vittorio gazed straight at her. His face was warm, golden in the light from the fire. He pressed the hairs of the bow evenly onto the strings of Violetta's cello. It was a different tone than his own instrument, but the same elegance rang out, a melancholic call from somewhere deep inside the wood, inside the player. His touch seduced the instrument until it vibrated with a yearning, which drew the family into a tight quiet.

Giacomo, Violetta, Francesca, and her brother looked on, drawn deep into the sound. It was all so easy for this family, to sink into this simple pleasure, to allow themselves to feel. It made Alba fill with the sensation both of being very much at home and grieve for what she may never have.

Vittorio's expression softened. Their eyes met again. A challenge? An invitation? Both perhaps?

The applause was genuine and unhurried.

"You always get your way, Mamma!" Natalia cooed. The family jeered and cheered. More brandy was sipped until Violetta and Giacomo left for bed. Alba stayed up with the others for a while, around the warmth of the fire, bottomless glasses of brandy in hand, doing everything in her power to pretend she couldn't sense Vittorio noticing her every move, a penetrating heat. An oscillating desire to fight or flee bubbled inside her.

"I think I'll head up," she said, rising from the soft squash of the red velvet sofa.

"You're not going to practice tomorrow too, are you?" Francesca asked.

"Of course she is," Anna interrupted, wrapping Francesca's arm around her stomach as she stretched out across the other sofa beside Alba's. "That's why she sounds so bloody amazing."

"You sound amazing to me," Francesca whispered.

"I'll head up too," Silvio said, "before I throw up."

Francesca threw a cushion at his face. Alba stepped outside and wove up to her room.

Sleep taunted Alba, dancing evasive tarantellas around her bed. She looked at her clock. The second hand ticked toward everywhere and nowhere. The little hand cut to three.

There was a soft rap at the door.

Alba froze. A second rap. She considered ignoring it. She knew who she wanted it to be and wished she didn't. A third rap. She flung the eiderdown away from her and stepped her bare feet onto the floorboards. One of them creaked as she reached the door. She opened it. Vittorio stood in the dark.

"Hi."

"Hi," she replied.

Neither moved.

"Can I come in?"

"Why?"

"I don't want to wake anyone."

Alba stepped back. He stepped in. His hand pushed the door closed.

They stood in the blackness save for the square of silvery light from the window stretching across the bed.

"Alba, I need to talk to you."

"So talk."

"May I light the fire?" he asked in a whisper.

"You planning on staying that long?"

"Give me a break—I'm standing here freezing."

Alba bent down and placed a squat log into the stove, then lit a twist of kindling. The flames lifted. They watched the light flicker across the low uneven white ceiling.

"Why are you acting like I'm about to pounce?" he asked.

"Aren't you?"

"No."

Alba looked into him, willing her expression to belie the nerves rattling around her ribs.

"You've been dodging me since that night."

Alba turned her face toward the flames.

Vittorio knelt down by the fire. Alba didn't move.

"It's really hard to put all this into words," he said. "Impossible perhaps."

"Try."

He looked up at her.

"Are you going to tower over me while I struggle down here? At least let's start on a level playing field, no?"

She crouched down and sat opposite him, hugging her knees into her chest.

Vittorio took a breath. "That night was exquisite. I think I terrified you. Or embarrassed you. Or made you feel uncomfortable for whatever reason and I feel horrible. And I ache to feel you again. And I think you hate me. Which makes me hate myself."

The flames licked a little higher.

"This is where you get to say what you're thinking, Alba. Or just leave me floundering."

Alba looked at his dark eyes. There was no malice there. She knew she should feel safe. "I sacrificed everything to come to Rome," she said, stiff.

He nodded, opening up the space for her to talk.

"I'm not going to have anyone rob me of that."

"Me neither," he replied. "Music is my life."

The conversation hit another patch of silence. They turned toward the light in the stove.

"That's why we get each other," he began, unhurried. "You think I can't sense you intuit my thoughts? You want to kid yourself I don't do the same for you?" A sardonic laugh sighed out. "I thought I'd met people I'd been connected to on a profound level, but now I think they were boyish impersonations of love."

The word punctured the thick air between them.

He watched her for a moment.

"I was seventeen," he began, his voice dipped in bronze tones, warm, burnished, "she was in her thirties. I didn't know it. She lied. Told me she was twenty-three. I tumbled into her. Soul suicide. It was delicious. And fake. And beautiful. And carnal. And all the things it had to be. When we broke up it took me a year to even notice another woman. And when I did, aged nineteen, I tried to have sex with anything that moved. I stalked my prey. And it felt good, for a time. And then I got into the school I'd been dreaming about since my aunt first took me there to listen to a concert when I was ten. And I meet you."

He stopped, looking at her as if he was breathing her in. "Your music flew out of that piano on that first day. You were inside me before I could stop it."

He fell silent.

Alba felt her heart speed up, an urgent scherzo between her ribs.

"And now I'm making you uncomfortable again."

Alba watched him, admiring the way he'd found the courage to say these things.

"One of us has to say things as they are, no?" he asked, his voice lighter now.

"Usually the man?" she answered.

He turned toward the fire. He didn't rush a reply. The idea of his vulnerability being closed away again made fear strike through her with brutal force.

"I don't want you to make me disappear," she whispered.

"I don't want that either."

"I don't know why you did what you did. I was confused. Am confused."

"You're allowed to feel how you feel."

"You don't have to tell me what I can and can't feel."

"I did it because I want to know you. Deeper than I know myself."

"My music comes first. Before anything. Any*one.* I'm not your prize."

Alba watched him pull in a deep breath. His shoulders grew

wider, his spine lengthened. There was the natural élan, which had caught her attention from the first time she'd seen him. It was softer now, braver, more open. He was more beautiful for it.

"Do I want you to let me in? Of course I do," he murmured. "That night was like a dream. You left and I couldn't decide if it had happened or not."

"I'd never felt those things. Not like that."

"And that makes you feel like I'm setting out to destroy you? What did I do to make you sense I was entering into battle? That it was a trap?"

She felt her chest tighten. "I'm terrified by the feeling that I wanted it again and again. I wanted you never to stop. That's dependency. That's the same as disappearing."

His eyes glistened. "That sounds like good practice. It sounds like how we feel about our instruments, an obsessive return to them, which are by their nature like an extension of ourselves, a way for us to see ourselves, no?"

"I don't know."

"Practice makes perfect. Or as near as any human can get."

She watched the flames twist shadows around the small room. His expression melted away the aching fear she'd felt moments before. Her doubts were rooted someplace else, the silencing of her childhood, the clouding numbness since the kidnapping. She had disappeared already. The intense pleasure Vittorio helped her reach spun a light around the quiet shadows of suffocated invisibility. That was what had terrified her. If she let him in again what was she inviting? A world of uncertains, a distraction that might lead her away from the one thing she lived for, had left everything for: her music.

They looked at each other. He eased forward.

His face inched closer to hers. One breath between them now. Neither moved, but hovered, on the precipice of the other. He eased closer still, till his mouth was soft on hers, reassuring, tuning into her shift toward him; a peaceful, playful, present kiss. Then he pulled away. "I'm as scared as you. And as ambitious. Meet me halfway?"

Alba felt a droplet blot her collar. He wiped her eyes, her

cheeks, then cradled them in his hands. His gaze took on the patient watchfulness as when he tuned his strings, everything was blotted out now, but her.

"Let me in a little?" he asked, his voice a murmur, a forgotten pianissimo note at the far end of the keyboard sustained into a fading ring with a press of the pedal. "We can be tourists around each other together?"

She laughed then, at the thought of them bumbling around each other, cameras strapped to their necks like the hordes she'd crush through near the Pantheon or huddled around the Trevi fountain throwing coins after harried wishes.

He leaned forward and kissed her again. This time her mouth opened. His arms reached around her and pressed deep into the muscles of her back. She felt herself arch. His touch spun in like a thread of gold. Alba felt her body rise up to the surface of itself. Her hand reached for his trousers. He stopped her.

"I don't want to rush," he said, easing her off him.

He stood up and led her to the bed.

She watched him take his shirt off, then his cotton pajama trousers. He slipped out of his socks. His movements were assured, relaxed. He bent down and fished a small foil package out of one of the pockets.

Alba looked at him.

"I don't think either of us want an immaculate conception, do we?"

He walked over to the side of the bed and reached down for her face with his hands. "I've dreamed of this. With you. The person I hear when you play. The person you keep hidden away at all other times. But I heard her. And it's impossible to get her out of my head."

She felt her hips tighten, then ease.

She watched him cover his penis with the contraceptive. He cradled her in his arms. Alba reached for his lips. Their tongues flickered around each other.

Their bodies shifted into a new and familiar dance. Not musicians, but instruments, played by a power far beyond their control; frightening in its complicit intimacy, sending shards of light through from the tips of their feet to the top of their skulls, sparks of harmonics, notes beyond aural comprehension, vibrating at a faster frequency than could be contained by their bodies alone.

The sun rose.

They turned toward the light, Vittorio's chest pressed against Alba's back, hearts thudding a gentle tempo into the dawn.

"My grandfather used to bring us to a place like this," he began.

"A musician too?"

"A frustrated one. His father didn't let him study, so he went into law instead. Built a house on a lake to keep his hands and mind busy. Loved wood, making things. Mamma says he was quite the violinist. Beautiful voice too they say. But I remember his smell clearer than anything else. Always a hint of tobacco. He taught me to whittle when we'd stay with him by the water. I loved the feeling of that sharp blade in my hand, forming a piece of tree into something else. Like our instruments, finely honed pieces of nature. We rip the raw materials from the sublime, our trees, and return there. Transcending the place it came from only to return. We arrive armed with code—black dots on a page. All so we can feel that original wisdom fly through us. Interpret something unspeakable. Alchemical mechanics."

He stopped short.

"Please, don't let me stop you. Clumsy poetics suit you so very well," Alba said, a smile in her voice. "Did they catch you off guard too?"

He kissed her ear. "You make me want to talk like that."

She swallowed.

"And you're self-conscious right now because I just said that. You may want to attend to that bad habit."

They surrendered to sleep. His arms wound around her, sheets twisted with pleasure and the delectable discovery of an unsung melody. Alba couldn't shift the sense that like any piece, however powerful, however stirring, it was bound to end. She pushed the thought away but it returned, like the persistent resonance of a final chord as the pianist keeps steady pressure upon the pedal, so that without any fingers dancing the keyboard, the piece sings on.

1978

17

Crescendo
a directive to a performer to smoothly increase the volume of a particular phrase or passage

For the three years that followed a world opened up at Alba's feet. Her repertoire grew beyond her expectations and her relationship with Vittorio fueled both musicians' ambitions. Their love didn't sap their focus, but rather pushed each toward greatness that they had only dared dream of. Their conversations were lively, stretching her mind and soul in ways she never thought possible. Natalia teased them for being the king and queen of their year where she and Leonardo mumbled behind like the pauper versions. Alba didn't notice the way others looked at her beside her lover, she was oblivious to their glances of admiration and barbed jealousy. Her and Vittorio's bubble was impenetrable, the cocoon they carved out in the middle of Trastevere, in the sheltered musical warmth of his studio where she spent a great deal of her time was her world now. She'd rebuilt her universe, one that replaced the haunting resonance of her estranged family and the Alba she'd relinquished long ago. She spread into her new identity.

Now, in the early summer of 1978, her graduation grew imminent. Three years of dedication, unswerving focus, edged toward its apex. Soon the real world would beckon. Alba postponed thinking about the woman she might become beyond the safety of the *accademia*. The uncertainty was too daunting. Perhaps it might not be so easy to keep on pause the return to memories of leaving home? Three years of not having anyone come to hear her play. Three years of pretending with a fiery determination that it wasn't agony to see spare seats in the auditorium for invited family.

Celeste scheduled a final one-to-one ahead of her students' graduating performances, which had thrown the entire year's intake into a state of deep electric focus seeing a steep drop in social engagements and a reclusive desire for personal perfection. "So, Signorina Alba Fresu," Celeste began, "I am three years older and you are three years wiser, no?"

Celeste's expression crinkled into her mischievous twinkle, the sparkle in her little green eyes lighting up the fine wrinkles that framed them. She eased back deeper into the leather armchair of her office.

"I don't know about wiser," Alba replied.

Celeste let out her breathy, knowing laugh, wafting from another world, a place where time wandered without aim nor end.

"I would say so, yes. Certainly your playing has deepened in a way I sincerely hoped it would. Now that we're just a little way away from your graduating concerts, I can say that when my dear friend Elena told me about a girl in her town who could play a phrase exactly after hearing it only once I didn't believe her. I certainly didn't need to tell you that you have one of the most astonishing talents I've known."

Alba felt a familiar sensation of claustrophobia. She could hear the words were positive, but all the compliments and encouragement she'd received these past three years made her feel put on the spot somehow, vulnerable, naked. Describing her playing was like an imprisonment that deadened the act. It became a subjective, once removed from the composer and then from the player, when all she craved was to disappear into the music, as if she weren't there at all. Descriptions of her playing style never came close to how it felt to play. That's why, she realized, listening to Celeste that morning, the words always felt like a betrayal.

"I know how much you hate me talking like this, Alba, I just need you to know. Because the next few months will be grueling.

The business side of our art is not the cocoon we've had here. There will be people out there who will want a piece of what you have, of that I can be sure. And you can be sure that I am always here for advice, like a compass, if you'll excuse the whimsy, should the seas become choppy."

Alba tried to land somewhere inside her body rather than watching it all from a step beside herself, like a translucent memory of herself, a blur in a mistimed photo, snapped moment in a haze with several others preceding, stuck somewhere in no-time space. "Thank you."

"Your personal life may witness some shifts too," Celeste added, her tone dipping into conspiratorial, signaling she knew it wasn't within her jurisdiction to mention in the first place, though Alba and Vittorio's relationship had come up in their conversations with regularity.

"This place gave me life," she replied, the words slipping out without effort.

"I am glad."

The conversation floated on a pause. Alba's eyes traced Celeste's shelves and scores and noticed a smaller photograph upon her wall of her seated at the piano next to another woman. The profile looked familiar, but Alba couldn't say why she recognized her from where she sat.

"I was very much in love when I graduated," Celeste began. "It's not easy for two musicians married to their art to allow space for anything or anyone else sometimes. Not impossible. Just not easy."

Alba watched the brief flight of images soar through Celeste's mind, feathering away as fast as they appeared.

"Thank you for all your wonderful work, Alba," she said, straightening, "and for making sure the faculty could find no fault in my decision to grant you our scholarship."

There was a knock at the door. Celeste cleared her throat. "My next student, Alba. I won't see you until your concert performance. I will be thinking of you."

"*Grazie.*"

Alba stepped outside into the corridor, a polished world away from the disorientation of that first week. The three years had sped through sonatas, composers, repertoire that spread from early music to modern classics, the Romantics and the Impressionists. All the pieces stayed with her well after she'd been assessed, like family members with their unforgettable quirks, idiosyncratic poetries, and the stories that led to their creation. Soon she would be leaving this family of the *accademia*, but she would take this other family with her.

Every step along this corridor, once a quotidian rhythm, now took on new meaning: every scuff one more farewell, like ever-increasing circles rippling in water around the weight of a plunging stone. The building fizzed with an electricity she'd never felt before, or perhaps never noticed. Her year group was about to graduate, performing their final pieces for an invited audience and assessment. Despite what the teachers told her, she felt like the adrenaline scoring through her wouldn't by necessity mean she would run headlong off this cliff and take flight. Nerves might take her in the end, her self-belief might fail her and all the other branches of anxiety might strangle her.

"Didn't it go well with Celeste?" Natalia asked, stepping in beside Alba.

"It was lovely. As always."

"Why the long face?"

Alba stopped and turned toward Natalia. She looked at her, open and available as she always was, the light blue of her eyes like a pale breeze-kissed sky. Alba longed to not envy her that, the freedom she'd known all her life, the ease of family, their unwavering support. She wanted to tell Natalia that there would be no one in the audience who had come especially to see her and it was breaking her heart. Three years of shunting her family out of her mind had reached its end. The return to facts was brutal.

"Is it Vittorio? Leo has been like a bear the past few weeks. We've decided to not see each other every night until after the concerts."

"It's not Vittorio."

Natalia took an unhurried look at her friend. "You've excelled these three years without your family. They can't stop you now, right?"

"I want to believe that."

"You're hurting today."

Alba nodded.

"Gift yourself that? We're always taught to be so stupidly happy. Your music wouldn't be what it is if you didn't feel things like you do. It's a kind of superpower. I envy you that. Everyone does."

Alba sighed a fading smile.

"Come to mine for dinner? I'll cook something light. We can eat outside—the new boys renting upstairs let us come through and sit on the flat roof."

"I'm working late tonight."

"I know. Just know my door's open, *sì?*"

Natalia blew a wisp of hair off her face. Nothing about her demeanor suggested that she was preparing the hardest concerto for her final assessment.

"If you need company I'm there, okay?" Natalia added, off Alba's silence.

She wrapped her arms around Alba and gave her a squeeze. Her patchouli scent was as pungent as always. It would always remind Alba of their Christmas together. She watched Natalia stroll down the corridor toward her practice room, violin case in hand, the world light upon her shoulders.

"A little more vibrato here, Alba," Goldstein said along the puff of smoke, the gray clouds like wafts of dragon's breath. "Don't look at me like I'm talking nonsense. We return to the same idea that it's never true that once you've played a note you're committed to that sound. Let it ring further. And here"—he walked over to her from the window and traced his fingers along the score upon the music stand on his piano beside hers—"I want to hear absolute pathos. Beethoven wrote these first chords as a sforzando, like a sharp consonant, then we have the far-off echo. Make it a voice, Alba."

She repeated the measures, striking into the keys on the opening chords and reaching deep into the sound for the pianissimo answer, rolling her fingers with deft precision.

"Yes!" Goldstein exclaimed. "This is the place, Alba. Now lean into the improvisatory adagio when it appears. Let us really feel you too don't know what you will play next. Beethoven writes this sonata, 'The Tempest,' with some liberty deep into the score. Honor this."

Alba returned to the same measures, coloring the first chords darker still, filling the echo with yearning and sorrow. He stopped her again. "So tell me about dynamics with Beethoven."

Alba no longer feared his questions in the same way she did in her first year. In fact, she'd come to long for them because it made her feel like she was never still, but probing for further information. She'd lose hours deep in reading at the school's library, a cocoon of knowledge that brought the world into her mind and kept her shielded from it at the same time. Inside the rows of books the composers' lives unfolded, intertwining with their music, clues to how passages could be interpreted, liberating her ideas of what she could bring to them, how honestly she could share their vision. "We know Beethoven only wrote four types of dynamics, very loud, loud, very quiet, and quiet," she replied.

"And?"

"And it's up to me to choose what happens in between. Sometimes, like here"—she let her fingers caress through some of the fast descending groupings of notes—"the lack of direction is enigmatic. I can paint my own color."

Goldstein took a drag on his dying cigarette. "It's good to know that I haven't wasted my breath on you after all."

Alba allowed herself to smile. A mistake she knew better than to do. He always pounced harder when he spied too much relaxation.

"You grin like an imbecile. Remember this: You can be feeling anything you like, but if we don't *hear* it, it's just smoke and mirrors. A detestable performance of performance."

He stubbed his cigarette out on a porcelain saucer and knocked back the final dregs of his espresso.

Alba began again, this time launching into the opening chords like an arrow darting through space, focused, direct. Then she broke off, and the treble answer whispered from the higher notes. Goldstein didn't stop her this time so she brushed on through the slurred pairings, remembering how he had directed her to not give even sound to each, but, as in the words of Beethoven, dusting the keys, a flip-flop flick of the ivory, not equal groupings but casual, some notes more important than others, like the natural patter of speech where not every syllable holds the same weight or tempo. In the adagio section she let her hands grow heavy, the chords echoing the first melody, now played as if underground, ominous, pressing her foot down on the pedal halfway to sustain the rumble. An allegretto finished the piece. Alba looked over at Goldstein.

He shook his head. "It is a great responsibility, your talent. I hope it doesn't kill you."

It would be impossible to become accustomed to his unexpected darts, however much she'd tried.

"It may not, because you're stubborn enough to finish things," he added. "Hold on to that, Sardinian girl, always hold on to that. Keep working. Keep asking questions. Keep hearing me in your ear, when you start to get comfortable, when you start to believe what people tell you about your playing, that's the danger zone and all of us are lured by it. Don't go there. Stay with the text. Stay true to what is written in front of you. That's when you will make music."

Alba hooked her hair behind her ear.

"Are you ready for next week?" he asked.

"I think so."

"Say more."

Alba pressed her lips together and rolled them back out. She took a breath. "It's what I've been working for all this time."

"No one said it wasn't. I'm asking if you're ready."

"As ready as I can be. Ready enough to forget my practice when I'm in front of everyone. Ready enough to see what happens. Ready enough not to expect anything."

He nodded, answerless.

She waited.

He flicked open his packet and popped another cigarette into his mouth. Then he stood and walked to the window.

"All will be as is," he said, with a snap of his lighter.

Alba looked at the clock. It was time to go.

"Yes, Alba, our lessons are done."

She stood up and walked toward the door. Before she opened it she turned, knowing that any thanks would be returned with a stiff silence at best, a cutting remark at worst.

"I wish my family wanted to hear me," she said. Alba watched the statement land with the tiniest shift in Goldstein's rounded shoulders, his regulation light blue short-sleeved shirt poking out from his red cotton woven vest. She left before he could answer, snapping shut the door behind her as her eyes filled up with tears she would not let fall.

The bus was late, as always, and the warmth of the June evening did nothing to relax her. She dashed out of the bus as it approached Trastevere and ran along the cobbles toward the main square. That's when she saw a swarm of police cars. There was a crowd gathering around the front tables and officers yelling for people to stand back which fell on deaf Roman ears; in her five years in the city she hadn't once seen anyone do much of what an official asked of them, in any capacity.

Across the group she saw Dario. He waved at her. She wove through the muttering bodies till she reached him.

"Remember what I told you when you first started?"

"I don't know," she answered.

"Get yourself home and wait for me to call you, got it?"

"What's happening?"

"Police got wind of Antonio's little meetings. Turns out the Red Brigade have quite the cozy home upstairs. Or some story like that. I knew stuff was going down, didn't know he was so high up in it."

"Are you talking about the group who assassinated the prime minister?"

"Well, I'm not talking about Mickey Mouse."

"There he is!" she said, seeing her boss being frog marched out of his bar, hands clamped behind his back and being bent down into the police car.

"Get out of here, Alba," Dario said, raising his voice over the sirens.

"See you tomorrow?" she yelled back.

"I think we both know we'll be looking for another job by that time. Go home. I've been told to lock up and give them the key."

Dario turned away from her and moved toward the bar. She watched him slip inside. Alba squirmed out of the crowd, thudding in her chest, heading for Vittorio's, pounding away the creeping panic on how she would pay the next few months' rent. Her heart was racing. She didn't need this extra pressure as she began her career. Vittorio would ease away her worry. Perhaps he'd rustle up a quick feast, bring her back into her body and back down out of her squirreling mind.

He answered after the third ring, creaking open the door looking like he'd just woken up.

"Hey," he croaked. "Why aren't you at work?"

"Boss got arrested."

Alba waited for a response. He ran his hand through his hair.

"Can I come in?" she asked, "I feel a bit shaky."

"Not a great time, Alba."

She felt her jaw clamp.

"I mean, sure, I'm at a critical point in the composition."

"I won't stay long. Just a bit of a shock, seeing that."

He turned and walked toward his apartment door and she followed him.

His room was an explosion of manuscripts, which on careful observation were stacked in apparent order but left little space on the floor. There were several whiskey glasses perched on various flat areas, upon the mantel, his desk and the coffee table among them.

He let out a frustrated sigh. It put her on edge.

"Alba, I'm fucking drowning here!"

She walked over to him, wrapped her arms around him. "We're all tense. Even Natalia didn't look her complete self."

"This isn't just about the projects, Alba, we've worked this whole time for this moment. The walls are inching closer. I can't breathe."

Alba interlocked her fingers into his and ran her other hand up the muscles of his forearm.

"What, did you just run round here for sex? Got a fright and think if we make love everything will be fine? It won't! This is our fucking lives at stake here."

He snatched her hand out of his.

"Why are you being like this?"

"Why? Does it suit you for me to always be available? You come around when you like, never mind if I'm deep in something."

"I'm not going to stay long."

"You want me to smooth your back and say you'll find another job? You're about to start your career as a pianist, who cares about a shitty waitressing job?"

"Some of us have to work to eat, Vittorio."

"Is that why you're here?" He let out a louder sigh. "I don't know what you want from me."

Alba considered replying, but when Vittorio began twisting through his whirlwinds there was little to stop him. She turned for the door.

He pushed his hand onto it with a thud. It gave her a fright.

"That's it? Interrupt my flow and then leave?"

She turned to face him. He didn't move his hand.

"I just— I don't know what I wanted. I'm sorry."

His eyes softened with remorse. "My God, I've become a stereotype. Does it happen that quickly?"

Alba watched a wry edge of a smile unfurl.

"I want to kiss every inch of your body, Alba." His hands rushed up inside her shirt. It made her breath catch. His fingers wrapped around her breasts. He licked her neck without haste. It sent shivers over her body. When he moved inside her, pressing her against his wall, his breath almost blocked out the tumble of thoughts fighting for attention, the way he'd received her, the way he'd accused her of using him, the way she felt invisible as he moved inside her with smooth strokes. He pulled out, rolled off the contraceptive with a tissue, and chucked it into the bin in the kitchen. She tossed on her clothes and watched him kneel down before his manuscripts upon the floor.

"You got what you wanted. I suppose you'll go now," he said without looking up.

Alba felt the heat rise in her chest.

"Why the pout? You want more?"

She knew she should walk out right then.

He stood up and walked back over to her. Unzipped her jeans and eased them down her legs. He buried his face into her pubic hair. She pushed his face away.

"What?" he said, looking up with the familiar gleam of mischief.

"I don't want that."

"Let me in, Alba."

She retracted her hips from his mouth.

"Please?" he asked, sinking back onto his heels.

She bent down and pulled her jeans up.

"You come here but you're not here," he murmured.

She looked at him without moving.

"I was an idiot a minute ago. I'm sorry. Just they're putting me under a lot of pressure. Or I'm doing it to myself."

"We're all the same," she said, her voice somewhere far away.

"You want me but you don't show up, Alba. You keep yourself in a small box, locked, hidden. You see me get vulnerable all the time. I cry. I shout. You just stand there watching. It makes me feel idiotic. I want you to show me you, too."

Alba nodded. It felt like a feeble apology, for what she didn't know.

He shook his head, rising up to standing. "We've been through this," he said, kissing her ear with soft unhurried lips. "You've got stuff to do, so have I. And I love you with every fiber of my soul and I wish you did too."

He held her face. His eyes glistened now. It was always hard to tell if it was overwhelming love or frustration.

"I do love you, Vittorio."

"Maybe you do. But sometimes you're not here. Your body is, but your spirit is somewhere else."

The familiar accusations swirled around her but didn't penetrate. She was accustomed to his speech every time deadlines loomed; she suspected his search for her soul was always more about seeking his own.

"You want my spirit to show up every time you're reaching a deadline?"

"What's that supposed to mean?"

"I don't know. Forget it."

"You swing everything around to me!" he yelled, lifting his pile of manuscripts and sending them cascading onto the floor. She looked at them at her feet, a silent clang of discordant notes.

Vittorio started to pace. "I'm talking about you not being open with me, not being adult enough to be vulnerable, and you switch it to my faults?"

"Shouting at me isn't going to make me want to be vulnerable!"

"And screaming at me is?"

"You go out of your way to make people boil. You push. You think making me feel like this shows you to be a good human?"

"Better to let everything out. I don't do an Alba Fresu, no, making out like I'm this enigmatic untouchable. Like I'm too good for anyone."

Alba froze.

"Truth hurts, no?" he sneered. "Time to grow up and talk, Alba. You know, like people who love each other. Like *grown-ups* who love each other."

There was no essence of love in his words. The intonation was stark, out of tune, a crass bow in a drunk hand.

She left.

18

Colossale
to play in a fashion which suggests immensity; tremendous

The Day arrived.

Alba waited in her dressing room, the sound of the audience filling the auditorium gurgling out from the stage monitor speaker on the wall. She turned the volume down, then clicked it off.

It was the loudest silence she'd ever heard.

Phrases of Chopin's scherzo toyed in her mind, flashes of purple light, flecks of his passion. Her mother's face fought for attention, but she willed the images to dissipate, breathing deep into her abdomen. She was a young child again, hearing the echoes of Signora Elias's home, feeling the light stream in on her face.

A knock at the door brought her back into the room.

"Places please, Signorina Fresu," a voice called from just outside her door.

She rose, tucked her chair in under the desk, and caught her reflection in the mirror that ran the length of one side of the dressing room. The woman in the glass had a confident, unpredictable gait, her black velvet dress hugged in at her waist, her arms long and muscular by her sides. Her eyes, outlined with black pencil, looked straight into the face looking at her. It was like meeting someone she'd once known and hadn't seen for many years.

Her footsteps clacked through the expectant silence, the heels of her flats marking time. As she reached her stool the room filled with applause. She let it die down, retracting from the room into the quiet.

Her breath fell deep into her abdomen. She was back with Elias, listening to the record for the first time, letting the dreamy yearning of Chopin swirl around her, his phrases unexpected, playful, full of longing and detailed description. Her hands lifted. She flitted across the lower notes, a whisper, a hint, a suggestion of a phrase. Then she swept up to the higher notes and stretched into broad chords. Back again to the bass and a second return to the majestic chords. After a breath she relaxed into the next phrase, her fingers running down the keys with effortless precision as she played with the rhythm, dancing, as Goldstein had told her, with an insecure pace, improvisatory, as if she and Chopin were uttering this melody for the first time. Time drifted away. The walls of the auditorium disappeared. There were no bodies now, no peering eyes, no judgments. Alba was not there. Alba was inside his Scherzo no. 2. She was the oranges and yellows of the allegro, the mischievous phrases, light, golden, playful. Her family fought into her mind now, whilst her fingers traced the melody, their consistent rejection permeated her physical memory and Alba remained powerless to stop it. Their refusal to love her as she was, the bitter disappointment she brought them poured into the deep reds, purples, and onyx of Chopin's sforzando, strident, rageful, full of disdain and declaration. She eased into the middle of the piece now, spreading golden rays over the keyboard, singing out the simple melody over the top of a rolling bass of arpeggios, bronzes, copper warmth, an easy summer's day, a meadow by a river, yet a sadness floated above it, a wistful sense of things that might have been but weren't. And as she approached the final section, her hands stretched, charging up and down the keys, reaching the length of the board and racing down, again and again an unstoppable waterfall, brutal, determined, cleansing. And she was alone, at the center of herself, and nothing could touch her or drown her or make her disappear because the music was beyond all that. And so was she; for those final breaths, for those final defiant chords of strength and passion and freedom. At last nothing mattered. Not her, not her family, not what was shunted from her life as she'd known it. The music powered through her and around her and wove back inside like a golden anchor.

A chord. And another. And then the final.

The silence cracked open with applause. A light beamed out of her so bright that it eclipsed her own form, now rendered meaningless and powerful at the hands of Chopin. The people stood. She walked to the front of the stage. The sound rippled down her back as she bowed in thanks. She was laughing now, uncontrollable tear-streaked laughter, shudders from deep inside her that she couldn't stop. She had touched something beyond them all, and now their response lifted her somewhere just above her body, hovering on the wave of love. Three years of dogged, disciplined work had led to this moment. Three years of her family's betrayal and the abandonment she refused to let anyone in on, a secret she'd never share. Three years of not having a group of family around her to congratulate her, hold her, touch her, tell her that despite everything, she had made them so very proud indeed. She'd taught herself not to need this. She'd almost convinced herself. Her chest was heat and light. It scored through the darkness, the insistent worry that crept in like a tide as the applause began its fade. She pictured her mother's face, imagined her loving her music in spite of herself. She thought about her reaction beside Signora Elias, how uncomfortable it felt for her to allow her pride to shine through. As Alba stepped into the shadows of the wings, a terror gripped her so hard, so fast that her breath caught.

Vittorio was in her dressing room.

"Sublime. I have no words, my love."

Alba smiled and wrapped her arms around him. Their kiss was caramel, flecked with a fire she had come to crave in spite of herself.

"I fell in love with you all over again. I don't know how much more I can take," he murmured, easing his hands down her back. She stopped them.

"I'm sorry for the other night," she said.

"We both are."

"Yes," she said, without knowing why. It was easier somehow than to go into the truth of the quiet sorrow that filled even the happiest moment. It was an emptiness he understood, but she was happier delving into his than allowing him to fully see hers. Perhaps that meant she wasn't adult enough to conduct this relationship after all? His subtle but seemingly gentle criticisms filled her mind. She swept them away like a glissando, running her thumb up over all the keys at great speed.

The champagne reception in the foyer afterward was in full swing by the time she got there. A sea of faces turned toward her as she entered. It was like stepping into a surprise spotlight and the feeling wasn't comfortable, until a familiar face rose out of the wash of others'.

Signora Elias was before her.

Alba's breath caught.

She wrapped her arms around her. The noise of the reception faded into a single distant note.

"You wrote saying you couldn't come," Alba said.

"I didn't think I could. Then I felt up to the trip. I thought a surprise wouldn't be unwelcome. I thought I might make you nervous, to tell the truth. I always hated it when my teachers came to listen to me. Distracted me somehow."

"I am thrilled you're here."

"Not nearly as happy as I am." Tears streaked her eyes now, and she looked smaller than Alba remembered. "It is the most precious feeling, the one I'm having right now. All is well with the world when someone gets what they deserve."

Alba wrapped her arms around her again. Her eyes were wet now too.

"You've been with me, Signora, all these years right beside me."

"My name is Elena. We are both concert pianists now. Time to let go of your childhood names, no?"

Alba laughed and took Elias's hands in hers. Vittorio stepped in beside them.

"Are you congratulating my girlfriend, Signora? Might I have the pleasure?"

He stretched out his hand. Alba watched Signora Elias's face light up. Vittorio did look smarter than usual this evening. His crisp white shirt was open at the neck, hugging his svelte torso. His pride in her performance had lit him up.

"This is Signora Elias," Alba began. Signora Elias shot her a look. "Sorry, *Elena,* my first piano teacher. The reason I am here, Vittorio."

They exchanged pleasantries until Vittorio was called away by one of his fellow cellists. He kissed Alba on the cheek before he left.

"That boy is smitten I see," Signora Elias said.

"He's a wonderful cellist. He's going to be a conductor. His compositions are divine. He's had several meetings with agents already."

"Congratulations, Alba. I know all this was incredibly hard for you. I watched you sacrifice everything for it. I hope you feel like you made the best decision of your life."

"I think I do."

"You've made me so happy to be alive tonight. Sadly, I have to return tomorrow, I can only stay away for short periods these days. I like my routines, you remember that, don't you?"

Goldstein stepped in beside the two women. "Well, you didn't fail after all," he said with a chuckle. He introduced himself to Signora Elias and then turned toward the man beside him. "This is my friend Dante De Moro. He's an agent to some of the best talent in this business. He wants to talk to you. You'll want to listen. And if he offers you anything too good to be true, talk to me first."

The men laughed. De Moro stretched out his hand and shook Alba's with a firm grip.

"You made the audience fall in love with Chopin all over again," he began, "as if we needed to relearn that!" Alba listened to his voice, it had an effortless quality, like a wandering clarinet solo, but beneath, a metallic strength, a quiet confidence.

"This is my card. I'd very much like to meet with you at your earliest convenience. I think I can help you reach the audiences you deserve. And from what my friend Dimitri says, you have a work ethic that he thought only *he* knew. And that's saying something. I'm not accustomed to my friend waxing lyrical about many students. Quite the contrary."

"Thank you," Alba said, the words fighting to get out.

"I shan't keep you now, Alba, you'll want to celebrate with your friends. But I look forward to your call. At your earliest convenience."

De Moro walked away. Goldstein turned back to Alba as he did so. "This man doesn't give his card to people, Alba. Be sure you take him up on his invitation."

"Yes, Maestro."

He nodded, his eyes twinkling with a conspiratorial glee. At last, it seemed, one of his progenies had blossomed.

"Oh my God, did you just get introduced to Dante De Moro?" Natalia wafted into view, effusive, the chiffon fringes of her dress floating in different directions, which gave the impression of a passing colorful cloud. "Are you kidding me? This is the best thing ever. I'm so proud of you, you disgustingly talented sexy woman. I was literally weeping watching you."

"You weep at everything," Leonardo purred, stepping in behind Natalia.

"Seriously, Alba, that was beautiful. You deserve all the things!"

"You do," Leonardo added, "it really was the best I've heard you play. So deep, clear, passionate. I felt that piece afresh."

"Thank you."

Alba wanted to say more, but the words were stuck somewhere inside, the overwhelming happiness, relief, excitement just bubbled in her marrow, adrenaline coursing through her veins. Tonight was the best day of her life.

That's when a tall young man made a beeline for her. He was slim, with a suit cut to perfection with thick black-rimmed glasses that gave the impression of a fashion designer or an artist perhaps. He looked familiar but there was something about his confident élan that made him hard to place. When he raised his hand, waving it at speed, she recognized Raffaele. They raced toward each other. He lifted her up and spun her. Their voices were muffled in happy tears and shrieks. Alba didn't notice the people step away from them as they reconciled.

"This! This is the best night of my life!"

"No, mine, Alba! Oh my God. No words, my love. You are beyond them. I couldn't stop weeping. Let me hold you again!"

He wrapped his arms around her. How different this young man felt in her arms from the gawky teenager of their shared past.

Vittorio slipped in beside her. "I don't think we've met?" he asked, holding his hand out for Raffaele to shake.

"I'm Raffaele," he began.

"My best friend, *tesoro,* from home," Alba interjected, her voice dancing.

"And there I was thinking I was the only man to make your voice sing like that." Raffaele mirrored Vittorio's grin.

Someone tapped at Vittorio's elbow, he made his apologies and left again.

"Seriously?" Raffaele asked, his face alight.

"Where are you going with that thought?" Alba replied.

"All the places I shouldn't. He's gorgeous."

Alba shrugged. Then her best friend's expression darkened.

"What's wrong, Ra'?"

"Can we go outside for a moment? I need to talk to you where it's quieter."

"Of course!" she replied, still giddy from the froth of the reception. She realized someone had put a flute in her hand and it was already empty.

They stood in the shadows of Via Greco.

"I had planned to surprise you. Then I called home yesterday and I knew I had to be sure to get to you right away. I didn't want to tell you before the concert. I know how important that was."

"Ra', your riddles make me feel queasy."

"No easy way to say this." Alba watched him shift in the shadows. She felt a shiver spindle down her spine.

"It's your mamma. She had a routine operation for appendicitis but there's been complications. My mamma couldn't tell me exactly what, but the situation is critical. I wouldn't say this without cause, Alba. I think you should go home. Tomorrow."

Alba felt the blood drain from her face.

"I wanted to tell you right away but I didn't want to ruin this evening."

Alba didn't move.

"Say something? I can help you pack? I've got a ticket for you for the crossing tomorrow. Signora Elias is going back too. I took the liberty of arranging it so you'd have company."

"Does she know?"

"Yes. I called her to ask what I should do."

Alba's throat was dry. Her heart ached; tomorrow she had to return to face the world she'd fled. It felt like her family desired, by any means possible, to dim her light that yearned to shine.

19

Dal segno
a mark in a composition that informs
the performer to repeat a specific
section of the composition

Caffe Greco was an institution along a narrow *via* that led off the hordes of people clustered around the Spanish steps. The heavy clouds had broken at last and now the tourists waved across the streets in messier swarms than usual, few looking prepared for the cascade.

Alba stepped into the café, and through time it seemed, landing somewhere circa 1870. Inside, the red padded walls were strewn with heavy framed paintings and drawings. There were sculptures balanced in elegant poses on nooks in the walls of the small warren of interconnecting rooms, each lined with red velvet long-backed benches and small granite-topped tables, most of which were occupied and strewn with tall, fluffy, creamy cakes and dainty china cups of teas and coffees, beside cut-crystal glasses of water. Alba wiped the wet hair off her face and shook her overnight bag. A waiter in black tails looked her up and down, judging her to be yet another tourist escaping the downpour.

Her eyes caught sight of Signora Elias waving from the farthest room. Alba wound through the tables, past the golden display cabinet of unfilled cannoli, large *bavarois*, *rhum baba*, and Sacher torte, smaller powdered custard-filled pastry puffs and fruit tarts. The tailed waiter stopped following her, once he'd realized she'd met a well-dressed friend and was not about to steal the furniture.

"I took the liberty of ordering a little something already, Alba, hope you don't mind. I know this is not what you think you should be doing right now, but I think some sustenance will help the crossing—the food on board is not what I would describe as appetizing."

"I've never been here. It's like a palace," Alba said, shaking her light overcoat and hanging it up on a brass hook just around from their table.

"You deserve this, Alba. Last night was a triumph. Today, you will need all the strength you can get."

"Signora, your selection," the penguin man said with a flourish, his team of other flapped servers weaving behind him, all looking with ferocity at somewhere in the near distance as they chased cake orders and pots of tea.

Alba turned her gaze toward the tower of tiered plates, laden with fresh sandwiches and tiny cream cakes. "This is for a queen, Elena. Thank you."

"They do like to pretend they're in Vienna somewhat. If this place was good enough for Mendelssohn and the rest, then it's downright good enough for you, I'd say, no?"

Alba's smile was a tentative line, erased as soon as it appeared.

Signora Elias poured Alba a cup of tea and slipped in a thin slice of lemon. The swirl of steam was comfort in a cup. "Did you manage to sleep?" Signora Elias began.

"Not really. I stayed with Raffaele until he caught the late train back up north."

For a breath she returned to the darkened piazza where she and Raffaele had sat beside a fountain and shared the same bottle of whiskey after convincing the nearby closing bar to sell them an entire one, something Alba knew from her time at Calisto was a sackable offense.

"I can imagine what you must be feeling," Signora Elias comforted.

"I think I did all my feeling last night. Now I'm numb and empty."

"When I last saw your mother she was looking very well."

"You saw her? At market you mean?"

"Not exactly, no," Signora Elias replied, swirling a white sugar cube into her tea, watching it dissolve for a little too long. "Your mother came to see me. Fairly often, I suppose. Not every week of course, as before, but perhaps every month or so."

Alba looked at her, willing her to continue.

"She never stopped wanting to know if you were alright and doing well."

Alba swallowed but the tea had done little to wet the dryness of her throat.

"Today it seems like the right thing to do. Tell you, I mean."

"She never replied to any of my notes."

"Your mother wouldn't have been able to write a reply without asking for someone's help. She was too proud to ask me. It made us go deeper into the betrayal I'd committed already, and which she paid for dearly. She made me promise I wouldn't tell you either."

"Why?"

Signora Elias gave a gentle shrug. "Your mother has fixed ideas about most things, Alba, this we all know. I suppose that way she could ease her conscience without the threat of your father finding out. She couldn't risk you telling him anything either." Signora Elias shook her head as if wiping away the thought. "What I'm trying to say is that although it may not have been obvious to you, your mother has never stopped loving you. This, I must tell you."

Alba took another sip of tea, trying to let Signora Elias's words slip into her with the same warmth.

"She wanted to be here last night. She'd bought her ticket. Told your father she was visiting her cousins in Genoa, but they had to operate immediately. She gave me this pressed rose for you."

Signora Elias pulled out an envelope from her bag and handed it to Alba. Inside was a single red rose, flattened and dried. There was a faint memory of its scent clinging to its papery leaves. It was shocking more for the uncharacteristic sentimentality than even the love behind the gesture.

Alba nodded her head, but her lips fought off a reply.

They walked to Rome Termini station to catch the train to Civitavecchia port, the streets shiny with the fallen rain now gleaming in the return of the summer sun. The air was clear and the tourists had returned to their steady gawking. The train led them through Rome to the west, creaking through Ostiense and then Trastevere. Alba felt a pang as they pulled out of Vittorio's area, toward San Pietro, and decided to try and give him another call later. She would have liked to hear his voice before leaving. He might have reassured her that she would be back soon, though in truth she knew he would offer his own particular brand of sarcastic swirl about Sardinians and their mammas, which they'd both know not to be true in her case, but they would laugh together anyway. His humor always felt like a mini test. She liked the challenge of it, even if she'd never shake the sense that it was his gauge of people's intelligence, an armory of defense to monitor the worthiness of a possible friend. Leonardo had passed with flying colors.

They pulled into the port and the passengers disembarked. Signora Elias walked at a measured pace. It made Alba feel anxious and relieved at the same time, drawing out the inevitable. As they approached the ferry Alba spied a line of pay phones. She signaled to Signora Elias and she nodded in reply.

Alba dipped her hand into her pocket for some *gettoni*, thick coins needed for the pay phone. At last her fingers wrapped around the ridges. She lifted it out, slipping it into the slot, watching the telephone symbol at its center being swallowed into the machine. It rang. She pictured Vittorio's phone in the corner of the room, surrounded by last night's bottles no doubt. He'd wanted her to stay with him last night after the performance. She'd wanted to fall into him too. But after Raffaele gave her the news she couldn't relax into their plan. She'd watched him be swept up with a group from their year, with a loose promise of connecting later, but time slipped away. Raffaele had walked her home. Back in her room she'd squeezed a few things into her bag. She'd reached for the shutters to close up her room properly before she left. The aqueduct had looked resplendent in the rays of the dawn, hitting the tiny bricks against the troubled gray sky full of summer rain behind. A minute angle ensured that water ran hundreds of kilometers along this aqueduct for those ancient Romans. It felt no different with her family and her own trajectory; one shift and she too was trickling away.

She hung up. Then tried again.

Nothing.

She replaced the handset, feeling like she was already walking on a moving deck.

The sun began its descent as the passengers boarded.

"Do let us sit outside before it gets too dark and cold, *sì?*" Signora Elias asked.

Alba nodded. Fresh air sounded good, away from the crowds and traffic driving onto the hold, full of the first loads of holidaymakers at the start of the summer season on the island. They chose a metal bench toward the bow.

As the ship pulled out of the port, the amber light dipped through midnight blues and now etched toward the purple black of night.

"When Celeste and I graduated from Santa Cecilia, I remember coming home under not too different circumstances. It felt like everything I had worked for was at risk of slipping away somehow."

"That's how I feel."

"Whether you're an eighteen-year-old with rebellion in your heart who doesn't know how to fight other than through music, or a young woman at the start of a very promising career, or an old woman sitting beside her protégée, feeling like everything she'd ever done had led her to this point—perhaps there's perfection in every moment."

"I long to look at the world through your eyes."

Alba looked across at Signora Elias, the ink of night around them, her eyes twinkling in the soft light of the lamps on deck. The air was brisk now. It made Alba's eyes water a little.

"Oh, I don't know about that, Alba. I just try to always steer my ship—if you'll pardon the metaphor given our current environment—because in our business it's essential you stay open to surprise."

"As a concept I kind of understand that, but have no idea what it will actually feel like. Right now I'm trying not to panic about how I'm going to pay the rent next month."

"Perhaps some things are far beyond our control?"

Alba looked at Signora Elias's expression. She'd missed her wistful smile lit with mischief.

"Why don't you talk to me about my favorite old chestnut?"

"Music?"

"Actually, I thought I might distract you by asking about love?"

Alba felt her eyebrow lift in mock defense. She wanted not to be thinking about what Vittorio was doing now. Why he hadn't called to ask if everything was alright. Or swung by her apartment. He knew the situation felt like an emergency to her. He was celebrating her with his friends. Where had he been all day when she'd try to reach him?

"It's clear that you two are intertwined deeply."

"Vittorio loved meeting you. I could tell. He's normally quite aloof when he first meets people. Not with you."

"I dare say he misses his grandmother or some such. I don't have quite the effect on young men as I used to."

She cackled at herself. Her laughter eased and they took a couple of breaths looking at the thin black line of the horizon smudged into the smatter of stars. The sounds of the water rising up against the sides of the ship as it cut through sloshed beneath the silence.

"I fell in love at the *accademia*," Signora Elias continued. "I fell into someone with such a force it almost knocked me off course." She giggled. "I'm sticking firm to my metaphor."

Alba smiled a soft laugh. It was a tonic to be seated beside her mentor again. It made her forget why she was returning and filled her with the same courage it had taken all those years ago to leave in the first place.

"Tell me," Alba said, tentative.

"Oh goodness, you don't want an old woman boring you with her stories."

"Actually there's nothing I'd rather listen to."

Signora Elias reached for her hand and squeezed it.

"I'm excited for you, Alba. For me, love had a way of complicating the business, my practice. I found it so very hard to divide my attention. And there were other concerns too, but primarily sharing my lover with my instrument, and theirs, was, well, in the end, impossible. We stayed friends. For this I am eternally grateful. But at the time, my heart was split."

Seeing Alba's expression Signora Elias's tone softened. "Don't misunderstand me, I'm not saying you and Vittorio will necessarily meet the same challenges."

"I think there's a price to pay when entering into a love affair with a musician, no?"

"Perhaps. Sometimes they become your secret lover, and they yours, because the true love is music. And we know how much time that requires. It leaves little space for another."

Her tone dipped into a quiet melancholy, cool, simple. Alba had never heard her speak like this before. Her words were little shards of light illuminating thoughts Alba had witnessed inside herself and hidden.

"What's he like, Alba?"

"We understand each other."

"And he is clearly in awe of you."

Alba tried to let her words soothe but the ferry gave a lurch and her balance left with it.

Signora Elias smiled, giving the flattened hair on top of her head a quick stroke, then adjusting one of the pins in her bun.

"How am I going to face my family?" Alba whispered. "I can't shift the feeling this is all my fault somehow."

Signora Elias's expression relaxed. "You'll face them with the same quiet courage you've always tapped into. You'll try to accept that their health and happiness is not your responsibility alone. We all have a part to play in our own lives. Your family might try to suck you back in, they might be angry that you have returned."

"I'm not sure I'll cope."

"Maybe only fools believe they are invincible? I believe you'll do what you came to do without forgetting what you've worked for all these years."

Alba fought her brittle resolve against tears.

"You're still happy to stay with me?" Signora Elias asked, her voice a gentle embrace.

"I don't think I could be back in Ozieri without that."

Signora Elias smiled. Alba watched a trail of unspoken reassurances, thoughts, stories track through her eyes, but her mentor kept them locked on pause, withdrawing, as always, from the desire to offer unsolicited lectures. She stood. "Now, I think that's quite enough chatter from this old lady for one night, no? Do you mind if I take to our cabin? I'd like to rest a little before I see the dawn over my favorite strip of sea, if you don't mind?"

They tucked into their small cabin beds, the boat churning through the night, the rise and fall lulling Alba toward a second night of elusive sleep. When she took back to the deck, exhausted from grappling with the hope of getting some proper rest, the sun was rising. In the near distance rose the rocks of home, the spray of turquoise by the shore, the darkening blues of the deep reaching out to her. Three years she'd hidden this view from her mind. Now it greeted her as diffident and beautiful as she'd scarce allowed herself to remember.

Everyone she met in Rome informed her of her island's beauty, as if, being from there, she might have been too close to notice. Perhaps they were right, but the sensation of being educated about her home by outsiders never sat well with her. Now, in the sun's ease toward the height of morning, hidden within the metallic slosh of the water below and the rumble of the engine, she allowed herself to cry. All these years her mother had kept her love secret, whispered after her but never let it be known. Alba had left the tyranny of her father, leaving her mother to suffer it tenfold. Without Alba to bully, his rage would have fallen to her mother. Alba felt her heart ache, twisting with guilt, with anger, with that constant need to unshackle herself from the responsibility of his behavior, to escape.

It's what Vittorio whispered into her ear after lovemaking. Her Faraway, he'd call it. As if this pull were a phantom trailing her, another spirit he'd come to love. He'd honor it even. Sometimes he'd tease her, ask it questions. If they were at dinner he'd ask it what it would like to eat. She'd always reply how did he know it was an it and not a she? That would make his wry smile wrap his face in light and she'd feel adored. He'd run a finger over hers. Sometimes lean over and take her bottom lip between his. It would have been easier to not feel the allure of disappearing with his kisses. It was bittersweet bliss and terror.

Now, the galloping in her chest increased. She thought about her brothers, the look on her father's face, her inability to picture or plan for the conversations that would need to happen, or the Sardinian silences she'd have to rise over, step through, destroy. A concerto could be practiced, a sonata honed, scales were the ladders toward harmonic heaven. But this? How could she practice for this? There were no rules, no repetitions, no quiet study to be returned to, no solace. She hung on to the unexpected nature of performance. The way she'd leave her practice in the wings. They way she'd let the music carry her, staying in tune with her piano, allowing each moment to ripple through her and escape, without control, or judgment, but with the freedom to let the truth ring out.

Truths on Sardinian land felt far more dangerous.

Ozieri's hospital was a disinfected white. The nurses were starched, the floors and walls gleamed the same color. The air was crisp and bitter with ammonia. People talked in hushed tones. The nurses' white leather clogs squeaked along the plastic underfoot.

Alba turned a corner and then another, feeling like she was treading a labyrinth. A huddle of figures clouded the end of a far corridor. She recognized the two boys in an instant. They were taller, broader, but had the unmistakable profile of her brothers, that familiar shuffle, the hapless hunch. They looked up as she saw them. Her muscles injected with adrenaline. Her footsteps sounded loud, but her bag no longer felt heavy. Marcellino reached her in stunned silence. His eyes were red. He looked ashen, far older than the three years past. She stood before him, wanting to apologize but not sure for what or why, angry that those feelings crept up like ivy, her legs hollow, brittle, desperate to feel the ground but failing.

He shook his head. Disbelief? Refusal?

His voice was an exhausted croak.

"You're too late. She's gone."

20

Con dolore
with sadness

The sensation of her body falling away like scurries of sand began at her feet. It traveled up her spine, dissipating her form until all she could feel was the thud in her ears and the steady crescendo squeal of a thin high C. The voices along the corridor fogged into muffle. Familiar faces looked up at her now, friends and other family members who held guard outside her mother's room. She walked past her brother. Zia Grazietta's face sharpened into view. Alba turned away from her. She stepped into the room. There were hands reaching out to her, consoling or forbidding, Alba couldn't tell.

Her brother Salvatore looked up from beside the bed and locked eyes with her. His face was wet. Alba looked down at her father, his head buried in her mother's limp hand. His sobs pierced the violent silence, body shaking. One of her uncles was beside him, holding his shoulder. Her grandfather stood with his back to her, blocking any view of her mother. The room was dipped in a blue light, as it fought through the pale blue curtains. It sharpened the sensation of watching everything unfold before her as if through a pane of glass more tangible still. This was an enactment of grief, someone else's room, a perfect composition of a family torn. Perhaps if she blinked the figures would disperse, disappear.

Her father looked up. His expression struck her with a brutal blow of sadness. Alba watched the men around him straighten, as if he might charge across the bed, across his dead wife, and send his daughter to join her. Words fired out of his mouth now, sparks of sound that enveloped Alba in a hurricane of grief.

"What are you doing here?" he whispered, taut.

"Mamma," is all she could manage before her own tears fought out.

"Go home, Alba." A friend beside Bruno placed a gentle hand on his back.

"You've come to gloat?"

His tear-stained face folded into a grimace that made the volume of Alba's drumming heart pound louder in her ears. Her tears felt cold on her cheeks. Someone moved in front of her now, blocking her mother's body further still, forcing Alba into a web of memories that interlaced through childhood, the silence of her time in Rome, the look of Giovanna's face when she'd first heard her play, the realization that her mother never deemed her enough, always less than what a daughter should be. The thoughts cloyed; a spider's sticky silk.

She was ushered outside the room. "Your father is very upset, Alba," she heard a voice say. "Leave him now, you'll have your own time to say goodbye."

The door closed behind her.

"You should go, Alba," Marcellino murmured.

Alba looked at him, the stubble prickling his chin with newfound manhood, which he wore with as much grace as his adolescence.

"I came as soon as I knew." Her words trickled out, the last droplets after a tap has been twisted shut.

"She never recovered after you left, Alba. You should leave now before Babbo starts into you. It's only a matter of time."

Grazietta pulled on her arm now. Alba's body was being walked away from her father, her limbs like thin matchsticks balanced with precarious hope, click-clacking away from her dead mother.

Outside the sun blinded her with a mocking life-giving white light.

"I would have you stay with me, Alba," Grazietta began, "but you know your father. I don't know what he'd do." Alba turned toward the little woman. Her round wired glasses perched on the middle of her nose, her hair scraped back into a low bun, streaked with more gray than Alba had remembered. She saw that Grazietta was carrying her travel bag. She reached for it now.

"I'm so sorry, Alba," her voice fought out in scratches, breaking through the simmer of throaty tears. "Oh, my poor friend." Her cry loosened. "They said with the aneurysm she suffered it was quick. She wouldn't have been in pain for too long. I dreamed this all last night. I just knew." Her fingers clutched the wooden rosary beads in her hand, the silver figure of Jesus swinging in time with her breath. She fished out a tissue from inside her dark gray apron, which lay above her layers of skirts and cotton petticoats. Alba watched a droplet fall on her long sleeve shirt, tiny white daisy patterns speckling the black cloth.

"I have somewhere to stay," Alba replied, wondering why she did so, as if this woman needed to know, when everyone would rather she'd not appeared in the first place. Perhaps it was her way of assuring Grazietta that she had no intention of doing whatever her father asked her to do. That his grief appeared to leave her untouched when in reality that vision of him fought for her attention like a skipping record scratching over a two-measure refrain. Grazietta kissed her on each cheek and left Alba standing blanched in the scorching morning sun.

A sound of hurried steps drew her round. Mario was squinting beside her, panting from running.

"I'm so sorry, Alba," he puffed. "I got your dad here just in time. We got the call at the *officina*. Scrambled over. I'm so, so sorry."

She sniffed his words for the snide she'd once been accustomed to hearing from him. There wasn't any. She hadn't noticed her own slide toward adulthood as much as she did his.

"*Grazie.*"

He looked down at her bag.

"Where will you go? I heard he wasn't too pleased to see you."

She shook her head, as if waving off the memory, a dog spraying off water from its drenched coat. She wished she wasn't crying. "I just want to see her."

She felt his arm reach around her. Her body crumpled toward

the tarmac beneath her. She didn't remember how long she stayed down there, her breath wheezing out through tears. She wished he'd been colder, snubbed her like the rest, then the tears wouldn't have come, then she could have walked away in silence. Saved this collapse for the privacy and safety of Signora Elias's home.

"We're all at the house tomorrow of course. I can keep your father upstairs maybe when you get there. Give you some time with her?"

Alba nodded, disoriented. She stood up, furious for accepting his comfort, embarrassed, snot salty on her lips. She wiped it away with her hands, her cheeks puffy to the touch.

"You want me to walk with you?"

She shook her head before he'd finished the question. A young woman approached him from behind and snaked her arm around him. Alba took in her bright face, a cascade of curls reaching her shoulders, an effortless lightness to her gait. It came as no surprise to see Mario with a girl like this. She leaned her head in toward his chest.

"This is Antonietta, Alba," he said, trying to hide his pride in light of the situation but failing.

Antonietta held out her little hand and Alba shook it, wondering what the point was in these perfunctory motions of politeness. All she wanted was to curl up in Signora Elias's spare room, caring nothing for her tear-matted hair, her stinging eyes, the vulnerable puffiness of her face.

"I'm so sorry," Antonietta added, her voice resonating with a youthful innocence. She looked back up at Mario as if the statement needed qualifying.

Alba picked up her bag.

"I meant what I said, Alba," Mario added, urgent.

Something flickered across Antonietta's face. Perhaps it wasn't customary for her boyfriend to have conversations without her at any time.

"*Grazie*," Alba said, then turned and left without a goodbye.

A line of people stood outside number 27 Via Galvani the next day. Some hushed as Alba walked past them. She ignored their mutterings about whether it was her or not, whether she'd be allowed in or not as the sounds rippled into the air underscoring the women's murmur of rosary. Her brother Salvatore saw her as she approached.

"Babbo's in there. He's not in his right mind," he warned, shifting from foot to foot nervous of the inevitable fight ahead.

"I want to see Mamma," Alba answered, feeling her eyelids blink over her eyes, rubbed dry of tears, aching with the night's elusive sleep.

"Maybe wait a little while?" he answered.

"I'm going to say goodbye to Mamma."

"He'll kill you."

"Alba!" She turned toward the voice. Mario was weaving through the crowd. "I thought I might be too late. Let me go in and Salvatore and I will take your dad upstairs with some of the men."

"What are you talking about, Mario?" Salvatore asked, fearful.

"Let your sister say goodbye, for Christ's sake."

Before Salvatore could argue back Mario strode forward and into the house. He peeked out of the doorway soon after and nodded to Alba. She stepped toward the door she didn't know if she'd ever see again. She crossed the threshold, prayers incanted in her periphery. Within, the atmosphere was still. She entered their front room. There the table, the sofas, their lace doilies untouched from when she left, the stone walls that had suffocated her. In the center two trellises topped with a thick light blue velveteen drape hung toward the tiles. On top was the casket. The lid was removed. Behind the coffin another drape hung, an embroidered image of the Madonna on a golden shield-shaped piece of material was sewn onto the center like a crest. The gray light rippled along the softness of the folds, alternating light and shadow. Two tall candleholders stood either side of the head of the coffin and two more toward the feet. The stands reached up toward the top of the casket and the candles rose high above that, topped with determined, unmoving flames.

Alba stepped forward. Her mother's skin was smooth, eyes closed in a gentle sleep. The corners of her lips turned up at a near imperceptible curve. It was like looking at a statue of her mother, admiring the craftsmanship of the sculptor's hand without comprehending that the figure described truth. This was the artist's impression of a woman named Giovanna, who spoke too quickly, thought a beat too late, was cowered and bolstered by superstition, threatened by anything new, fortified by wealth, betrayed by her daughter. Alba's chest grew tighter, clawing into a blistering crimson sting. At once the sensation of watching the scene from a step outside her body invaded every particle of her being. The feelings rose and broke away, like a tide failing to reach the shore. In its place, a displacement, a quiet disappearance. The piercing guilt was muffled, happening to another Alba, a discombobulating emptiness in its place, a thoughtless floating feeling. The silence was heavy and horrific in its simplicity. Inside the wooden box was someone posing as her mother. A body, no more. The act of acknowledging the stark reality signaled the start of a rush of heat from her feet up to her chest, like the virtuoso runs of a Chopin, or the intricate unstoppable recapitulations of Bach's fugues, melodies returning, overlapping echoed in new forms, rippling out from the original into new versions that held the core of the initial but permutated into something else, like a mother and her daughter, who begin at the same place but twirl into opposite directions. I was inside her once, Alba thought. She couldn't have played without her, couldn't have described the brutality of diffidence upon the keyboard without having betrayed her mother, without having rebelled against her wishes she wouldn't be on the precipice of her concert pianist's trajectory. Alba wouldn't understand superstition, paranoia, God-fearing witchcraft wanderings without this woman. The body that was her mother offered no reply to her thoughts, no further suggestion of where her mind should land, how to understand what these bitter sensations were. Anger? Fear? This couldn't be grief. It was too ambiguous. It wasn't torrents of tears, loss, yearning for a sweet past that was no more. This was silence, brutal, nature's impossible vacuum. Alba stood in it, gazing at the face that would once growl at her, switch-blading from ferocity to maternal overfeeding, to panic, to pride and back through the spectrum of her mother's contradictory colors. A reeling guilt filled her bones. In her chest, a licorice black, bitter, furious.

The door opened.

"Hurry, Alba, he's coming down," Mario said, breathless.

Alba made to move but it was too late. Bruno was inside. He froze.

"What's she doing here?" he whispered through clenched teeth.

"I came to say goodbye to Mamma, Papà," she answered, without moving, her voice firm, belying the terror in her legs, the quivering in her stomach.

"You left this family. I watched your mother wither in front of me. Every day, a little piece of her changed. Her hair turned gray in a week after you left. This is what you did."

"Come on, Babbo," Marcellino murmured, "we're all broken."

"You won't tell me what to do, you hear?"

That's when her angry tears fell, currents running across her cheeks.

"I'm her daughter."

"You left her. After all she did for you."

Marcellino placed a quietening hand on Bruno's shoulder. He flinched it off.

"Leave. Now."

"She heard me play, Papà. She knew. You can't take that away. However much you try."

A few more men stepped inside. A priest followed them.

"Signor Fresu," the priest began, "we must move to the cathedral now. It's time."

Bruno nodded, the men turning him away from the room. They filed out. Six other men stepped inside and Alba moved back toward the wall. She watched them lift the cover onto the coffin, then her mother onto their shoulders and out onto the street. Another came in and snuffed the candles. The singing began, a rhythmical rosary that followed the casket all the way to the cathedral, along the uneven stones of their *vicolo,* around sharp corners where the houses lined the streets close enough for neighbors to almost reach across the alley into the opposite window.

The cathedral was heaving. Everyone in Ozieri needed everyone else to know that they respected the Fresus. Her mother disliked many of the people inside, this Alba knew. What would she think of them all gaping at her now, eyes bowed, heads shaking, thanking the grace of God that they did not pass in her place.

The priest began the mass. Her brothers and father sat in the first pew. Alba scanned the crowd along the back of the cathedral filtering down the steps beyond the entrance of the *piazzetta* where more stood to pay their respects. Signora Elias was in one of the last pews. Alba slipped in beside her. Signora Elias reached for her hand and squeezed it. She'd dressed Alba that morning in the black clothes she had, rather than the shorts and T-shirts Alba had packed in haste before the crossing. Alba could smell Signora Elias's perfume on the collar of the shirt she now wore.

A group of women sang beside the altar steps, their Sardinian melody haunting, simple. Alba felt the notes reach her like a memory. Her eyes scanned the congregation for Raffaele, who caught her eye from the opposite side. His wan smile was a brief tonic. On the opposite side stood Mario, beside Antonietta, her hand cradled in his.

The mass ended. The people left the pews and lined the church aisle, shuffling toward the Fresus at the far end by the altar, touching the hand of all the well-wishers, receiving the river of condolences, hand after hand. That's when Alba saw the piano to the side of the altar steps hidden earlier by the singing women. She broke off from Signora Elias. She walked the side aisle of the cathedral, past the mini chapels of the once wealthy landowners of Ozieri, along the marble swirl underfoot. Past Madonnas, laughing Jesus, dying Jesus, mournful Jesus. Past the frescoes in the style of the Renaissance masters, others with the pomp of baroque, beneath the priest's lectern, up narrow marble steps to a wooden perch, ornate with carved wooden frames, till she reached the instrument at last.

She lifted the lid. Her fingers ran over the silent notes. She pushed the stool a little farther back. Her wrists lifted. Her fingers eased into the nocturne she'd played to her mother that morning at Signora Elias's. Her left hand rocked arpeggios like moonlit waves, the melody stark above. Onward the piece undulated, hopeful major chords, sinking back into the minors, flecks of grief. The sound rose like a crystal light, toward the high stone ceiling of the cathedral, echoing over the rumbles of voices that hushed to the sound.

The crescendo began, the melody yearning to be heard, swallowed into the left, rising above in octaves now, insistent, falling into echoes of the same, quieter, unanswered questions trebling into the stone. The left hand somber, a return to the quiet loss of the first simple rhythm just before a brief cascade of notes from high on the keyboard, a run of chords, tumbling with an inevitable, scurrying flow toward the base. Another chord followed, until at last, the unavoidable conclusion; simple, stark, pure, honest.

Like death itself.

Alba lifted her hands, her mother's eulogy complete.

The silence filled with warm applause and tear-stained laughter. She looked up at the unexpected sound, feeling interrupted, revealed, craving the applause to stop. This hadn't been her performance, it was the dedication she was banned from giving.

Raffaele was near her, his eyes glistening. She saw Mario across the opposite side of the aisle. She recognized that expression: the same as the one he'd revealed when he'd spied her practicing that day at Signora Elias's. The frame was older, but the eyes shone with the naivety of that afternoon, as if they hadn't quite understood what they'd seen, a quizzical curiosity. He held her gaze for a moment. Someone tapped him on the shoulder. He turned away.

Then Alba's eyes landed on her father's. For a moment he may have been the man who told her stories to stop her being swallowed by fear in their wilderness. For a moment he might have been proud even. Then his eyes hardened, shiny onyx stones on the shore. Chopin couldn't undo the years she'd chosen to be away, the years Giovanna had been too scared to reach her, the years Bruno had held fast to his belief that Alba's choice to follow music was a deep snub against everything he'd worked to achieve for his family. Yet the measures brought them to an equal plane of vulnerability. For a breath, father and daughter acknowledged what they had both lost. It wasn't Giovanna alone. Alba watched the briefest hint of regret streak her father's face. Then Bruno nodded at his audience. The moment dissipated as quickly as it appeared, droplets of rain evaporating after the storm.

* * *

That afternoon Signora Elias's doorbell rang. She stood up from her seat on the terrace beside Alba where they shared a pot of tea with lemon. Silent sips, no hurry to mop up Alba's grief, rather a simple seat inside it.

Raffaele followed Signora Elias onto the terrace after a little while. The friends held each other for a moment. He sat down beside Alba. "How long will you stay?"

"I don't know. Everything feels frayed."

"Of course."

"I've paid a high price for following my music, Raffaele."

"You're not responsible for your mother's death."

"In my mind I know I shouldn't feel that way. I don't have anything but my music, Raffaele. If I leave Ozieri now I don't know if I can ever return. Not with how my father and brothers are."

"Sardinians don't forget easily. We know that. But you didn't take all that risk and stand on the precipice of success just to leave it all. Not now. That would be the real betrayal. You think that's what your mother wanted?"

"Your friend speaks sense," Signora Elias added. Alba watched her pour a cup for Raffaele. "Alba's been asked to participate in the Chopin competition next month. I'm so very excited for you. The Signor de Moro called again this morning, I told you, didn't I, Alba?"

Alba nodded.

"You must feel dizzy," Raffaele began, "everything is coming at once."

They drank in silence for a moment.

"Did you see how you changed that cathedral this morning, Alba? I'd never felt the atmosphere in there like that before. It was electric. Beautiful. Better than any speech a person could make. We all felt the love for your mother. Your hands spun a poem. I can't do it justice."

"Thank you, Raffaele."

Alba looked at her mentor. Her eyes were twinkling, open to the pain of her student, her own. Alba lit with the courage she saw there.

"In your short time on the planet, Alba, you've had your fair share of pain. Don't hide it away. It's a gift. To feel deeply. Past the power of words alone. This is a musician's superpower," Signora Elias said.

Alba sighed a half-hearted laugh.

"Don't shy away from what is yours, Alba," Raffaele added, his eyes a deepening brown, the awkwardness of his youth a faded whisper now, in its place a quiet strength that he'd once masked beneath his geeky juggling of numbers and algorithmical nonsense talk, as she used to think of it.

Alba turned away from them for a moment and took in the yellow plains of Ozieri. The sun was easing toward the start of its descent, the land golden in the afternoon rays, a herd of sheep tinkled their tin bells in the distance, charging alongside one another ahead of their shepherd. Alba had no idea how to operate from empty, but she knew her life was no longer here.

21

Capriccioso
capriciously, unpredictable, volatile

Alba returned to her room in the apartment to find a huge bouquet of white flowers upon her desk.

"They came yesterday," her landlady, Signora Anna, said, her face the picture of polite restrained grief. "I'm so sorry, Alba."

She leaned forward and kissed her on both cheeks, an act that caught her off guard as she had never hinted at doing anything close to it in all the years she'd lived there. Theirs was not a familiar relationship; Signora Anna did well at keeping a professional distance. It was the reason Alba felt comfortable to stay so long.

"You take your time now, *si?*" Signora Anna smoothed her apron and turned toward the corridor that led to the kitchen at the far end. "Anything you need, just ask." With a nod to refrain from sharing her tears, she turned and left.

Alba let her overnight bag slide to the floor. She reached for the small envelope and read the message, not expecting Vittorio to have undertaken such showy a performance of chivalry.

Sending you all my love at this difficult time, Alba.
May we meet this week as we had planned so I can
give my condolences in person? Yours, Dante De Moro

Alba reread the note and scanned the telephone number along the bottom. Goldstein's friend was in no mind to let her grieving stand in the way of his plans for her. She thought about her recital examination evening, the way Goldstein had made her promise not to look this gift horse in the mouth. That fairy-tale evening, where life, for a breath or three, was a song, legato, effortless, sparkling. Excitement and guilt cramped her stomach. People offered condolences for her mother's death. What they didn't know was that it felt more like Alba's entire family had disappeared, or worse, that they had never been there in the first place somehow, that the charade of being part of that tribe was like a forgotten refrain. This was the ache. She would do anything to flee from it. De Moro was offering her the world back again and a place in it.

Alba decided to walk to Vittorio's. It was a hot day, the buses were brimming with sweaty bodies, the trams the same. Romans' predisposition for patience ebbed even further under these temperatures and it wasn't a fight worth having today. She wanted to be cradled by the man she loved. She wanted a shelter from reality, a brief respite. He of all people knew grief better than her. He didn't answer right away. As always. His voice sounded croaky on the intercom. He buzzed her in. She walked down the corridor to his door. It creaked open. His apartment was darkened, save for the one shutter half tilted open to the morning sun sending spidering shafts across the wall. She stepped in. He wrapped his arms around her. There was whiskey on his breath. They stood there, on the precipice of his studio for a breath or three, nothing but the thud of their hearts against each other.

"I'm so sorry," he murmured into her hair, his voice warm, a welcome home, her safe place. She let herself cry. The first tears since seeing her mother. He wrapped his arms tighter, his hands strong on her back, easing her into the sensations of flying and drowning at the same time. How long had they stood like that? When he led her inside, when their clothes slipped off, when their limbs stretched along the rug before the unlit fireplace, its fibers rubbing on her legs and arms, the weight of him inside her lifting her high out of herself. How long did she cry afterward, how much whiskey had they sipped, when she crawled on top of him and eased him back inside her? Was his glass still in hand? Did she crumple some manuscript paper? Did he hold her breasts a little tighter than she would have liked, did his finger claw too deep into her flesh? Did she care to say anything or did the twinges close to pleasure but nearer to pain silence her grief so that she welcomed it, yearned for it even? Were his movements more jagged than she had remembered them? Did she silence the sensation that his drinking had started that morning, not the night before? All she cared about was the white noise canceling out the past few days, the past few years. For a moment, there was nothing but their breaths, snatching together as one, and that's all she needed. A flash of white inside, her thighs clenched and relaxed, a breeze flew through her. She folded down onto his chest, then rolled off him and lay beside him looking at the light and shadow across his ceiling.

"I'm not going to fill the hole," he said at last, his tone slurred. "Pardon the clumsy pun. Or don't, whatever." He turned his head to her, burning his dark eyes deep inside her. She loved his fearlessness, this welcoming of all things awkward. He thrived on it even. She may have envied him that. "Your mother. *That* hole. No one will fill it. And it won't go away. And I won't tell you it gets better, because it doesn't. But the scar tissue is strong. Especially when you're as stubborn as you."

"Or you," she added, licking his top lip. He opened his mouth and wove his tongue inside her mouth. She could kiss this man forever.

He pulled away, and laid his head back down on the rug, his fingers caressing her bare breasts.

"Dante sent me flowers."

"Course he did. You're going to make that man a millionaire."

Alba thumped him.

"You're fierce, talented, sexy, exotic—you know, from the bandit country—it's the perfect package."

She raised her head on her hand. "You make it sound cheap."

"It is."

Her throat tightened. "What have I been working for all these years if not this? Why are you putting it down? You sound jealous."

"I'm never going to be a concert pianist. Why would I be jealous?"

"Who knows how your sordid little mind works? You sound pissed off even. Like one of my brothers!"

She sat up, curled into a ball. Then she jumped up to her feet and started to get dressed. "Why were you seated in the dark like this?"

"You going someplace?"

"I asked first."

"We're aiming for playground chat, are we? Here's a question then, why didn't you call me? Straightaway? Why did you just keep me out? I tried reaching you. Had to get the info from your madam."

"Stop calling my landlady that."

"It's a joke, for Christ's sake, learn to take them."

"Forget I said anything."

"You didn't. You were just asking me what I thought of De Moro and his courting."

Alba stopped. She shook her head with a terse sigh.

"Face facts now rather than later, Alba. There are sharks out there, right?"

"At this minute it feels the only shark is you. Look at me! I'm drinking whiskey with you midmorning, screwing on the rug like a teenager, telling you I'm going to meet with the biggest agent in the business and you sully it all. I don't know why I came."

"Because you know no one knows you like I do, that's why. Because I'm not going to talk bullshit with you. I'm going to call you on stuff that you don't want to see. That's why."

He stood now and walked to the kitchen, his naked body like marble in the gray light, his muscles rippling beneath the surface. She wished she didn't find him so attractive. Her mind sent arrows toward his back, but her body knew it wouldn't divert the impulse to feel him against her. Their postcoital arguments were born from that sliver of terror she felt for loving him too fast, too soon, too deep. It made her feel like she had edged out of her body and lost a part of herself inside him. *Un petit mort,* he'd called it one afternoon after making love, the French name for orgasm. She'd thought about it for days afterward, realizing that for her, each time she climaxed with him it felt like another part of her had been ignited and swallowed up. At what point would all of her be used up?

He lit the back ring and set a pot of coffee upon the heat. She didn't move.

"So storm out like you always do," he said, without looking at her, "or let's talk like people who want the best for each other."

She slumped into the chair by the window. "How's the composition?"

"Which one?"

"The one you're going to convince the festival of new writing to showcase. Full orchestra."

He threw her a grin. "It's a bit like you. Comes flying in like a storm, takes all of me, and then leaves. There are these waves of notes I wake up in the night with thrumming in my head. Then the silence. If I could make it coffee and lure it into comfort like I do you it would make me happy."

"Can I open the shutters?" she asked.

"So all of Trastevere can see my naked body?"

"There's such a thing called clothes, you know."

"Really?" he said, sliding across the room to her. Alba watched him kneel down before her. He buried his face in her crotch. She pulled his head back by his hair.

"Life goes on, Alba," he said, his lips darkened as they always looked after making love. "That's the biggest head fuck. The pulse, the verve, that unstoppable passion has to go someplace. All that love you didn't share with your mother is bouncing around you like an electrical current and you're scared to touch it because you think it might burn you, kill you even, but it won't, and you'll run to stay ahead of it but no one can, not really, not for long."

Alba dipped her head and tasted his mouth. She let his hands peel away her trousers. He wound his tongue deep inside her whilst the coffeepot spattered for no one.

"I hope you don't mind sitting on the street," Dante began, pulling out a chair for Alba to sit on. He moved to the other side of the table, his crisp pale blue suit luminous in the sunshine. "It's a glorious day and I always think food tastes divine when the sun is shining—oh dear, now I sound like an Englishman who doesn't see it often, no?"

Alba smiled, wishing she felt less on the spot than she did.

Dante sat down and removed his sunglasses, folding them with precise movements and placing them down upon the linen. "I'm so sorry about your mother. Mine passed away only a few years ago. She was elderly. A dragon in fact. But it aches all the same. Of course. I might carry on and say a whole list of clumsy condolences, but I think I'll stop there."

"Thank you," Alba answered, as the waiter swung in beside them and placed a basket of fresh bread and thin homemade grissini beside them. He filled her glass with a crisp Frascati and a flourish.

"I'd suggest the carbonara," Dante began, "it's really one of the best places to have it." Alba hadn't been taken to a restaurant by a Roman who hadn't insisted theirs was the best place to eat the city's famed dish. Dante signaled to the waiter, who seemed to intuit his decision. This was his local haunt after all.

Alba was glad for Dante's ability to ease them through lunch, filling her glass before it got empty, sharing wondrous anecdotes of the some of the greats he had looked after over the years. The waiter arrived at regular intervals, strewing the table with fresh grilled vegetables and crisp salad, which Dante dressed as if he were no stranger to cooking. He ordered two coffees before she knew she fancied one and waited till the end, when her mind was warmed with wine and sublime food, to share his proposed schedule of concerts. She looked at the list. The words Paris, Vienna, Madrid, Verona, Palermo, Brussels were one after the other. And at the bottom, the two words that formed the name of the city she'd always dreamed of playing: New York. Her heart was a frill of trilling notes. She looked up trying to hide her astonishment and failing. Her hands were clammy with excitement and overwhelm.

"Yes, Alba. You didn't believe me when I said that your performance was the start of an incredible career, should you choose to work with me."

"These are suggestions?"

"They are bookings."

She swallowed hard. The sudden clangs of the narrow Roman street around her did little to drown the whirring inside her.

"The schedule begins next month, so you'll have time to hone your repertoire. Of course, they are most interested in your handling of the Romantics, and I told them we'd stick to that program. There was a mention of Tchaikovsky too, that's in Paris. It's part of an emerging artists series. There are young graduates from all over the world attending."

Alba looked down at the list again not knowing how to contain her thrill.

"To the start of a beautiful partnership, *si?*" Dante offered.

"I would love nothing more," Alba replied. Freedom from her grief was typed in black-and-white upon the sheet in front of her.

The following months were like a riding a carousel at great speed, watching the world whirr about her in Technicolor splendor, shades of fairy-tale reds and yellows, the silvery shimmer of applause, the golden opulence of the concert halls all like smeared paint on a crazed artist's palette. Her feet brushed the floor long enough to know it was still there but no more. At the center of the circling haze was the blissful silence of her practice mind, and deeper still, the molten core of performance, the moment when all the noise dissipated and Alba swam in the sensation of freedom and simplicity that her piano gifted her in return for hours seated by her side. Her days were solitary, filled with diligent practice and one good meal in the middle of the day, where Dante made sure she was well fed and cared for as he accompanied her on the tour. One evening in Vienna she woke with a start, which was not atypical after a performance and the celebratory meal afterward, where Dante encouraged her to liaise with the rich and powerful music scholars and bookers in town, something she'd grown more accustomed to, but still recoiled from the idea. After a few months she'd learned to mask her reserve with an impressive performance of relaxed ease, but the effort left its toll the next day.

She reached for the phone and dialed Vittorio's number. His voice was sleepy.

"I just wanted to hear you," she said.

"Are you sure that's all?" he asked. She could hear his smile.

"No. But that will do for now."

"Mr. Manager scheduled this call or is it playtime?"

"This is me ignoring you."

"Stick to concertos, you're much better at it."

"I love you." Her words hovered like a golden ball, her lips tingling.

His reply was silent.

"Vittorio?"

"Yes?"

Her swallow sounded loud over the phone, it was easier to focus on that rather than the crackle of self-consciousness creasing her body.

"We'll see you in Paris tomorrow afternoon, yes?" she asked, brushing off her uncertainty.

"Of course."

She could hear his breathing down the line.

"Last chance for you to admit that you asked them to have me conduct?"

"How many times do I have to tell you, Vitto', I only mentioned how amazing you are. If anyone had something to do with you being asked to be part of this new artists program, it's Goldstein. He loves you. You don't know that yet?"

"I know you don't want me to feel like you're my sugar mamma."

She sighed a laugh. It was useless to try and persuade him any longer. Besides, perhaps being a sugar mamma wasn't such a bad prospect. "Have you made peace with performing the Tchaikovsky at last? I don't want you throwing any tantrums now," she giggled.

"I can't wait to hold you," he said, his voice weaving a luscious thread through her bones, sewing her vertebrae in light.

Paris seduced Alba in an instant, at least the little she was allowed to wander. Dante's schedule at the opera house was grueling and saw the orchestra, her, and Vittorio inside the theater rehearsing for most of the three days ahead of the concerto.

Vittorio tapped his baton. The violinists looked up. "May we go from here again please?" he said, flipping the huge pages of the score back to the opening measures.

"Alba, let's keep the resonance of the first time you played it."

He turned back to the orchestra before he registered her expression. He'd never given her a correction like that, especially not in front of all the others. The orchestra were also recent graduates from the academy in Paris. The fact that he and Alba were a couple was not lost on them, especially the first violinist who took it upon himself to comment on the first whiff of the lovers' tiffs at any chance he could.

Vittorio lifted his baton, as he swung down the orchestra's brass burst with the opening melody of Tchaikovsky's Piano Concerto no. 1. The strings replied. Vittorio's arms swung in large circular motions. Then a silence. Alba watched his upbeat and then her piano percussed the opening chords, sweeping up the keyboard, as the orchestra and piano swelled together.

Vittorio threw his hands down. The musicians fell silent.

"We can't go over this again, Alba, there's no time!"

She took her hands off the keys.

"Back in twenty minutes everyone—is that okay, Pierre?" Vittorio called out to the stage manager seated in the wings.

"Of course!" he yelled back, charmed by this young conductor's attention to timing.

Vittorio came over to the piano and leaned his elbow on the side.

"What are you playing at, Alba?" he asked.

"I was going to ask you the same thing."

"You're holding back, trying to slow me down. We've talked about this. And still it's like mud. I can't keep us from the Russian saccharin of this piece if we do it this way. You want to have your freedom in the midsection? You need to earn it here at the beginning. Why are you resisting?"

"I won't resist if you talk to me like this. Don't give me notes in front of everyone, yes?"

"Keep your voice down, they'll think we're not grown up enough to do this in the first place."

Alba felt her lips tighten.

His voice dipped into a conspiratorial whisper. "Plus, I've just found a delicious spot beneath the stage where I'd like to make love to you."

Alba didn't let his gaze penetrate her. His finger traced hers.

"Stop it," she whispered, urgent, rising from her stool. "I'm going for a little air."

He caught up to her.

"Alba, *tesoro,* forgive me—I'm so giddy to be here. I'm like a boy at Christmas. More, even!"

He stepped in front of her. "I want you to shine. Don't misunderstand me out there. It's all about the piece."

"I hope so," Alba said, easing away from her impatience. He slipped his hand into hers and led her toward an unknown door in the corridor that ran the length of the back of the stage, glancing behind to make sure no one was following. The darkness beneath the stage wrapped them in a conspiratorial quiet.

"What are you doing?" Alba said, pulling back against his hand.

"It's fine, no one's here."

"This is totally unprofessional, Vittorio."

He stopped and faced her, cupping his hands around her face with unexpected tenderness. "I just wanted you to see this. Before it gets crazy up there. Before we don't have a second to even talk to each other. I wanted to feel you here."

He eased her skirt up over her thighs, she pushed his hand down. "I'm working, Vittorio, not thinking about this."

"When I hear you play, I can't think of anything but this," he replied, easing her against the brick wall beneath the stage, slanting strips of light fighting in from above.

"Vittorio, stop!"

He did.

"Sorry, Alba. I thought you'd find making love under the stage delicious."

"It would be. But we're guests here. Someone walks in? Then what?"

He planted a soft kiss on her cheek. His tongue slid down her neck a little. "I want to share what we have, out there," he whispered.

She kissed his neck. "That's cheesiest thing you've ever said to me."

He pulled away and looked into her. "I would make love to you all day. You know that, don't you?"

"Maybe."

He kissed her, his lips pressing hard on hers, fleshy and ardent. She didn't need him to tell her in words, the feel of his mouth expressed everything she wanted to know.

"Twenty minutes is almost up," she murmured with a smile.

"You've always kept perfect time."

Raffaele Sanna
Via Ambrogio Spinola, 27
87349 Milano
September 3, 1978

A good luck note for your Parisian adventure! I'm so jealous it's untrue. Most especially because I've just fallen in and out of love with a French guy and I can't get the idea of swanning around that beautiful place out of my mind. Send me a letter with all the gory details. You and Tchaikovsky were born for each other. Hope lover boy does you both proud. Lap up every moment, my beautiful friend!

Miss you!
Ra
xxx

The performance was electricity. Vittorio's body swung with the music, the rhythm effortless through his bones, and she let herself be led this time, not fearing his lead, not fearing the orchestra but melding as one big breath of music. They eased into the mellow center of the piece, Vittorio affording Alba extra freedom of tempo, his body angled always toward her seated at the grand piano in the central front of the stage. The end of the piece approached, Vittorio silenced the orchestra, Alba raced her hands high up the keyboard stretching her palms to reach the challenging octaves, zigzagging up and down the white and black, streams of crisscrossing currents of arpeggios, a plethora of waterfalling notes cascading down toward the final refrain which Vittorio eased the orchestra back in with seamless effort alongside Alba. The final measures were bold, beautiful, startling the audience into an impromptu standing ovation at the end.

Vittorio walked over to Alba and kissed her hand, then looked up at her. "I love you, Fresu."

The deafening applause would have drowned any reply. He turned away and led them to the front of the stage, where a young girl rushed on from the wings with a huge bouquet of red roses for Alba. She bowed to thundering applause. Vittorio squeezed her hand a little tighter. Alba scanned the smiling audience. As her eyes flitted to the wings she saw Dante nodding with pride.

A few weeks later Vittorio convinced Alba to move out of her room at Signora Anna's and into his studio so that they could form a bona fide Love Nest, as he called it, or Hive, depending on her mood. Alba felt like they were beginning the story of their lives together in earnest at last. Perhaps there was room for both them and their music to harmonize together after all.

New York deafened her with an assault on her senses so violent Dante had to insist she explore only a few hours a day. Between the oppressive humidity and the dubious smells emanating from the trash cans lining the streets Alba didn't know whether she'd just stepped onto the set of a movie or a warped dream. Dante spoke of jet lag, but Alba knew that with more distance from Europe her grief had time to permeate her with brutal determination. The discombobulation of being so far away from anything familiar made her feel lost, unanchored. Dante ensured there was a piano in her suite, air-conditioning, and a steady supply of fresh fruit and chilled drinks. Whilst she practiced her thoughts were silenced into oblivion, but as her fingers lifted off from her regimen the waves of nauseous memories filled her. The adrenaline soaring through her after the performance at Carnegie Hall so soon after the euphoria of the concerto with Vittorio merged into the delirium of travel so much so that Alba couldn't shake the sensation of being several steps behind her body.

"My fingers are slow," she told Dante.

"It's normal to feel this way, Alba," he'd reply, without concern, defusing her anxiety with a smooth wave of his manicured hands. "Don't practice for the next hour and return to the instrument after that."

She heeded his advice to the letter, watching him harden when she spoke of Vittorio.

"You don't like him, do you, Dante?" she asked one afternoon, biting into a piece of fresh melon so cold it made her teeth hurt. The honks from impatience along the streets of New York below reverberated up the walls to the fifteenth floor.

"He is a talented young man."

"But you don't like him."

"That's not for me to say, Alba. As long as he doesn't affect your professional life, he can be as lovely or as nasty as he wishes."

She took a sip of coffee, missing the tar espresso of home. "They have offered him a placement in Paris. For the next year."

"I hope he thanked you."

Alba laughed. She had grown to love Dante's spice, the way he could dissect anyone in a quip or two.

That evening when she and Vittorio spoke, he sounded distracted as usual, funneling his attention deep into the piece he was working on, monosyllabic about the composition they had commissioned him to create.

"You sound far away, my love," Alba said, her voice sleepy, trying to quash the feeling that she wished him to congratulate her for playing one of the most important stages in the world. Somehow the conversation had steered back around to him.

"I'm several thousand miles away. And there's an ocean."

"You want to hear how it went?"

"I know how it went. You're a star. They loved you. Never heard the Romantics played with such honesty. You're a breath of fresh air."

"You're a snarky twit."

"I know what's good for you."

"Do you miss me?"

"No."

Alba listened to him chuckle. "You really are a fool."

"Yes. It's my saving grace."

"Good night, lover."

"Good night, starlet. I'd love to kiss you now."

"Good," Alba murmured, then placed the handset back before she said anything more.

Dante tried to suggest she needn't surprise Vittorio in Paris the following day. He gave a list of reasons, money and sense being top of the list, but Alba knew she'd earned a few days' rest and she wished to spend it beside Vittorio, underneath his covers, hidden from the world, which was becoming an increasing loud and blurry place.

The plane touched down in the early morning, just in time for her to swing by his local bakery and pick up some fresh pastries. She spent the last hour of her flight choosing what she would wear to greet him, a new folly that seemed to have crept up on her with the aid of Dante, who had some strong opinions about how she would best describe her form to her ever-growing public. He respected her lack of desire for revealing outfits and supported her taste for classic lines, sharp blacks, demure purples, anything that left her body free to express how it needed to when she performed. As they traveled, fashion houses approached Dante, wishing Alba to wear their garments. Now she rifled in her hand luggage for a shirt that didn't reek of travel and tiredness. She went to the bathroom and applied a little eye makeup, buoyed by the anticipation of feeling Vittorio against her, of retreating from the merry-go-round of schedules and performances to the quiet of their hidden world.

Pastries and luggage in hand Alba swung down the Parisian avenues to his apartment on the third floor of a beautiful block not far from the opera house. She rang his bell twice. No reply. It was early after all. She found jet-lagged patience for a moment or two, then rang again. The door swung open and a neighbor ushered herself out, hair blow-dried in impeccable waves, her makeup applied with an artist's hand, her shoes the exact same maroon shade as her leather handbag. They exchanged nods. Alba held the door open and stepped inside. She tapped up the wide marble steps to the fourth floor and stood before his door. She rapped at the door. After the third attempt, she heard the click shift and the door opened. Vittorio looked more beautiful than she remembered. His black curls zigzagged with sleep, his light skin smooth alabaster.

His eyes squinted into focus. His expression fell.

"This is me being a romantic, Vittorio!" She laughed at herself, giddy with the travel and the plan well executed.

A figure stepped in behind Vittorio.

A sheet wrapped around her naked body, auburn hair crinkled in a messy mass.

Her smile faded with his.

"*Que se passé t'il*, Vittorio?" the woman purred.

He almost shook his head. Alba felt her bones harden.

Was it Vittorio's voice ricocheting down the hallway as he jumped two steps at a time, a towel around his waist? She couldn't hear the words, the tone, the desperation woven inside. It was a wash of out-of-tune strings, twangs of a clumsy hand. The sun was glorious outside, as her feet percussed the sidewalk, as she stepped inside a taxi, as she boarded the fast train to Rome. The weeks of phone calls, letters, pleading apologies, poems written with a tired sleep-deprived hand, in her honor, in praise of everything he knew her to be were not kept. Alba burned them on his stove. She finished his whiskey. She stopped herself from smashing all his plates and glasses, his beloved remnants of his mother. All the terror she'd felt now came blasting forth, burning black, hot treacle.

Dante helped her relocate to a quiet suburb of Rome and she ensconced herself in her new hideaway of Prati, in an apartment that looked out onto a lush courtyard beyond her living-room window. When Vittorio fought for attention in her mind, she looked out there and counted the fringes on the palm until she sank into sullen silence convincing herself that he, like everyone she'd loved, was nothing but a murmur of memory.

III Movimento

Rome

1988

22

Cadenza
in a concerto, a brilliant, unaccompanied solo section, once improvised by the player, now more often already composed. It enlarges on the themes set forth in the work and exhibits the player's technique.

Vittorio's betrayal sent Alba flying toward her music with a fervor that reviewers described as one they'd never had the delight to witness before and doubted they would again. Over the decade that followed, Alba brought a flair to the Romantics the public had never heard, an improvisatory quality, playing with a ferocious passion that breathed exciting, fresh energy into the classics. In academies across the classical world, the Fresu Style was talked about, described, assigned as a bar against which brave new students should set themselves up. Professors would lecture that Fresus only happened every decade or so, should the classical world be lucky enough, and that her virtuosity was nothing short of ethereal in quality.

Dante, on Alba's request, kept her reviews from her. She didn't want to start living for the kind words, she didn't want to live in the shade nor sun of their remarks. It made the act of playing less creative, less personal. She chased a schedule that would leave even the most prodigious player out of breath. The pressure fueled her, thrilled her. The silences of her quiet hotel rooms were deafening, and whilst she abhorred the frothy conversations she had been expected to become good at in the gala nights and suppers hosted in her honor, it was always better than real life. Music was her safe place, the only time she welcomed solitude and connection. It reached people, but at both a safe distance and with a brutal intimacy. It was a heady concoction, one that wove into her like a lover, whose touch she yearned for, always leaving her needing more.

Goldstein's favorite trattoria was tucked down a side street close to Rome's Parliament. He knew Gino, the owner, on a first-name basis, and whenever he'd taken Alba there, he had swayed his arm as if he were swatting flies, which signaled to the waiter that Gino bring him whatever he thought best that day. There was a picture of Goldstein with his arm wrapped around Alba behind the cash till beside the front entrance alongside other stars of the opera and television. This was the almost secret hangout for the most successful music stars in the city. Goldstein chose a table in the far corner. He could spy all clientele entering and leaving from there. Their conversation meandered through Alba's commitments, she filling Goldstein in on Dante and his impeccable handling of her schedule. They feasted on carpaccio and *tortorelle,* wide, hollow spaghettilike pasta, creamy with *cacio e pepe,* the quintessential Roman sauce of oozing pecorino and cracked black pepper, followed by the most tender steak Alba had ever tasted, flanked with charred vegetables and bitter chicory sautéed with caramelized garlic. It wasn't until they were sharing a tiramisu and coffee that Goldstein brought the conversation around to the real reason he wanted to treat her to dinner.

"The academy needs a new piano maestro. I'm pretending I'm not too old to do it. I'm pretending I'm grieving for the lack of Fresus in this world. This is the sorry truth. My Greek-Jewish melancholy has broken through the thirty-year dam and I can't do anything to stop it."

He flicked his gold lighter and lit his pungent cigarette. He took a deep drag and breathed it out in a plume of smoke toward the ceiling.

"I think you're what the institution needs."

Alba heard her cup clink to the saucer.

"It's a wonderful post. You will be able to keep up your concert commitments of course and teach a maximum of one hundred and fifty hours a month. It's been the hardest and best job I've ever had."

"I've never taught. I don't know if I know how."

"You've had the best to set an example, no?"

He smoothed his beard with his unmistakable grin.

"That's what worries me," she replied, mirroring his expression.

"Don't answer before you've finished your coffee. I'm not dying just yet. I can hold it down another few months. But don't beat around the bush. You either want to have a go at this or tell me no, but I have a feeling you would make a fine mentor to some unsuspecting rat out there. It may be the tiramisu talking, but teaching you was one of the highlights of my playing career, make no mistake."

Alba licked her spoon. It was sweet with a few fading granules of sugar and the bitter cream of the end of her coffee.

"I think that is flattery."

"You know me better than that, Fresu."

They stepped out into the mellow warmth of the Roman night. The quiet was an antidote to the cavernous noise of the trattoria, satiated voices ricocheting across the vaulted mural-adorned ceiling.

"You'll let me know next week, yes?" Goldstein asked, lighting up another.

"I thought you said I could take my time."

"Time is something concert pianists gamble away, no? I know Dante's in favor of you doing this."

The idea of Dante being so in charge of her schedule made a crackle of claustrophobia bristle up her spine. Between the recording contracts and performances it felt like time was an illusion gifted her once. Goldstein was offering a respite, a chance to further her development. Perhaps this was the perfect moment to add another dimension to her relationship with her instrument. Give something back to the place that made her what she was today?

"It would be an honor to become a maestro, Maestro," she said, the decision slipping out before she had a chance to change her mind.

"It is, Fresu. You will touch our students deeply. Whether they like it or not, is none of our business, that's their own journey. You will show them the road, but they will have to walk it."

"If I can teach them half as well as you did me, that will be a bigger achievement than watching the audience in Milan stand for my version of Rachmaninoff's piano concerto."

"I can't promise that, Fresu. But it is a good choice you've made. We'll talk soon."

He kissed her on both cheeks, leaving his Gauloise-scented breath in the air as he did so. Then he turned and raised his hand for a taxi. As he climbed in, Alba noticed his movements were more angular than she'd remembered, his age apparent all of a sudden, his shoes large ones for her to fill.

Raffaele Sanna
Via Corso
Emmanuele, 19
28763 Milano
18 August 1988

Darling Alba,

How was Zurich? I sent two colleagues to watch you. They said your playing was sublime. I told them you still owe me commission for helping you all those years ago.

I've met The One.

His name is Luca. He's from Switzerland. I've been able to tell him things I'd have been too terrified of doing with others. The drug trial doctors have altered my dose now and they're really happy with how I'm reacting. Still early days, but they're really hopeful. I celebrated the fact, obviously. With said Swiss-man. When do I get to see your face next? You need to meet him.

All my love,
Ra
x

Alba picked up the pot with one of Natalia's handmade holders and poured them both a generous shot into two mismatched cups. They took them back out into the living room. The Roman afternoon was warming toward Alba's favorite time of day, the laid-back bronze light of those early summer evenings, that delicious time between afternoon and evening where the bars would line with *aperitivo* drinkers taking a moment to slip with ease toward dinner. She loved that hiatus, it was the time she'd stop her daily practice and afford herself some fresh air, either on her terrace or in the courtyard below, sometimes, if time allowed, sipping an *aperitivo* herself at one of her locals. It was a syrupy pause, like the edge from sleep to awake, the golden breath before the start of a new movement during a piano concerto.

"When do you go away next?" Natalia asked, leaning on the counter.

"Next month, after the concert here."

Natalia stepped over and wrapped her arms around Alba. Their hug was unhurried.

"It's so good to see you. Are you going to fill me with stories of the Austrian audiences? Tell me about that awful rich guy in New York who keeps hounding you? No, what about that one in Madrid you told me about?"

"No stories to report."

Natalia untwisted her bun and wrapped a new one off her face. "Shall I pretend I don't want you to meet the kind of lover who will sweep you off your feet?"

"Please."

"Shall I pretend I don't notice you not sharing all the gory details because you think I can't cope with them, and secretly I feel really left out?"

Natalia pulled out the sugar from the cupboard by the stove.

"That would be nice, yes," Alba replied, feeling the warmth of familiarity fill her. This was the only home where she felt she belonged. Even after all these years, the gaping hole left by her family could only be filled here and it ached that she couldn't come over as often as she'd like, sometimes for several months at a time.

"Fine, I'll blame it on the oxytocin," Natalia continued. "I swear when I feed Matteo, I literally feel high, woozy. It's a pretty addictive sensation I have to say." She spoke of her youngest son and her face took on that blanched tenderness it always did when she did so. He was the fourth of the brood, and, Natalia had promised, the last. In the room down the corridor, Alba could hear the other three squabbling through play.

They flopped down onto Natalia's huge sofa, plump with cushions of various shades and fabrics. Something sharp poked into Alba's leg. She pulled out a windup toy from underneath it. Matteo's eyes lit up. He charged across to her, grabbed it, and then drove it over every piece of furniture.

"I'm so excited to play with you, Alba," Natalia began. "How long has it taken for this to actually happen?"

"Too long," Alba replied.

"My orchestra has been great," Natalia added. "Schedule-wise we've actually managed to make it work this time. Leo's so busy at the *conservatorio* and with his orchestra that sometimes it feels like we're long-lost relatives."

One of their daughters' cello music swelled, doing little to drown the bubbling conflict in the next room or Matteo's gurgling sounds of a motorbike engine.

"Your home makes my apartment seem like a morgue when I go back."

"Swap for a day or two anytime you like, my friend!" Natalia gave her cup a swirl and downed the contents. "So Goldstein just laid it out like that, out of the blue?"

"Exactly."

"So does this mean I get to cook for you more often?"

"You can twist my arm."

The sounds of the front door heaving open sent the children running out into the corridor. Leonardo stepped into the living room, small children attached to him like barnacles.

"Look who it is, *famiglia!* Zia Alba has arrived at last! Do you have any idea the musical royalty in this room, my friends? Of course you don't! You just care about whether I brought you cakes from our favorite bakery, no?"

Squeals in the affirmative.

"Which I did!"

More shrieks.

"I spoil them, Alba, so that I get to be the favorite," Leo said, kissing her on each cheek. "Natalia is wrangling all day and I swan in like one of those cowboys who's found Californian gold. Cheap, no? Works a treat."

His face creased into his olive-skinned grin, eyes twinkling more than before, as he swung his viola off his shoulder and placed it down with care in a safe corner by the piano at the far end of the room. The children ran after him into the kitchen, then reappeared with fresh crème puffs in hand, marching back to their various stations. He placed the cardboard tray of the remainders down on the coffee table, moving aside a pile of books and the fruit bowl loaded with medlars and tangerines.

"May I sit between my two favorite ladies?" he asked, plonking himself down and taking a big bite of his puff. A little icing sugar powdered the tip of his nose. Natalia signaled for him to wipe it. He kissed her instead and left the remains on hers.

"You really are a pig, Leo," Natalia said, through a giggle. "Those children will not eat their dinner now."

"Just scoring points because I'm feeling guilty I left them for a few days for work last week, right?" Leonardo looked over at Alba with mock guilt.

"You're going to let me cook for you tonight, *sì?*" Leo said, rubbing his hands together.

"The two of you seem to be fighting over the challenge."

"Did you read that huge spread on Vittorio the other week? The article was like five pages long."

Natalia shot Leonardo a look.

"Come on, Natalia, enough time has passed now. He was a shitty boyfriend, yes, but that can't take away from his talent, no?"

"You think he's saying the same about you, Leo?" Natalia prodded.

"I try not to care. I do miss him sometimes." He twisted back toward Alba. "Am I being insensitive?"

"It was a long time ago," she replied. "Besides, I love it when you get all soppy."

Alba almost believed her laid-back performance. That much

was true. It had been hard to ignore the rise of Vittorio. She liked to think it was just as hard for him to ignore her own. She ought to thank him in part perhaps; his betrayal had fueled her commitment to her music even deeper than it already was.

"Ignore him, Alba, he just wishes he had a four-page spread too." Alba smiled at her friend. Her cheeks were rosy despite the rambling mess around her, seated beside a man who did everything to make sure his family was happy and well cared for. Behind her, the walls were lined with snaps of her and Leonardo in various exotic and remote places of the globe where they'd traveled to share, teach, and learn music with children. Alba's favorite was of them in the humid forests of South America, surrounded by a crowd of grinning, budding musicians. She remembered receiving their postcards throughout their travels, an almost ignored twinge of envy of their freewheeling adventures whilst her schedule became ever more full and demanding. They'd set their own timetables, taken time to explore the world, expanding their comfort zones, and returning deeper in love than they'd left. They wore their lives with honesty, a breezy acceptance of life's fluctuating rhythms. She admired them that, and always left their home bolstered, replenished somehow, even if she didn't give voice to those secretive lurks of jealousy that pierced her mind, not for a family that she'd never wished to have, nor a domesticity she never chased, but because unlike her, they still held control of their daily lives, despite the mess, the anarchy, the never knowing whether the bills would always match their income; their buoyancy was never threatened.

In contrast, Alba clung to her packed schedule, the pressure of having to deliver: The tight turnaround between concerts was addictive, it made her feel like she was in a race and winning. Yet after the drastic dip of adrenaline that followed the ebb of celebratory dinners and drinks after a concert, a recurring emptiness threatened. Little anchored her beyond her music. Without its song, her closeted memories fought for attention, the silent, brutal rejection from her family ached, quashed only by a passionate return to work and the music that provided the sole way to express all that was too painful to revisit away from her instrument. It propelled her to chase more commitments. Freedom lay onstage alone, by her keys; through the paired-back preludes of Ravel, or woven into Bach's thoughtful melancholy, complex intertwining of crisscrossing themes, a mathematical breakdown of life in all its brutality, pain, and beauty. There it was safe to visit these feelings of quieted grief that she kept cloistered with fastidious care. In contrast to the music she lived onstage, real life could feel like a bland white wash.

Matteo drove his truck over the precarious pile of magazines on top of the table. They tripped onto the floor, the center one opening to a large glossy picture of a man standing by a window of an opulent palace.

"There, you see!" Leonardo laughed, pulling himself off the sofa and grabbing the picture. "Speak of the devil. Always had that knack of popping up, no?"

He twisted Vittorio's portrait toward him. "You're right, Natalia. I am jealous. Tell me I can do the brooding thing as good as him, no?" He switched the picture back to the two women and pulled his hammy version of sultry. They laughed. Alba loved pretending she didn't notice the way Vittorio's age had brought out the best in his features. She loved pretending that she hadn't read every word of that article before throwing it away, recording the name of his opera star wife, Clare Veritiero, the British-Italian starlet taking the opera scene by force, an elfin woman with the voice and charisma that made reviewers quiver. Her eyes lingered on the headline and subheading:

VITTORIO DEL PIERO ON HIS MOST REWARDING ROLE TO DATE: PLAYING ONE HALF OF THE OPERA WORLD'S ADORED POWER COUPLE

23

Da capo
a directive to the performer to go back to the beginning of the composition

Alba stepped inside the large double doors of the *accademia*. The receptionist called out to her as she reached her window.

"May I help you, Signora?"

"Yes. I'm here for Dimitri, he's expecting me."

"Are you Signora Fresu?"

Alba nodded. The receptionist's cheeks flushed, perhaps with embarrassment for not having recognized her. Alba was familiar with the look. It was a caged knowing, a gaze with a childlike openness and closeted masking at the same time. It hadn't become a comfortable sensation to witness even though over the past decade it was a regular occurrence. Nevertheless she gave the receptionist a polite smile.

"He'll be waiting on the first floor, Signora," the receptionist replied, placing down the handset from her ear after calling him.

Alba walked on through the next set of double doors, which opened onto the courtyard. The familiar patch of grass greeted her. The space reverberated with sounds from the adjoining *conservatorio*. Celestial marimba from the percussion rooms on the ground floor ran up the pinkish stone toward the sky like invisible footsteps racing up the plaster, vibrating the air with pentatonic glissando. Hands on an upper floor flew over a short passage upon an organ. Cutting through it all, the vibrato of a young opera student from the smallest rooms on the uppermost floor rose like a streak of silver.

It was good to be home.

Alba took a left and walked up the wide staircase, forced to take in the iron gated lift where Vittorio often jammed the cubicle on purpose by trying to open the door a little before it reached the requisite floor so he could kiss her, whilst furious grumbles of other students trying to fix it echoed down from the upper floors. The memory smarted. She let it evaporate; a half-hearted phantom worn to nothing, its host killing it with a gentle but determined rationing of regret. With each step that wound around the shaft Alba felt the pictures slip away, back into the neat pile snapped shut inside the metal case she'd fashioned somewhere upon the forgotten shelves of her mind, the place everything was stored for some other day, some other life. Not the one she had now, the world-trotting existence she'd enjoyed these past years, the lovers she relished like delicious meals, for sustenance, with reverence, appreciation, but void of the cloying claustrophobia of intimacy, not a whisper of the delectable marriage with her music, that ephemeral place where she lived in fullness. Her lovers didn't drink her essence as Vittorio had. That was something that she'd made a pact to never repeat.

The office to the *accademia* entrance stood before her now. She opened it and a woman with an explosion of black curls greeted her with open arms and a warm but firm handshake.

"An honor, Signora Fresu, we are so happy to have you here!" Her tempo was brisk, excitable. "Maestro Goldstein has spoken so highly of you. Welcome."

Alba nodded in thanks as another man came out of an adjoining office, his glasses perched on the end of his nose, extending his hand in welcome alongside his colleague. Then Goldstein appeared, triumphant.

"So she decided to show up on time for once, yes?"

His staff laughed loudly.

"Manuela," he began, talking to the lady *con brio*, "bring in some coffees to my office, yes? Let's ease the *signorina* into the day, no?"

He turned toward the room and opened the double doors into it. Alba had never been in here as a student: the secret meeting room of professors only. Large framed pictures of all the past presidents hung at regular intervals along the fabric-lined walls. The raised golden patterns upon it caught the light from the window at the end streaming the space with sunbeams. At the center of the pristine parquet floor stood a vast mahogany table, its top polished to gleaming, high-backed chairs around it.

"Rather grand, yes? I remember sitting around this talking about you, Fresu."

Alba looked up at the chandelier, crystals dripping with sparkles.

"This is where we will meet regularly with other members of the *accademia,* yes? We schedule it to coincide for when you are here teaching so it won't interfere with your scheduling, don't worry. Follow me."

He led them back out through the reception and down the corridor to his corner office. She stepped inside. The familiar blue walls greeted her, the smell of his smoke engrained within them. The window was open to the sounds from the street below rising up to smudge with the strings that could now be heard from the practice rooms above.

"It's good to be back, I see," he said, reading her inscrutable expression in the way only he knew how.

"It's like yesterday and once upon a time all at once."

"Careful, we'll be mistaking you for a quantum physicist."

"I should like that," she replied with a broad smile.

Manuela entered with two little porcelain cups of coffee.

She placed the tray down on his desk with care. Goldstein nodded and she left, flicking Alba a sunny smile as she passed.

"Without Manuela, Alfonso, and Alessandra, this place would be sinking. They are special people. Treat them with care and they can't do enough for you. Here, down this coffee, it will stop me talking to you like it's the first time you've been here."

Alba sprinkled a little sugar into her cup and twisted it in to dissolve. She drank it in two sips.

"The students are eager to meet you. We have an interesting selection. Some very serious types, they're traveling from different cities once a month to be here, starting out in the business, you know, a few concerts here and there of course, a little teaching maybe. One of our graduating class has decided to relocate to Rome. Quite an interesting young man. Born in Russia, raised in some industrial town in the States, no less. He makes my hair stand on end sometimes but he urged me to let him have a few sessions with you, and, perhaps a little selfishly, I agreed because I thought it wouldn't do any harm to have you work with a few people before you start properly in September? He could do with some guidance from someone with a quiet rebellion inside."

Alba raised an eyebrow. Goldstein chuckled.

"So you are awake, I thought I'd talked you into silence."

"I have missed you, Goldstein," Alba replied, "more than I care to admit."

"Excellent."

"And I'd be happy to start with this Russian."

He opened his office door and they climbed to the next floor toward his main practice room. They stepped inside and he pushed the shutters wide open, just beyond the familiar terraces that flanked her and Goldstein's lessons. The two Steinways gleamed, as if expectant.

"Are they the same instruments?" she asked.

"Immortal keys touched by the sublime, yes. I have to remind the students to wash their hands afterward even though they want to fall asleep with your fingerprints plush on theirs."

Alba laughed and sat at the right one. So many hours were stamped onto those strings, hammers softened by the repetition of section after section, endless measures of words and silences Goldstein fed her, drawn out pauses filled by her unanswered questions. Each time she'd studied alongside him tiny beads of confidence strung together on tenuous invisible ribbons. Her body now lit up with adrenaline, or nostalgia or caffeine, she didn't care to decide which.

There was a knock at the door. Goldstein barked a welcome.

A young man poked his head around the slight opening. His face looked flush, a crushed petal of lateness or tension upon his cheek. Alba recognized the pre-Goldstein look. He ran a hurried hand though the tight wave of his blond hair, blue eyes sparkling with a simultaneous childlike curiosity and mature intelligence.

"Ah yes, I had forgotten to mention that I have a few coaching sessions today." He turned back toward the young man at the door. "I can't teach with you at the door, can I, Misha?"

Alba stood up. The student's eyes shot to her in surprise.

"Alba, this is our very own Russian novel chap I was just speaking of, in fact," Goldstein said, beginning his introduction. "He's flown in from the States so he likes to think he is American, but both he and I know better—the way he plays is more Uncle Vanya than Uncle Sam."

The blond adult-boy bubbled an embarrassed laugh. He straightened and reached out a hand to Alba. His touch was firm, no hint of nerves, confident not puppy dog. "I'm a huge admirer of your work, Maestra Fresu." He stopped for a breath but not quite long enough for her to answer. "I'd hoped I wouldn't blurt it like that, but there you go. My speech is very much American. I think afterward."

"Nice of you to notice at long last, Prince Misha," Goldstein trod on. "Now be quiet and make a different kind of noise."

Goldstein nodded for Alba to take a seat.

"Maestra Fresu will be listening for today, to see what on earth she's got herself into. Don't let that make you want to show off more than you usually do, Misha."

"I wouldn't dream of it, Maestro," he threw back, with the kind of wry grin Alba would not have expected any student to be brave or stupid enough to flick Goldstein's way. Any suspicion of Goldstein's mellowing over the years was brushed aside within the first few minutes, however, as he desecrated Misha's interpretation of Mozart. He tapped his floppy wrist, cursed his elegant handling of a pert section, asked him why he hadn't leaned on logic for more sensible fingering. It was like watching a flickering reel of her own lessons with different voices dubbed over the top, a jagged interpretation of a foreign film.

Throughout the onslaught, Alba found Misha's poise compelling. He had lightness to his gait. Despite, or perhaps in spite of Goldstein's intensity—Alba intuited a diffident streak the boy kept under control—he weathered his corrections with implicit precision, void of the defense of ego, filled with an attack to implement the direction with an energy Alba related to in an instant. His back was long, strong, moved with ease, but his hands drew her eye like a magnet. They moved with delicacy, at odds with their size, a feral freedom matched with an intelligent sensitivity. She couldn't help but wonder whether his appearance must belie his years.

The hour and a half lesson passed in a heartbeat. Alba retrieved herself from the mathematics of Mozart, the elegant flourishes and expression, aching to hear more, sensing the areas where this student yearned for further development, his natural flair for the dramatic coupled with an innate sensibility, pillars of a great musician, but with room for deepening practice, a greater attention to finer details, perhaps an encouragement to broaden his creativity in the passages where he sounded a little held. The room eased back to Via Vittoria, not without some effort. It took several moments before the feeling of looking at the scene through a jar of honey began to retreat.

"It was a pleasure to meet you." Misha's voice light, warm, and buoyant cut through her syrupy memories. "I'm very much looking forward to working with you, Maestra Fresu."

"Roll your tongue back into your head, child," Goldstein jeered. "No amount of sucking up will change the way you hammer Beethoven. Maestra is a master of the Romantics, so if you can manage to sop up some of the chocolate goo you've laid over your Chopins, it might mean you'll leave your next lesson in one piece."

Misha looked to Alba. Something flitted across his expression she couldn't identify; a rogue note slipping into a fast trill or run, a minuscule slip unidentifiable to the lay listener but an instant, if brief, discordance to the trained. She pretended the hairs on the back of her neck hadn't twitched to attention.

She reached out her hand and Misha shook it. "I look forward to it too, Misha." The sound of his name on her lips was like a foreign place she'd lost herself in once before, darkened wintry streets lit by memory or the wistful warmth of an unknown audience. He left, taking a little of the air in the room with him.

* * *

When Alba returned to her apartment that evening her mind was alight with ideas of which students required what kind of development. All fears of her knowing whether she was adept at the post had disappeared, replaced by a passionate drive to implement the observations she had made. The day had flown past, ideas rushing to her whilst she listened, watched how their bodies moved, which parts of them appeared restricted, less pliable, which parts intuited the music. She was struck by how much a pianist revealed of themselves seated there at the keys, something she had reveled in watching musicians whom she admired, but now in the intimacy of the *accademia* she couldn't wait to participate in the challenge of helping others. It was as if windows had been thrown open to a bright day, filling her with life-giving energy that she'd sensed she'd denied herself for too long.

She switched on a few lamps in her main living area that sent a glow along the sideboard where her favorite pictures stood, concert halls that had left the deepest, fondest memories: Dante with her at an opening in Venice, Natalia when she came to visit her in Vienna with her mother, Raffaele beside her when she'd played Milan. She opened the doors beside her grand piano, letting the air of the evening terrace waft over her face, the toasted early summer evening air warm on her skin. She walked into the kitchen and poured herself a glass of wine, then returned to the instrument. It looked beautiful in the suffused light. She took a sip and placed her glass on the flanking book shelves. Her fingers eased onto the keyboard. She improvised a lazy line, a triplet of gratitude. Chords unfolded with ease, a laid-back hum. She fed the day into those twisting lines of nowhere melodies, warmed honey. She couldn't remember having felt like this in a very long time.

A blinking light on her answering machine caught her eye. It was the first place she always checked when she came in, but tonight was different. She had kept her pager on her at all times, like she always did, but Dante had no reason to reach her and this brief sensation of lightness was addictive. The machine flickered with the number three. She walked over and pressed play. The first message was Dante, checking in to see how her first day at school went; his voice had the frayed twists of laughter on it, and it made her smile too. Next was from a French classical singer she'd met in Naples several months ago and with whom she'd shared various unhurried nights, both clear in the understanding that their intertwining was casual, two laces held in a loose bow. He was in Rome, he said, his lilt inviting yet cool, and would she like to meet up?

She skipped to the final message.

Her heart lurched. Salvatore. He never called unless it was Christmas, and even then it would be an awkward voice message to which she would reply in the same manner. Still, she was touched that he would reach out over those holidays because she knew Marcellino forbade it, as his father's chief guard. Salvatore had always been the most susceptible out of the three, neither the eldest nor the longed-for girl, and now he still hovered in the unseen shadow of his siblings. She played his message again straightaway to allay her panic that something had befallen someone at home. The sensation sent a shiver of guilt rippling through her. By the third replay she was ready to really listen.

"It's your brother," he began, his voice tentative but not without his unmistakable swagger. "I'll be in Rome in a few weeks' time, for business. Can I see you? Hope you get this message. You know my number. Call if you can."

Alba looked at the grandfather clock holding court in the corner. She'd bought it after the first time she'd performed in Germany. It reminded her of Signora Elias's room. The sudden panic of something having happened to her mentor sent ice through her veins. Perhaps that's why he'd called? The business visit was a ruse? After all, that's how she'd received the bad news from Raffaele about her mother years ago. She balked at the slipshod angles of her thoughts. The clock chimed eleven. Too late for her to call Salvatore back now. The thought of speaking to him, let alone seeing him, filled her with optimism and dread at the same time. He'd sounded stilted on the answering machine. She knew he hated to leave messages. He'd reached out though. He could have chosen not to. He wanted to see her and it was this that made her feel wary, her stomach crinkle with nausea. She had no desire to cover old ground, old mistakes, nor taste the bitterness she'd left behind all those years ago. But her family seemed compelled to crawl back somehow, crackle through her happiness, as if tied to some invisible antenna that made them tune in just when they lost her signal, desperate to regain control. She blew off the thoughts as a prickle of mania, admonished herself for it, swirled her wine, and took another sip. They didn't hold that power, it was her own fear of being stifled, her own voices, not theirs, and she loathed the way their echoes made her own resonate, vibrating her shadows into life, like oblique silhouettes of cutout puppets, grotesque angles jerking a clumsy yet terrifying fairy tale.

The second hand ticktocked the evening away. She didn't want to be alone tonight. She wanted to float on the feeling that had filled her at the *accademia*. She told herself it was the music, the return to the source of where she'd begun to spread her wings, retracing her steps, completing the circle. She didn't give any air to the thoughts that the feeling had more to do with how the room dipped into toasted ochre as Misha played, than the simple return to her musical infancy. When she asked her French singer to enter her later that night, those thoughts were an ache she disguised as pleasure.

24

Prelude
a short composition for piano

a movement or section of a work that comes before another movement or section of a work. The word also has been used for short independent pieces that may stand alone, or even for more extended works, such as Debussy's *Prélude à l'apres-midi d'un faune*.

"From the midsection again please, Signore *e* Signori—measure twenty-nine," the conductor announced as the orchestra ebbed back into quiet. Gianni Conte was a small man with a verve that Alba found electric, and she adored playing with him. A powerhouse, he whipped the air about him with a ferocity that ignited the orchestra with such a deep understanding of the music and its textures that Alba could speak to him about the score for hours before and after performances. His wife, Anna, was a delightful human too, an exquisite violinist who treated Alba like a sister and fed her like a mother. Whenever they had the chance to work together Alba jumped at the opportunity.

Gianni sent her a look. They inhaled at the same time and the orchestra rose to glorious life. Then their tone eased into a silvery line of soft strings. Conte looked toward her, judging the entrance of a second melody to marry with seamless perfection to her piano's entrance, fading the strings to silence as her score led her up to the top of the keyboard and back down in a jagged arpeggio toward the return of Rachmaninoff's glorious melodious line, smooth and fine as a voice, rising through the quiet. Conte's baton tapped his podium again. All fell quiet.

"*Si, mervaiglioso!* I'm happy with that for today. See you all at the concert!" He stepped off his podium and walked over to Alba. "Glorious, Signorina, as always, and of course you don't need me to tell you, but take as much time on the adagio melody as you wish, we will be right behind you, *si?*"

"*Grazie,* Gianni, the orchestra is sounding heavenly."

"They work hard, no? Today they didn't eat too much for lunch, I think." He chuckled then, as Natalia stepped in toward them. He kissed her on both cheeks. "Wonderful Signorina, you are my favorite first violinist."

"You say that to every violinist, Maestro Conte," she laughed.

"Perhaps," he replied. "Oh, I almost forgot, Anna insists you join us for dinner afterward, Alba."

"I'm not sure. I may be meeting my brother."

"He is most welcome to join us. I insist. We have a few friends in too, the more the merrier. I think it will be a special table."

He left before Alba could reply anything to the contrary.

"You talked to Salvatore?" Natalia asked.

"Eventually. Took several attempts. It wasn't as awful as I'd thought it might be," Alba replied, leading them down the corridor behind the stage toward her dressing room. "He sounded pretty relaxed, grown up. I suppose at some point I have to accept that people change as much as I have."

"Alba Fresu getting all philosophical. Going back to school has shuffled some stuff up, no?"

Alba laughed at herself. Natalia hit home.

"That look on your face says I'm right, Alba. It's wonderful to see you like this. Really. And to sit next to you and play is, well . . ." Natalia's eyes watered. "Ugh, look at me, I'm mush every time I feel even a twinge of emotion." Her laugh was spilled out through her teary smile, unguarded. "I'm going to go now and mop myself up, see you at the performance."

Alba watched her leave, feeling overcome with gratitude. She was playing the hardest concerto in her repertoire for the first time in public with her favorite conductor, alongside her best friend. How long would this feeling last?

Alba wasn't anticipating Misha to be waiting outside the practice room when she arrived later that afternoon for their first session. She noticed herself talk a little too quickly, jarred speech she attributed to someone interrupting what she'd planned on being a little quiet time ahead of the session.

"I can come back in a little while, Maestra, I'm just going through the score some more. My colleague needed the room I was using."

"I'll take a moment, yes," Alba replied, regaining her center.

Misha stood and closed his manuscript. "May I bring you a coffee?"

"I don't think we're on coffee terms just yet, do you?" She'd meant it to come out as pointed as it did but thought the flicker a little brittle. She wasn't here to be another Goldstein. "The fact is," she added, "I'll be thinking faster than I can speak, and I don't care for that this afternoon. See you in five."

She entered the room and closed the door behind her. The windows were open, afternoon warmth filling the room with the golden hum of silence. The pianos' black lids were lifted. She sat and looked through Misha's piece again. She knew it well, but somehow fixing her gaze to the page made her forget their awkward greeting, silence the doubts that perhaps she wasn't prepared to be a teacher at all. She played the first section; its spare yet profound introduction sent light down her spine. She adored this Debussy piece and knew why Goldstein had advised Misha to work on it with her; it was deceptive in its simplicity but required a great deal of thoughtfulness and precision to make it sing. She let the first few sounds of footsteps in the snow hover in the air above the strings of the piano. This was one of the pieces she'd played during her first few months at the school. It was a piece Vittorio loved her to play for him. She had interpreted his love of the spare as a signal of his controlled passion, a disciplined nature she found compelling but later understood what it was in truth: a narcissist's compulsion for control.

She stood up from the notes and walked across the room and opened the door for Misha.

"So, here we are," she said, swinging the door open and walking away from him toward her piano. "I love that Goldstein has suggested you begin with Debussy. He is a favorite of mine."

"I've listened to this piece since I was a child," Misha began, setting his satchel down on a chair and placing the score on the righthand piano.

"Your parents are musicians?"

"Engineers."

Misha looked over at Alba, and she observed his eyes had the kind of openness it was easy to fall into, void of cloying naivety.

"That's the look most people give me, yes," Misha said, in place of any reply. "I just loved music from the beginning. My brother was obsessed. I heard it because of him, I guess." His voice had an American twang but with throaty Russian vowels: a contradictory impression of modern confidence and old-world melancholic romanticism.

Alba nodded for him to begin. She sat beside him a distance away, watching how he dealt the weight of the notes, how he let the tone deepen. She didn't interrupt till the end of the piece. She watched him skirt the tension, ease toward the profundity, then circle it instead.

He finished and looked over at her. His gaze was penetrating but not provocative or defensive. She wondered if she'd ever looked at her professors in that way.

"You know the sense, Misha, but I think you are not counting entirely correctly. You have to be precise with Debussy. There is always the danger of being a lazy watercolor with him. He is not that. This piece is about coming home. Yes, a walk through the snow, but which snow? Where? When? What is the protagonist returning from? For me, this entire piece is about loss. And that requires you to dig a little deeper, Misha."

She watched her guidance land.

"Take it from here," she began, leaning over him to signal the section she wanted him to revisit. "This time I need you to clarify the pictures in your mind. We are reciting poetry here; you can't just make a general poetic sound. You need to know what it is you are craving to express."

She could have spoken more but wanted to see how far he would go with just a little prodding.

He began again. This time his feet looked heavier upon the wooden floor. His legs were active, she could see the muscular indentation through his jeans. His back lengthened and when he pressed into the keys, his touch was more descriptive. This time the rhythm was pared down and precise, this time the sense of an interior world was alive, inviting. Then he lifted his hands up, abrupt.

"Like so?" he asked, his full lips scrunching into uncertainty.

"Until you stopped, yes," she replied. "You found the tension, Misha. That's what every piece requires. These notes are like pearls, yes? We can't admire the necklace without the string of tension that links them."

She surprised herself with the analogy. It was something she'd always thought about, but it was the first time to hear the words in the space. It occurred to her that this was the first time she'd felt so open talking to someone she didn't know about music. Over the years she'd trained herself to do so with the string of journalists salivating over her words as if they were minute gospels. She hated the feeling of her thoughts being tied down into black and white. She avoided the sessions where possible and as the years went on became better at refusing to speak to many point-blank. Because of her fame, Dante now acquiesced, though they both knew he would rather she were more communicative. In the recording sessions she'd often leave during the breaks and get as far away from the studio as she could, where the hosts would have prepared food that was left to go cold. Now, in this quiet room, she could have spoken for hours. She heard her voice lift, in effortless waves, free, and Misha let every word land, not interrupting, not submissive. His active engaged listening was a quality she found more attractive than she would have wanted to. His hair was golden in the afternoon light and she wished she didn't notice it quite so much, nor his athletic poise. A quiet embarrassment began churning inside her.

"Try again," she said.

This time the nerves of his first playing had been stripped away. He found an unhurried touch. His tone had deepened. But what struck Alba most was the melancholy that rang through, the complex palette of wintry sensations, the darkening blue of a late afternoon winter sky, the swaying silhouette of iced cypress trees in a freezing wind. He captured it all. They were transported from the warmth of this room at the center of Rome to a land far away, inside a frigid landscape, the loneliness a result not of harsh surroundings but of punishing interior ones. He was no longer playing note by note, but shade by shade, easing from one to another with confidence. A low chord, rumbling the bass notes, heralded the start of the final measures. For his final touch, a chrome shiver filled the space; an icicle of sound.

Alba let the silence fire the emptiness between them. They hovered in the quiet, lulled and lost by Debussy.

"Yes, Misha. That is what I mean."

He looked up at her, the afternoon light dipping his pale skin into a warm sienna. "Thank you for not terrifying me into it like Maestro Goldstein." His smile was unhurried, unguarded, the kind of smile that invited one inside.

The feeling smarted. "I don't want to be nice. I want you to develop the deepest interpretation you can."

She looked down onto the open width of his jaw. "You hold some tension in your central cervical spine. You'll need to address that."

She placed her palm on his back, just below his shoulder blades toward his spine. Her fingers stretched to find the place where she could see his muscles were clamping into mild spasm. He let out a sigh.

"I know this," she said, "because I had to work on this too. We don't just work with the head, Misha, we need to give as much time to the body. You know this, of course."

He smiled in recognition.

"It has been a good first lesson, *sì?*" she said, brisk, pulling her arm away. "I will see you next month before your final graduation concert. Keep chasing the quiet center of this piece, Misha, it is a great vehicle for you to show off your natural lyricism."

He stood up.

She hadn't realized how tall he was until now.

"Thank you," he said, his voice warm, not sycophantic. He stretched out his hand. She felt it wrap around hers. If she didn't know better she might have misjudged his touch for someone trying to say more than how grateful he was. The idea was ridiculous. She admonished herself for even entertaining it. When had she become a grown woman who let herself keel toward this kind of ridiculous vanity?

He nodded and turned to leave. When he reached the door he looked back as if to say something. Their eyes met. He thought better of it and left.

Alba waited at the center of Piazza del Popolo, gripped by a sudden irrational fear of not recognizing her brother. They'd arranged to meet at this central point, which was often less crowded than other parts of the city. Offering him an *aperitivo* also meant she could manufacture plans for dinner if it was uncomfortable to be in his company, or stretch out to another local place if it felt like he was open to the idea. She looked around again. *Caribinieri* were parked at the entrance to the piazza. Tourists shuffled around the central fountain and Egyptian stone needle, more took photos from the Villa Borghese gardens that rose beyond. A steady stream of people promenading from Ottaviano and the Vatican strolled in from *via* that rose on the opposite side of the piazza. The arch of Flaminio bordered the commuter chaos beyond it, and behind her, her favorite spot for an *aperitivo*. The waiters knew her there and gave her a few special bites of the chef's improvised follies that were never shared with the tourists. She decided to take a table ahead of Salvatore coming and trust she would spot him from there. As she approached one of the waiters waved at her and signaled for her favorite table.

"The usual, Signora?" he murmured. She nodded. He left.

Several more minutes past, each prodding her as if to say she'd made up the whole thing, that her brother hadn't called, twice, to make the plans, that he wasn't able to get out of his work commitments or some such. The waiter placed her Negroni upon the table. She swirled the large hunks of ice around the crimson liquid, then took a sip and let the bitterness calm her senses. That's when she spied a familiar silhouette. She lifted her sunglass onto the top of her head. Then she stood up. It was him. She walked out in front of the bar. They met halfway. Salvatore took her hand and gave her two kisses. All fear of awkwardness evaporated.

His expression hadn't lost any of that little boy lost masked with as much zeal as he could muster. His clothes were grown up, well ironed, sleek, and expensive; he smelled of aftershave and he'd lost all the chubbiness of his youth. His face too was slimmer, clean-shaven, his hair was coiffured into obedience. He looked like someone who'd come into wealth and was very much at peace with it.

"You look like a movie star!" he said, his voice with the same bubbling enthusiasm and mild jealousy of their childhood.

"Thank you?" she said, deflecting the apparent compliment. She'd never felt at ease with people commenting on her appearance. It made her feel like a cutout, imprinted with the other's judgments and standards of beauty. It had little to do with whatever was inside. She wanted to know if people could see beyond a picture. Of those, there were few. Alba led him back to her table. He lifted a hand and ordered a beer from the waiter.

She took another sip, more to fill the hiatus than anything else. How were they to navigate this conversation? She fought the need to steer it, or sink into silence, as she always did when nerves gripped her. Perhaps it would be best to lift the sails and just see where the wind would take them?

"It's really good to see you, Alba. I've wanted to come for a long time," he added, a twinge of teenage angularity in his voice, "but it's not easy at home. A lot of changes since you left. Almost fifteen years now, no? Shall we not talk about home for a bit?"

Alba smiled. He'd become more sensitive a man than she'd remembered.

"Thank you for calling," she replied. "It means a lot to me. I have a lot going on right now. I'm glad we could find this time." She noticed herself flexing her regular defenses and get-out clauses. She'd already laid down an out, even though he had not mentioned anything about monopolizing her time. When might this habit die?

"*Un momento,*" he replied, standing to his feet and waving in the direction of the fountain. "I hope you don't mind, I asked Mario to join us. There's only two of us over this time from the *officina*, and I didn't want to leave him alone."

Alba followed his gaze to another man making his way toward them. His shirt was pale blue, his hair jet-black, his skin a deeper olive than Salvatore's. The walk looked familiar, even the outline, but it was like a vague memory, a pencil drawing smudged with an eraser. It was only when he was almost at her table that she recognized him.

Mario took her hand and kissed her on each cheek, hints of citrus and musk.

"I had no idea," she replied, hoping it didn't sound as feeble as she thought.

"Me neither," Mario answered, "I told him to call every time we'd come but you were always abroad working."

Salvatore waved at the waiter again signaling they wanted another beer.

Alba looked at her brother for an explanation, but he averted her gaze.

"He's working as a partner now," Salvatore said, slipping into easy chatter. "I need him with me on these trips. He's got a knack with the folks on the mainland." His voice was assured. Perhaps the swagger of his youth still spiked the fringes of his personality, it was difficult to tell what was charm and what was confidence. "Mario's got us out of a lot of scrapes here and there," he added, pointing toward a tight relationship beyond their professional one.

Alba wondered what to ask next. It was clear the two would be able to steer the conversation around work and other less personal subjects, but she longed to cut through to the center of this reunion somehow. It was the thing she disliked so much about everyday conversation. Music required her to get to the emotional truth, but in everyday life, it was acceptable to skate on the crisp icy surface. It was why she felt lonely in the appreciative crowds who fawned on her. They didn't care to share the emotional truth of a piece of the moments following it, thinking it had been her inner life that had ignited them when in truth it was always their own.

"I was terrified of meeting you," she blurted.

"Mario is terrifying," Salvatore teased, "you should see him in the mornings."

His expression softened with unexpected sincerity. "Truth is, a lot of us miss you."

The table fell silent for a moment. The waiters placed their beers down.

"Papà is not doing well," he began, his tone dipped darker, "forgetting things. Small stuff. But it's not good. That's another reason why Mario's here with me. Marcellino has to make sure Papà doesn't make any more mistakes at the *officina*. His brothers are causing hell. They hate the fact that he's doing this victim rehabilitation crap. Some nonsense that hippies set up from the capital. They arrange regular meetings with bandits that kidnapped people. They say it helps both sides to heal. Can you believe it? I say it's a load of rubbish but Babbo is evangelical. Seriously, he's like those old biddies and their daily mass. You wouldn't recognize him." He shook his head, embarrassed for having confided everything too quickly and in one breath.

Alba struggled to paint the pictures in her head that matched his descriptions of this new father. "Is it working?"

"Who can tell? I've been at the house when Mesina, the main guy who led the attack, swans in to chat with him over some homemade wine. Awkward as hell. But Babbo's happy so that's okay, I suppose?"

Alba let the idea ripple toward her, but it didn't penetrate. Her brother seemed to intuit her reluctance.

"Salute to that then," he said, with a sardonic grin, raising his glass. They clinked. Mario's eyes locked with Alba's for a breath. She remembered that mischief. The memory of her swinging her fists at him burned into view. It was like watching a girl she once knew.

"I know a good place for dinner," Alba answered, knowing she couldn't let these men go before filling in the silence of the years past in case they changed their minds about seeing her.

25

Agitato
a directive to perform the indicated passage in an agitated, hurried, or restless manner; excited, fast, agitated

The audience peeled into applause as Alba stepped onto the stage, the sound splattering the space like sheets of rain. She never tired of hearing the listeners, alive, bristling with anticipation, filled with energy she could tap into. Tonight was different though. Somewhere inside the auditorium were her brother and Mario; tonight she was not just performing the hardest concerto in any pianist's repertoire but able, at last, to show her brother the reason she'd left, that he might understand her choice. She did not long for forgiveness. Her father, not her, with his temper and stubborn vindictiveness had broken up the family. Tonight's performance would allow her to be heard. It filled her with something close to optimism, not a childlike need for approval, but the exquisite anticipation of taking the space to express, to share what her life had been up until this point and why. She was ready to let her brother in. It was the closest she'd ever get to reaching her father, connecting on some level, not hooked to him through their mutual disdain alone. Her music had distanced her from the family for so long now that, at last, it was washing them toward her. It was time for the tide to roll in.

Gianni flashed her a warm smile, his body slipped inside a smart dinner jacket that emphasised his diminutive stature whilst outlining his fierce energy. She adored his playfulness, the way he stood on his podium with the wonder of a child and the strength of a lion. It filled her with confidence. A sliver of excitement twisted up her spine like a metallic helix, her skin tingled, her body hot, alert, and ready. For close to fifty minutes she would place all her trust in Gianni and the orchestra around her, hoping to express every shade Rachmaninoff painted, the fire of his virtuoso runs up and down the keyboard, the melancholy within the pensive piano solos, then the dazzling galloping finale, kaleidoscoping clusters of chords that challenged the greatest of performers.

Gianni raised his baton. A silence filled the space, eating up every sound, every murmur. He took a breath. The orchestra played their first entrance. The violins began, their silvery murmur, purring couplets to create an inviting bed of sound for Alba's piano to sing above. Her breath filled her body. Her feet tapped into the floor beneath her. Her hands lifted and eased down onto the simple melody that rang above the strings, pared down, concise, yet full of a yearning, the syncopated rhythm tripping across the bar line that always made Alba imagine someone lost, searching for a home they'd never find. Beneath the piano, an undulating build from the orchestra as the melody expanded, as they took over from the piano and she undercut with trickling notes, chrome waves of starlit longing, sepulchred memories, moonlight clawing through darkened Russian woods, twilight wanderings. The sound grew, fattened, and layered.

Then the orchestra fell silent.

Alba's piano was alone, singing a passage without strict time. Gianni tuned in to her every impulse, watching with care to know when to bring in his orchestra once again. Her tempo ebbed—here was the section where Alba allowed her piano to take control, the melody humming through pensive glides from chord to chord. The flute player now joined in, twisting around the piano's notes with his breathy lilt, weaving around her melody with the papery wings of a butterfly. As it fell away, an oboe took its place, woody now, deeper, pressing. As it fell away, the French horn sounded, the pensive echo growing confident, not defiant but urgent. They swelled together, each led by the other, two lovers searching for each other from afar until the orchestra swelled and they sought once again in vain. The next forty minutes flew by on a breath. The adagio, mahogany and unhurried, the finale a potent last display of virtuosic playing, Alba's arms fired with all her might, her feet deep into the ground, her back long and responsive to each impulse. She percussed the final chords, the horns echoed. Again and again the seesaw defiance, as the instruments fought for the last word. Gianni's body cut through the space like a tornado, sweat dripping from his forehead. The players onstage were lost in one another, rushing toward the ending, a herd of wild horses charging downhill, unbridled, fearless, muscular, and free, making the earth tremble beneath their hooves till the final note filled the auditorium.

Crackling applause electrified the space like a blinding white light.

Alba rose to her feet, half propelled from the physical exertion of the ending and also to reach Gianni, clasp his hand, and thank him for the glorious ride through the hardest concerto she'd always longed to play. As he kissed her cheek he whispered, "An out-of-body experience, Alba. We did it!"

She walked away from the podium and stood by her stool. The audience were on their feet now. The applause reached the ceiling, cascading down like sparks, and inside the shattering noise, an elusive quiet. Somewhere out there was her brother. Where did the music take him? Did he join her ride? How was his different? How would he describe this evening to the others? Would he even mention he'd seen her? At the end of their dinner that first evening he had asked her lots of questions about her life in Rome. She'd described what she could, but it was difficult to color her descriptions with a complete picture of her daily rhythms. Salvatore was part of such a different world, to him her life was precarious in some way, an unknown that unsettled him. She had quickly turned the conversation around to him and the family, gentle prods to paint a clear vision of what had befallen them all since she left. When he left, he'd seemed excited to watch her perform, though

Alba knew he would not have expected to be seated in so large an auditorium with such a passionate audience. Perhaps it was a streak of vanity, but she was glad he saw how her playing was received with such profound love.

Now the orchestra stood and took their bow, followed by single bows for the soloists. Natalia shot a look of joy to Alba. Her cheeks were flushed, her smile reached the edges of her face, eyes twinkling. Once the bows had repeated in the same order, and flowers were placed in Alba's arms, they filed off through the noisy wings, chattering with post-performance adrenaline.

An assistant led Alba to her dressing room. A huge fruit basket from Dante was upon her table, as he always arranged after every performance, beside a bottle of champagne on ice. She closed the door for a breath or two, her accustomed pause before inviting anyone inside after performing. She breathed into the quiet. A twirl of an idea smoked her mind. After this concerto where could her performance take her next? A new world had opened up, one where she would reach students and watch them unfurl before her. This concerto had been the apex of her ambitions for so very long, and now restlessness crept in. She blew away the preemptive thoughts, admonished herself for not enjoying the present moment of glory, opened the champagne and her door, signaling to the assistant outside that guests were now welcome. Dante strode in and wrapped her in his arms and praise and gushes.

He held both her shoulders. "How do I start then, Alba? I've listened to that piece since I was a child and I know I have never heard it like that and I know that they are going to sell millions of copies from the recording and it fills me with joy because so many people will be able to feel what I've felt in the comfort of their homes."

"I don't think you stopped for breath, Dante!" Alba chuckled.

"Yes, tease me as much as you wish. I don't care. You made music history out there and you know it, and it's my job to make sure everyone else knows it too."

A knock at the door.

He paused.

"I will see you at the restaurant. Gianni's given me the address, I have some people I need to talk to out there, *si?*"

Laughter frothed out of her. "Talk is something you do so marvelously, my wonderful Dante!"

He took her hand and squeezed it. "It's wonderful to see you like this, Alba. It's been too long."

He left before she could neither agree nor disagree.

Goldstein was in the doorway as Dante opened it.

"The king has arrived, Alba, will you see him now?" Dante said, flashing Goldstein a grin. The men hugged. Goldstein stepped inside. Alba handed him a fizz filled flute.

"To Rachmaninoff!" he said, clinking his glass to hers. "For allowing us to swim in the depths of Alba's soul."

"I think that Russian has made us all dizzy tonight. Wasn't the orchestra sublime? I've never had a night quite like this."

Another rap at the door. Gianni poked his head around it. Alba raised another glass for him. Her room filled with ebullient praise, ping-ponging from person to person, as effervescent as the champagne they sipped. Some of Gianni's guests were introduced and then left. Goldstein followed.

"Don't keep us waiting, Maestra," Gianni said with a smile, "my wife is hungry and that's never anything others should suffer."

He closed the door behind him.

Alba turned to the mirror. She'd asked Salvatore to come to see her in the dressing room. She could imagine him now, reticent about asking for directions to the artists' entrance, overcome with that familiar shyness he'd tried to outgrow. She'd seen it when he'd spoken to her over dinner, the quiet angular tics that crept up when the conversation steered away from business or their father and toward her world. She'd noticed the way Mario had listened with a steel silence and it had surprised her. Perhaps her brother's awkwardness served to make Mario appear open, interested, fascinated even. She'd tried to keep descriptions of her life to date to a minimum. The only way they could see what it had been was to watch her play. Then all the colors of that life would tumble out, fill the air, sift into their senses without pause, without words, that always carried with them the risk of being misunderstood.

Perhaps he'd hated the concert? He was delaying coming to see her because he wouldn't know how to say that to her face. It was longer than many other concertos she played, but melodic and easy to understand in places. It was filmic, even, a pastime she knew he adored. She scrolled her lipstick back into its holder and zipped up her long gown. It was simple, black, but with an understated elegance and glamour that meant her movements were neither self-conscious nor stilted.

The assistant assured her that her car and driver was waiting for her whenever she was ready. Alba thanked the young woman and made her way down the corridors toward the artists' entrance. Outside the air hung heavy and humid. The crowd she had grown accustomed to being greeted with was bigger than usual, voices cascaded over one another for her autograph, as they held out their programs. She made her way down the line, trying to connect with as many as she could permit herself, conscious that somewhere amongst them must be Mario and her brother and she didn't want to keep them waiting, nor have them watch her speak with her fans as if she enjoyed the spectacle of attention. She noticed a young man standing a little bit away from the crowd, his back to her. Across the street her black Mercedes waited. The crowd dissipated, after the flashbulbs from several cameras lit the narrow street that ran the length of this side of the auditorium. Hands were shaken, well-wishers began to make their way home. As she reached the kerb, the young man turned. Misha's face lit up. He held out a bouquet of damask roses.

"It may be corny, but they were too beautiful and I knew my tongue would be tied so I thought if I just pushed them at you like a schoolkid you'd take some element of pity on me and accept them with grace."

Alba received the flowers in her hands. She looked at his wry grin. "I'm so very curious to hear what you sound like when you're not tongue-tied."

He laughed at himself then, the streetlight catching the mischievous twinkle in his blue eyes, his face creasing into the kind of smile that made Alba feel like all was well with the world. Around him she noticed the crowd commit his face to memory too. His kind of smile was one she wouldn't mind waking up to or falling asleep beside. Their expressions relaxed. Neither spoke for a breath. An unhurried pause filled the narrow space between their bodies.

"They are, indeed, beautiful," Alba said at last, without hurry, wondering when they might have time and space to talk without having to be somewhere else, someone else.

"I wrote a note," he said at last, his voice dipping into a warmer, maroon timbre. "It's a little less stupid than the way I'm acting right now. But not much."

"I'd never describe you as stupid, Misha."

"Good. It was a trope to get you to tell me all the things you like about me so that I wouldn't start holding you up any longer after you've been so kind to this gaggle of fans. I need to tell you that your performance makes me want to play all night and also never touch the piano again."

She liked the way he made her laugh with ease. It had been too long since she'd been close to this youthful giddiness, this ebullient dance. It struck her that she'd never known it at all. Perhaps she was adult enough to be childlike at last?

"For the sake of others, I do hope you wouldn't consider giving up your piano just yet," she said.

Misha's cheeks flecked with something like embarrassment or happiness.

Alba shot another look to the car across the street. Where was Salvatore? How long would she disguise her prolonging the conversation with Misha as waiting for her brother?

"We're probably at the coffee stage I'd say," she blurted. "You know, now that you've done a little sycophantic dance. I suppose I'm as much an egomaniac as the next concert pianist after all."

Their laughter mingled, notes jangling in space, hovering golden in the night air like two glowing spirals of light.

"I have to go now."

"I see that," Misha replied.

Neither moved.

Someone called out Alba's name. She spun around. A figure was running toward her. Mario was flush like a man running late for his train. He held her shoulders and kissed her on each cheek. His skin felt clammy.

"I've been trying to find my way around this warren. Are all auditoriums like this? It's like a small labyrinth. Anyone would think they don't want the commoners to get to the stars or something!"

Alba filled with a spicy mix of joy and trepidation. Had they enjoyed the evening? Where was her brother?

"I was a bit nervous of coming alone, I have to say," Mario began, in between panting for breath. "Salvatore got held up at the conference, but I didn't want to miss it."

Alba felt a knot twist in her stomach. She turned back to avert her expression from him for a moment. Misha had gone. The mild disorientation that followed irked her. She felt the gaze of the driver. And Gianni's words rang in her ear.

"They're expecting the three of us at dinner," she said, not wanting it to come out as clipped as it did.

"Don't worry, Alba, I know this is a work thing for you. I just wanted to tell you how wonderful it was. I don't want to encroach on your night."

"It will be worse if neither of you show up, especially as they're already waiting for me."

Mario straightened. Alba willed her disappointment to disappear, but it was as uncooperative as her pride.

"I didn't mean to blurt it out like that. Salvatore really wanted to be here." He shook his head, waving off the clunks of their almost conversation.

Alba softened. "I don't mean to be short with you. We should get going."

Mario looked her square in the eye. It was impossible to trace the idiot she'd once longed to pummel. Why was it so difficult to accept others' changes but expect everyone to accept her own? The hypocrisy made her bristle.

"Please come and eat with us," she said, a little calmer, "it will be a table of big personalities, but they're good fun too."

Mario's features softened. "I'd like that. Don't know if I can keep up with the conversation?"

Alba shook her head with a smile and started to walk across to the car. Mario held the door open for her. "If all else fails," she began, "just tell them about the time I almost knocked you out cold in the marketplace."

They scooted onto the back seat. Alba exchanged pleasantries with the driver, apologizing for keeping him waiting. He pulled away, rumbling over the cobbles of Rome through the streetlamp-lit *vias*, out toward the hills in the periphery where Gianni's favorite haunt looked over the moonlit city, its terrace stretching the length of the venue. Alba knew he would already be seated holding court with a chilled Frascati in hand, waving his arms through another anecdote, behind him an unadulterated view of San Pietro and the surrounding *cappellas*, gleaming in the midnight blue of the Roman midsummer evening.

26

Delirante
instruction to a player to play in a mad, frenzied way

As Alba stepped onto the terrace of Ristorante Anselmo all the guests around Gianni's table stood and began applauding. She waved the entrance off, swatting away the warm but embarrassing welcome. Other diners from the adjoining tables looked up. Several appeared to recognize her. She reached the table and a waiter held out a chair for her. Someone gave her a glass of wine.

"Thank you so much," Alba said, taking her seat, "now please let's get back to Gianni's story—I'm sure he was painting some elaborate picture about the Berlin Symphony orchestra or some such."

The guests laughed. The more well known she'd become, the funnier her lighthearted quips appeared to be.

"Ladies and gentlemen, this is my friend Mario. We grew up in the same town."

The guests rumbled their welcoming patter. He took a seat beside her, and the lady next to him launched into an instant conversation. Romans had a fascination with Sardinia. Alba had grown accustomed to the slight wariness and awe of the city dwellers interrogating the islander for knowledge on how life is like the other side of the water. Many had spent lavish holidays there and were keen to display their knowledge. Alba sensed Mario was neither intimidated nor patronized by the attention. It put her at ease.

"Alba, darling," Gianni said, walking over to her side of the table, "let me introduce you to Francesco Maschiavelli." The man beside her reached for her hand. He wore a blue artist's linen jacket with a silk scarf wrapped around his neck, splattered with various shades of purples and blues. His skin was fair with a shake of freckles along his cheeks, his hair white with age, but his blue eyes sparkled with a youthful humor.

"*Tesoro*," he began, "I can't believe we have never met in person. It's a farce, really. I have all your records. I've listened to every one of them and each time I hear something new. It's like staring at a painting and noticing the minute details that make up a masterpiece. Not just the broad strokes, but the smallest flecks, the minuscule handling of light, the courageous handling of the dark."

His words hung, shimmering in the air. Alba wasn't sure if he was the sort of person who would welcome conversation or like the sound of his voice as a virtuosic solo. Alba stepped into the gap. "That is the most beautiful way I've heard music described to me. Words are not my friends."

"That's why you play," he replied.

"Francesco is working on a new film about a pianist," Gianni added. "He's coming to the *conservatorio* and *accademia* to listen to some of our students over the next few days."

"I haven't decided who my protagonist will be. At the moment, the script is about a young girl who discovers music. We've heard musicians up and down the country but no one has revealed what I'm looking for just yet."

"That must be a difficult process," Alba replied.

"It's like looking for a needle in the proverbial haystack, my dear. Each time I feel like I want to give it all up, to be frank."

"Don't say that," Gianni's wife, Anna, chimed in from the other side of the table. "Your *Don Quixote* was the most beautiful thing I ever saw, I remember you saying the same thing about *that* auditioning process. Imagine if you'd never given me the pleasure of watching that, my darling Francesco."

The guests murmured warm appreciation. Alba watched him deflect the group's spotlight off of her and toward him. Another night she might have minded, but she was so dazzled by his personality that she welcomed the opportunity to observe him from the safety of not being attacked with praise from the others.

"I'm working with a sublime composer," he continued, "all original work around the classics of course, but I wanted something fresh." He swiped his gaze across the guests. "Where is he, Gianni?"

Gianni straightened from where he was leaning on the back of Francesco's chair. "He's gone to call Clare, I think he'd said, no?"

The name rang out like a bell. Alba brushed off the ridiculous spark of irrational jumping to conclusions. There were other women in the world with the same name as Vittorio's wife, after all.

"Oh yes," Francesco replied, "that little British woman keeps him in line alright—darling bird with the voice of a comet and a temper to match. Breeders can't be choosers, I suppose."

The two younger men beside him cackled at that. He threw them a wry look. Alba's chest felt hot and tight.

"These are my assistants, Florin and Armand," Francesco plowed on, oblivious, flopping a hand toward them like an afterthought. They appeared to bow their heads a little, and Alba realized she was indeed in the presence of filmic royalty. Of course, she too had watched all of Francesco's films: They were decadent, passionate, elaborate in design and pomp, a feast for the eyes and the soul. His time working in opera had lent him a keen sensibility for the grand, sweeping tragedies that worked well on film.

"Pleasure to meet you all," Alba replied. "This night continues to thrill me."

Gianni went back to his place and raised his glass. "To music and the power it has over us all!" Everyone cheered. Mario clinked glasses with Alba. "I think I've made a new friend with Mrs. Countess here." His face twisted into a sardonic grin.

"Here he is at last," Francesco began to the entire table, as if they had all been waiting for someone, "the henpecked artist, back from the Signora Veritiero front, the walking injured, love or world weariness creases his brow, I don't know which." His flanking men sniggered. Alba turned, following his gaze.

Vittorio met hers.

"Nice to see you, Alba," he said, effortless, as if they were business acquaintances familiar with regular meetings in work environments. He stretched his hand out and shook hers before she could register the shock.

"Darling boy, you always have this effect on women?" Francesco teased. The men in waiting giggled. Francesco turned out to the company. "Honestly, it's a liability. No wonder your wife is calling you at every minute."

The guests rippled laughter. Vittorio sat down beside Gianni, opposite Alba.

"You alright, Alba?" Mario's voice chimed in from somewhere far away, an echo over the sea.

She turned to him, feeling like her movements were slowed down to an abstracted speed, paint smudging before it has dried, rendering a picture a mess of brown blur as the pigments merge.

Before she could answer, should any words have risen to the surface, the waiters entered with vast boards of prosciutto and slices of melon, halved figs drizzled with honey and topped with shavings of Parmesan. The conversation steered around the feasts that followed, creamy risotto, large fresh porcini mushrooms grilled and sprinkled with olive oil and parsley, an obscene Fiorentina steak—in honor of the Florentine film director—large enough to feed the entire table, flanked with Romanesco cauliflower, stuffed zucchini flowers filled with ricotta and anchovies, hunks of pecorino, crisped open fried artichokes sprinkled with coarse salt, and a mound of *cicoria* greens sautéed with garlic and chili. The colors wafted into view, the smells mouth-watering, salty, savory, deep and full in flavor.

Alba couldn't taste a thing.

Vittorio hovered, unmoving, in her periphery, however much she concentrated on the reams of anecdotes Francesco filled the air with, or the delightful stories of Gianni and the witty interjections of Anna, who wouldn't let him get away with any exaggeration, much to the delight of the crowd. Francesco's double act added their own spin, as Florin and Armand added their comic echoes to everything that was said to laughter, which failed to blot the screeching claustrophobia pounding in Alba's chest.

How she and Vittorio had managed to avoid each other for all these years was a feat she was proud of. Now she could feel the power of his gaze without even turning her head. What game was he playing? She chided herself for even wondering. He wasn't playing a thing. His presence alone had churned her back to her ignorant years, when she didn't read the people the way she did now, when she allowed him to invade her. In all these years she'd forgotten to forgive him, she'd shelved her hurt and now it came blasting through her body like a finale, emphatic, unforgiving, craving attention.

She would have liked to leave. She would have liked to behave as breezy as he. That was always his trump card, playing the nonchalant, the unaffected, as if nothing around him moved him in any way whatsoever. One would think he was void of feeling altogether, perhaps except for an arrogance that people who didn't know him attributed to Tuscan pride. Alba knew better.

"Perhaps I can have you hear a little of what Vittorio has created for me?" Francesco asked, leaning in with a conspiratorial color to his voice.

"I don't think I'm the right person to offer an opinion on that, Francesco," Alba replied, noticing Vittorio make a woman beside him crease with laughter.

"Nonsense. I would value it above anything. I can give you some of the written music? If you would consider playing it for me I would be indebted."

Seeing Alba's look he backtracked in a hurry. "Forgive me, my darling, it does sound like I'm hiring you to be my repetiteur! Good heavens quite the contrary. I just think Vittorio and I would benefit so from having another ear give it a sounding. Would you consider making me the happiest man in Rome and do so?"

Francesco was a hard man to refuse. Alba had met her fair share, and if she wasn't a fan of his work, it would not have been difficult to say no. But she couldn't silence the part of her that was intrigued to hear how Vittorio's music had developed. Her spiteful streak imagined pecking at his phrases, hoping to be disappointed and reveling in the fact that he hadn't become the star he'd longed to be. She blew off the folly of thoughts as churlish and childish. She convinced herself that offering a professional opinion, relating to the person she'd avoided in all forms since the day she ran out of his Parisian apartment building, would be the best way to put his memory out of reach, create one afresh; one where he didn't hold her tied in strings.

"I would be happy to have a look, Francesco. Of course, I can't carve out too much time to do so, but equally I can't say no to the only man who has made me weep at the cinema, can I?"

Francesco's face lit up. He called out to Vittorio across the table. "Wonderful news, boy! Alba will take a glance at the score when we visit the *conservatorio*. My favorite pianist will be playing through my favorite composer's work. I think I just died. Salute Romans!" His voice rose above the crowd now. "Waiter! Fill these people's glasses with the finest champagne you have and don't let the nasty conductor man pay for it, do you hear?" More laughter. "You have to watch a man with a stick, you know!"

"We all know!" Anna replied from the other side of the table. Everyone followed Francesco as he stood. He lifted his glass as three waiters ran around to fill everyone's. Their voices echoed down the hillside beyond, above them a full fat moon. Alba thought the face she spied there, with wine-infused sight, rolled its eyes over her pathetic return to her younger years, tipped off-center by the boy who had taught her to never give herself away like that again. This ought to be *her* night, but Vittorio's presence eclipsed the joy that had filled her but moments ago.

Their eyes met.

An invisible tunnel of silence formed, around them watercolor voices turning bland and indiscriminate as if more liquid dissolved over them, diluting their pigment and power, leaving two people standing in a frozen moment of time and space. His face was the same, age creasing the edges only a little, a mature breadth to his chest, which Alba had tried to forget. Something flickered across his expression; a spark of contrition or invitation? It disappeared as soon as he'd seen her notice it. If she was as much an adult as she claimed herself to be, she should smile now, show how little of a scar he had left, but the burning sensation of wanting to launch what was nearest to hand at him made her fingers hot. It was a painful anger, because she knew it was directed more at herself than anyone who could ever put it right.

Mario touched her arm with a gentle hand. "You look a little pale, Alba."

"I'm exhausted," she replied, topping up half the fib with truth.

"I bet. You were a rocket onstage."

Alba let his words ease her away from the glaring pull of Vittorio. The sound of his voice, his accent, took her away from the table in an instant. She was on the Ozieresi streets, screaming out the rules of childhood play.

The guests started to mingle around the table, in an effort to talk to people they hadn't had a chance to yet, and in the hopes of digesting a little of the foodie onslaught they had just confronted.

"So this beautiful man then," Francesco began, tapping a drunk hand on Mario's chest, "what's the real story?"

"The real story, Signore," Mario began, "is that Alba nearly killed me when we were twelve."

"Ladies and gentlemen, attention!" Francesco yelled. "There is gossip afoot."

The crowd turned to Mario. Alba watched him face shyness and let it melt away. "No gossip, Signori, just childhood friends reuniting for a meal after many years."

"I told you they weren't lovers," Florin chimed in.

"Only because you'd already planned your line of attack," Armand followed without missing a beat. The guests laughed, then simmered back to their separate conversations.

"Francesco, I hope you won't think me rude," Alba said, "but I am absolutely shattered. I need my bed now. I used to be able to stay out all night." She noticed there was more honesty in the statement than she'd imagined.

"I've heard the stories, my darling," Francesco quipped. He took both her hands in his and kissed each. "It has been a magnificent pleasure to sit beside you. Your passion, verve, courage, openness at those keys makes me almost believe in God. It was beyond beauty, my *tesoro*."

Alba let his gush run over her without penetrating.

"Vittorio!" he called out. Alba watched him walk to his side. "You will listen to what this goddess has to say about your ideas, yes? Don't be a pouty little boy as usual, no?"

Alba enjoyed watching Francesco tease Vittorio on his petulance; there was some warped justice to the evening after all.

"You told me you'd gone to every one of her concerts, no?" Francesco asked. Alba couldn't tell if he was teasing. "So don't tell me you're not going to follow her advice, *sì?*"

Alba found the resolve to face Vittorio. He didn't look as diffident as she'd imagined him throughout the meal. His demeanor relaxed beside Francesco. If she wasn't mistaken, his expression softened, not quite friendly but something close to it. Which one of them was going to mention they had spent years together at the *accademia?* Why didn't Francesco appear to know? Was it her place to keep up the pretense, as if it hadn't been important? Should she take the adult lead and lift his guard with force? Staying silent was like upholding some kind of secret pact, playing into Vittorio's lead as always.

"Only one part of what you said is true, Francesco—I've enjoyed all your performances, Alba—but don't confuse that with me taking any musical suggestions lying down," Vittorio replied at last. His voice was as rich as it had always been. It wove a whisper of memory through Alba's bones, a desert storm lifting the sand, leaving her unable to throw away a lighthearted mention that they had been lovers, a flick of a thought as if he'd left no dent.

"Well, good night, gentlemen," Alba said instead, shaking Francesco's hand. He pulled her in and kissed her on each cheek. She stretched her hand to Vittorio, determined to have the final, clear-cut gesture. He reached in and kissed her on each cheek. His lips pressed her skin, she felt their fleshy touch soft against her, not skirting the air as was customary for polite farewells. The blood beneath raced up to the spot. She hated the bristle, the twinge of pleasure, an exasperated adolescent's overexcited reaction. Her body betrayed her. She let the feeling rise and fall, out of her control, refusing to give in to the fear of it unfurling her buried feelings.

Alba turned away. "Would you like to accompany me, Mario? I don't really want to be alone just yet."

"My pleasure," Mario whispered, "you're helping me escape Duchess woman."

They said their farewells to the other guests and moved away from the table, winding through the now empty tables of the restaurant, stepping out onto the street outside.

"I could have called a car," Alba began, cradling Misha's bouquet. The flowers had opened a little in the heat and now let off a heady scent. It made her think of his face outside the artists' entrance. "Do you mind walking? It's the only thing to make that food digest."

Mario ran a hand through his thick short hair. It made Alba think he was searching for a polite way to end their evening.

"Oh goodness, you have work early in the morning, don't you? How selfish of me. Here, let's go back into the restaurant and I can call a car for you?"

"I'm relying on you to give me a whistle-stop walking tour of this sexy city."

Off Alba's look he corrected himself. "Did I just call a city that? The wine was strong, no? Perhaps this Sardinian shepherd can't handle civilization after all."

"Is that what that woman called you?"

"Pretty much. I wouldn't mind but she was flirting and her husband was right next to her."

"Perhaps it's their thing," Alba replied, as they began a gentle saunter downhill. They walked in silence for a little while, just the tapping of their feet along the tarmac, the city a pool of twinkling lights below them.

"I can see why you don't need to come home," Mario said, his voice full of the Sardinian melancholy Alba allowed herself to admit she'd missed.

"My father made it clear he didn't want me there. It stopped being home after that."

"He's really in a worse way than Salvatore says. He loses his temper."

Alba made to reply but Mario stepped in. "I know he always did. But now it's different. He sees betrayals where there aren't any."

"Always did."

"Maybe. But now he flips out at the tiniest thing. It's hard on your brothers. He lives with Marcellino, and his wife is not the kind of woman who is easy, let's just say."

Alba let the words lift and settle, crushing underfoot like crisped autumn leaves.

"I'm speaking out of turn. I know this. I also know you deserve to know the truth. I don't think it's right they don't tell you. That's why I insisted Salvatore find you this visit."

"This visit?"

"It's an annual conference."

Alba took a breath and let it out with a sigh. They were approaching the outskirts of the Villa Borghese now, wandering along the piazza that overlooked Piazza del Popolo, the fountain pouring water out onto the turquoise stone pool below.

"I've felt responsible for my father's anger for too long." She wiped a hair away from her face, noticing how warm the night air still was, how much she longed to get into a nightshirt and out of her dress.

"I don't know why I'm telling you this," she said, clamping shut.

Alba watched something cross Mario's face.

"My apartment isn't far away, let me give you some whiskey so we both have a terrible headache tomorrow?" she asked, a peace branch for pushing away his attempt to reach out to her, to be the spokesperson for her fractured family. It was the least she could do.

"You drink whiskey, Alba?"

"You have an opinion on what women drink?"

"Not anymore. You've got that look of violence and Antonietta will not be happy if I come home with a black eye, especially from a woman, then I'll have a story to try and escape out of."

They walked a few steps in silence.

"That was quite a crowd tonight," Mario said, turning the conversation away from his home life and back to her.

"The people you saw tonight? Not all Romans are like that." Alba was unnerved by how relaxed she felt in his company. "Thank you for being such a good guest. I know a lot of folk from Ozieri would have felt pretty awkward."

"Now who's being patronizing?"

Alba twisted an embarrassed smile.

"And yes, you're right," Mario qualified, "I'm being an idiot. It's true though, our lives in Ozieri always seem predestined, sheltered, you know, laid out nice and neat."

"How do you mean?" Alba asked, willing him to carry on, understanding what he meant in an instant but needing to hear it from his perspective. She liked the way his head cocked to the side when he thought through a sentiment. It gave him a humility, a gentle wonder. It wasn't like the definitive way of talking she'd remembered from most of the Sardinian men around her father's table.

"You're born," he began, as they wound down the steps through the park toward the deserted Piazza del Popolo. "You're the boy, you learn to be a Boy, capitalize that, stake your territory, protect it, make sure everyone knows you're the big guy. Then you hit puberty and you're expected to want to jump into the forest with every girl you can chalk up. You meet a girl who is pretty serious, anxious to get on with the proper thing and it seems attractive, you know, the idea of being adored forever, of providing, of becoming the man you were always designed to be."

His voice trailed off a little.

"I didn't mean to put you on the spot," Alba said.

"You haven't. I've just never talked about this before. There's no time to sit and think at home. If I started talking like this people would think I was losing it like your dad." He stiffened. "Shit, sorry."

"It's the truth."

He sighed a half laugh. "I suppose what I'm saying is that you didn't do all that. You did the opposite of everything expected of you."

"I paid a price."

"Don't we all?"

"I don't know. I think we can judge our debt. Depends how much we let ourselves off the hook, forgive, forget."

"Sardinians aren't famous for either of those."

They laughed again. They turned off toward Flaminio and began the walk up toward Prati. It felt wonderful to finish the evening in the company of someone who had known her before all the pomp, all the success, and for whom she had no other feelings other than the comfort of childhood familiarity. They reached her apartment block.

"Actually, I'm going to head back, Alba, we have two more meetings first thing. But I could stay here and talk all night."

"Thanks for walking back with me."

She turned to put the key in the large wooden door that opened up to the courtyard within, palms streaking the night sky with spiky silhouettes. She twisted back to Mario and kissed him on each cheek.

"Thank you for coming tonight."

He nodded.

"Best hundred thousand lire I ever invested," he said, turning to start his walk away from her palazzo.

"What's that?" she called out.

He turned back to her. "I said it's the best money I ever spent."

Alba wondered whether he'd drunk more than she thought.

"When Raffaele came to me in a sweat," he began, just far enough away to make the distance from her edge toward awkward, "not knowing where to find the money he needed to help you, I pulled a few strings."

Alba froze.

"I'm glad to see he kept to his promise of not telling you. Seeing your expression now has made it even more worth it."

"Mario Dettori, are you telling me that you were the one who raised the money for me to come over and study?"

"I don't think I could make it up if I tried."

Alba opened her mouth to speak.

"Don't thank me. And don't pay me back, if that's what you're about to say."

"I've no idea what I was about to say."

He held her gaze.

"Watching you play has been the highlight of this trip. This year. Congratulations, Alba. You escaped and made a fairy-tale life. I'm trying not to be jealous."

Alba felt the desire to let him in on the harsh reality of her day-to-day life, the hours of solitude, her resistance to being alone at other times, the lovers who fed her but little, the magnificence of music that made quotidian life at once confusing and dull. The way she chased the immensity of those emotions and dodged them, and that the boy who had taught her the trappings of love almost ruined her entire evening tonight after the hardest concerto of her life.

Instead, she thanked him, words not coming to her rescue in the easy way she would have liked, the sensation of being teenage Alba creeping up again, awash with gratitude for her best friend and the boy she'd trained herself to hate all those years ago, for helping her.

"Keep doing what you're doing, Alba. It's making the world a better place."

"Now you sound drunk."

"I don't care, because it's true. You let people feel things we can't in day-to-day life. For that, I thank you."

He turned then and began walking away, disappearing around the corner, the echoes of his swaying steps echoing along the silent cobbles.

Alba stepped into her darkened apartment. She poured herself a whiskey from a decanter upon the sideboard, threw in ice, and stepped out onto the terrace. She switched on the string lights that she'd hung across it. The hunk of ice hit the edges with an inviting clunk, swelling the whiskey from side to side. She took a sip.

Her eyes floated across to the olive tree in the large terra-cotta pot, the small trickling fountain at the far corner and then along the collection of succulents growing out of an array of mismatched pots, curving in toward the terrace along the periphery.

Alba felt the alcohol begin to turn to sugar. After a large whiskey she always felt a rush of energy, restlessness, a hunger for company. She looked at Misha's bouquet, lying on the piano stool. In the kitchen she placed them in a vase of water. The note slipped out onto the floor. She opened it.

I fell into you after the first note you played. You may not feel the same, but here is my number if you do. You can call me anytime. I usually work through the night. Sleep is not my friend but the moon, it seems, is.
Misha

Alba looked at the clock. It was almost three. A splintering electricity zigzagged through her; it was the whiskey, the concerto, seeing Vittorio, finding out that Mario was responsible, in part, for the success of her departure for Rome, Alba knew all this. She recognized this sensation, it followed her performances every time. It was when she'd call her singer, the artist in Berlin, the banker in Milan, or allow herself to enjoy whatever lover offered a night of lovemaking without commitment that particular evening, wherever she found herself performing. She loved the rush of these clandestine interlacings, they were ephemeral, the closest thing to a fleeting performance at the piano, something you couldn't recreate, would never become real, nor repeatable.

When Misha arrived at her apartment half an hour later, he looked more radiant than she'd remembered. They took a bottle of wine out onto the terrace but neither of them needed to drink. She switched off the lights and let her naked body wrap around his on the cool of the tiles on her terrace. She felt the moonlight caress the curves of her breasts and surrendered to each sensation. The dawn sliced the sky, tentative pinks and oranges as they wound back onto her bed, as she invited him deeper inside, as she fed all the night's energy through her body, chasing her pleasure, guiding him to the center of her without fear, and, at last, to the quiet that wound round them like a silken cocoon. Sleep overtook them and the entire night faded into a dreamed past.

27

Dead interval
interval between the ending note of one phrase and the first note of the next

The *accademia* looked resplendent a few mornings later when Alba returned, ahead of the summer break, to teach her final one-to-one sessions before starting on the faculty in September. The courtyard at the end of the entrance corridor was bathed in light, the rays stretching through the surrounding walkway as far as the first set of glass-paned double doors at reception. Alba adored the smell of Rome at this time of day, ahead of the humidity of mid-morning, when a laurel-infused freshness renewed the air, creeping jasmine hedges scenting it with a heady perfume lingering from the night. On her stroll to work the bars clinked with stocky espresso cups, saucers slammed onto granite counters, air sugared with fresh pastries as she passed, snippets of passionate politics spitting out from caffeine-charged Romans, putting the world to rights, or throwing their arms up in disbelief at the insanity of their new government.

Manuela was waiting for her, a crème puff and espresso in hand.

"*Buon giorno*, Maestra Fresu," she said, standing up and lifting the plate toward her.

"Goodness, I'm not going to be treated like this every time I come to work, am I?" Alba said, in reply, smiling. "I'm not sure I'd do well to get used to that."

"Perhaps not, but it is your last day and everyone is overexcited for their summer break."

"*Grazie.*"

"Misha has checked in already," Manuela added, "then the enrolled students will follow. I've printed out the schedule for your morning. The auditions are being held later today too, for Signor Maschiavelli, they'll be using one of the lower rooms."

Alba took the paper and scanned the list of names. Goldstein appeared at the double door leading to the offices. "Well, look who graces us once again," he said, walking over and kissing her on each cheek. "I'm gushing because I meant to thank you the other night, but you were surrounded by adoring fans picking apart every quarter note of your performance—by the way, whatever you did to that student from the other day, keep doing it."

Alba's eyebrow raised.

"Don't act coy," he continued. "The German girl, I've been trying to get her not to play everything as a march since last year and only after an hour with you she's finally popped her lyrical cherry." He sent a grin to Manuela. "Sorry, don't mean to be crass."

"Of course you do," Alba replied, "and thank you. It was my pleasure. It's good to hear that—she appeared terrified throughout our session."

"You must have learned from the greats," Goldstein concluded, twisting back to the dark corridor from where he'd appeared.

Alba finished her coffee, wrapped the pastry into the napkin, and headed upstairs. All the practice rooms on her floor were silent apart from the farthest one. It was Misha's favorite room. Though he didn't like to admit it, he'd become superstitious about that space, he'd told her, as he had lain beside her on their night together, hair ruffled on her pillow. Something about the light, he'd lyricized. She'd teased him then, asking whether his Russian persona was studied for the benefit of foreigners. It had made him laugh, as he rose onto his elbow and kissed her with the most unhurried touch she'd ever felt. It made time slip away through the floorboards, an intimacy she'd not allowed herself to dip into for longer than she cared to remember.

She walked toward her room for the day, opposite his favorite space. A ribbon of melody wove out from underneath his door, nothing of the Schubert or Brahms they had run through before. The haunting tune pinned her to the spot. It had reflections of Debussy's descriptive, atmospheric themes but coupled with the complexity of Bach's fugues, interweaving impressions at once compelling and improbable. It was an artist painting an abstracted version of a classic, the *Mona Lisa* in unexpected flecks, or Botticelli's Venus, floating to shore on weeping acrylics. Beneath the main theme, a longing that almost brought tears to her eyes. She caught them before they fell, admonishing herself for infusing the sound with her own version of adolescent folly, standing as she was by his door, hanging on his every note, a soppy sight. She ought to move, she knew that, but the music kept her rooted.

It shifted to minor now, edging close to unexpected harmonies that held both the quality of a church chorale and a fierce yet restrained passion. It was unusual to use the time ahead of lessons to practice one's own compositions, or perhaps even improvise something new. Maybe it was Misha's way of reaching calm, refreshing his approach rather than hammering what they would be focused on for the next hour. A part of Alba wondered whether he was playing their lovemaking, a musical code just for her. The sound was tender, creative, unexpected, everything he had been at her apartment.

The handle lowered. The door opened before she could move.

Perhaps they could laugh off this awkwardness, with the same ease they had made love?

Vittorio looked as surprised to see her as she did.

An instant shiver of embarrassment rippled from her center.

He smirked. "There's probably a word for professors who skulk outside doorways listening, no?"

"If anyone knows it, it would be you, I imagine," she replied. He opened his door a little more. A young woman was folding some music at the piano and filled her satchel with it. She stepped out from behind him, effusive. "Thank you so much for your time, Signor del Piero," she gushed, her voice light and clipped, as if a small bird was trapped somewhere high in her chest. Vittorio's effect on young women had not changed. "I'm very much looking forward to playing for Maestro Maschiavelli."

He nodded, giving little away. When the young woman disappeared through the double doors, Vittorio turned back to Alba. "Another hopeful. Giving most of them some direction before they see Francesco, in the hopes that at least one of them will understand what the hell I've written. Were we so square when we trained?"

His face lit up then, breezy, inconsequential, tempting Alba toward their shared memory, as if chasing a mutual acknowledgment of a quaint interlude from the past. Had he decided their enactment of love was nothing but an immature romp after all? His sideways smile said as much, always the provoker.

Alba took a breath to reply when Misha bound in through the doors.

"I'm so sorry I'm a few minutes late!" he called out, stomping down toward them. "I got held up downstairs with one of the students."

"Your next victim, Maestra Fresu?" Vittorio teased. His eyes scanned Misha for details. "They all this pretty? Keep him away from Francesco, for God's sake. You have no idea how long it takes me to get anything done with that man."

Alba brushed off the sensation that Vittorio had intuited this young man was not a student alone. She'd forgotten that tone of his, the charcoal roughness to it, bold, easy to smudge between meanings.

"Some people have a hard time keeping their folly intact," Alba replied. Misha caught her eye. For a flicker he led them back to her room, disappearing somewhere together through a silence percussed with breath alone.

"*Buon giorno*," Misha said, reaching out a hand to Vittorio. "The school is electric with your name, Signor del Piero. Quite a frenzy having Signor Maschiavelli here. It's an honor, really."

"Well, it's lovely to be complimented by the youth. It makes me believe in my genius. And my age," Vittorio replied. "Does he have the same effect on you, Alba?"

She'd forgotten the way he'd lift his chin at a slight angle when he spoke to new people. In all these years his defenses were still intact. She would have expected them to have eased away. He had nothing to prove here. Yet a twist of something close to territorial slipped in between his words, as if he was trying to exhibit their supposed friendship in front of Misha, the opposite of how he'd behaved before Francesco.

A silence stitched the space.

"Let us begin, Misha," Alba cut through, with a fleeting glance back to Vittorio. "Best of luck with your auditions today, Vittorio," she said, determined to have the last word, to show his throwaways left her unmoved.

"I'll need it," he said, holding her gaze a little too long, before closing the door behind him.

Alba and Misha stepped inside.

"Are we expected to conduct this lesson without me wanting to peel everything off you?" he murmured, wrapping his arms around her and moving in to kiss her.

She pulled away. "How would you like me to answer that?"

"Without words," he replied, kissing her neck.

She stepped back. "This is our last hour to work together. Don't waste it."

Misha emptied his satchel and placed a couple of manuscripts on to the piano's music stand. He lifted his hands as if to begin, then held the pause. "I love it when you call the shots," he whispered, sideways.

"I love it when you stop leering and play."

He sat down with a grin. "I can still taste you."

"Don't make me repeat myself."

Somehow they managed to focus on their music, ignoring the sensations running through them. All the while Alba convinced herself she wasn't aware of Vittorio in the room across the corridor, shifting the sense he might be listening to their session, marking where and how she worked. More uncomfortable than that was the quiet desire that he do so, that he acknowledge what she had become. How ridiculous to even care a breath of what he thought, it made her dislike his memory even more than before, for unstitching the story of her stepping out from the remnants of their love affair, woven with care, embroidered into memory so she would believe it. With him only meters away in the next room it was like a lamp was shining on a tiny figure carved in his form, rendering it a giant shadow, looming like a grotesque threat, begging for attention.

At the end of the session Misha turned to her. "This is bittersweet. Hellish actually."

"We knew it would be."

He reached for her hand, wove his fingers between hers.

"Misha, please, don't."

"We're grown-ups, Alba."

"Our night was beyond beautiful, Misha."

"This sounds like an opening to something longer."

She looked into his blue eyes. A welcome whisper of breeze wove in from outside, tickling the tips of his golden hair. "You have a magnificent journey ahead of you, Misha."

He cocked his head with a shallow swallow.

"I'm not going to stand in the way of that," she added.

"That's good," he replied. "I wasn't planning on you doing so."

She could feel him bristle, a slight petulant tone to his voice.

"I'd like to buy you lunch," he said.

"I'm not hungry, Misha."

"After all the snotty students about to saunter in here like they own the planet you'll need fresh ravioli under some trees, and I know where that place is. Brief though. I know your day is full. And I've got an afternoon of practice lined up."

Alba took a breath, allowing his beauty to lure her, memories of their night together swirling in her mind, creased sheets, the moonlit floor of her living room, the darkened terrace.

"Please?" he asked. His smile was knowing, hopeful, almost resistible.

"Okay. I suppose I would like that, Misha."

He leaned in and kissed her. The sunlight fell on her face, the press of his lips ardent and sincere. It wasn't guilt that urged her away from him, rather the memory of how Vittorio had once drawn her so far in. Knowing he was just the other side of the door unfolded those memories through her body, like a trim of concertina paper garlands unraveling, falling to the floor in a heap, ripping from the thin string that connects them. A familiar sensation of claustrophobia fought for attention, even though she knew this young man wanted no more to snap her wings than she did his.

"You are the most wonderful kisser, Misha."

"I know," he murmured, his voice spun sugar, fine, a little cloying.

"Modest too."

"Meet me outside, Flaminio?"

"I'll be there for one thirty," she replied, watching him leave.

Alba took a swig of her water, and a moment to compose herself ahead of the next student.

There was a knock at the door.

"Come in," she said, eager to begin work with the next student, who was tackling a Liszt.

Vittorio stepped inside.

She tensed at his presumption. "You're not the German girl I'm expecting."

"Thank God for that," he replied. "Here, just wanted to drop Francesco's note to you. I feel like one of those gofers in a Shakespearean play."

He walked over and handed it to her, casual, as if they were friends. "He's inviting you over for drinks, but don't eat before you get there, he has a tendency to force-feed people once they're over the threshold."

She looked down at the note. It was for tonight. "It's rather last-minute."

"I tried to tell him that, but he's a hard man to refuse."

It was a level playing field of sorts. "I saw that the other night."

They filled the space between them with a breath, less barbed than before, almost comfortable. His face relaxed. "It's great to see you, Alba."

She didn't reply.

"Perhaps I'll find the chance to apologize for being such an idiot."

She held his gaze.

"Or not," he added.

She scanned her spiraling thoughts. Was he waiting for her to perform the woman scorned act? How he assumed she was steaming after all those years infuriated her. She said nothing.

"Fact is I was an utter idiot," he began, reticent for her answer, "an ego-driven boy trapped in a young man's body. It went to my head, the whole stupid show of it. It's why I was so thrilled to work like this for Francesco. I needed a break from the opera, leading the orchestra in Paris all those years was incredible and drained me of every ounce of humanity."

"I have students coming now, Vittorio."

He straightened. It felt good to cut his flow. This was her space. Why did he invite himself inside without doubting whether he ought to? She'd pretended she wasn't hoping for him to come into her room. She'd imagined them being in a room alone together for months, years after she'd fled from him. Now time had delivered, but the feeling was a world away from her dreamed-up, stifled version. It was raw. She hadn't given herself space to feel this. Rather it wedged in by force like a stubby angle of wood holding open a heavy door, small, yet potent, letting all matter of emotions fly in and out.

Vittorio nodded, looking straight into her.

She didn't shift her gaze until he'd shut the door behind him.

Flaminio was cooking in the heat. Misha was by the arched entrance to the Villa Borghese gardens, his sky-blue shirt setting off his light skin, sunglasses reflecting the busy street back to her.

"I was beginning to think you'd forgotten," he said.

It wasn't the kind of conversation starter that appealed to Alba. Misha was behaving like a boyfriend, and the idea felt contrived. They strolled in silence for a little while, uphill.

"Are we headed to the little kiosk at the top of the hill, Misha?"

"I think it's the only place I know where you can breathe in Rome at this time of day."

They fell into step. She allowed his hand to wrap around hers, his fingers strong, comforting.

They sipped Frascati under the trees at a metal table for two. After their plate of homemade ravioli drizzled with sage-infused butter Alba asked for two espressos.

"You are absolutely gorgeous, Misha. I'd love to trap you in my apartment and never let you out."

"Don't tease me."

"I'm not. But I need to tell you that how I feel and what I need are often polar opposites. It's something I've learned to live with."

Misha scooped the last dregs of his coffee. "So now you're going to tell me that you're too old for me, that I need someone younger, that you feel guilty for following your instincts."

Alba felt the hairs on the back of her neck stand to attention.

"I feel no guilt. Why is there the assumption that a woman my age must have shame attached to sex? That idea is absurd to me. Especially from someone so young. I thought society had moved on from this."

"You're twisting my words."

"No, Misha. We had a momentous night. But I'm not looking to share my life. I've tried it once, and I know where it leads."

Misha undid another button of his shirt. He signaled for the waiter to bring the bill. "Can we walk and talk? I'm feeling like an idiot seated here."

His resistance to approaching the conversation with calm made her tunnel through.

"This is what I fear. I've been in love with musicians. It's a slow torture. For both involved."

"Now you do sound your age. Bitterness doesn't become you."

Alba took a breath. "I know what I want and what I need. And I have a sense it's not what you do."

He stood up. She didn't move.

"I've embarrassed you, Misha."

"Actually, you're breaking my heart."

Alba stood up. Misha looked away, aware of the diners around him now. He leaned on the back of the chair and dropped his voice.

"I feel like you've brought me here so I won't make a scene."

"You invited me, Misha."

The waiter cut through with a dish of chocolate thins and the bill. Alba put down the money before Misha could beat her to it.

"I invited you—let me get this," he said.

"Let's walk," she said, leaving the table.

He followed and paused by the kiosk window where a crowd had gathered lining up for fresh-squeezed juices. They staggered downhill back toward Flaminio.

"I'm sorry I lost my cool," he said.

"I need to be brutally honest with you and myself. That's the cold truth."

"There's nothing cold about what's happening between us, Alba, and you know it."

She drew to a stop. He walked a few paces ahead and then turned back.

"I won't do this, Misha. These pulls and tugs. We barely know each other and already our conversation is unraveling."

"What do you expect, Alba? For me to run away with my little boy tail between my legs? You can be honest about your feelings, and so can I!"

Alba nodded, her jaw tightening.

"You want honesty?" he asked, his voice rising. "I think I've loved you for longer than I care to admit. I don't want to lie down and let you walk away without a fight, no." His face hardened. Alba witnessed her feelings rise high in her chest, followed by a swift coolness. Like a parachute in reverse, Alba was being pulled high above from her body, sucked up on the wind, observing herself from afar, a speck on the ground as her view became ever more distant, Rome's giant pines now little bushes under the swirling air beneath her feet, the deafening silence of the cloudless sky suffocating her.

"Say something, Alba! Say you don't have feelings for me, you're scared. I'm scared too but I know we have the kind of connection that only happens once in a lifetime."

Alba loathed these ultimatums, this idea of people having one chance at something sublime. She willed her breath to deepen. "I want the world for you, Misha, and I don't want to share mine. I don't want to qualify my decision, my reasons. I don't want to be held to account. I'm acknowledging our fierce connection, of course I am. I felt it the moment you stepped into that sunbathed room at Santa Cecilia, it scorched through me from your first note. I feel I understand you and that you understand me. These things never die."

He puffed out a sigh.

"I'm saying we are not obliged to act on it. But we did. And it was mind-blowing. And I choose not to continue. For both our sakes."

Misha ran a frustrated hand through his hair. She knew the feel of it on her face, on her stomach, between her thighs. The sensations returned from another time and place.

"Why stunt us before we even know each other?" he spat.

"Why not accept that I don't want what I think you need?"

"That's it? You call the shots and your lovers obey?"

He wasn't the first stubborn male to diminish and ridicule her point of view, but she refused to take the bait. "Misha, let's be gentle with each other."

He bit his lip. "I'm feeling so many different things right now I can't even begin to explain which is hurting the most."

"I am too."

"You're standing there like marble, Alba, watching me disintegrate like a fucking idiot."

"I'm asking you not to misconstrue my honesty for cruelty. It cheapens us both."

He shook his head. His tears fought over the edge of his lids now. He wiped them away.

"You know what's the most fucked-up thing about this? I feel like you're the one person I'd ever want to cry in front of like this. You're being a cold bitch but I don't want to be anywhere but here. Maybe it's for the best, you're screwing with my head and we're not even real yet." He sighed and wiped his nose with the back of his hand. "Shit!"

Alba held the space. Misha took a sharp intake of breath. "So what, I say goodbye now? Storm off like a moody teenager, is that what you're expecting?"

"I'm expecting nothing."

He gave another short, sharp sigh. It sounded bitter. If she didn't know it before, it was clear her decision was the right one.

He looked at her, his eyes flashing with anger. Then he turned. She watched him storm downhill until his form was swallowed up into the crowd around Flaminio station, his hurt enveloped by the noise of the shoppers haggling over the flea market stalls and the hordes of tourists swarming toward Piazza del Popolo.

28

Con slancio
with enthusiasm. This can also translate to "dash," "leap," "burst," and "abandon," directing the musician to play in this manner.

Francesco Maschiavelli's villa lay on the southern outskirts of Rome. A black Alfa Romeo picked Alba up, on his insistence. She'd sat in the back seat, replaying her exchange with Misha, watching the figurines act out their scene, flattened paper cutouts that fell away, tumbling like a house of cards. The driveway up to the villa was long, flanked by flowering oleander bushes splattered with fuchsia, white and pale pink blooms. The driver pulled up in front of a porch that stretched the front of the cream stone two-story home, now golden in the early evening light. Bougainvillea crept up the arched walkway, paper blossoms folded in translucent pastel shades, punctuated by Roman statues in marble, twisting in contorted poses to best display their musculature. A large, low terra-cotta pot with a tumble of succulents stood beside the door, beneath a wall-mounted marble fountain that trickled a delicate spray over a dancing nymph; a hedonist's hideout. Florin appeared at the door, waving his arm as if welcoming a long-lost relative. As Alba stepped out of the door he flew to her side and kissed her on each cheek.

"*Benvenuta*, Maestra! We're so happy to have you," he gushed, gesturing for her to come up the steps and through the thick wooden door.

It took a moment for her to adjust to the dark inside. The corridor was lined with paintings and Florin led her straight out to the rear terrace, a large wooden table dominating the space, laid with linen, a huge vase at its center filled with purple-blue hydrangeas, cream roses, and a delicate spray of bougainvillea. Francesco appeared at the far end from another door, wearing what looked like a light denim poncho, blue silk scarf tied around his neck.

"Darling! This is wonderful. Florin, come along, give Maestra my best!" Florin left the terrace and Armand appeared a moment later with a tray. A bottle of prosecco leaned at an angle inside an ornate silver ice bucket, beside it a bowl of large green olives, a glass filled with delicate hand-twisted grissini, a board of thin sliced pecorino, and a plate of tiny crisped bread topped with ricotta, minute twirls of anchovies dotted with capers and a grind of pepper. Alba's mouth watered.

"*Grazie*, now leave us awhile, boys," Francesco said with a wave of his hand. The men retreated.

Francesco lifted the bottle of prosecco out of the silver bucket and poured them each a glass. "What a delight to have you here, Maestra."

"Alba, please."

"I've never met a Sardinian with a name like that."

"Me neither," she replied, taking a sip. "I was born at sunrise. I blame the post-birth hormones, or some latent act of rebellion on my mother's part. In every other respect she was as traditional as they come."

"You ought to have been named after a saint like everyone else."

They laughed. Francesco nodded as if the information revealed the answer of a long calculation.

"I've spent several days at the *conservatorio*, as you know," he began, smoothing his thinning hair with a deliberate hand. "It's been the most difficult few days. Casting is a horror. I think I had expected to find young Albas chomping at the bit."

"And instead?"

"Instead, I found them lacking the intensity required for the part. Some had an inkling but quite the wrong look, others appeared to be just as I pictured the part but their playing lacked ferocity. I don't want to make a story about a butterfly. I want a lioness to lead this project. I want to make something different from anything I've done before. I'm even thinking to make it without dialogue, or at least pared down to the skeleton of words. I want this picture to have a French sensibility and an Italian rendering of beauty in all its devastating forms."

Alba took another sip and reached for an anchovy crostini, the saltiness a perfect match to the dry sparkle of the prosecco.

"In short, Alba, I want you."

Alba swallowed just before the contents of her mouth spluttered out in shock.

He looked at her square. She threw her head back with a throaty laugh.

"Exactly!" he cried. "I want abandon, a woman with life, who takes her music seriously, passionately, but can laugh without a care."

"Francesco, that's the most ridiculous thing I've ever heard."

He filled her glass. "It's the smartest thing I've ever said."

"Getting me drunk is not going to convince me of anything other than you're teasing me."

Francesco's face relaxed into a studied thoughtfulness. Alba wondered if this was the face he'd pull when having portraits taken for newspaper articles.

"Trouble is, Alba, I'm not. It came to me like a bolt, how all my best ideas arrive, from the cosmos, darting across space and time and I follow like the hungry disciple I am. Maestra, I'm asking you to be my star."

Alba shook her head. Noticing his expression, she straightened. The man was serious.

"Francesco, I'm so touched, truly, but I don't know the first thing of your world. It would be like me asking you to play a concerto."

"I'm not asking you to perform anything other than what you

do. I've looked through my script and realized it's an abomination. I've written a fairy-tale version of you, in essence. I don't want a young girl doing a brutal impersonation. I want the real thing. A grown woman. A woman who knows herself and is not scared of the fact. Who doesn't need to fit in, or prove herself, is not lost in vanity, or the desire to be desired, does not label herself by anyone's standards but her own. And above all this, chases only the compulsion to lose herself in music, follow it, unpick it, lay it out for others to understand and feel things we all scarcely allow ourselves to do in real life. She *is* music—the only universal truth that exists."

The words hit her like a dart. The sincerity with which he spoke lacked posturing, theatrical swagger, his tone honest, a melody with the deceptive simplicity of a Ravel before the orchestra swells.

"I think you love music as much as I," she answered, feeling a complex complicity strike between them like a splinter of electricity.

"I'm tired of doing what is expected of me, Alba, or what I've come to expect from myself," he confided, "and I wonder if we haven't met, by some delectable twist of fate because, perhaps, you are too?"

A delicate fringe of lyricism gilt his words. For a moment she second-guessed his truth. But the words hit home. It was one of the first thoughts she'd had after the Rachmaninoff night. It was what had propelled her to pull away from Misha with the same power as she'd raced toward him. The prospect of doing something so improbable did seem exciting for a flash. Perhaps she'd drunk too fast.

"You're wondering whether I'm insane. Perhaps I am too? But this is how I see it," he offered. "We couch the story on your terms. I want this to be about a pianist's process, as if we've opened the door into a pianist's private world. I want to give my audience a sensation of being inside a woman's inner musical world, not just the bravado of performance but the arduous practice, the inner barriers to overcome in order to express what the composer requires."

Composer. The word made Vittorio crash into her mind. His mesmerizing score filled her. "Francesco, it sounds extraordinary. But I am not an actress."

"Exactly. I'm not interested in performance. This will almost be a documentary of sorts, with a poetic lens. It's genius. It's the perfect way to allow your fans to see more than you at the piano."

"Why would I want that?"

He smiled, unhurried. "Because you're a trailblazer, Maestra Fresu. We have a chance to bring your music not just to the people who can afford the concerts, but to those who don't know that music even exists. We can bring the celestial to the real people of Italy. To the world. It's time. We've stayed in our artistic bubble too long."

Florin popped his head around the door leading to the terrace. Francesco looked up. "Seafood, I think," he said. Florin nodded and disappeared once again.

"You don't need to agree this moment, Alba, but at least tell me you'll consider it. We could make something so very beautiful."

They clinked to that, Alba's head fizzy with prosecco and the prospect of even considering following this maestro's lead. Armand, Florin, and several other young men performed a miraculous dance of gastronomy soon after, laying down plates of thin slices of sea bass carpaccio followed by charred langoustines and then a twist of linguini with the most delicious lobster sauce Alba had ever eaten. This was trumped by a bowl of steamed clams and mussels dripping with garlic, parsley, and wine-infused juices and a crisp salad of leaves and tomatoes grown, Florin announced with pride, in their vegetable garden beyond the terrace, which he promised to offer a tour of after the meal. Armand filled their glasses for the last time.

"Francesco, is this what you do for everyone you wish to work with?"

"This is what I do for those I adore," he replied, wiping his mouth with the linen napkin and standing up. "We'll take coffee and liqueur in the other room, boys, *sì?*"

He signaled for Alba to follow along the length of the terrace, past his fruit trees dotted throughout the large garden and into a powder pink walled room. In the center stood an oval Victorian settee, with padded velvet seating all around. On either side, large antique sideboards were crowded with black-and-white signed framed photographs. Chaplin leaned on his stick with a personal message to Francesco, beside Gina Lollobrigida and Sophia Loren, every opera singer Alba admired, Paul Newman, Marlon Brando, and almost every icon imaginable had their image and message preserved for all to see. Alba was a child in a candy shop.

"Wonderful people, all of them," Francesco began. "I am so very lucky. I've worked with true artists. I'm drawn to them. They are drawn to speak our truths. This is beauty. As Keats, the darling little English man, said when he came to our beautiful city to die, 'A thing of beauty is a joy forever.'"

Alba looked over to him with a smile.

Armand entered with a tray of fresh coffee, a plate of biscotti, and two glasses.

"Vin santo, yes?" Francesco asked with a grin. "To bless our holy plans."

He lifted a glass for her and they clinked. His grand piano had pride of place in the window. "She's a beauty," Alba said.

"I'm not going to ask you to play," he said, "I've already put you on the spot enough for one night."

Alba felt the sweet dessert wine warm her cheeks. She welcomed the spin, the surprising conversation, being in the proximity of a living legend and having the opportunity of working with him, it was a heady mix. She lifted the lid, wound the stool up a little, touched the keys. It was an antique, restored well with carved swirling ornate legs. Vittorio's music whispered inside. Her fingers wandered up the keyboard from the center. As they fell deep into the notes, the wash of sounds from outside his room rippled through her, those melancholic flecks she'd heard, the push and pull of the left hand in counterpoint to the lyricism of the melodic line rushed through her. It was as if she'd already played it. She waded deeper into that memory. She knew this tune; Vittorio had painted their love affair with notes. There was the familiarity, the pain, the elation, the brutal beauty of their love beneath her fingers, new and revisited, a grief and celebration. It was fire and air and space and loss in an incessant twisting turn of runs, luminous chords, angelic tones, earthed bass.

Her hands stopped.

She looked at Francesco.

His eyes were moist. "I shan't beg you, Alba, because that is cheap."

They held the pause, Alba surprised at her willingness to dip into that musical space, her body leading her toward the place her mind put up an abject, now losing, battle.

"I'll give you some time to think, of course," he murmured.

"I think my answer frightens me."

Francesco's face lit up. He brought her glass over to the piano and they clinked to artistic terror.

When Alba returned to her darkened apartment the alcohol and food was shifting toward a headache of excess. She poured herself a large glass of water in the kitchen and returned to her living room to drink it. Another evening she might have dialed someone for company. Perhaps those escapes were avoidance tactics after all? Diversions. She'd always refused to see them couched in those terms. Her lovers satisfied a drive, which was her right to explore, enjoy, and then abandon. Now her head flitted toward the fascination of Francesco's film. If she chose to go ahead would she be reaching more people like Francesco said, or attracting more attention for the sake of what? Adoration? Exhibitionism? Rampant extroversion?

She picked up the phone. Dante answered after a few rings.

"Yes, I heard he was going to wine and dine you into an offer you'd find hard to refuse."

She always loved the way Dante plowed into the middle of a conversation as if they'd just left one room and carried on talking into another.

"He told you?"

"He insinuated. But I've been around people long enough to

sniff out a motive. Should have me on one of those TV detective shows."

"What do you think?"

"I think it sounds amazing. Terrifying for you I'd imagine. But worthwhile."

"Did he feed you too?"

Dante chuckled. "As always the ball is in your court. I know you've been restless these last few months. I can feel it. You like to tackle things that are going to stretch you. This will do this. And some."

"Isn't it just vanity? A little ego dance for the concert pianist who fancies herself a starlet?"

"Call it that. Or call it an impulse to explore, a dive into the unknown. What's that word the Americans keep saying in their interviews now, oh yes, a challenge. If we face the facts, the record companies know you're not keen on doing any more recordings for a while. You've been wanting to cut back on your concert schedules. I'm sure you're not ready to ease back on the little luxuries you enjoy though, no? Perhaps taking this artistic gamble will bring you just what you need right now?"

"I think I've had too much good food and wine to think tonight."

"I'm your *digestivo*."

"Thank you, Dante. I would be lost without you."

"You would be someone else's favorite client is what you'd be."

She could hear the smile in his voice. "Now you're talking to me like I'm one of those fragile opera stars."

"Sleep on it, Alba."

"*Grazie, buona note*, Dante."

She hung up and saw her answering machine blinking with messages.

She pressed play. Raffaele's voice sounded weak, his vowels more prolonged than usual. She listened to him asking when she'd next be in town. Would she come and see him sooner rather than later?

Then he clicked off. Her apartment fell silent.

Her regular visits to him in Milan had become erratic over the past few years, but they made time to talk on the phone at least one a month. She'd met his partner, Luca, several times. He was a beautiful banker who took pride in his physique and kept himself to himself. Raffaele did the talking for the both of them and Alba adored watching their gentle dance, Luca creating in the kitchen, listening to Raffaele's stories with that Swiss-Italian reserve of his. Precision oozed out of Luca, his every movement deliberate, efficient. It was hard to picture him breaking a sweat, though it was clear the man spent hours training his body into an athletic form a professional would envy. They'd met on the trading floor, Raffaele had explained, and had navigated the same circles until entering into a relationship. Raffaele was besotted. He lit up when Luca was with them and when he wasn't, a large portion of the conversation was devoted to relishing the delightful details about the well-planned romantic surprises Luca came up with, which to Alba's mind involved a lot of spending and a great deal of outdoor pursuits followed by fine dining; one weekend in Paris, another in the Swiss Alps, escapades to Amsterdam, Seville, Barcelona. It was wonderful to see her best friend living his very best life.

She looked at the flashing number on the machine. She'd catch a train the next morning. It would be the perfect opportunity to see her choices from afar and devote some well-needed time to her friend.

Luca answered the door. He wasn't the resplendent male specimen Alba had come to know. His face was a shade of forgotten stubble and his cheeks lacked the inner glow he cultivated. He was wearing a light T-shirt which may have been pajamas. Off Alba's look he apologized, "Thank you so much for coming, Alba. Raffaele's going to be delighted."

"No need to thank me, Luca, I'm always happy to see you two, I had a few days free too, which was an added bonus."

Luca didn't reflect her grin.

"Come into the kitchen, will you?"

Alba followed him down the wide corridor, past Raffaele's original artwork acquisitions, strange bronzes, paintings that lured and repelled. She teased him for the fact. He'd call her a pleb. She'd call him a poser.

"Luca, is everything okay?"

"No."

He leaned against the counter, arms folded.

"You can tell me anything, Luca, you know that."

"The drugs have stopped supressing the HIV virus."

The room became marble. Frozen in a singular breath of sculpted time.

"Maybe weeks," Luca said, tears fighting out now, dripping off his chin.

Alba wrapped her arms around him. His tight torso pressed against hers now, shuddering tears. She was glad for it. Hers caught in her throat, stones in her chest, that couldn't fight out even if she wanted them to.

They pulled away.

"Is he sleeping?" Alba asked.

"He was. He's so anxious to see you."

Alba nodded. The movement loosened something in her. She felt the heat of tears wet her eyes now.

They turned back along the corridor and into the lounge. Her shoes clicked across the granite floor toward the bedroom. Luca opened the door.

Alba's best friend was disappearing into the bedsheets. His skeletal frame lifted and fell, the space between each breath erratic. His skin was gray, hanging on to the bones like thin paper. Beneath she could see the enlarged lymph nodes at his neck and along his chest swell with disease. His eyes opened in the half light, rays clawing in through the narrow cracks between the shutters.

She sat down and took his hand. A wan smile stretched across his face.

"Day, made," he said, his voice weak, gone the babble she knew and loved.

"*Tesoro*. Thank you for calling me," she said, willing the tears to disappear, willing her panic to dissipate.

"You can cry, Alba. Everyone else has. Me included."

She laughed then, tears spattering out the corners of her eyes.

"Laughing's good too," he said.

"You're a jerk, Ra'."

He swallowed with difficulty. Luca dipped a small stick with a foam sponge on the end into some water and moistened Raffaele's mouth. There were several sores in the cracks.

"I'm not scared, Alba. I thought I would be. But I'm not."

"I am," she whispered. "I love you."

"I love you more. Present company excepted." He smiled at Luca. "I don't know how I'll feel when it's here, but I feel I'm already there, you know?" His arm waved into the distance. "I've done enough hallucinogens to appreciate where I'm going."

Alba let his words wash over her. He'd been so open with her about his life on the gay scene, the hedonist lifestyle of the rich traders in Milan, his freedom to enjoy every whim at no cost, until his diagnosis. She'd held him when he'd sobbed, some latent Catholic guilt searing through him, as if his HIV was some kind of retribution. She'd fought him out of it, sat with his bouts of depression over the phone wherever she was working, listened to lengths of silences, tidal waves of joy, of manic energy, high on life, or cocaine, or any other substance that was in vogue at the time.

They breathed into the space for a moment.

"It's all such a beautiful act of surrender, Alba. We've talked about this before. Now I know what that means. In my bones."

Alba's tears fell. She slipped her hand into his.

"I'm going back home," he whispered. His breathing became a little more labored then. His hand felt clammy. Alba and Luca watched him slip into sleep.

She spent the rest of the day in that room. That night she slept in their spare room. The following day she did the same. She called Dante to rearrange a recording of Chopin's nocturnes, but he could stall for another two days, no more.

"He's really serious about going home to his parents," Luca said, resigned, over coffee whilst Raffaele slept.

"You'll go with him?"

"Masquerading as his nurse."

Alba nodded, a familiar grief filling her.

There was a noise from the bedroom. When they walked in Raffaele was seated up on the edge of the bed. They rushed to him.

"I think I need to throw up again," he croaked, struggling to lift himself off the bed. They hooked their arms under his and helped him toward the bathroom. Alba felt his bones against her, his spine poking out like scales along the hunching curve of his back. He refused to let them inside. "I can do this alone today, honestly," he said, closing the door behind him.

He came out after a few minutes and reached for her hand. They walked across the room on fragile steps, then she eased him onto the bed and lifted his feet up till he was comfortable again. It took a minute or two for his breath to return to normal.

"I've found myself doing the proverbial list of regrets," he whispered, his throat scratchy. "Not coming out. Not always jumping into the unknown. Not like you. I'm so very proud of you, Alba."

"I don't want to go back to Rome."

"Don't put life on hold, Alba. If I've learned anything these past years it's that."

"I don't want to say goodbye."

"So don't, my friend."

She reached for his hand, then kissed his forehead. He felt cool to the touch.

"You're brave, Alba. Don't leave it too late with your dad."

Alba looked at him without reply.

"The blessing of dying—I'm free to say what I think, shift a few truths before it's too late."

"Will this hurt, Doctor?" she asked, trying to match his glibness.

"A little."

"I'm in no position to refuse you, am I?"

He laughed at that. Alba noticed several of his teeth were gray with decay.

"You're pretty similar to him."

Alba ignored the bristling up her spine.

"Fear runs your life in more ways than you think. Like your father you've been protecting a broken heart for too long."

"My father?" she said, trying not to argue and failing.

"You saw him at his most vulnerable and he can't forgive you that. Lover boy Vittorio saw you at yours, and since then you've made sure you've called the shots."

Alba shifted in her seat.

"You can get angry even though I'm sick, Alba."

Her voice was glassy, brittle. "I'm nothing like my father."

Raffaele looked at her, eyes smiling. It was irritating and comforting in equal measure. There was no time for her to feel affront and he knew it. It was why he was saying these things in the first place.

"Women are judged harshly when they don't follow the rules, Raffaele."

"And men aren't?"

He looked over toward the picture of him and Luca framed on his bedside table. "No one is invincible, Ra'."

"You're telling me?"

Alba took his hand in hers.

"Your dad asked me about you. The last time I went home."

Alba looked at him without blinking.

"He didn't want me to tell you. I guess I'm not holding my promises these days."

Alba's chest tightened.

"He showed me his framed picture of you. It's of your concert in Venice in 1989. One of the ones that had been televised, no?"

Alba nodded.

"Maybe it's time, Alba."

He struggled for breath. Luca rushed in and administered some pills. Raffaele seemed woozy after that. She watched him fall asleep, the gawky teenager she'd lain upon the forest floor with fighting for view, a stranger she'd known once. Luca stepped inside.

"I'll arrange a nurse to help you when he gets home," Alba said under her breath.

"His mother has already done that."

"Do they know?"

"Everything."

"How are you?" She shook her head. "Stupid question."

He shrugged. "Strangely calm. Trying to hold on to the tiny moments. He's teaching me how to deal with all of this, really."

Alba smiled, feeling the three days of broken sleep catch up with her. Her legs were hollow, her thoughts misting like a slow-rolling fog.

"This has been special for both of us, Alba, thank you."

Alba stood and hugged him. "I don't know how to be strong right now," she whispered into his shoulder. The sobs jerked out of her. He didn't move. Her tears ebbed before Luca spoke. "Everything feels momentous and simple. Death teaches us life." He laughed at himself then. "Stop me before I sound like one of those hippie books, *sì?*"

"I'll call every day," she said, straightening.

Alba pulled away, nodded her head, pretending her tears weren't streaming, knowing that each moment near Raffaele made it harder to step away. She took a breath and walked out of the apartment. Luca closed the door behind her.

The stairwell underfoot fell away with each sob, nothing but the air beneath it, the sensation of falling without the possibility of hitting ground, a purgatorial tumble, unending numbness, spiked by waves of tears that surged through her, tidal, brutal.

Outside, the world rushed by her, like painted scenery. She felt Raffaele's words course through her. She stopped in at a payphone and dialed Dante's number.

"Get me out of the recordings, Dante."

"Fine, how are you?"

Alba's breath sped up.

"Are you okay, Alba?"

"No. I'm awful. I don't want to give some greedy record company one more minute of my time. I'm going to stay in Milan with my best friend because he's dying, Dante."

"You know how this works, Alba. You pull out now and we're in breach. It will cost you. Literally, not just figuratively."

"I'll settle it with some of what I'll get from the film?"

"Some?"

"My best friend is dying."

Alba heard him take a few breaths, easing them into calm.

"You've already changed this contract twice, I don't know how patient they're going to be."

"So get your film negotiating cap on and help me out of this fix."

He fell silent.

"Sorry, Dante. I'm a mess. Seeing him like that. I can't leave. I know I can't delay the record company either. And more than that, I'm going to play like an imbecile if I record now."

She listened to Dante take another breath.

"You absolutely sure this is what you want?" Dante asked.

"It is."

They said their farewells, Dante's voice sounding more reticent than she'd hoped. When Luca opened the door to her a little while later he looked confused.

"I'll stay down the street somewhere if that's easier. I don't want to impose on your time with Raffaele. Put me to good use. I'm not great friends with a washing machine but I can learn? I can help with the preparation for his return home? Remind you to eat?"

Luca's face lit with a sad smile.

She'd teased Raffaele for sounding like a monk in training, but his words were beautiful, lotus leaves floating on a still pond, delicate like its blossom, compelling, deceptive in its apparent fragility. In a few days she had tapped into a new world of fear. For the first time in her life she was forced to acknowledge that it may have been driving her more than she'd admit. Her music was unconditional love. Perhaps it was time to find a way to devote herself to other aspects of her life, with the same care and passion? Driven not by the quest to protect herself, or others, but by tapping into the courage to unfurl toward the unknown, embrace vulnerability, and, more than all this, to honor the example set by her best friend as he looked death square in the eye. She did have more of her father's qualities than she would have had the bravery to admit until now.

Three days later Luca and Raffaele set sail for Sardinia. Alba accompanied them to the port of Livorno with a chauffeur-driven car she'd hired for them. The last memory of the boy she once lay beside under the spindle leaves of their *pineta* was his balding head tilted toward Luca's hand, wrapped around the handle of his wheelchair as he pushed him along the gangway.

29

Seconda volta
often repeated sections of a composition will have different endings

Heat waves zigzagged skyward from the scorched tarmac of Catania Airport. A driver waited for Alba beyond the luggage carousel and escorted her to his large black Mercedes. They wound through the parched Sicilian countryside toward the hotel on the coast by the town of Noto. Parts of the scenery reminded her of Sardinia, the long yellow grasses cooked dry in the heat; the rocks seared by the same; tree trunks gnarled with age, creaking out of the ground at acute angles, twisted in the temperature like human figures contorted in contrition. They reached the resort where Maschiavelli's assistant directors had informed her she would be staying along with a filming schedule mailed to her a week ago that appeared to be a feat of human engineering in and of itself. Her suite looked out over the Lido di Noto, a wide bay now dotted with the winding-down crowds of late September, with children back at school, but summer's hold still clasping the crowds in its torching clutch.

There was a knock at the door. Alba opened it.

"*Buona sera*, Maestra Fresu, my name is Giulia, I'm the third assistant director, I wanted to welcome you to the shoot. I'm here to make sure you have everything you need. I'll be your point of contact on set too, whilst the second director is on scheduling and our first, Gianluigi, is Francesco's mouthpiece, in essence."

Seeing Alba's look she backtracked. "*Scusa,* Maestra, you must be tired from your travel day."

"No, I'm fine, it's just you're speaking another language somewhat."

Giulia's face lit up with a smile, highlighting the deep dimples in her cheeks. Her hair was cropped short and lent an efficiency to her bright demeanor.

"I'm sorry, I should have simply said, please ask me for whatever you should need whilst we're working together. I'll see it gets done. We have an appointment scheduled for costume and makeup ahead of shooting, just to go through a few things before we begin. It's in the schedule I'd sent to Dante for you?"

"Yes. I'd read through that, Francesco had said I would be wearing my own stuff?"

"That's fine. We just have a few things for you to try, and Francesco and you will discuss your preferences, of course. A car will be here for you in the morning, Maestra. Your driver is Tomaso. He'll be your personal driver for the shoot during filming and around those times. He's on call for whatever you need."

Alba smiled, a little overwhelmed by the onslaught of information.

"Signor del Piero gave me this package for you also. There are some changes to the score that he wanted to let you have as soon as he'd made them. I know Francesco has spoken to you about the likelihood of changes as we go through and so forth."

"Yes, he has."

"I'll leave you in peace now to rest, we're all delighted to have you on board. Don't be alarmed if some of the crew are a bit tongue-tied, I'm sure you're used to that."

"I'll be the tongue-tied one, you can be sure of that."

The women looked at each other. Giulia's green eyes were alive with the energy of a young woman set to move up the ladder of her career with an inspiring drive, the focused verve of youth. She reminded Alba of herself at that age. Goldstein poked into her mind, a sly comment about her serious approach to music sometimes standing in the way of her exploring the unexpected flair she found as she matured during training. Looking at Giulia she felt a sharper understanding of his sideways comments, even more than she had already.

The next morning Alba arrived on set to a Giulia who looked like she'd already been up for most of the day even though the dawn had just started to peek out over the valley. She offered Alba a coffee and then escorted her to her trailer, parked beside several others within the grounds of a magnificent crumbling villa, complete with a courtyard and long drive. Inside Alba made herself comfortable on a long sofa, sipping her espresso. A few moments later Giulia escorted her to the trailer where Luigi, a makeup artist, set to work on her face with the flurried brush of a painter and Marianna, the hairdresser, twirled her hair to look like her usual tussled mess but with a few more self-conscious flicks. She looked at herself in the mirror when they were done and wondered how they had managed to formulate a more high-definition version of herself. It was as if they'd put her under a magnifying lens, extended a length here, focused the eye there; she was a photograph of herself with the shutter finger holding the power to expand details often hidden.

Vittorio stepped in and stood behind her reflection.

"They've done the same to me," he said, sipping his coffee, "only far less glamorous. Francesco wants me in some of the shots, I guess." Alba met his eyes in the mirror. It looked like they'd emphasized his eyes somehow—had they given him the eyeliner treatment too?

"You're everything they warned me of," Luigi said, looking at Vittorio's reflection, voice dancing.

"Never believe everything you hear, lovely Luigi. I'm even worse than they said."

Without breaking Alba's gaze, he replied, "Ask the maestra."

His expression relaxed then, whilst Alba struggled to hold on to the absurdity of the moment, seated in a makeup chair at the crack of the day, a makeup artist flirting with her first love whilst he shot her conspiratorial looks in the mirror. She drew her mind toward the composition they were filming that morning. Vittorio seemed to intuit her shift because he sat beside her whilst Marianna combed a few stray locks.

"Did you see the corrections I'd made?" he asked.

"Yes, I liked the changes, I think they give a different modulation to the midsection, it cuts through the linear passages of chord progression."

Alba waited for a reply that didn't come. Then he nodded, mulling over her words. "It's such a pleasure to have you with us, Maestra," he said at last, in that infuriating way he'd always had of flipping out an answer in such a way as to be construed as neither truth nor joke.

When Luigi released Alba at last, Giulia was outside waiting to escort her to her trailer even though it was no more than ten paces away.

"It's fine, Giulia, I can find my way."

"No problem, Maestra," she replied, shy of curtsying with her body as well as her tone, before leaving toward the costume trailer.

"She's just doing her job, Alba," Vittorio said, under his breath, "go easy."

"Alright, Vittorio," Alba said, spinning to face him. "We're working together for the next few weeks, in closer proximity—"

He stopped her flow before she could continue. "I don't think I need everyone overhearing us, do you? Come into my room a second, okay?"

"No, not okay."

"Alba, we have work to do before Francesco calls us in and starts messing with my score again. It will be helpful to the both of us. I'm not trying to shut you up."

"Fooled me."

He opened the door to his trailer, beside hers. She took a reluctant step inside, annoyed that her nerves ahead of the first day of shooting were getting the better of her and more so that he knew it.

"Make yourself at home, Alba, they won't call us for a while."

"You seem quite at home."

He paused a beat. "I'm scared shitless," he said.

Alba laughed.

"You knew that already," he added, joining in her laughter.

"I just wanted to see you have the courage to say that, Vitto'. Now we're having an actual conversation. Next time don't keep me waiting so long."

He ran a hand through his hair. Alba noticed him take a swift glance at his reflection.

"I think you missed a bit," she said.

They settled into a new silence.

"I love the changes," she said at last, "I adore the entire score."

"I didn't think you'd be here if you hated it."

"Don't brush off my comments, Vittorio."

"I'm trying to keep you talking."

Alba fell silent for a breath. He looked luminous in this light. It was nothing short of being back in his studio, the taste of his skin, the feel of his breath on her body. That was what she loved about the score. It was a timeless entry into their private world, matrix of codes, melodies, and silences interwoven like a helix, vibrating, luminous, coming from somewhere deep inside each of them. His music allowed them to make love in public. Would she ruin the newfound openness between them by stating the fact?

"It feels fresh and new and familiar and potent. I just want to do it justice," she said.

"I don't know anyone else who could."

They stepped in the protective cool of this coded language. Neither needed to articulate what was written on those staves in words. The morning light caught the fullness of his lower lip, the sharp-edged outline of his mouth. Neither moved their gaze.

Time slipped through the gap.

A knock at the door clipped the pause.

Giulia opened it, revealing her sunny face on the other side.

"Oh, Maestra is here, wonderful, we're ready for you both on set."

They stood and followed Giulia out past the other trailers, the breakfast truck, the electricians carrying in several lights, smoking and joking and arguing as they did. Francesco's entourage surrounded him as Giulia reached the room where they were filming. Alba took in the high vaulted ceilings, decorated with delicate putti twisting through the clouds. Three sets of double doors were cranked open a little, letting light in through the peeling shutters, spidering strips of shade along the aged wooden floor. At the center of the bare space appeared a large black grand piano. Her fingers tingled.

"*Buon giorno*, my darlings," Francesco said, shooting a look to the crowd around them. A hush fell. He led Alba a little way from them. "We're going to do some test shots of the section where I'll cut back to you playing the second movement. We may interweave this with other parts of the orchestrated section, but don't worry about that now. All I would love to see you do this morning is really just get at home with your piano, play through Vittorio's composition in the sections we've talked through, yes?"

"I've recorded in studios before, Francesco, but this looks like you're trying to make me a pop star."

"Don't insult me, Maestra. You couldn't be bubble gum if you tried."

He kissed her hand. He nodded to a young man beside him who bellowed for silence. "That's the first assistant director, Alba," Vittorio murmured. "Does the shouting so Francesco doesn't have to."

After the First's announcement Marianna and Luigi rushed to Alba's side, buffering their work that to Alba's mind hadn't altered since she'd left them a few minutes earlier. Then Giulia ushered Alba to her stool. She took a moment to adjust the height. Another bellow from the First and a small army of electricians stepped into play, cranking the lights up or down, twisting their angles. Alba felt her face heat in the light. Another pair of men twisted the lights from the windows so that now she saw the sunlight was aided by artificial means. Another two adjusted a statue by the double doors so that it was more in view. At a final command the team withdrew in unison. She was alone in the space, a crowd watching from beyond the camera. The First yelled for the camera to roll. A man beside the camera leaning over the man looking through the lens shouted, "Rolling!" A few beats later another interjected with "Speed!"

Silence.

The First's voice dipped into a gentle invitation. "Whenever you're ready, Maestra."

Into the golden hush Alba sounded the opening of the adagio, a pared-down tiptoe through a minor scale with the injection of occasional incidental notes. It was a love letter of few words, a wish, a whisper, a hidden hope. She left the space, disappeared somewhere inside the faint waft of smoke coming from a machine by the far wall, twisting to catch the rays of light rendering them solid forms across the space. She stepped inside the narrow gap between her face and Vittorio's, the silent hum before a kiss, the complicit emptiness thick with expectation. She played the pause they'd sat in a moment ago inside the trailer, the unspoken space, craved, remembered, mourned. She played his touch, tender, precise, tentative, knowing, urgent, unpredictable. The feeling was the cool of a summer's night, filled with the heat of the day, a balm and a memory. The camera didn't cut until she had pressed down into the final note, high on the keyboard, a sigh from far away, an unrequited ending.

Francesco was by her side. The crowd burst into applause, which echoed in the stone-walled room. "Absolutely divine, my darling," he murmured, "I need no more. We'll move on to the next setup now. Thank you, Maestra." His eyes were wet, smiling. He moved off, swallowed into a group of men around the camera.

Vittorio leaned on the piano top. "Thank you, Alba."

"It's my pleasure."

"Yes," he replied, "that's what I wrote."

Francesco darted over to them. "I'd love it if you took a moment to go through the changes with Alba, Vittorio, yes? Gianfranco, my director of photography, will just ease himself here"—his hand gave a generalized twist in space—"but this is not for the camera, we're not here, if you like."

A distinguished-looking gentleman stepped out from the camera, bronzed skin, wearing the blue cotton coat of a hillside watercolorist, and shook both of their hands. "It's a deep pleasure," he said, his voice a purr, his white hair folded over in a neat line, with the demeanor of someone with infinite patience and acute powers of observation, something Alba suspected were intrinsic qualities for anyone working beside Francesco.

Vittorio placed his score upon the stand and reached over Alba to scribble on it, signaling the section they were to alter. Alba could smell his skin. Beneath the cologne, and products they'd powdered his face with, was the unchanged scent she'd purged from memory. The scent she'd found herself summoning when another lover was beside her. It felt like the welcome shade of a forest. Vittorio made a joke now, which crashed her back to the present. The scurry of memory evaporated. The First shouted, "Cut!" and Francesco congratulated them. Vittorio left to return for the hotel soon after and Alba didn't see him the rest of the afternoon, as they continued through the score till the day reached an early wrap and Francesco announced plans to take her and Vittorio for a well-deserved dinner. "I have some things to run through with Gianfranco, but I will see you in the foyer at eight o'clock, *si?*"

Alba waited in the foyer. Vittorio's voice drew her round. He walked up to her and kissed her on both cheeks. No hidden intimacy this time, a clinical press, as you might kiss a distant relative, or colleague. It made Alba wonder whether she hadn't imagined the tender touch back at the dinner after her concert. His black curls were tame, still a little damp from a shower perhaps, and his skin looked like he'd spent the late afternoon in the sun, while she was at the villa being interviewed on camera; at least, his demeanor, if not his golden glow, pointed toward the fact. It was good to see him like this, gone that terse edge she remembered preceding social gatherings. A picture of him surrounded by his manuscript papers on his studio floor unfolded in her mind. She creased the memories into a tight pile and shelved them.

"Francesco just called me and says to go ahead without him. He'll join us a little later perhaps. I think he wanted to go through some stuff with Gianfranco. Not like him to miss a good dinner, must be important."

Alba felt her body tighten a little.

"We can get through one dinner just the two of us and pretend it's not awkward, right?"

Alba sighed. "I'm hungry. Pretending sounds like a sensible option."

They set off into the night with Alba's driver, who had been instructed on where to go by Francesco's driver, on the understanding that he would join them in a little while. They wound toward the hills inland and then toward a farther coast till the seawall promenade gave way to narrow cobbled alleys, so tight Alba worried the car might scratch the side of the small fishermen stone cottages that lined it. At last the car drew to a stop along a shingle beach where a handful of wooden glass-sided huts stood on thick trunks upon the water. The driver pulled up beside one of them and signaled for them to walk along a rickety jetty to one of the huts. Inside the tables were rammed with locals. Alba introduced herself to the owner by the door, whose invisible feathers puffed out in anticipation of their esteemed guest, whom she explained was delayed. The man wiggled his way through the narrow space between the tables to one at the far end, in a corner secluded from the other diners, facing the moonlit sea. He announced they were invited to dive into the long table of seafood antipasti and that Signor Maschiavelli had already ordered their signature seafood linguini to follow.

"Apparently, if you don't eat at least one sea urchin, they put a mark on your family's name," Vittorio whispered as they approached the delectable array of shells on offer. The urchins were halved, their orange flesh inside on show, long purple-blue spikes poking out toward the dishes that surrounded them: fresh squid with sliced potatoes and parsley, thin slices of rare tuna, fillets of sea bass drizzled with olive oil and fresh black pepper beside a bowl of prawns that reminded Alba of the interminable wedding feasts back home.

"It's so great to be around eaters," Vittorio said, without looking at her. "When I'm out with Clare there's so much I can't eat because she has severe allergies. She's also not partial to kissing anyone who's eaten garlic within the hour." He scooped another helping of clams onto his plate.

She looked at him.

"Stop staring, Alba, it's rude," he replied, with a soft smile. "This is me trying to make this process as enjoyable as we can, I'm making up for the tripe I spouted at the *accademia* the other day."

She replayed Misha's session, the sensation of Vittorio working on the opposite side of the corridor, the way his familiar scent had spiraled through her like a golden splinter of energy, ricocheting along the pearls of memories stringing them together in one direct thread before she could stop them.

"I think Francesco is interested in exploring the relationship between composer and pianist," Vittorio began as they sat back down.

Alba shot him a look. His lips lifted in a sideways grin.

"But we're still keeping with the culmination of a live performance at the end of it, no?" she asked, straightening with a brusque shift to business.

"Certainly," Vittorio agreed, echoing her tone. "The dancers are rehearsing every day with our choreographer, but we will film that at the very end of the shoot. The idea of a live piano concerto with original choreography on film is going to break the mold."

They ate in silence for a moment. Vittorio wiped his mouth and his hands, then filled Alba's glass again.

"*Grazie,* go easy," she said, signaling for him to stop pouring. "I've a full day tomorrow."

"Francesco can't believe you've actually agreed to all this."

"Me neither."

"I admire you for jumping into something out of your comfort zone. I've been surrounded by people who are engrained in their routines for so long, I'd forgotten what that felt like."

"Really? Clare is a comet from what I've heard. You both are."

"From the outside things always look different, no?"

"Maybe," she replied, taking another sip of the rich red wine.

"The truth is so subjective, right?" The warmth of his tone eased them toward a conversation she wasn't sure she was ready for.

"Always," she agreed, deciding they had both decided to dodge anything anchored in their past.

"Truth is, my wife yearns for every new tenor she meets. At first it was a bit of a shock. My ego took a bruising."

Alba tried to mask her expression and failed.

"I felt pretty much how you're looking at me right now."

"Egos need checking on a regular basis."

Vittorio nodded.

"Don't misinterpret that for insensitivity."

"It's honest."

Alba wiped her mouth, silencing the thoughts that he was laying a trap for her, twisting the story around to his victimization so she might break down and revisit the pain he'd caused her. She hadn't come to dinner for that. He would leave dissatisfied if that was his goal. His back lengthened. He seemed quite the opposite all of a sudden, eager to let her in to something it appeared he hadn't unburdened to anyone else.

"I'm not grasping for sympathy, Alba. She's away a lot. She asked for space and I gave it. Didn't figure on having to deal with this in return. First time it was like my world had crashed around me. Then we found a way to live with what we both needed. In the end, we both realized that if both partners have the freedom they need and the courage to be honest and respectful, then their marriage actually has a chance of survival."

"Francesco described her as quite a different woman."

"That's her great game. She likes to make people think she's the insecure opera star, trailing her man. But the opposite is true. We both keep up the mask. Maybe that makes us both brave, or really stupid. I'm still deciding."

Alba prized another clam out of its shell. "You think she'd appreciate you talking about her to me like this?"

"She adores being talked about. In the beginning, finding this new way to make the marriage work was liberating. I'd learned the hard way, by being an idiot with you, and I didn't want to gamble her away in the same selfish way. We talked about how it would work, and for a time it brought us both happiness. Now, I'm not so sure."

Alba dipped her bread in the garlicky oil, hoping it might mop up some of the tension in her body too.

"Didn't mean to hijack the conversation like this, Alba."

"So don't. We could talk about the weather. Or politics? That always brings dinners to abrupt ends."

"I'd actually planned on talking about your sublime playing, but I'd imagine you wouldn't take that too seriously."

"Hearing the details of your marriage doesn't feel appropriate either."

Alba watched him soften, grateful his humor tiptoed through. The moment eased away.

"How do you protect your happiness now?" she asked at last.

"I thought you didn't need to hear the gory details."

"I'm nosy."

"Fine. Details: I pretend I am. That's the stark truth."

He gave his mouth a stiff wipe.

"Living with our choices is probably the most adult thing people can do, no?" Alba offered.

"Don't mistake this for a plea for sympathy."

"You're not getting any. I think we're both rather spoiled."

He smiled. "I'd forgotten how easy it is to talk to you."

"I had too."

"Talk to yourself a lot?" His smile was unhurried. It made her feel seen, without judgment.

The waiter cleared their plates and announced that the second course was being prepared. Alba craned to look for Francesco. "Do you think he's standing us up?"

"You know how these things go. I sat in on a meeting with Gianfranco and him the other day and it was midnight by the time we ended. He gets on his creative waves and there's no stopping him."

Alba sighed a laugh.

Linguini arrived suffused with wine and seafood juices beneath a tumble of garlicky crustaceans. They opened a second bottle of wine. Hands sticky and happy, Vittorio launched into a wine-rosy speech. "I've watched your every performance, Alba. Thought about leaving a note every time. Some anonymous bouquet perhaps. But it was cheap. I realized it wouldn't make you hate me less."

"It's not important now, is it? That was another life."

"I need you to know. I want to be able to say that without feeling corny or that you'll feel hemmed in."

He straightened and took a sip of wine.

"Are you admitting you've been stalking me or is this a clumsy way of telling me you think I'm fabulous? Either way I don't think you'll come out unscathed."

She let her fork rest on the side of her plate without a sound. He emptied the last droplet of wine into her glass and caught her gaze. A split second of silence; they returned to the cloistered quiet they once knew, this time as wiser adults, no demands, no regrets, disarming for the compelling sense of liberation within it. In the breath of hush, his honest, unswerving gaze made him look luminous against the blackened sea streaked with watery moonlight.

He signaled to the waiter for the bill.

The moment dissolved as quickly as it had snapped to attention.

They stepped outside. The air was still warm. She looked toward the driver parked at the far end of the jetty.

"You want to sit out for a bit, Alba?" he asked, in the tone of voice she'd pretended to have forgotten but which sent a faraway familiar song twisting through her bones.

"I'd like to, yes," she replied.

Vittorio walked over to the driver and explained they weren't quite ready to leave, then reached her and they stepped down onto the beach and crunched across the shingle toward the shore. The cove was lower than the seawall promenade, sheltering it from view. The moon was a huge luminous cream ball hovering above the midnight-blue horizontal. She fell in beside him. "So we're standing in the light of the archetypal moon," she began, inviting and shirking the moment. "A little trite, no?"

"You're breaking the romance of the moment," he teased, his wry lilt waving through his voice. They watched the water crawl up over the stones and slink back into the deep.

"I want to let you into the truth of my marriage because I ended up with the person most opposite from you, clutching to that daydream so I could blot you out."

Alba felt her chest burn. They stood in a wave of silence for a moment.

"I think we've drunk too much. We'll say things we don't really mean," she said at last. "How many men weave tales about their wives? I'm not into the victim thing if that's where this is headed.

Sounds like the life you've made suits you both. No life is ever going to feel perfect all the time."

He didn't turn toward her, but let his words trickle out into the shadows. "You and I are only together for the next few weeks," he began, "and I might be about to screw up whatever budding professional friendship we have going, but a part of me needs you to know that my relationship with Clare is a mask I wear, that we both wear. It suits us. The idea of divorce is a complicated mess. We've reached a friendship." He bent down and picked up a few stones. "She has her life"—he threw one—"I have mine." They watched the pebble skip moonlit ripples toward the thin onyx line of the horizon. "Together we're musical royalty. We know that. It's a carefully constructed sham. Two consenting adults in a charade, performing it masterfully."

He looked toward her. Alba refused to reply.

She didn't want to urge him on.

"Why do you need me to know?"

"It's a quiet torture," he said at last.

"You chose your façade, Vittorio. You both have."

"No. The torture is hearing the music I created played by the person it's about."

Alba felt waves of ice and heat trace her skin.

"I wrote it for years, Alba. It's us. I know you know. I can hear it when you play."

She'd fallen back inside him at the first bar spiraling out from Misha's room, and now she knew he knew it too. Her mind had shut him out for so long, even after seeing him back at that dinner, all the way until the music met the air. The sound of him, of them, of the space that hummed in the heart of their connection could be expressed in that score alone. She straightened, holding fast to her determination. "*This* is the conversation that's going to screw up our professional relationship, Vittorio."

"I disagree," he murmured, reading between her words, sensing the pull between them and not shirking it with sarcasm this time.

"You'll make me disappear all over again if we carry on," she whispered.

His face softened, his voice smooth, almost a murmur, as if the sea were listening. "I want to breathe so much life into you that your feet won't touch the ground, Alba." Gone was the sound of a man trying to prove his point. This wasn't someone yearning for sympathy. "I want your light to shine so that it eclipses everything else and I can bask in it."

Alba stood motionless. "Easy words, Vittorio," she said at last.

She watched him draw a breath. He looked into her. "I've never stopped being in love with you. Stubborn, powerful, unpredictable you."

She didn't want the tear to streak her cheek, but it left its watery trail, an embossed admission that she might feel as much as he.

"I've been writing this piece since I met you."

His fingers wrapped around hers. He lifted her wrist and kissed the inside of it like the first time they'd touched in his studio.

"We don't have to act on this feeling, Vittorio."

His eyes lifted to hers. "Tell me to stop."

Her lips found his. His tongue wove around hers.

Twenty years of forgetting and remembering flooded her body.

He pulled away. "I'm scared, Alba."

She let him see her. "Tell me to stop," she answered.

She reached for his hand and led him toward the rocks that huddled at the far end of the cove, beneath the seawall that rose above. She pressed him against the cool of their stone. He pulled away, bending down to kiss her ankles. His tongue traced her thigh. His mouth stopped a breath away where it met the other. She could feel the heat upon her but not the touch of his lips. He didn't move. Neither did she. Then his face rose to meet hers.

Their lips sealed a pact.

Their breaths filled the shadows, the sole witness to their lovemaking the moon, drowning the memory of their tryst as it disappeared into the black sea.

30

Glissando

a continuous sliding from one pitch to another (a true glissando), or an incidental scale executed while moving from one melodic note to another (an effective glissando)

The crowd around the camera sprouted as Noto's market rose to life. Giulia and her assistants worked hard to keep the onlookers at bay. News of Maschiavelli's shoot had made a fast loop of the island. Alba found herself being photographed when she least expected it, the taste of what film stars might have to endure a sour introduction to a different world and one she longed for no permanent place in. Francesco cooed in her ear, "Giulia and her team will keep the people away, you're not to worry about them, you understand?"

"I do, but I'm struggling to understand why the shot of me strolling through the market is so necessary, Francesco?" Marianna gave a third twist to one of her locks toward the back of her hair, spindling it around the thin point of her comb, whilst Luigi passed a second brush of translucent powder over her cheeks. "Isn't it a little contrived?"

Francesco shooed the makeup and hair duo away, dipping his voice into the reassuring tone he used to great effect. "What we're achieving with this shot is a sleek look into the process of making this film as well as the performance aspect. It will give grit. Authenticity. And it will be quick. We're only here for a few hours and then I'm taking you for lunch to my favorite little spot."

Alba didn't want to be lured by food. She brushed away her impatience in order to get on with the task in hand. Tiredness was seeping through. She and Vittorio had skimmed the night, lifting from their slumber to fill her bed with pictures of the light off the bay skimming his outline, the taste of his mouth, the scent of his skin clinging to her. Francesco gave her a twinkle that reminded her she was in safe creative hands. The quicker this was done, the better.

He traced what he wished her route to be through the market; past the huge trunks of wood upon which fishmongers slammed their enormous tuna steaks, past the carts festooned with lemons, knobbly unwaxed skins beside towered crates of blood oranges, some spliced open to reveal their ruby crimson fruit inside. On "action" she replicated his route and onward, past tables loaded with nuts and nougat, tiny darkened bakeries snuck beyond squat wooden doorways, the smell of their fresh loaves making her mouth water. At last the First called "Cut!" and Giulia announced lunch.

The crew, whom Alba had come to love for not just their work ethic but their incessant stream of food descriptions that underpinned the breaks between takes—what they'd eaten that morning, on other shoots, whose grandmother cooked the best sauce—now headed toward the food truck. Large polystyrene boxes were distributed to the line of hungry men. Inside, the usual array of smaller boxes containing fresh pasta, a meat dish, a vegetable side, bread rolls, cheese, and a small glass of wine. Giulia reached Alba as she walked toward the line to join, as usual. "Maestra, we'll be walking to Francesco's trattoria, it's this way." She signaled for her to follow.

"It's a select group of people," Giulia added, under her breath, "the crew is staying behind." It was clear Giulia was keen to point out the selection included her too. Alba was glad. The young woman brought a little sunshine wherever she was, and Alba appreciated being able to rely on her to keep her in the loop at all times. She had a fierce, quick intelligence, the ability to build a tight rapport with both the crew and the performers with an effortlessness that Alba knew was no mean skill. Gauging from the balance on set, it was clear, as always, that women had to work twice as hard to gain the respect and acumen of men their equals, or inferior even in skill, within this industry as much as it was in her own.

Vittorio appeared, crisp white linen shirt open just enough to reveal the taut outline of his clavicle and an edge of muscle on his upper chest. He walked across the street toward Alba and took her elbow in the gentle cradle of his hand, planting a kiss on either cheek. "I didn't want to wash you off my skin this morning," he whispered.

Giulia walked over to welcome him. He turned away from Alba and greeted her with the same kisses. Alba invested nothing into the stirring of her stomach. This ridiculous spike of possessiveness had no place in whatever had reignited between them that night on the beach, nor the delicate dance they had welcomed each night since. Alba observed her adolescent knee-jerk impulses at a comfortable distance, like weather, watching them pass from afar, listening to the quiet beyond, understanding their connection went far deeper than any mild flirtations at work, which she, more than most, understood was a necessary part of living and working alongside people in close proximity. In this industry the lines between professionalism and a tactile attachment to colleagues were even more blurred than in the music world. Everybody on set kissed one another, even if they were greeting each other again after lunch hour. Colleagues embraced at the simplest remark and laughter was always loud. Francesco was clear to set the bar on that point.

Francesco led the group down several twists of alleys until they filed into a tiny cave of a trattoria, low ceiling curved above, one single table taking over the space. The owner danced around Francesco, his male entourage fluttering beside him. Wine, homemade, of course, Francesco announced, came pouring out in a chain of carafes from the tiny counter at the back followed by pasta alla Norma, ridged tubes coated with a robust red sauce and fried cubes of eggplant with enough garlic to ward off ills of any kind, supernatural or no. After this, the table was filled with large platters of seared tuna steaks, a finger thick, pink in the middle and doused with nutty olive oil, a squirt of fresh lemon, and a generous crack of pepper. Fresh salad plates were dotted beside, bitter pan-fried *cicoria* drizzled with chili and oil and bowls heaving with more steamed artichokes than they could eat. The party mopped their plates dry with fresh rolls and when the coffees were passed around a large tray piled with tiny cannoli accompanied it, brought in from the *pasticceria* next door on Maschiavelli's insistence, which, he announced, swaying more than usual, cheeks purple with wine and grappa, was famous for these miniature delicacies. When no one could move, the owner insisted everyone have another shot of his family's limoncello. There was an ignored collective groan, then a toast to his hospitality.

"On the last shoot," Giulia began, half to Alba across from her, more toward Vittorio seated beside, "Francesco threw the most outrageous wrap party. I've seriously never seen so much food. Not even at my cousin's wedding!"

Vittorio sniggered at that, flashing one of his winning smiles. He didn't offer them to many. "I think Alba knows something about overfeeding, no? Sardinians trump the lot of us when it comes to that?"

Alba felt her eyebrow rise.

"Oh, I don't know," Giulia added, before Alba could reply. "The last time I was in Florence I ordered a Fiorentina steak, and it literally could have fed my entire family."

"Don't believe the mock modesty of a Florentine, Giulia," Alba quipped. "It's what they call humor." She shot Vittorio a snigger, which Giulia mirrored. He pulled a face.

Giulia wiped her mouth for the second time. Alba found her to often feel more comfortable discussing timetables and pickups than casual conversation. Did Signora Elias spy the same in her at a young age? She recalled the way she would offer gentle advice about loosening up every now and then, which Alba ignored, of course.

"So," Giulia began, swerving the conversation back to business, "Francesco is going to move setup back to the villa now, neither of you will be needed till early evening. He'll be taking a look at the rushes later too before the night shots, he'd love you to watch with him?"

"Rushes?" Alba asked.

Giulia flashed her a smile. "Sorry, the rough cuts, from the other week. The first shots from the villa. We view them in case we need to retake, you know, before they're developed and graded and so forth. I saw a few the other day. You are absolutely wonderful, Maestra."

"You don't have to stroke my ego. I think I should be doing more of that to you. Do you have any idea what an amazing job you're doing?"

She watched Giulia's cheeks turn a darker pink.

"Have you always been drawn to this business?"

"Since I can remember. But my first passion was music. I studied at the *conservatorio* and then when I finished my ten exams, I went to university instead. My dad wanted me to be a lawyer."

"Everyone wants their kids to be a lawyer rather than work in the arts, no? That's the contradiction of our society. We prize ourselves as the birthplace of all the *belle arti*, but when a young adult expresses a professional interest it's as if they're from another planet, imbeciles even. We Italians are marvelous at hypocrisy."

"Says the speaker of the people who just ate like a queen—at someone else's expense."

Seeing her expression, Vittorio flashed Giulia a smile to reassure her he was joking.

"Here's some unsolicited advice—"

"More?" Vittorio interjected before Alba could finish. "The poor girl's back at work in a minute!"

"Only listen to the father when he talks sense," Alba overlapped without giving Vittorio another moment's attention. "The rest of the time, just follow your gut."

"Yes, Giulia, do listen to *Signora* Alba. Didn't you just watch her follow her gut through lunch?" Vittorio teased.

Giulia stood up and pushed her chair in. Alba felt the uncomfortable sensation that somehow the young woman had intuited something more about her nights with Vittorio than she cared to acknowledge. After all, she did seem to know what was happening to everyone at all times, why would they be any different? The rest of the table began to rouse to professional life once again. "I'll call your drivers?" she asked, once again her usual breeze.

"No need," Vittorio interrupted, standing up too. "I've made some arrangements for the afternoon, if that's alright with you? We'll get to the set for our call time tonight."

Giulia nodded, her cheeks flush with good food and wine. Vittorio let her take a step out of earshot before squeezing next to Alba as the crowd began to file out, hooking his arm in hers. "Taking Alba for some fresh air, Maestro!" he hollered back to Francesco, catching his questioning look. "The feast was beyond description—now I need to walk it off!" Alba joined in his laughter and let him lead her outside.

"What is going on, sir?" she asked, letting her hand reach up toward his bicep.

"I'm escaping small talk. God, I thought I was going to fall asleep over lunch. She's a sweet girl and does her job well but there is only so much I can listen to when all I want is to run a finger along your delicious thigh."

His arm wrapped around her waist and their pace sped up.

"Are we late for something, Vittorio?"

"Etna is a bit of a drive away, but if I've calculated correctly, we'll be back just in time."

Alba drew to a stop. "Excuse me? You're taking me to a live volcano?"

"You're keeping up, well done."

"Have you told Giulia? She'll be in trouble if they find out. It's her job to know where we are, you know."

"That's why I've hired my own car. No one will know a thing, unless you've cultivated a habit for gossip?"

He gestured toward the two-seater Alfa Romeo Spider parked before them, its top rolled back. Alba shook her head with a laugh. "Is this your finest performance of my Italian lover? We must be more middle-aged than we'd like to admit."

"Cynic."

"Learned from the best."

He cupped her face in his hands and kissed her before she could stop him. What did it matter if anyone saw? The gesture caught her off guard. She would have liked to relax into it more, but the idea of making such a public statement didn't sit with her. Not yet.

She pulled away. "I don't think I need anyone to know, Vittorio."

"That's a shame," he replied, opening the door for her. "I want to yell it from the rooftops."

Alba shot him a look.

"Sorry, too overtly Italian for you, Ms. Control?"

"Get in and drive."

Together, they left Noto, heading north for the foothills of Etna. When they arrived a few hours later and started to hike, Vittorio didn't stop until they reached the first expanse of blackened hills, undulating granules of dried lava stretching out toward cloudless blue, tufts of fuchsia flowers sprouting at unexpected intervals, clumps of trees creating shade, reaching up out of the fertile rock beneath. He reached for her hand. Their feet scuffed along the black dust, giving way to it as it fell downhill off their steps, tiny rubble tumbling. Patches of green gave way now to a horizon curved with black dunes.

"It's like another planet," Alba murmured, her tone hushed in the formidable surroundings.

"I wanted to share it with you. It reminds me of us."

Alba turned to him. "Destructive?"

"A force beyond our control."

She looked at his face, lit with the golden rays of the afternoon. "I like the poetry in your music better."

He pulled his sunglasses up onto his head. His fingers now a gentle cradle around her face. He kissed her eyelid. His lips lingered there. "This," he whispered, "this intimate space, Alba. I've never shared it with anyone like I can with you."

"I've never heard a volcano described as intimate."

He pulled away and planted a full kiss on her cheek now. "Alright, glib it off, Alba, come on," he said, reaching for her hand, leading her back down toward the roadside where he had parked. They crossed it, walking toward a small bed and breakfast opposite. An elaborate plan was unfolding before her and she was caught between the thrill of him having organized their interlude and feeling like she'd rather have had a say in the matter.

He stepped into the lobby and checked them in. Perhaps there was no harm succumbing to the adolescent excitement of whatever he had in mind after all? What was the harm in posing as Mr. and Mrs. del Piero for an afternoon anyway? Inside their small room Vittorio opened the shutters to let the view of Etna's hillside into their space. Alba watched him undress her. She let him revisit the first time he'd tasted her. This time she didn't flee. This time she welcomed her pleasure without confusion, nor guilt, but with the outspread wings of a woman who chose to open. This time they were equals. Each touch was like a conversation, a piano piece for four hands composed in real time; no longer a semitone away from the truth.

They lay beside each other, the blackness of Etna beyond their naked bodies.

"I wanted to make some space for us, Alba, rather than sneaking into each other's rooms like naughty children, scared Giulia would discover one of us in the other's place."

Alba turned her face toward his. He was beautiful against the crisp white of the pillow, his black hair a stark frame for the face she could stare into for longer than she was ready to say.

"Can we have space? In the end, this is blissful make-believe, no?" she murmured.

"I don't think I'm ready to share you."

They looked at each other for a moment.

"Perhaps you have to be. I'm sharing *you*," she said.

"I'm not going to mess with this. Not again. It's too precious."

She let her lips reach his. Her hips rose over his now. He slipped inside her.

She stopped moving. "So let's not mess with it," she said, feeling the sting of vulnerability and leaning in to it. His hips rose, pressing himself deeper inside.

"Take all of me, Alba," he said, his abdomen tensing as he rose higher still, his hands reaching around for her back, pulling her mouth down onto his.

Their foreheads pressed together. Their hips moved with tender strokes.

The afternoon eased into early evening before they made their excuses at reception and drove back to set, his hand in hers, like the promise they'd always wished to gift one another.

Giulia greeted them as they pulled into the driveway of the villa and parked beside the makeup truck. "Did you have a lovely afternoon, Signori?" she asked, fresh with the glow Alba had come to expect of her first thing in the morning, rather than this late at night. She was indefatigable, and it made Alba want to remind her to not let anyone sap her of it.

"Wonderful," they answered in unison.

"How sweet, Alba," Vittorio added, with a sardonic slur, "we've even started to speak as one." Giulia led them through to a trailer where Francesco was waiting for them.

"Ah yes!" he exclaimed, as they opened the door to the darkened room. "Come in, my darlings, I'm looking through some rushes, I want you to see the gorgeous work for yourselves. I thought it might put you at ease somewhat, Maestra." He turned to Giulia and nodded for her to close the door. Gianfranco, the cinematographer, clicked a switch on the projector at the back of the space. A beam stretched over their heads. Alba's face now filled almost the entirety of the back wall. Her eyes were half closed in concentration, her body swaying to the music. Then the frame juddered to a different section. "Yes, let's cut to the two shot, Gianfra'," Francesco called back.

Here was Vittorio now, beside her at the piano. She watched him lean into her projected self. She caught her expression as she looked up to his gaze. Within the frame he returned it. Alba felt naked. There they were, overtaking the darkened space inside the play of light. Their connection captured on celluloid and splayed for all to see. There was no mistaking the inexplicable energy that filled the space between them. Alba's body tightened in her seat with the revelation lighting up the room. She looked over at Vittorio beside her, watching the light dance over his face, the shadows of their screen selves flitting across his skin. He sensed her gaze and turned to meet it. His expression was unflinching. There lay no defense, no mask, no arched silent comment. Francesco had spied their relationship and committed it to film. Now they witnessed the replay, knowing that this snatched moment in time had been captured for posterity. The feeling was the open-ended resonance of a perfect fifth, longing for the reassuring return to the tonic, the root note, the final chord of a symphony, ringing out with the inevitable resolution to home, one they were both ready for, at last. One neither could deny. It was plastered across the walls for all to see, and soon, across the world. Alba could have hovered in that dark quiet for a beat longer, looking into the man who knew her and searched her like a well-loved book, pages creased with rereading.

The beam snapped off. The lights switched on. With mechanical punctuation their love affair disappeared off the wall.

Francesco turned toward the two of them. "Quite the pair," he said, with the smile Alba had come to love but which now intimated he knew what they had been avoiding for too long. "Thank you, Maestros. You are making me appear far more brilliant than I ever will be."

He reached over for their hands and squeezed them in his. Then he jumped up with a flourish and the room rose alongside the gesture, bursting into work, filing out of the trailer and back toward the set for the night shoot.

Vittorio was swallowed into the crowd.

31

Col pugno
with the fist; i.e., bang the piano with the fist

Three weeks later the final day of the shoot loomed. The set sizzled with a mixture of excitement and delirium; night shoots had taken their toll on even the indefatigable crew, who no longer punctuated the stops between takes with their prolific stories about food. The team primed itself for the biggest shoot of the schedule. In two days' time Vittorio's finale would culminate in the recording of a live performance at Taormina's magnificent Greek amphitheater, Alba surrounded by a full orchestra, and onstage, brand-new choreography with a fifty-strong team of dancers, both classical and modern, in what was set to be the area's most ambitious performance of the season, if not ever. There had been a second unit in charge of preparing the space with a new lighting rig. It would illuminate over the course of the evening as the setting sun dipped into the sea framing the cliffside monument.

Alba had visited with Francesco and Vittorio a few days before and they had slipped into an awestruck quiet. She'd never seen an amphitheater so intact, so preserved, as if the players had headed to their dressing rooms for a brief respite thousands of years ago and forgot to return. Its magic all the brighter for sharing it with the two people raising her toward the pinnacle of her career to date, giving her the chance to perform the most beautiful contemporary music of the time in a form she had never explored but which she grew to adore more each day. On the daily review of the rushes, Alba had grown used to seeing her face. She no longer scrutinized the minutiae, cringing at her image. Now she had come to love the way the camera seemed to capture something unspoken. It drew out the most private thoughts, with a fleeting glance of the subject, the eyes revealing every flit of emotion. She felt ripped open. By Francesco and his probing lens, and by Vittorio's unswerving attentions.

She floated now on a delicious bubble of wonder and the liberation of letting others in where once she'd built defiant, fearful walls. She would be foolish not to admit that the constant care of Marianna and Luigi did not also add to it. The initial bombardment of unwanted touch was now a balm, a constant hug. If she didn't have a tactile mother, she was making up for it now, and it soothed a hidden need. Besides the makeup duo, the crew adored her readiness to socialize with them, and they danced on her every word, comfortable in her presence at last.

It was the family she had craved for so long.

Giulia stepped into the trailer and stood behind Alba. Her reflection was tense.

"Giulia *tesoro*, whatever is the matter?" Alba asked looking at her in the glass. "Have they run out of the coffee again?"

Giulia shook her head.

"Darling, just say whatever's troubling you," Alba cooed, as Marianna warmed her hands with a hand lotion loaded with essential oils renowned, she had preached, for their healing, anti-inflammatory properties, a ritual at the start of the day now, ahead of shots of Alba's playing.

"Your agent, Dante, called, Maestra, he says you're to call him back right away. You can use the office phone."

Alba turned to Marianna. "I won't be a moment, angel. It must be urgent, he knows not to interrupt me on set. *Grazie*."

She kissed her on each cheek, another new habit she'd grown fond of, and followed Giulia to the office.

Dante's voice was taut. He apologized for disturbing her. She gushed about her newfound tribe on set, described too many details of her day-to-day activities, apologized for not keeping in touch the past few weeks.

"It's Raffaele," Dante said, his voice a wisp. "I'm so sorry, Alba. I knew you'd want me to let you know. They tried your pager but weren't sure if you'd received the messages."

Alba's mind flitted back to her trailer where she'd left the gadget switched off for several days. She was absorbed into this world now, and didn't want anything or anyone to pull her away from it. Besides, as was now evident, when anything urgent would happen there was always a way to reach her. Her pager was for work commitments and she and Dante had agreed, after the shoot, not to take anything else on till the New Year.

"When?" she asked, her voice a rasp.

"Last night. The funeral is tomorrow."

"Oh God."

"I thought about waiting to tell you, but I didn't think you'd forgive me that. I'll speak with Francesco. He'll understand. That man can move mountains if he puts his mind to it. Got you to agree to do a film, for heaven's sake, I'm sure rescheduling some shots won't be difficult."

"Dante, it's not a few shots," she began, her tone spiking, "I'm playing the finale tomorrow night. Are you actually asking me to walk away from the biggest scene of the film, fly away like a diva leaving hundreds of people cheated out of the performance the island has been waiting for months? The theater is sold out, hundreds of people have been preparing for this for ages!"

Dante's voice dipped. "Alba, people will understand. Shifting it back a day or two is not going to ruin everything."

"Not for you, maybe, but these past weeks have been all headed to this point. Are you asking me to compartmentalize my grief? Run back, cry a bit, and then fly back and finish the shoot? It's not like running out to a bakery, Dante. I don't know how I'm going to get through today, let alone a live performance!"

Her tears spurt now, a brusque swipe of anger and frustration.

Dante knew better than to rush. "I hear you, Alba. Do you want me to come down? Would that help?"

Alba wasn't ready for anything from her life outside this world to interfere.

"I owe Raffaele more than I can express."

Dante swallowed. Alba knew he was scrolling through ways to come to her aid, as always.

"Take today to think about what you need," he soothed. "Let me know and I'll make it work."

"For once, Dante, I have to *not* do what I need. My needs are secondary to the entire team resting on me. I won't be one of those prima donnas." For some ridiculous reason Vittorio's wife, Clare, sprinted to mind. The night before, Francesco had described one of her latest outbursts to Alba, as relayed to him by a colleague working at La Scala in Milan. The picture Vittorio painted started to sound much closer to what the woman was like in real life after all.

"If you need a day or two you will not compromise your professionalism. Francesco will understand."

"I don't want to make him understand. I need to finish what I promised to do, after much persuasion. I'm not a flake. I can handle this. But I can't promise I can go back home, with all that entails and on top bury my best friend—that will break me, in more ways than you'll ever understand—then zip back and finish the most courageous project I've ever agreed to take on."

Another pause.

"Whatever you decide, Alba, will be the right decision."

"Yes."

She let her clipped answer hang in the vague white noise of the long-distance connection.

"I'm sorry I snapped, Dante. Raffaele loved me more than you can know. I'm terrified."

Dante made a reassuring hum. "If you want to talk I'm here. You know that. I'll support you whatever you need."

"I know. Thank you."

She placed the receiver down. Giulia stepped inside. If she had been her usual breezy self, Alba might not have cried, might not have crumpled into her arms, sobbing away Marianna's work, make-up dripping off her face in blackened streaks. The young woman sat beside her, holding her with a wisdom beyond her years, Alba sensing neither embarrassment nor panic from her.

"Thank you, Giulia," she whispered, wiping her face with the tissue she'd given her moments ago. "Someone's guided you well, Signorina, you're seated with a woman collapsing but it doesn't seem to faze you in the least. Certainly makes me feel a lot less pathetic, I can tell you that!"

"I've told Francesco that you need some extra time this morning. The First's rescheduled a few shots so they can accommodate that."

"*Grazie*. That was thoughtful."

"After everything you've taught me these past few weeks I think it's the very least I can do."

Alba looked at the young woman and let her in a little more. What would her life have been like if she'd been able to be so open and composed with her elders?

"Where's Vittorio?" Alba asked, straightening. "I'd like to let him know what's going on."

"I'll send him to you, Maestra, when he gets in, I'll tell Marianna to expect you too."

"You're a sunbeam, Giulia. Thank you."

Once Marianna and Luigi had reapplied the image of made-up Alba to her face, she waited in her trailer. Not long after, Vittorio arrived. He stepped inside and wove his arms around her without a word. She buried her face into the space at the base of his neck.

"I don't want to cry again," she murmured.

"I don't think it's up to you, is it?"

She pulled away and looked at him. There was a knock at the door. They stepped apart in an instant. Francesco popped his head around the frame. "*Tesoro,* I'm so so sorry, Giulia just told me. My darling, if you need to go, you need to go."

"Come on in, Francesco, please," Alba replied. The three took seats upon the two sofas within.

"I'm not going to do that to you, Francesco," Alba began. "You've been so wonderful to me these past weeks, everyone has, there's no way I'm putting that in jeopardy."

"He was your best friend, no?" Francesco asked.

"And he would have understood. Of all people. Being there at this time won't bring him back. If I'm to get through the performance I need to stay."

"I don't want you to get through it," Francesco replied, "I want you to feel comfortable, free, not clenching your teeth for my sake."

Alba met his eyes. The blue looked close to a pale gray in the suffused light of her trailer. She was touched by his genuine concern.

"*Grazie*, Francesco, really," she began, "but I know what's best for me. That means sticking to the schedule. I've never let anything get in the way of my performances. I'm not going to start now."

She noted the men seated at an awkward angle to her decisiveness. If there had been any whisper of doubt, it evaporated then.

"You are a consummate maestra," Francesco cooed, kissing her hand. "I won't forget this. And I am in debt. Of this there is no doubt."

Francesco stood up. "Take today to rest, Alba, we'll reconvene tomorrow."

Alba rose to meet him. "I would like to go ahead as planned. The idea of being alone at the hotel fills me with dread. Keep me busy till I have to believe it. Please."

Francesco took her face in his hands and planted a soft kiss on her forehead. "You are a warrior. I don't think I could do the same."

Alba felt a wan smile lift to the surface and retreat. Francesco left.

Vittorio's fingers traced a line across her shoulder blades. He kissed the back of her neck. "I'm here," he said, his voice warmed honey. "Do you need to be alone?"

"Not sure what I need other than to stay on track."

Her voice wavered then.

He pressed her back onto his chest. She could feel his heart beating behind hers.

Life pulsed on.

* * *

The day of the final performance arrived, proving to be the bolstering distraction Alba needed. Every fiber in her body was alert. There was no space within for a thought for anything other than the music, than the glorious finale of Vittorio's composition, a powerful celebration of love in all its brutality and tenderness. This section of his composition described the years they'd been apart, Alba's utter rejection of their relationship, a love kept sepulchred till now. Tonight she would be the conduit, and fill in the blanks with her own poetry, twisting the bravura of her interpretation around his celestial melodies so that the audience would alight with her.

She'd asked Vittorio to not visit her in her dressing room. However much the past few weeks had thrown her off all recognizable rhythms, the habits before a performance were fixed. She took her time to warm up her entire body, easing into her usual stretches. Marianna and Luigi sprang into action after that. A crushed velvet gown hung upon the clothes rack beside a window that looked out onto the sea, easing toward sunset, the water purple-blue, the surrounding hills rising up to frame it. The neckline of the dress swooped across her clavicle revealing more skin than she was used to when she'd first tried it on at the initial fittings. It was cinched in at the waist and then escaped toward a moderate train. As the lights of her dressing room caught it, violet undertones crushed in the beams. It was the most glamorous thing she'd ever worn to perform in. No one but Francesco and his stylists could have convinced her to wear it.

There was a knock at the door. One of the backstage managers apologized for inconveniencing her and placed a green box on her table. "I've been asked to leave this for you, Maestra."

She nodded. He slipped back out. Tonight, an army of local crew ran backstage, adept at hosting concerts there. They were the regular team in charge of the summer seasons in Taormina and led the proceedings with a flurry of efficiency. She opened the box, thinking it would be a gift from Dante, alongside the copious bouquets he'd already sent to the hotel, the masseuse he'd arranged to visit her room, and the baskets of fresh fruits, luxurious piles of dates and figs and prickly pears ripened to perfection. She and Vittorio had eaten most of them after they'd made love last night, his mouth sweet and tangy when she'd kissed him afterward.

Inside, a solitary glinting diamond sat on a bed of black velvet, refracting the bare bulbs surrounding her mirror. Beside it was a tiny scroll of paper.

She unfurled it and read the message.

Not an ultimatum, not a fence.
Nothing other than how you make me feel;
sparkling under pressure.
Your,
V.

She'd promised to save all her flow of emotion for her piano. She promised she wouldn't cave in to the wave of gratitude muddled in the murk of grief. She rose to her feet, as if the air would be thinner there, easier to breathe. She checked the clock upon the wall. There was plenty of time before she'd enter her preperformance concentration. Why did she forbid him from seeing her? It was ridiculous, superstitious, childish even. After all, in a moment they would be side by side, he upon his podium, unleashing the orchestra, setting the dancers alight with his music, she at his side singing out above the rest. She tied her silk dressing gown around her waist and left her room, winding down the corridors to his, which was one among the several trailers set up for the other musicians and dancers.

She knocked at the door. No answer.

He wouldn't mind if she slipped in. She turned the handle and pushed the door open a little. His lights were on, his suit hung on the rack. She could hear the patter of water coming from his shower. She brushed away her instinct to step inside with him, that would be no way to repay Marianna's and Luigi's attentive creations. She hovered for a moment, waiting to surprise him.

The sound of a woman's laughter lifted from the bathroom.

She froze.

A jealous imagination spidered out of control. His murmurs now. She knew those tones. They sang in her ear, under her sheets, cut through the dark inside and out. She needed to leave but her body had short-circuited a breath ago.

Then the door flung open.

A naked Giulia tumbled out.

Clouds of soapy steam fanned around her; Venus emerging from the waves.

It wasn't until Vittorio followed that the couple realized they had a visitor.

Alba's mouth opened without sound. Giulia grabbed a towel. It covered one breast and part of her abdomen but little else.

A clumsy snapshot.

Giulia started babbling something like excuses, apologies, embarrassed whispers filling the air Alba left behind her, as her body led her out of there, back past the huge columns rising up toward the far end of the performance space, as she wove through the walkways past the costume trailer, the dancers' dressing-room trailers, bubbling with excited chatter, the silhouettes of stretching limbs inside. She didn't answer when several of the local crew asked her if she needed anything, forgotten echoes in a distant past. Her heart pumped vicious beats, a runaway orchestra; the juvenile handling of an allegro, out of control, full of manic bravado.

Two women from the costume team stepped her into the gown and zipped it up. Several stage managers came in to tell her Signor del Piero was wishing to talk to her. She refused his audience, thankful that the barricade of crew was working—he didn't attempt banging on her door.

After half an hour a stage manager led her out of her room. He stood beside her in the darkened wings. Vittorio walked on from the opposite side of the stage. The audience was electric. It sounded high on the glorious evening, hugged in antiquity, gazing at the stage illuminated like a jewel, and beyond the wave of coast, a glassy sea, and the red ball of sun dipping into it sending streaks of gold across their faces. When the stage manager nodded for her to enter the applause drowned her like a wave. The lights glared in her face, making her feel more pale than she did already. Behind her the columns rose, their red brick deepening in the rays.

Thousands of people from all over the island and the mainland had come to witness this glorious illusion. Vittorio lifted his arm toward her, the ringmaster to his trained lion. She felt her spine prickle to pounce. His eyes shone black against the light, malevolent marbles. The applause swelled, tightening the vice, as she sat caught between the orchestra and the crowd. An A note was twanged, hummed, plucked, as the strings and wind instruments tuned toward the same destination; many versions of the same tone, a collection of half-truths.

They stopped on Vittorio's command.

A wave of silence rushed over the audience.

Alba sat inside the quiet, a breath outside herself, willing her shell to perform. The music was not their love affair. It was the seduction and obliteration of Alba Fresu. It was her greatest hopes and fears naked for all to rake through. The ones she'd offered to him beneath the sheets in his moonlit studio, now woven through incessant melodies, coded into unusual harmonies that made the listener's heart swell and recoil. It was the seduction of a Sardinian girl innocent to the ways of those who seek to sap the very life force that compelled her first love toward her in the first place. It was the score of the woman who was Vittorio's soul food and whom he'd prefer to destroy rather than being shunned from the deepest, guarded parts of her.

His composition was betrayal. Her performance, revenge.

Vittorio looked at her. She held his gaze, allowing herself to see the calculating mind within, the genius used to lure her back into his warped world, clawing to be as good as her, something she now understood had fueled his attraction in the very beginning. She was never the one person who wove deep inside him, she was the lover he'd never managed to conquer, and his life had led him back here through a sheer hardheaded determination. The unswerving focus she'd found so compelling was the very thing that would crush her; he'd played a very long game indeed.

The orchestra wheezed into bolstering sound that ran up the brick side of the amphitheater like a river, rushing back to the stage in waves. The dancers filled the space at speed, their limbs throwing lithe shapes, twirling around one another, passion scoring through from the tips of their fingers to the tops of their heads.

Vittorio lifted his arm to bring Alba in.

She followed.

They both knew she had no choice.

Her body played the melody, this time colored in shadow, this time scored with a ferocity the reviewers would salivate over the next day. And as Alba watched her fingers scurry through the lie, the image of them reflected back to her on the shiny black veneer was like looking at a mirror of herself both in front and behind, endless permutations of an Alba refracted until it was impossible to tell which one was real.

All life flew out of her, through the music, into the air, until there was none left at all. Until Alba stood behind herself, a listless phantom watching the adulation reach her from the audience, feeling the hand of Vittorio within hers, observing her entire world hover like an illusion before her. Tonight she'd given the pinnacle performance of Maestra Fresu. One she had honed for twenty years, one that had been reflected back at her. One fed to her by Dante, by Goldstein, and now by Francesco.

The audience stood. Flowers cascaded to her feet. It was the cheers of a wake, and the petals crushed under her feet as she curtsied for the sixth time. A dark hole opened up beneath her, just beyond the lip of the stage. The earth beckoned. The sounds at once treble and grating, snapping in her head like splintering glass. Vittorio took another bow. He held his hand out for her to follow. She turned to look at the faces. Tears coursed down her cheeks. Involuntary streaks leaving tracks of confusion. The applause deepened. Here was their artistry lifted to ecstasy through the sublime music. The dancers were standing, clapping too, and now the orchestra rose to its feet.

The amphitheater was a deafening light; Vittorio's victory charge.

Backstage the shadows filled with a sea of adrenaline and congratulations. Francesco was beside her at once, his voice a froth of compliments, his entourage giddy. A flute of champagne was placed in her hand. Responses to the inundation of delight fought to escape but without success. Her mouth remained mute. Someone told her she looked pale, it may have been Marianna as she applied some more rouge, or perhaps it was Luigi with a puff of a powdered sponge. The noise wove around her like a tornado, a forceful blur of delight, whirring until the sounds creased into a singular brown dirge of confusion.

She awoke in her dressing-room chair. Francesco held her hand. He fused into focus after a few blinks. "*Tesoro*, are you alright? That was the performance of your life. I think you pushed yourself too far."

Alba looked at him. Francesco had played his marionette well, now the strings were cut, the thick fingers of the puppeteer idle. Dante rose into view behind him and beyond, she could make out the black curls of Vittorio. She looked at her life through thick glass, her voice clamped far away, beside the real version of Alba, seated somewhere by the sea, alone, cushioned by the shore and nothing else.

When she let out a guttural cry they tore back. She lunged at Vittorio. Half of the clutter upon her dressing-room table flew to the floor, the carpet a crush of powder and petals. Somewhere at the center a despised gem. She watched Vittorio's face turn red as her hands tightened around his neck. She was in Ozieri now, the market square, the scuff of dusk dirt, the disorientation of utter loss of control, the shifting axis of defeat, blind-white wings of fear, flapping to nowhere, crashing a bird against the hard walls then twisting to thwack the same painful spot.

32

Deceptive cadence
a chord progression where the dominant chord is followed by a chord other than the tonic chord, usually the sixth chord

As the valley road from the coast snaked inland the cluster of Ozieri appeared in the near distance, past the parched yellow grasses of the farms in its periphery, beyond the trees, sundried and twisted in the heat spreading their branches skyward. The cicadas were in full song. Alba didn't turn on the radio. She'd wound down the windows since the start of the drive from Olbia Airport, the wind smashing against her ears with smacks of white noise. She needed a break from Rome, she told Dante. Her *accademia* duties didn't start for another month. She would call him from Sardinia. He would promise not to contact her before that.

As she wove uphill, the cemetery rose into view, its high white walls a blinding glare in the late morning sun. She pulled in across the gravel. It wouldn't be long before it closed for the day. There was a small hut selling flowers just outside. The woman working there had already begun taking the buckets of blooms inside out of the heat ahead of closing. Alba caught her just in time, buying the last two dozen roses, then she walked in through the arched entrance, the tall cypress planted along the periphery casting spindled shadows across the pine needle floor and tombs. The sun-toasted dusty air filled her with a brutal slew of memories, a childhood scuffed along the cobbled streets, hours spent in the shade of the trees of the *pineta* finishing homework with Raffaele, followed by the disorientation of being a balloon snapped of its string, rising aimless, caught up on the whim of the wind.

A janitor was filling up a bucket at one of the faucets. She approached him to ask where Raffaele was buried, her voice breaking midway through his surname. He pointed toward the far end of the cemetery. "He's in his family's monument," he added.

The sound of her feet upon the brittle needles felt like they reached her from far off, like the space between two radio stations, where the dial hits the crackle of frequency still fudged with the sounds of a distant presenter.

The sculpture of an angel contorted in a mid-flight twist rose into view. One foot leapt off the marble base, the other yearned for the sky. Its wings were outstretched and the detail of the sculpting brought Alba to a stop. At its base lay a spray of flowers, the first signs of decay at their tips since the funeral a few days before. Beyond, wrought-iron double doors that opened into a tiny chapel, enough space for a thin marble altar with a lit votive, and, in front, a pew for one person to kneel upon. Alba opened the doors and stepped in. On either side were enamel plaques of Raffaele's grandparents, and there, on the bottom was his sunny smile. She recognized the picture straightaway. It was a snap they'd caught on one of his visits to Rome about ten years ago. He'd just met Luca and was full of the fresh blush of love, the real deal, he'd said, as they sipped *aperitivi* in a little bar just above the Spanish steps watching the Roman sun dip across the city in streaks of amber and rose. They clinked to that, to love, in all its forms. Alba had thought of Vittorio that evening and let the image of him swirl into nothingness with the melting cubes, sending love to her younger self, forgiving her mistakes.

A fresh wave of rage rose.

She knelt on the cold marble. Her sobs echoed across the stone. When her breaths returned close to normal, she straightened and looked into the photographic plaque of her best friend's face. "I want to say sorry without crying at you, Ra'," she began, sitting back on her knees. "I want to do it with all my soul. Simply. Truthfully. But I can't, my love"—her tears fighting out between the narrow gaps—"I can't because the sorry truth is that I was flying and I couldn't think of coming back down to earth. I believed in the creation of an Alba I no longer recognized. I wore her like a brand-new coat, you know? And I looked good. I looked fucking beautiful. And everyone made me feel so special. I was a breath away from demigod, Ra'. I fed my audience so they would feed me, rather than come straight to you. And I don't know how I will forgive myself. I was taken up with the current. You knew that though. And you still loved me. You saw through all that crap. If I'd come maybe things would be different. Though of course, that's not true."

She wiped her wet face. Saying the words out loud helped calm fall over her like a veil. "So I'm back. I think that's what you were trying to get me to understand in Milan. But it took the complete breaking of me to really hear you, Ra'. I was swept up in lots of people's plans for me. I've escaped that for the time being. I've escaped escaping. I thought my running was the force of ambition. And it was, in part, but driving it was an unswerving need to escape some hard truths. I think it's time to face some head-on. I think it's what you'd always tried to get me to understand."

Her stomach twisted in deep knots. The pain was visceral, pummeling. Here was the grief she'd not allowed herself to feel for her mother. The grief she didn't allow herself to feel for the broken relationship with her father. It rattled her bones, a fierce resonance, each ripple ricocheting, brittle, against the first, sending grief's silent melody through her marrow. She might have sat there for longer, in the shade of the small mausoleum, but the rattle of the janitor's keys wrenched her out of her pool and she stood up, noticing the tips of her roses' petals had already started to curl inward a little in the heat. She placed them in a vase, replacing the bouquet that was already in it, then stepped outside, closing the iron gates.

With the click of the lock a voice called to her. She spun round, at once aware of her wet face, witnessing the impulse to clear it, hide it, a fleeting yearn for Marianna's cosmetic brush, letting the sensations drift over her without action.

"Alba?"

Mario was clutching a bunch of chrysanthemums in his hand, a spray of yellow before his spattered trousers, flecked with paint and oil.

"I'm so sorry," he murmured.

"Thanks."

They stood, her eyes wet, unblinking.

"I didn't think I had any tears left," he began through the hot quiet, "but now seeing you I think I'm going to start again."

He laughed off his stumbling with a sigh, shifted his weight. "I've come to see Papà."

Then he stepped in and kissed her on each cheek. He smelt of the *officina*, a metallic blur of car oil and coffee.

"Just swung by after work," he began. "You probably knew that already."

The silent heat of the afternoon closed in.

"You're a film star these days too, I hear?"

"Shouldn't believe everything you hear," she replied, regretting her throwaway straight afterward. "I mean, yes, I made a film. It's finished now."

"That's wonderful, Alba."

That the film was finished? That *she* was perhaps? She wiped her face, and with it the piercing thoughts, feeling how puffy her eyes were beneath her fingers.

He straightened. "I didn't mean to disturb you just now, Alba, sorry."

She noticed a few more lines around his eyes than the last time they'd seen each other. The weathered look suited him, lending a warmth and gravitas, which had eluded him till now. His tempo had relaxed. Perhaps Raffaele's death had stripped him down too?

"It's fine, really," Alba said, breaking the pause.

"How long you staying?"

Her eyes dipped for a beat, she found herself wondering why there were dried cracks of earth on his boots beside the splatter of oil. "Not sure."

"I'm taking your papà to one of his meetings later this week. You know the victim support circle I told you about?"

Alba felt her face wither. "Right."

"Sorry. Didn't mean to start, I mean—here." He reached into his pocket for his card and handed it to her. "Just call if you need anything."

She took it. It had the Fiat logo at the center and under his name, Partner.

"No one knows I'm back yet." Her words came out more of a warning than she'd planned.

"I won't spoil the surprise."

She felt her body tighten.

"I mean I won't say anything, of course," he added.

"*Grazie.*"

The stood in silence for a breath, the stone angel between them desperate for flight.

Alba turned and began a slow walk back to her car.

Mario called out. "Alba?"

She switched back. He reached her. Now he was no longer in silhouette against the sun she could make out the start of dark stubble along his jaw.

"Your papà's pretty frail these days. Just before his ministroke, they charged Mesina with drug trafficking. I think that's what caused it. Turns out Mesina was heading a ring. Big stuff. The reformed bandit, who invited your dad to his son's wedding even, was playing a stiff double bluff. Even went to my girls' school last year to educate kids on how not to succumb to a life of a crime. Quite the celebrity."

Alba felt a whirr of confusion and tiredness sweep through her.

"I just felt like you should know. Your papà's not the man you left behind."

"And I'm not that girl."

Mario's expression softened. "I'm so sorry about Raffaele. I can only imagine what you're feeling."

Alba nodded. She didn't want any more words, or any more tears. The heat had begun to weigh down her limbs.

"See you around, Mario."

"Sure."

She left him behind her as she reached the car, parked beside what must have been his motorbike because there were no other vehicles in the unforgiving scorch of the lot. Alba pulled out onto the road and followed it till the *pineta* rose and fell out of view, farther still, till she reached the house where it had all begun.

Elena and Alba took their post-lunch coffee on the terrace beyond the piano room, overlooking the plains that Alba had played to as a young girl, now bathed in blissful shade. Alba was delighted to see her aging mentor still at home in the kitchen, moving a little slower than before, her movements delicate, but not tentative, her eyes still fierce with that insatiable playfulness Alba adored.

"How do you do it, Elena?"

"Do what?"

"All this. Your house is immaculate, you threw me a lunch worthy of a princess. Your terrace is still in bloom and your garden looks like a painting."

"Well, I'll take credit for everything but the garden. I have help with that."

"You're an inspiration."

"I'm too stubborn to die, I think. Maybe that's it."

Alba laughed. "Thank you. For everything."

Elena's eyes filled. "It doesn't feel real, does it?"

"No."

"Dear Raffaele. Are you still outside your body a little?"

"Very much. Or outside the body I thought was mine. I don't know where to go from here."

"Has Vittorio tried to reach you?"

"I left my phone at the hotel. I have my pager for Dante, but he knows I'm keeping it off for the next few weeks. Should have heard how I spoke to him that night. I must have sounded deranged. I was deranged."

"I think you're entitled to that, no?"

Alba's mouth curled into a memory of a smile.

Her voice dipped into a whisper. "All I ever wanted was the music, Elena."

"That will never leave you."

"You should know."

Alba looked out toward the blue-green streaks across the hot haze of the plains.

"Did you run away in such a mess though?" Alba asked.

"I never had the fame you do, Alba. But the pressure put upon me by my agents and managers made me realize quite early on that I didn't want those things. And yes, my heart was split in two also. That has a way of making you realign your life story, no?"

Alba sighed a sad laugh and took a final sip of her coffee.

"I'll stay a few days only, Elena. Today I'll go and see Raffaele's parents. Then, I don't know."

"You stay as long as you like, you know that."

Elena reached for her hand and squeezed it. Her skin was papery, her fingers thinner than Alba remembered, but inside the grip remained the unwavering optimism of the woman who'd laid this world at her feet.

Raffaele's parents lived in the heart of Sassari, a small city twenty minutes from Ozieri. They owned a four-bedroom apartment in one of the new blocks that her mother used to complain about and long for. Inside, the corridors were lined with books, an academic mixture of their combined medical and law training. When his mother opened the door, Alba didn't recognize her. Gone was the elegant woman she remembered. She was dressed in a house smock and looked transparent. Grief had sapped her. They didn't speak for a second, but held each other. She was not known as a tactile woman but now her frame was brittle in Alba's arms. For a moment, the touch became the closest thing to feeling Raffaele; a hug once removed.

She led Alba into their living room. The furniture was unchanged from the 1970s. Echoes of her mother talking about it ricocheted in her mind. They had been at the cutting edge of modern living, she would say, flapping her arms in the air as she described the furniture, the obscure abstracts on the walls, the sculptures that looked both like naked dancers and random swirls, the lamps that stretched at peculiar angles and shapes. They knew about cocktails, a sideboard along the one wall testified to the fact.

Giovanna had described the place as if it were a palace. Now it looked forgotten, hovering in a time just behind the present.

They sat. Raffaele's mother spoke first. "Thank you so much for coming, Alba. We know how hard it is with your schedule."

Her voice was mouse-like. She'd always seemed so forceful when they'd been kids.

"I'm sorry I wasn't at the funeral," Alba began, "more than I can say, Signora. I don't think I will ever forgive myself."

Raffaele's mother straightened. She grew even paler. "But you must. If there's one thing our son taught us, it was forgiveness."

Alba didn't want to interrupt.

"I abhorred Raffaele's lifestyle. For a very long time. And truth be told, it made me sick. Nothing life-threatening, but a series of constant ailments I needed to attend to. Stress, they said. Such a fashionable word. Can't stand it. Truth was I wasn't happy, feeling this disgust for my child. It was like an automated reaction. Pathetic when I think about it. My husband was worse, of course."

"I didn't come to punish you, Signora."

"You're not."

Raffaele's mother took a sip of water. She placed it down, all her movements in slow motion, as if there was a possibility that she may break if they sped up.

"I punished myself quite enough. And then one day, Alba, I just decided that it was enough. I was causing the stress to myself. My choice of reaction, you see. I hung on to my reality whether or not it was making me ill."

Alba nodded, yearning for her to elaborate. Her pain wasn't a comfort, but it was good to sit with hers as well as her own. Just beyond the doorway to the lounge she could see Raffaele's room. From the little she could see it was untouched since he'd left. All his posters were on the wall still, his collection of Rubik's Cubes, the lamp with a Lamborghini as the base.

"He'd told me about Luca, you know," his mother began, "and I looked at my grown baby, standing tall over me, dressed impeccably, beaming, and I knew my feelings had been a farce. Seeing your child in love is better than being in love yourself."

Alba let the words hang.

"What I'm trying to say is, I forgave him. No, I forgave myself. I forgave myself for living with hate, I forgave myself for living in fear. It's almost impossible to forgive myself for him getting sick. Though any good doctor, or mother, I suppose, knows they cannot control everything, however hard we try. And I think he taught me that—the courage to forgive. Yes, that's the word. His legacy is courage. It's noble to forgive, Alba, but I always thought it weak, like I was giving in to something I knew was wrong, but the truth is, it's courageous."

The words were a dart.

"Sorry, I didn't mean to go on," she said.

"I'm glad to listen."

Raffaele's mother nodded and returned to the stiffness Alba remembered.

"I won't take more of your time, Signora. But please, if I can do anything, you will ask me, *si?*"

Raffaele's mother rose and took her hands. "My son loved you so very much. I had wished you two a life together, we all know that. We're all so proud of you. What you accomplished."

Alba couldn't muster more than a wan smile. It would be some time before her achievements would become more than a shield she had used to keep some truths at a safe distance.

"My husband used to tell me how your father would tell his customers about his concert pianist. When he was still well enough to work there."

"Signora, with respect, we both know he hated me for leaving."

"He hated you for not doing what he knew he could control, yes. And I was guilty of that too. Raffaele was almost too ill to forgive me my hatred. Don't leave it till it's too late, Alba. No one but a parent can understand the agony of their child despising them."

Alba's throat tightened in rage. "My father feels nothing but spite. He hates what I've achieved."

"He hates that he doesn't know you even more. I was one of those parents. I know."

Alba stood up. "Thank you so much for letting me see you."

Raffaele's mother nodded; in the suffused afternoon light netting in through the linen curtains she caught the same slant of Raffaele's eyes. A fresh wave of grief began to rise. She didn't want to cry here.

They reached the door. The women promised to stay in touch.

Alba got in her car and left the city behind her. As the road curved through the mountains, Raffaele's mother's words pounded in her mind. An unending free fall of fear opened up beneath her, deep as the rocky ravine to the side of the tarmac. Forgiving her father would leave her tender to hurt all over again, just like with Vittorio, one that she may never recover from.

Alba returned to Signora Elias's home and curled up in bed right away. She didn't wake till late afternoon, when a clatter of banging rose from the garden. Alba creaked one eye open. Her body ached. Her hair hurt. Her face felt caulked, dried in the heat, flaked plaster. In the bathroom mirror she caught sight of this vision of disappearance; a hollow trunk. The tiles were cold and shifting underfoot. She was a question mark; a character in search of an author.

Something called to her, a quiet hiss of thought, wordless yet urgent, like the steam fighting out of a coffeepot. She had been running her whole life, so fast, so focused on winning the race. Now she stood past the finish line, the cheers of the crowd ricocheting in her head like hammers. She gazed back at the starting post, her escape. A young girl stood looking at her, wearing the T-shirt from the night Marcellino was taken to the cave in her place. She'd left her so far behind. Chained her back where she belonged. And as the grown Alba squinted in the bathroom mirror, the other began a slow walk toward her, her twelve-year-old legs shuffling across the runners' lanes till she could almost feel her breath upon her. She stood in Alba's shadow now, slipping across the tiles in a faint silhouette. She was a powder of memory, the swerve of dashed hope in a dream, disorienting, insistent; in her voice the strangled call of home.

Another clang of a dropped hammer. A yelp. A man's voice cursed, before the teeth of a saw bit through some wood and further percussive jitter jiggered through the still of the afternoon. Alba swung her legs off the side of the bed and went to the window, tipping the shutters open just enough to see who was making the racket. Mario's vest top was streaked with sweat. She opened the shutters fully and poked her head out. He was beneath Elena's olive trees, building what looked like some kind of support. She was about to retreat back to her bed, her skin still felt gray and her body didn't crave company, when he stood and looked up, catching her before she slipped away.

The second time he'd seen her feeling at her worst, she thought.

"Sorry, did I wake you?" he asked, running a quick hand over his black hair.

"Shall I lie?"

He laughed then, the lines around his eyes deepening, the easing afternoon sun casting olive tree dapples over his face. "I promised Elena I'd finish up the job this afternoon for her, before I head back to the *officina* later."

"Everyone knows better than to argue with Elena," Alba replied. And with that she stepped away from the window and closed the shutter once again. She threw on her silk dressing gown, sat to put a little cream on her face, then left her reflection forgotten instead and headed downstairs. She filled a coffeepot and decided to start the day all over again.

"I've made you *papassini* too, Alba," Elena said, walking in, wearing the apron she always wore for garden work. "Dear Mario has been a lifesaver. He does the olives now. Makes oil for me from them. Patience of a saint."

Alba shot her a look.

"I know. Miracles never cease."

Alba twisted the coffeepot shut with an extra turn.

"You imagining it's someone's neck?" Elena asked.

Alba smiled.

"He is so kind, really," Elena continued, sitting down at the table, "what with everything going on at home."

Alba leaned against the counter waiting for the lit ring to do its magic.

"His wife left him for a dreadful man in Pattada a few years back. He's fought to keep the girls. Your brothers had a lot to say about that I gather. His parents aren't around anymore as you know, and I think he looks on me as the grandmother I doubt he ever had."

"All of us do," Alba replied, knowing that the simple act of being in the presence of this woman alone seemed to make life better.

"Still, mustn't sit here gossiping, the grapes need some attention this afternoon if I'm to have any wine this year, and the geraniums for that matter. I'll take this jug of lemon water to him," Elena said, opening the door of the fridge and grabbing the glass handle at an awkward angle so that it almost slipped out of her grip. Alba took it out of her hands.

"Here, Elena, let me," Alba said, reaching for a glass from an overhead cupboard. She left the kitchen and headed onto the terrace, walking down the steps to the olive grove where Mario was fixed on the task in hand.

"You winning the fight?" she said, placing the jug and glass on a stump beside him.

He stood up with a grateful sigh. "Not anytime soon." He took the glass, filled it, and downed it in one go before refilling. "*Grazie.*"

"Thank *you* for helping Elena."

"It's my pleasure." He took several more thirsty gulps. "She's been good to me."

Alba tightened the knot of her dressing gown a little, as it threatened to slip undone.

"Didn't know you were staying with her. Should have figured that," he said.

"Haven't thought my plans through yet."

"What do they say about the best laid plans?"

"I'm taking a sabbatical from the 'they.'"

Mario's face eased into a wistful smile. "Smart."

They stepped into a sliver of quiet for a moment.

"How are the girls?" Alba asked, knowing she was prying.

"Lunatics."

"Good."

He smiled for a brief breath, then took a final gulp of his water, set it down, and looked toward the trees. Alba watched his expression tighten into sharp lines. He was a different man than the one she'd walked beside in Rome. He still had that relaxed swagger about him but also a quiet weight to his speech now. Perhaps he had been trying to tell her about his situation back then? When he had spoken about the predestined lives of Ozieresi she'd taken it as just another person starstruck with her fame. Had she let him say much at all that night? She was so wound up in her performance she doubted she'd left space for anyone or anything else; Francesco had filled her with daydreams and Rachmaninoff had given her wings.

"I didn't know you were into all this?" Alba asked, willing him on.

"My dad loved the trees."

Alba felt the blood color her skin for the first time that day.

"And he passed on his gift in spades," Elena interjected, reaching them with a tray balancing Alba's forgotten coffeepot and two cups. "Do pardon the pun. They've made more fruit in the past two years in the hands of this handsome human than they ever did for me. He talks to them in tones they understand. I'm best with the begonias, but don't tell anyone, will you?"

She filled their cups with the hot coffee, insisted they inhale a *papassini*, then left, declaring she would be deadheading some geraniums in the front driveway should they need her.

"She is a marvel," Alba said, spooning sugar into her cup and offering him some.

"Thank you, just the one," he answered. "More than a marvel—lifesaver."

"Thought that was the trees?" she teased.

They stirred their coffee, melting the sugar, both welcoming the sweetness this miraculous woman brought to their lives, even in the bitterest days.

33

Fermata
a prolongation at the discretion of the performer of a musical note, chord, or rest beyond its given time value

Alba wound along the periphery ring road of Ozieri, downhill from Elena's villa, around the *pineta,* down toward the main Piazza Cantareddu, where all the buses arrived from out of town. The piazza was long and wide with *gelaterie* and bars along the width, customers spilling out onto the pavements before them, sipping midmorning coffees, some starting their drinking already with small glasses of ice cold beer or *aperitivi.* From there she began the steep climb toward the other side of the funneled town, passing the narrow Piazza del Cantaro to her left, where straggles of teenagers huddled in the shade of the trees, the same *piazzetta* where she had leaped over the embers with Raffaele all those years ago, the memory of the smell lingering on the tips of her hair floating into focus. She arrived at the next main junction of Ozieri and took a hard right to begin the near vertical hairpin turn. As she glanced in the rearview mirror her town spread out in the midmorning sun, the cathedral's spire glinting. The incline of Monserrato rose ahead, beyond the convalescent home for nuns.

Mario had explained that her brothers had built a house each, beside Bruno's brothers' homes. They were at the top of the hill, just before the tiny chapel at the apex, where Ozieresi would stroll the feast of Madonna of Monserrato, intoning their prayers and song on the steep path where it narrowed to a white road beyond the houses as they performed their musical pilgrimage till they reached it. Alba remembered doing it with her mother once, under duress, the only pleasure garnered from spying the tiny stone plaques carved into the rock retelling the Madonna's story. It always sat at odds with her, this worshipping of a problematic mother figure; virginal, inimitable, omnipresent yet distant. She'd never forget the expression her mother pulled when she tiptoed around her confusion in conversation after her first and last pilgrimage. They'd never spoken of it again.

The new Fresu houses were built one next to the other, all similar in shape, with an undulating thick white wall that linked them and framed their driveways like castle barricades. Their newfound wealth had been expressed no different than she might have expected.

Her father's was a little beyond, finished in the early eighties, named Villa Giovanna in dedication to his late wife. The tile said as much, in twirled font, stuck upon the brick support of one of the tall black metal gates at its driveway entrance. Alba parked her car outside on the street, pretending her heart wasn't galloping, ignoring the quiver in her fingers as she pressed the buzzer at last. She didn't call ahead. She didn't want to give him the option of refusing. This time a meeting would be on her terms.

She waited a beat or so, then rang again.

A clipped female voice answered. "Who's there?"

"My name's Alba. I'm here to see Bruno Fresu."

"In regard to?"

"I'm his daughter."

There was a click and the electric gate began opening. The driveway stretched ahead of her, paved with thick chunks of granite puzzled together in a pleasing zigzag of country idyll. Either side, succulents draped themselves over the boundary walls, oleander bushes streaked the white with bright pink blooms, geraniums poked out their pink and purple blossoms, and beyond, in the garden that seemed to wrap around the house, large medlar, fig, and almond trees. The floral fruity scent would have been uplifting on any other day. The sun streaked down across her shoulders, but her palms were cold.

The woman on the entry phone appeared at the door of the house, the glass panes reflecting the wide panorama of Ozieri nestled at the base of the surrounding valley. The balcony above which stretched the length of the house, must have views even beyond that, toward Tula and perhaps even Lake Coghinas, where her father used to take her and her brothers to fish. Alba's mind bounced toward any distraction available, only to ricochet back to the business at hand, like a jarring change of key signature mid-piece.

"*Buon giorno,* Signora," the woman said. "I'm Teresa, Signor Fresu's nurse."

Alba shook her hand. Teresa's touch was firm, no-nonsense. She was wearing a full nurse's uniform, which put Alba on edge; was Bruno more vulnerable than Mario had described?

"He's not expecting me," Alba began.

"That's quite alright," Teresa replied. "Do follow me."

She opened the glass-paned door a little more and they stepped into the stone cool of the entry room. Paintings of traditional farmers lined the walls of the space, which was more a formal sitting room than a hallway. By the door was a huge wooden dresser stacked with porcelain. There was a chest of drawers toward the opposite end, upon it framed photographs of Marcellino and Salvatore and a number of children, which Alba presumed must be her nieces and nephews. Her eyes took in the space and landed on a collection of three paintings just to her right by the doors. They seemed to be designed upon dried slabs of cork or leather, the bright turquoise and terra-cotta hues at odds with the subject matter. In the first, a man was being led away from the spectator's gaze, head covered in a sack, two armed men beside him. In the second he was inside a cave, bent over scraps of bread. In the third he seemed to be embracing one of his captors. Alba couldn't tear her eyes away. Seeing their terrorizing episode immortalized in a blatant, bizarre trio of art made her feel dizzy.

There was no daughter in any of the pictures.

"Signora?" Teresa asked the motionless Alba, who snapped back into the room. She followed the nurse toward the darkness beyond the door at the farthest end of the entry room. When her eyes acclimatized to this new room, cooler and dipped in more shadow than the first, Alba made out an enormous table that stretched the length of what looked like a *taverna*. It could have seated at least thirty people at a swift guess. At the far end there was a wide stone hearth, the walls either side hung with a comprehensive collection of copper pans, deep, shallow, small, large, even one on a long handle with holes in it, which Alba recognized as an antique bed warmer. At the end nearer the door where they stood was a bar, complete with a marble countertop and sink and enough bottles of *mirto* and *grappa* to keep several wedding parties inebriated for days.

"Bruno was quite the entertainer," Teresa began. "My father has a tale or two of him and their friends over the years, and many more he probably doesn't remember!"

Alba struggled to hear her over the television blaring out the obnoxious trill of a game show. As the cheers subsided, Teresa walked to the other side of the table and over to its far end. That was the first time Alba noticed the thin crescent of a bald head rising over the tip of a high-back armchair facing the television. Teresa stood in front of it. "Bruno," she began, in the tone Alba had heard adults address children, "you have a visitor."

Her father's voice was a muffled whisper.

"A visitor," she repeated, louder this time, enunciating with more of her lips. "It's Alba."

Teresa straightened and smiled at Alba, who tried not to receive it as a threat; it was a teacher's smile, more warning than welcome.

"Come on in," she insisted, "you have to face him so he hears you."

Alba followed Teresa's pathway, past the hearth and the pots, past a huge mural of her mother pictured cooking at this hearth, a double vision of surreality; her mother would never have seen this house and yet was immortalized in his view forever as if she had. The noise of the sequinned girls now gyrating in front of the game show host upon the screen screeched into the room.

Alba turned the corner of the table.

Her father looked at her.

Then he turned to Teresa. Alba felt her body become rigid; she tried to not prepare for a fight, for a dismissal, or worse, utter indifference.

He took a breath. "Come to gloat?"

Alba's throat tightened.

"It's Alba," Teresa replied, taking his hand in hers, warm, but professional, as if her touch might anchor him back. He flit his eyes back to Alba. They looked gray in the light until Alba realized they both had cataracts. His skin was sallow but well shaven. His body looked comfortable, especially underneath the two blankets wrapped tight around his legs.

"He gets horribly cold," Teresa explained, noting Alba's look. "Can't move around too well, so I keep him warm." She turned back to Bruno. "Lunch soon, *sì?* Then off to bed."

Bruno chuckled. His sense of humor alone was intact.

His body was smaller than Alba remembered. He sat, strapped in by Teresa's cocoon, the garish drivel from the screen ahead of him now frenzied on account of someone winning a food blender.

"Here," Teresa said, "sit on this chair beside him, Alba, he'll hear you better. I'm just going to prepare his insulin and medications in the bathroom just here, if you need me."

Alba didn't react as quickly as she would have liked.

Bruno's eyes were glued to the swish of half-clothed dancers, twirling around a second appliance that the contestant was under threat to win.

"Babbo," Alba said.

Bruno didn't move.

"*Sono* Alba, Babbo."

Bruno threw his gaze with surprising speed. A flicker of recognition snuffed as quick as it appeared.

Alba cleared her throat. "I wanted to see you, Babbo."

"Why?" he grunted, his voice hoarse. "You've done fine without me all these years."

Alba sat, waiting for the teary reunions she'd read about, watched in films, some kind of saccharin closure she didn't want to crave.

"I didn't come to fight."

"Never knew anything else. All your life you've been a fighter. No one can talk sense into you. I gave up years ago."

Alba fought the need to walk out, to forget her pilgrimage to this place.

"I came here because I need to talk."

Bruno gave a half-hearted nod, a Sardinian shrug signaling to a talker that the listener was not convinced.

"I've been punishing you all my life," she blurted, because there was no sense in a warm-up, or a segue, or any kind of logical approach to conversation. Their relationship had no foundation in logic. It was barbed love that had no way of being expressed other than through hurt or caged anger. "And I'd like to stop. Because it's made me hard. And I don't like the person I've become."

"Oh, you came to blame."

Alba felt her leg twitch. She gave a glance to the mural. Her mother looked down at her with a fake, painted-on smile.

"No change there then. You show up like a storm, stomp around like everyone's wronged you. No one in this whole town treats me like you do! They tell me how nice I am, how fair, how kind. Christ, I've probably kept the whole economy of this place going for years. But my own daughter? She treats me like I'm dirt."

Teresa swept in. "Keep it easy, Bruno, you know what the doctor said the other day, *si?*" She placed a tray down loaded with boxes and small plastic medicine cups. Inside a few there was a collection of multicolored pills. The game show's theme tune began calypso-ing through the stone room. She administered the pills and turned for the kitchen at the far end. "Lunch in a few minutes, yes?"

Bruno turned back to the television.

Alba grabbed the remote and switched it off.

"What are you doing?"

"Trying to talk to you. Trying to say sorry for not having the courage to reach out earlier. Trying to say that I resent the fact you open your heart to a group of strangers at that victim group but freeze me out. You tell them *that?* That the one person who needed you most was abandoned?"

His face contorted into defiance. "I did everything to keep you here. Why? So I could give you a life to be proud of. You stop and think how it feels when people tell me about seeing you in the paper, about this and that and I wonder whether I'll ever speak to you. I see fathers and their daughters, their grandchildren, and it rips me apart." His expression clouded now.

"You could have called me."

"A father should grovel to a daughter for attention?" He licked at his dry lips. "What kind of logic do you live by? You're an artist, what would you know about that? Swanning around the continent. You don't know real life."

The word artist was slung like a weapon. Had he spoken to the painter who had immortalized his late wife upon his wall that way?

Teresa stepped in with a bowl of broth and *pastina*, a fresh roll, a hunk of cheese, and a small salad. "Here you are, Bruno, I'll be preparing your bedroom now, *si?* After lunch you'll take your nap."

She left. The woman was a tornado. Alba had never seen a woman talk to her father like that. Some warped justice at last.

He tipped a small ramekin of Parmesan into his soup and gave it a swirl.

"I have no idea what you went through," Alba said, at last, choosing not to take the bait, the hit, his cruel default to put her down.

"You don't care."

A familiar tightness gripped her middle. She noticed it without clinging on to the feeling.

"I was the child. You were the grown-up. Did you ever think of that?"

"I don't want to talk anymore."

"I need to."

"You need to feel like you're right."

Alba took a breath. She willed her muscles to relax, finding a quiet inside the rage. "I'd like to feel like my father loves me." She felt her voice become thin but refused to cave in to the feeling of drowning. "That's all it comes down to. And bigger than that, I'd like to find a way to let myself love you too. Because this hate, this silence, has made me brittle. There's so little time now."

Bruno stopped swirling then. He looked at her. "You planning my funeral already?"

Alba shook her head. She didn't move as he took a mouthful.

"I miss the man who told me stories before he thought he would be left to die in a cave." Her face was streaming now. Droplets fell onto her trousers.

He couldn't eat now. Ripples in the soup fell to stillness.

"The little girl I made those stories for left a long time ago," he whispered now. "Was she ever there at all? There was a lot I didn't teach her right."

She could hear the crack in his voice and the tears he would never let fall.

"You sent me away."

"It was your decision to go."

No-man's-land.

"I could have demanded you acknowledge my success. I preferred to shut you out."

"You've done more than I could have ever dreamed of," he added, "and not once did you let me share it. How do you think that felt?"

The words landed hard. His first admission of feeling something beyond rage opened up a sliver of space between them. She felt herself soften a little. "I never thought to think about how you felt. All I've known is that you've hated me for most of my life. You hated the fact I saw you at your weakest. You've never forgiven me for seeing you like that."

Bruno nodded, deflated. She fought away a whisper of guilt for cracking open this old man.

"So you've said your piece," he said at last. "Happy now? Go on running back to the city."

"My life in Rome is finished."

He looked at her. It wasn't an expression of gratefulness but his diffidence looked tempered. "You look tired."

"You look old."

Bruno gave a half-hearted chuckle.

Alba watched him eat. His hands were shaky and sore, and she could see the gnarls of arthritis on his middle joints.

"I want to change," she said.

"You're too old to."

"I was waiting for you to forgive me. To say sorry for everything you'd said and done to me. But I'm sick of doing that. I'm going to do it first."

Bruno looked at her. "Just like that, after all this time? How?"

"No idea."

Bruno sighed.

"Do we have to know?" she asked.

He didn't answer.

Alba stood up. "I'll come again."

Another islander shrug. Sardinian for do as you wish, or I couldn't care less, or I care so much I don't want to let on in case I'm ridiculed.

Alba bent down and kissed him on his cheek. The impulse caught both of them off guard. She looked down at her dad. She was her father's daughter. They both knew it. And were both too stubborn to admit it.

She walked through the doorway back out to the hall toward the entrance door. Teresa came out of the downstairs bedroom, just as Alba's eyes landed on a framed picture she hadn't seen on her way in. It was a record sleeve. She was seated beside the Berlin Philharmonic's piano during the live recording of a Schumann concerto. It had sold more copies than any classical album that year. She looked at herself, mid-run, her back long, poised, alert, her hands cupped and strong, about to race through the allegro. A fitting oscillation from the kidnapping documentation on the other side of the door; here was music, there was silence.

"He's told me all about you, Alba," Teresa began. "You'll come again?"

"Yes."

"Your brothers come but they never stay long. They don't talk to him. I see him decline because of it. When you get to his age you need to be stimulated, be part of something. They're just pushing him out."

Alba let the words sink in.

"I'm speaking out of turn, I know. They're paying me after all.

But I'm here to care for your father and I know what he needs. I do what I can, but I don't work here all day, of course."

"I see."

"Anyway, it was a pleasure to meet the famous artiste at last. I've never met a professional musician. There used to be lots of music here in town. Broke my heart when the local studio closed. There's a call for it, just not the money for people to invest. Our kids all leave for England, the mainland. What are they supposed to do here? Wait for the season and work on the coast, yes, thank God for the hospital, that employs a lot of them, if they have the time and money to study, of course."

"I haven't been back in many years. A lot has changed, obviously."

"I'm sure. We're hardly the bustling Roma, no?" Teresa straightened. "I won't keep you, of course. But do come again. I'm here every morning."

"*Grazie,* Teresa."

Alba stepped out into the heat of midday. The stones were blanched in the rays. Her eyes crunched up in defense. She slipped her sunglasses on and looked out toward the valley. There was no man left to punish. Where there was rancor was now an empty page.

The peculiar nothingness flew through her bones, followed by a lightness, until the weight of twenty years of fury raced out in tears. She rifled in her bag for a tissue, wondering why she hadn't thought ahead to bring some in the first place. A rumble of a car drew her attention. It rolled up toward the door and came to a stop. A woman stepped out, makeup plastering a mural across her face, her wrists heavy with bracelets and bangles and a gemstone sparkle across all fingers.

"*Dio mio*—Alba?!" she gasped.

The voice of Marcellino's wife, Lucia, sharpened into focus. Alba didn't recognize the gilt persona before her. Where was the young woman who had blushed at the wedding-party table, playing her demure role to perfection?

"*Ciao,*" Alba said, reaching for her hand, receiving two kisses that almost touched her cheek.

"Marcellino!" the woman cried. "Your sister!"

Marcellino now rose into view, stepping out of the driver's seat, slamming his door with a tired swing, loosening his tie. His girth had expanded with wealth and wine, and his skin was tired, someone who smoked too much, the golden sheen of youth now gone. He shifted his gaze at first, someone adept at carrying secrets but not without effort. He walked over to Alba, frowning in surprise.

"I came to see Babbo," Alba said, as he kissed her on each cheek.

The couple's faces unfurled into confused smiles.

"Why did no one tell me anything?" Alba asked, hearing a wisp of anger hiss out on her breath.

"It wasn't serious. He's fine. The doctors said a ministroke at his age is pretty common. Not life-threatening," Marcellino replied. "You weren't exactly on speaking terms. Didn't think you wanted to know."

"I'm here now."

"How long are you staying?" Lucia pouted.

"I don't know yet."

"Your brother and I are pretty exhausted with all the ferrying. Hospitals, doctors, appointments. We do our best."

Alba shook her head in disbelief. "I just wish you would have told me sooner."

"You're busy, Alba, playing to people all over the world. What would you have done?" He shifted. "Is that why you came back now?"

Alba felt her body tighten. She wasn't about to explain what had brought her here any more than he was about to let go of the older brother's throne.

"You come every day?" Alba asked, deflecting the rising tempers.

"I'm running all three *officine* now. The one in town and the two in the next region. I travel two hours back and forth every day to the center of the island and back. I pay for the care. That's all that sorry bastard is getting from me. Treated me like shit all these years."

Alba looked into his eyes. "I know the feeling."

Marcellino shook his head. He looked like he needed an argument but didn't want to give Alba the satisfaction.

"I work in Sassari at the lab," Lucia added. "Our schedules are heavy. It's been brutal."

They stood in the hot silence for a moment.

"It's a shock," Alba said, at last, "that's all." Her guard drifted away like a fallen veil. "I'll be back another day. Perhaps I can help? With money of course, but perhaps other ways?"

Marcellino and his wife shot a glance to each other.

"I'll call later. When it's cooler. When *I'm* cooler," she added.

Marcellino gave a terse nod. He left for inside. His wife followed, then turned back to Alba. "We've given that man everything, you know," she began, a statement that Alba knew in all probability reflected half of the truth, "and when his friends come round, you know who he boasts about? The piano girl. You have any idea what that does to your brothers? They've sweated their lives for him, chasing after his approval, but *you?* Abandon the family, do what you like, when you like, cut everyone out, and still, the *star*. It's hurt me, watching Marcellino suffer that."

Alba had no reply. A younger Alba would have settled the matter right then and there, with hands, perhaps. This Alba stood tall and calm: unbroken but pared down to the core.

34

Rhapsody
a work that is episodic yet integrated, free-flowing in structure, featuring a range of highly contrasted moods, color, and tonality. An air of spontaneous inspiration and a sense of improvisation make it freer in form than a set of variations.

Alba didn't drive straight back to Elena's house. She wove farther uphill to the church of Monserrato instead, as if the circular view of the plains surrounding Ozieri might lend her an altered perspective on the disorienting visit. By the minute chapel perched at its peak, there was indeed more air than down below, and the lunchtime breeze wove across the large stones of its courtyard surround. When the sun beat down harder, the whimsy of seeking out a higher view left her with nothing but the feeling of being the archetypal artist still grappling with a yearning for poetic justice. In the near distance, a herd of sheep with metal bells around their necks clanged their lunchtime symphony, random rhythms she'd forgotten. Alba stopped by her car just before getting back inside. She tuned in to the welcoming sound, a Sardinian chorus of sorts, rugged, unselfconscious, music born of practicality, echoing across the stillness of the afternoon, bouncing off the crags and boulders of her childhood countryside. The flock's tinny treble resonated. The modesty was compelling, and it was what had lain at the heart of her attraction to music in the first place: Simplicity was what Alba craved.

A ball of grief hardened in her chest. Just beyond this hill was the shadow she'd been fighting for so very long. She was ready to hang up her gloves.

Alba caught the delicatessen just as the owner was hurrying to close for lunch. She took her few *etti* of sliced meats, a hunk of cheese, a bulb of fennel, and a couple of bread rolls to the *pineta* and sat in her and Raffaele's cool spot to eat, easing herself toward a thoughtless state, listening to the delicate taps of the needled branches overhead.

When she stepped into Elena's house it was already early afternoon. The first sound she heard was her piano, a tentative tune being chased with a new pianist's hands. She followed the song to find a young girl upon the stool, Elena beside her sipping a coffee, offering gentle hints as the girl stumbled through a central section. It was a Burgmüller study, Alba recognized it at once, an arabesque, she had played it herself early on in their lessons. She'd loved that piece, the A minor key lent a morose urgency; a drama that she'd locked in to from the first phrase Elena had played her. This girl had a muscular touch, a little tentative in places, but there was a bounce to her rhythmical understanding that made Alba feel like she was watching an old piece of footage of a life she'd known.

Now the girl shook the hair off her shoulders, its thick waves twirled down her back in defiant angles. Alba decided to accept this entire day would be a wade through the past. She rejected the impulse to sort and categorize, instead, at last welcomed the sensation as if she'd tipped an entire case of old photos onto the floor and sat at its center witnessing the sensory onslaught.

Elena looked up and saw Alba watching. She smiled and with a silent hand, motioned for her to come inside. Alba sat down upon the settee beside the piano. The girl stopped and looked at her teacher, then the stranger. Her eyes were an unusual shade of brown, vivid as the reddish bark of the cork tree's trunk when they were stripped of their bark. It wasn't the color that was compelling so much as the spark of intelligence within them. This child was afraid of nothing, it would appear, a flash of the girl shooting an arrow with precision pierced Alba's imagination; she had the outside about her, the feral strength of mythical creatures. Either that, or the heat and grief of the morning had melted Alba's brain at last.

"Good afternoon, Alba," Elena began, "do let me introduce you to a very special young lady. This is Chiara." Elena nodded toward her student, who twisted toward Alba and flashed her a smile. She shook her hand. Alba was impressed with the confidence of her grasp.

"Nice to meet you, Chiara. You're playing one of the first pieces I learned."

"Really?" Chiara answered. "Did you keep messing up this middle bit too?"

"Of course!" Alba replied. "Sometimes I think that's why he put it there. To trip up students, see if they had the gumption to keep at it. The hardest things are usually worth it in the end."

"You sound like my dad," Chiara replied.

"Those are the words of a very famous concert pianist, Chiara," Elena corrected, her voice golden with pride.

"Who?"

Elena gestured to Alba. "This one. My best pupil." She glanced toward Chiara. "So far."

Chiara grew a little taller. "Do you get to play for lots of people?" she asked, her voice now dipped into a youthful naivety at odds with the verve of her physical presence, which bore a confidence beyond her years.

"I do," Alba replied. "It's a wonderful job. Hard. But wonderful."

"I want to do that when I grow up. Papà says I have to do well at school first."

"Yes, because she talks too much in class and gets in trouble every day," the voice of another girl chimed in from the other side of the room. Alba hadn't noticed the second girl, who didn't look up from her coloring book as she spoke, fingers searching over the tub of pencils for her next color.

"Now now, you know my rule on bickering," Elena interrupted. The young artist looked up from her book at the sound of her voice, her cheeks smeared with dirt, her hair tugged into a ponytail that looked like it had been at the center of her head once and now wilted across at an angle. Wisps of hair tweaked out of its grasp, fairer and thinner than what Alba presumed must have been her sister's.

"That's enough for today, Signorine, go on out and see if Papà needs some more help, yes? And take the jug of cold water to him from the fridge, *sì?*"

"Did you make *sospiri,* Signora Elias?" the small one piped, just before Chiara elbowed her into silence.

"Of course I did. My best pupils always get my finest. Wash your hands first though, Donatella."

The girls disappeared into the kitchen. When Elena looked at Alba, her teacher's eyes were dancing. If she didn't know better Alba might have thought she was plotting.

"Remind you of anyone?" Elena asked.

Alba smiled, feeling it slip away as quickly as it appeared, a surface ripple in water.

"Mario does a wonderful job with them. I'm not saying he didn't need some convincing to let them learn with me. I told him it was as much for my benefit as theirs. I miss teaching horribly. I don't have the energy I used to, but I love watching children develop. Always have. There's a simplicity and a passion that we learn to tame as we grow. Some of us fight it better than others, of course."

She flicked Alba a sideways grin.

"If you want to talk about the meeting with your father, I'm happy to listen."

"I'd like to know where to start. I think grief is a self-fulfilling prophecy and a bottomless pit."

Elena nodded without comment. Alba heard the girls call for Mario.

"I tried to believe him dead for so long," Alba said at last, "I don't know what I'm grieving for exactly. It's like a drone." She looked at Elena now, her vision blurring with tears. "He masked everything he felt with a rage that lasted till now. How many times do we have to hear the idea that we hurt the ones we love the most? It's true, isn't it?"

"I can't speak for your father," Elena began, easing toward Alba, "but I do think he ached more than we'll ever understand. It doesn't justify the way he expressed it, but we know he never wanted to harm you as much as he couldn't live with the idea of not being able to protect you, not here, not in Rome, not from your mother's death."

Alba took a deep breath and looked out toward the plains. The girls stepped in from the kitchen before she could carry on. It forced her to swallow her tears. Now she could see their startling resemblance to Mario. They had that same quiet sagacity about them, Chiara perhaps more than her sister, and their physicality was similar too, assured, centered, strong.

"You look like you need help with that, Signorine," Alba said, walking across to Donatella before the *sospiri* met a sticky end upon the floor.

"*Grazie,*" Donatella said, relieved to have had the responsibility abolished.

Out in the garden Mario was putting the final touches on a tool-shed beneath the shade of a couple of almond trees.

"You've made that shed into quite the chalet, Mario," Alba said, feeling the earth crunch beneath her feet.

"It's what Elena wanted," he replied, taking a couple of *sospiri* and downing the glass of water from Chiara.

"This lady is famous, Papà," Chiara said, swinging herself up into a nearby tree and sitting in its crook. Her sister followed, hanging upside down along another branch.

"Pay attention, Donatella. I'm not rubbing your flat head again today," Mario said, taking a seat upon one of the two stumps he'd placed on the shed's porch.

"Mario, they're sunbeams. *Complimenti.*"

He nodded a silent thanks.

"And they're into music, no? Wonder where that comes from?"

Mario gave a heaven-bound shrug.

"Don't give me that Sardinian shoulder, Ma, you forget that I heard you sing your heart out at the Festa di San Giovanni."

"What's that?" Chiara asked, leaning back against the trunk to size Alba up at a new angle.

"We got to jump over the fire. Your papà had spied me at practice with Signora Elias and I was terrified he would tell my father, which would have got me into a lot of trouble. The next day I saw him sing with the male choir. He had a solo no less."

"Sing it now, Babbo!" Donatella squealed, swinging like a bat.

"Sit up when you eat," he replied. Chiara yanked her up.

"Can Alba come with us to the sea tomorrow, Babbo?"

"Will you come, piano lady?" Donatella echoed.

"I don't think that's up to me, ladies, sounds like your papà has a day planned for the three of you."

"Please, Papà?" Chiara asked.

Donatella echoed with her own version of puppy dog, which looked more grimace than she intended.

"Can you put up with these two for longer than five minutes?" Mario asked.

"I don't want to interrupt your time with your girls, Mario, I know it's precious."

Chiara jumped down off the tree and stomped over to them. "Now you're just being polite, Signora, Babbo makes the best barbecue in Ozieri. Signora Elias always says so. She always comes with us. I think you should eat it too."

"That is a hard offer to refuse," Alba said, smiling at the chef in question.

His face eased into a modest grin.

"We usually leave early, don't we, Papà?" Chiara plowed on.

"I don't love the heat," Mario answered, half turning toward Alba.

"It's settled then," Chiara announced, skipping back to her perch, victorious.

The next morning Mario arrived with two very excited girls to pick up Alba and Elena for a day by the sea. Alba sat behind with the girls, who sang the entirety of top hits at the top of their lungs, including several in English. Their version of Queen's "We Are the Champions" delighted Alba for its blissful, passionate delivery, in spite of dubious pronunciation. They arrived at Lu Impostu beach, greeted by a sheet of breathtaking turquoise stretching out toward the rock of Tavolara. Mario turned right, away from the beach, and they parked beside a tiny house just on the bend of the cove, sheltered by pine trees and facing an uninterrupted view of the water. They clambered out of the car, the girls dashing toward the hammock that hung between two pines at the far end of the garden.

"Mario, this is stunning," Alba whispered, the strips of darker blue cutting across the water pinning her gaze to the cerulean horizon, mountains rising up to the left.

"*Grazie.*"

"You told me your great-grandfather built this before the rich moved in, no?" Elena asked, sitting down on the seat Mario brushed down for her. "It must have been marvelous coming here as a child, I bet there wasn't another house around?"

"You're right, Signora," Mario answered.

The girls dashed back up to the narrow strip of tiled porch where the adults were.

"Can we go to the beach, Babbo? Can we go now?" they frothed.

"Give me a moment, girls, I have to start the fire."

"I'll go," Alba said.

"I didn't bring you both here to babysit my girls."

"I thought you'd brought them to babysit us, Mario!" Elena replied, taking their hands and walking down toward a little gate beside the hammock. "Its this way, isn't it?"

Mario shouted back. "Yes, come and get your towels, girls!"

Alba walked over to the car and reached in for their beach bag. "My pleasure, Mario, honestly," she said, waving it at them to signal they didn't have to come back to fetch it.

"*Grazie*, Alba," he said, heaving a bag of chopped wood from the boot and carrying it on his shoulder toward the brick barbecue just beside the house.

The two women and girls spent the morning afloat. Elena's swimming belied her years as much as everything else she did. Chiara and Donatella ran rings around Alba and by the time they prized themselves off the beach for lunch they had become firm friends. Chiara had pummeled her with questions about her job, Donatella had swung on her arm, shrieking to be thrown in from her shoulders over and over again.

"That smells divine, Mario!" Alba called out, wrapping her towel around her middle as she reached him by the head of the table. He was stood cutting several chops into manageable sizes, sprinkling the meat with a generous amount of coarse salt.

"Ribs for me!" Chiara yelled, reaching over her sister to grab some.

Mario swatted her hand away and began chopping the sausage. Alba watched the juices seep into the flatbread beneath it all, which lay upon a wide slice of dried cork bark. The table was set with paper plates and cups and a bowl full of fresh-cut vegetables, which everyone helped themselves to.

When they had filled themselves with Mario's barbecue, he brought out an enormous slice of watermelon and divided it into smaller pieces. After an espresso, the party slipped into a much-needed afternoon slumber, the girls reading on the hammock, Elena snoozing on the bed inside the singular bedroom of the cottage.

Alba wrapped up the paper tablecloth and cleared the final remnants of lunch whilst Mario put the leftovers in the fridge. She lay back onto the deck chair facing the water below.

"Absolute heaven," she said.

"*Grazie,*" Mario answered. "You may come again."

Alba sighed a smile. "I'm honored. I bet not everyone gets to sample the Mario hospitality that often then?"

"No."

Alba pulled the deck chair up a little straighter. Mario unfolded one next to her.

"I wish they'd told me about Papà," she said.

"I tried to."

"Yes."

They looked at the water for a moment, the lazy ripples catching the afternoon sun. The shade of the garden enhanced the luminous celeste of the sea at this time of day.

"I should have asked more questions," she began. "It was easier to cut it all out from my life than deal with it. I stayed away for as long as I needed. To survive. I couldn't face the rejection a third time. I won't take responsibility for what he did but I can take responsibility for what I do now."

"Makes sense," Mario replied, unhurried, without prying.

His silence invited trust. "The thing that moved me most?" she asked. "I saw the frail human in there. One that was guarded for a very long time. One that was protected by rage for so very many years. I made him feel more vulnerable than any parent can bear."

"Probably," Mario replied.

"Have you ever screamed at your girls after they hurt themselves?"

"Most parents do."

"You scream at them for not being more careful. What you're actually fighting is your own failure to save them in time. You take it out on them. My father went through that on a scale that I can't fathom. And I saw him at his weakest, overpowered by those strange men, and I think he never could forgive himself for that. Not ever. He protected me as well as he could, but he couldn't protect me from his weakness and that nearly killed him. And it might have killed me too. So I escaped. Now all his self-loathing, his pride, his fear, can't hurt me anymore, because that person is gone. That was a man-child I saw yesterday. Vulnerable. Dependent."

Mario nodded, his body relaxed, a person who had found his own way through his own thistle relationships.

"He doesn't know who I am, Mario."

Alba watched him reach into his pocket for a tissue. He handed it to her. She wiped her face.

"I didn't want to cry just now. It creeps up on me when I'm not expecting it. Raffaele, Babbo, the way I left the mainland. Now I sit here today, looking at this slice of heaven, and I think I was running away from the one thing I had the power to shift myself. You ever want to swap heads?"

Mario laughed at that.

"You know what I mean. I want to take myself off the hook. I want to start again. And I want to build my life where it all started. Here."

Mario turned to face her, his cheeks a deeper brown than that morning. "You'll walk away from everything you've worked for?"

"No. I'll do it on my terms. I'll travel to Rome once a month for my *accademia* duties. I'll take on one or two concerts a year."

"And in between?"

"Grow olives?"

Mario shook his head with a fading laugh.

"What?"

"You'll be bored after one season."

"Is that a challenge, Mario?"

"People don't change as much as they'd like to."

"Exactly—I'm as hardheaded as I was when I left. If I set my mind to buying that dilapidated villa down the road from Elena to turn it into a music studio for the musically starved children of Ozieri and the surrounding villages, then you can bet I will, Signor Cynic."

His eyebrow lifted and sank back down. "I don't think anyone could stop you."

The following summer the Fresu School of Music opened for its inaugural summer camp, which attracted over fifty children from Ozieri and the surrounding towns. The Raffaele scholarship was in place and gifted to three children whose parents could not afford the nominal fees. Alba had hired Mario to project manage the renovation, which had hammered through the dank winter and reached completion a week before the camp. Alba's days throughout had been divided into visits to her father, at a set time, on the advice of Teresa. His health had deteriorated at a rapid pace. Alba paid for round-the-clock care, though her brothers refused to allow him to move into the rooms above her music school despite her pleas.

One morning she sat opposite him, sinking into his oversized throne, swallowed in blankets and daytime TV and wiped memories. Then he shook his head, as if a sudden recognition crashed into focus.

He straightened. His eyes were haunted. "Where do you live?"

"Here. I used to live in Rome."

"Rome?" he asked, the edge of confusion fraying the tone of his voice. "Your mother let you go by yourself? Who's your mother?"

Alba opened her mouth to speak. Teresa stepped out of the bathroom with a metal tray loaded with his morning's doses. "Are you alright?" she asked, putting the tray down and reaching an arm around Alba.

"No," she replied, fighting for breath. Teresa sat her down by the hearth.

"I didn't know what to expect," Alba began.

"He's very happy, the meds keep him comfortable."

"My father is not here."

Teresa rubbed Alba's back, a clinical sweep away of tension.

"Stay until he's eaten? Then I must ask you to leave while I get him to bed."

"*Grazie,*" Alba murmured, watching Teresa begin her lengthy rituals of injections, drops, pills, and syrups. She hooked her arm underneath Bruno and walked him around to a place at the end of the table where he could still see the television. Alba sat opposite him. Thirty empty chairs stretched out around them as Teresa placed a bowl of broth and *pastina* before him and tore in some *pane fino*, giving it a swirl of Parmesan.

"Bruno, lunchtime now, *sì?*"

She tapped the spoon a little harder than was necessary and it hooked his attention toward the task at hand. Alba watched him slurp a few spoons into his mouth, trying and failing to find the man. All these years she'd fled the shadow of the bully who now sat hunched over the gingham tablecloth before her, drinking the soup like an obedient small child.

Bruno looked up and saw her staring. She held his gaze.

"They didn't give you any?" he asked.

Alba shook her head.

He slurped another two spoonfuls. "You should eat all the food they give you." He concurred and bowed his head toward his bowl.

Teresa wiped his mouth, switched off the television, and asked him to say goodbye to Alba who had come to visit him and wasn't that nice of her and shouldn't she come again soon? Alba kissed her father on each cheek. His skin was cool, clammy. He smelled different.

"Please excuse us now, Alba," Teresa explained, "he needs it quiet to get to sleep."

"I can let myself out," Alba said, feeling the air seep out of the room faster than she could stop it. "Will Babbo be well enough for the performance, do you think? Tell me what additional help you'll need and I'll arrange everything, okay?"

"*Grazie.* I'm looking forward to it very much," Teresa replied.

Alba watched them shuffle the length of the table, around the far end and into a room off the hallway room. The door closed shut without a noise. Alba stood for a moment, searching her body for a feeling where none would surface. A pervasive numbness spread through her limbs. Her father had died. In his place was a meager impression, a hollow puppet, frail, lost, lines half learned and mumbled.

A few weeks later, before all the families took to the sea and whilst the heat was still manageable, Alba directed the children in an end-of-camp performance to mark the achievements of her students. Excited parents filled the lower room, which she had divided with sliding doors to enable the space to enlarge or reduce to suit the requirements. All the doors were folded back against the walls for the show and the large windows were thrown open to the view of her olive grove. At the center stood her grand piano. Alba rose to her feet from her stool and signaled for the children to stand up from the benches that lined the farthest wall. She would conduct them whilst accompanying.

Chiara and Donatella stood at the center, flanked by their closest friends and responsible for the success of this starting project, so insistent were their selling techniques that it didn't take any time for most of their classmates to sign up to study with the famous concert pianist who once beat up their dad and used to live in Rome.

They took a breath in unison. Alba nodded. The concert began. Alba made a new arrangement of a typical Sardinian folk song, "Non Potho Reposar," the lyrics a swoon of longing for a true love left behind, which she then blended into a medley of livelier songs till her studio was thrumming with the beam of children's voices, lifting like a flock of birds, angling together, swooping and diving and rising in unison. The audience stood and filled the room with applause. After three bows, the children sat back on their benches.

Alba faced her piano. She took a breath and let her hands retrace the piece she had played for Celeste and Elena that afternoon when she'd slipped into an audition without even knowing it, when the wheels of the next twenty years of her career were set in motion. Not a sound filled the space, but the gentle waves of Chopin's Nocturne. No breath, but the space between the phrases, the hush of anticipation where one arpeggio sank and another surfaced.

The tides of that first tune had brought her home.

When the audience cheered, she didn't hear them, she didn't see their grinning faces, their reverence for one of their own who'd brought the music home. She saw only the small man in the wheelchair in the front row with a dutiful Teresa on one side and a proud Elena on the other. She saw his unmoveable body, inexpressible thoughts and feelings locked somewhere deep inside, betrayed only by a singular tear that ran down the thin skin of his cheek. She felt only the golden heat of forgiveness, but not forgetfulness. She felt the hot remembrance of all things past, the importance and futility of it all.

In the quiet of the evening, sparse for the disappearance of the vital energy of the afternoon, Alba handed Mario a cold beer out on the terrace. The echoes of Chiara and Donatella's play rose up from the olive grove below.

"*Salute,*" Alba said, tipping the neck of her bottle onto his.

"Congratulations, Alba," he said, taking a gulp.

"I had no doubt I would win the bet to get it done in time. I have your daughters to thank for bringing me the students though. You think they'll ask for commission from now on? If Chiara hasn't already made out an invoice, that is."

"You might be a bad influence after all."

"I hope so."

Their swallows percussed the comfortable silence, beneath the hum of the cicadas, and the gentle swish of the olive tree leaves.

"Don't let this go to your head. Because a job is a job. But the sorry truth is, I couldn't have done it without you, Ma."

"True."

Alba slapped his arm. "That's all you have to say for yourself? I knocked down my fair share of walls too, no?"

"Are you talking about those five minutes when you made a dent in the plaster?"

Alba laughed and took a sip of her beer. The evening was perfect pink-purple stillness. The air was clear, heated with the promise of summer, the mountains dipped in dusk.

She turned toward Mario, his skin lit with the damask light. Stubble poked at his chin, the start of gray at his temples noticeable against the black of the rest.

"I liked knocking down walls with you, Mario."

"Good," he said, with a soft smile, neither an invitation nor a polite retreat.

She looked out toward the view of her countryside.

"I think I'd like to knock down some more walls with you sometime," she added.

She felt him turn to her. Alba faced him. His gaze was unblinking.

Neither spoke. Neither moved.

Alba watched his expression soften.

The dimples in his cheeks etched a smile.

His voice a wistful Sardinian husk in reply, "I think I'd like that too."

Audiences are not important
for me now and they never were.

—Martha Argerich

ACKNOWLEDGMENTS

Heartfelt thanks to John Scognamiglio and his colleagues at Kensington as well as Lisa Milton, Dominic Wakeford, and their lovely team at HQ. Deepest gratitude for my indefatigable agent, Jeff Ourvan—the best person to answer tricky creative questions with. The steady and gentle support from all of the above has enabled me to breathe life into this story.

I want to thank the theatrical team (Ellie, Eddie, Pickles, et al.), who invited my husband and me to perform Shakespeare at the Globe Theatre Rome. Losing myself along its streets was the birth of this story.

I'm indebted to the kindness of Antonio Pappano's assistants Lottie Johnson and Loreto Santamaria alongside Melanie Allmendinger at the Royal Opera House. Thank you to Andrew Sinclair for encouraging me to reach out to them and for wine in a sun-dipped Australian theater lobby. Deep gratitude for the lovely Angelica Suanno and her amazing team and professors at L'Accademia di Santa Cecilia in Rome, who opened their doors and minds, educating me in all the wondrous training that happens within. Many thanks to Maestro Benedetto Lupo, for granting me the honor of observing his fascinating work as well as sharing his own music journey with me. Thank you to Giovanni Auletta for a seat in one of the magnificent meeting rooms as he shared his world of music to me, and to the students of L'Accademia di Santa Cecilia, who were more than happy to share stories, coffee and carbonara, and their amazing talent. *Grazie mille*, Patrizia and Sara Godoli, for giving me a room with a stunning view of Roman antiquity, and good company, always.

Mum and dad, thank you for all those evenings you ferried me to sit (and dance!) beside Mr. and Mrs. Martin and their daughter Anne as they guided my first (and further) steps into music. Thank you to pianist Emilio Merone for nurturing a deeper understanding of fifths and all things improvised. Big shout-out to dance teacher Adele Maxwell Miles and actor/writer Bella Heesom, two women who invited me to share my music with a larger audience beyond my parents and pets.

Finally, thank you to the handful of young students I've had study at my piano; you taught me as much as I did you, if not more. Two of those are my own sons—your music inspires me more than you'll ever know.

Thank you to my husband, Cory, for his untiring support and song: You have Music enough to match the lot of us.

To all the marvels who discover, make and share
the superpower commonly referred to as Music:
please never stop lifting our hearts and minds.

A READING GROUP GUIDE

A ROMAN RHAPSODY

Sara Alexander

ABOUT THIS GUIDE

The suggested questions are included to enhance your group's reading of Sara Alexander's *A Roman Rhapsody*!

Discussion Questions

1. What was your favorite part and why?

2. What prejudices are explored in the story around the notion of what it requires to be a successful artist in the music industry?

3. What is the role of the music in the story? What does it allow the author to explore? What is its central purpose in your opinion?

4. Which characters resonated most deeply for you and why?

5 If you had the chance to ask the author one question about this book, what would it be?

6. Which character would you most like to meet and why?

7. Is Alba's development of her innate talent and passion commendable, successful, or escapist?

8. Do you think the challenges of following a life in music are different or similar for a woman than a man in the 1970s? Are they different today?

9. How did you relate to the world created in this story?

10. What do you consider to be the author's purpose in writing this book? What central ideas are embedded within the story, its colors, and its characters?